THE DOGS OF THE KISKADEE HILLS

BOOK 1
HUNT FOR THE LYNX

Eve Marko

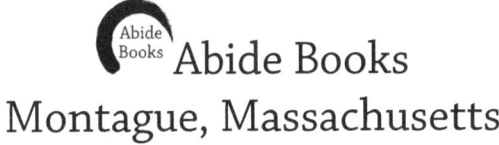

Abide Books

Montague, Massachusetts

The Dogs of the Kiskadee Hills
Book 1
Hunt for the Lynx

Copyright © 2016 Eve Marko
Print First Edition ISBN: 978-0-9969703-0-3
Ebook ISBN: 978-0-9969703-1-0
www.evemarko.com

Publisher's Cataloging-in-Publication Data

Names: Marko, Eve. | Epstein, Bianca Beth, illustrator.
Title: The dogs of the Kiskadee Hills : hunt for the lynx / Eve Marko
    ; [illustrations by] Bianca Beth Epstein.
Description: Montague, MA : Abide Books, 2016. | Series: The dogs
    of the Kiskadee Hills, bk. 1.
Identifiers: LCCN 2016931663 | ISBN 978-0-9969703-0-3 (pbk.) |
    ISBN 978-0-9969703-1-0 (ebook: EPUB)
Subjects: CYAC: Dogs--Fiction. | Social acceptance — Fiction. | Survival — Fiction. | Bullying — Fiction. | Science fiction. | Mystery
    and detective stories. | BISAC: YOUNG ADULT FICTION /
    Apocalyptic & Post-Apocalyptic. | YOUNG ADULT FICTION /
    Dystopian. | YOUNG ADULT FICTION / Mysteries & Detective Stories. | GSAFD: Dystopian fiction. | Science fiction. |
    Mystery fiction.
Classification: LCC PZ7.M33969 Do 2016 (print) | LCC PZ7.M33969
    (ebook) | DDC: [Fic]--dc23.

Printed in the United States of America

To Rocky

Kiskadee Hills

The Cliffs

Golden Mesa

Setters' Haven

Dobie Dells

Deerhound Downs

Flatheads

Bloodroot Hill

The Bottoms

Mixed Country

The Bottoms

Poplar Ridge

The Flats

Goliath

The Cliffs

Bassett
Bluffs

Ridgeback
Rise

Poet's
Vale

Woodchuck Hill

Pine Grove

Adamant Tor

Beau

TIMELINE

Distant Past: The Great Slavery

2112   Magogs' Calamity.

2115   The Great Liberation: Arden brings dogs to the Kiskadee Hills.

2116   The Ravages.

2118   Arden retreats to Glade of Remorse atop Adamant Tor.

2119   Arden returns to form the Great Alliance of Kisdees.

Beginning of New Cycle

1   First meeting of Kisdee Circle. Arden becomes first Noble One and finds swalas.

3   Brancken Dukes Lexor and Brancken Dukes Viktor become first Enforcers.

218   Gawls banished to live across the River Curl under Noble One Engelhard's Sartorial Jacko.

656   Gawls become haulers under Noble One Starry Slim Pomper.

735   Wordsworth meets Ruwena.

CHARACTERS

Ancients

Arden (Fearsome Arden). Known as the Great Liberator, he freed dogs from Magogs and brought them to the Kiskadee Hills.

Ruwena. An Ancient who appears to Wordsworth and commands him to find Beau.

Gawls in the Flats

Beau (Fireside Stomping Beau). A Mixed Akita Gawl rescued by Wordsworth from the Flats.

Charlotte (Prissy Miss Charlotte). A Pit Bull Gawl trying to escape from the Flats.

Hanna. A Leonberger Gawl condemned to die.

Rathbane. A one-eyed Wolfhound Gawl who escaped the Flats, thought to be the murderer of the Kisdees of the Hills.

Gawls of the Hills

Just Daniel. Leader of the Gawls.

Pandora. Just Daniel's companion.

Kisdees of the Hills

Anifa. A young Saluki member of the Kisdee Circle, one of the hunters for the lynx.

Babylon. A Puli, Prophet of the Hills.

Birdy. A Giant Schnauzer and Wordsworth's friend.

Corley (McDoon's Riverbend Corley). Head of the Tug-a-Lug family of Wolfhounds.

Dreden (Brancken Dukes Dreden). A German Shepherd who is Head of the Enforcers.

Goralac (Forever Fighting Goralac). A Bull Terrier who represents all the Terriers in the Kisdee Circle, one of the hunters for the lynx.

Lalo (Awuna Mapa Lalo). The head of the Malamutes. *Lala* is his wife.

Margaret (Dizzy Birdsong Margaret). A Black and Tan Setter, the second Kisdee murdered in the Hills.

Marima. Head of the Borzoi clan and one of the hunters for the lynx.

Markus (Brancken Dukes Markus). A German Shepherd and an Enforcer.

Odate. Head of the Daimyo family of Akitas. *Kiku* is her daughter.

Priam (Silver Bear Priam). A Great Dane, the Noble One of all Kisdees.

Vagabond (Moody Sunshine Vagabond). Head of the Moody Sunshine family of Golden Retrievers, Wordsworth's family.

Voldakov. Head of the Vizslas and one of the hunters for the lynx.

Wordsworth (Moody Sunshine Wordsworth). A lame Golden Retriever who leaves his family to recite poetry and becomes known as the Bard of the Vale.

Zebu (Brancken Dukes Zebu). An Enforcer and Dreden's younger brother.

PROLOGUE

Dizzy Birdsong Margaret, a Black and Tan Setter, lay fast asleep beside her brothers and sisters in a cozy hollow beneath a rocky ledge, until a soft breeze tickled her feathery chest hair and woke her up.

No one called Margaret Dizzy or Birdsong, only Margaret. She wanted to go back to sleep but her brown eyes willfully stayed open, so she sighed and sat up. Margaret was a serious, unremarkable young hunter who never did anything exceptional if she could help it, yet she now considered getting up, leaving the others behind, and walking into the forest's shadows. Like most of the other dogs that lived in the Kiskadee Hills, she tried to never be out at night. But she was hungry, and a full moon was splashing pools of light on the small promontory of wet earth further up the slope where she had hidden a cache of swala bones. All it took was a bound and a skip up the rise, and a few quick steps to where she had buried her treasure.

But Margaret wasn't much for bounding and skipping, so she searched around, licking her lips. True, she had the bones for exactly this kind of emergency, and there was so much light up the slope she could see every ridged tree trunk, every clod of uneven earth. She couldn't remember a night that shone like this one.

Treading loudly on the dry leaves, she walked heavily up the shimmering rise, expecting her cousin, Dizzy Bawler Letitia, to wake up too. No member of the clan howled louder than Letitia, though of course she would want a few licks of the bones herself. But no one stirred below, not even Dizzy Browser Bob who had the best hearing of them all, so she hurried over to the wide overhang. The mound of wet earth, secure and untouched, lay at the intersection of two mammoth sentinel rocks glistening silver with moonlight. Behind them drooped the branches of an old, graceful elm. Scraping quickly with her forelegs, she soon retrieved a thighbone encased in dirt. Slowly, thoughtfully, she gave it a few licks, went down on her belly, and began to gnaw.

The breeze tickled the hairs at the tip of her tail. She looked up and saw the elm branches wave gently over a small dark shadow in the middle of one rock. She sniffed briefly before going back to her bone, but several studious licks later she glanced up again. The second rock was turning dark too. Was a thick, winter-brittle tree limb ready to fall? Kisdees had died from large, dead boughs suddenly cracking overhead and smashing down on their unsuspecting skulls. But there was nothing above, just a radiant flush of moonlight.

She returned to her bone. The night was turning chilly; soon she would go back to the den. Her long ears flapped at the rustling of the drooping branches and she looked up again. Strange, their tips were churning madly though there was no wind. She snuffled in the frigid air but there were only familiar scents, nothing she hadn't smelled again and again going up and down that soft-earth ledge day after day. The sentinel rocks had turned darker—in fact, they were now pitch black—and it was so bitterly cold that she trembled under her rugged, wavy coat, which didn't happen even in the frostiest days. Her head drooped forward; she was getting sleepy.

Margaret was no longer interested in the swala bone, but when she went to place it back by the mound of dug-up earth the ground was covered with mist. A fog collected around her, yet just outside the rise, all along the slope, the moonlight seemed as golden as before. Margaret rarely growled, but she did now, wrinkling her nose, for a sudden odor of smoke and rot assaulted her wide, diligent nostrils. She sat back on her haunches. Fire! How was that possible when she felt so cold?

Get up, Margaret, she told herself. She was a staunch Black and Tan, not flurry and fluttery like her Red Setter cousin, Fret & Frazzle Tonia, who by now would have been chasing her tail from excitement. Besides, what was there to worry about? Her family was slumbering close by, ready to awaken and charge up the small hill at the slightest cry.

There was a piercing sound, broken off at the very end. Then everything was as quiet as before, only the branch tips above her were still flip-flopping wildly and the two sentinel rocks were ebony as night. What's creating that shadow, she wondered dully, body drooping down once again. Her eyes almost shut, and then, alerted by her hunter's instinct, they opened again and her earflaps shot straight up.

A large, dark shadow stood further up the rise on the other side of the mound. An Ancient! She'd never seen one before, and yet how could she not recognize it after all the tales she'd heard. They were bigger than dogs, with larger paws and narrow muzzles. This one was black and almost twice her size, and if she weren't so sleepy she'd be up on her paws crouching low, tail down, and showing deference every way she knew. But her belly was already flat on the ground, and anyway, it was common knowledge that Ancients were the guardians and benefactors of dogs. As it moved close, she could see nothing but tender concern in its two yellow eyes.

Her tan chest swelled briefly with emotion. Ancients appeared but rarely to Kisdees, but one was now paying close attention to her, Margaret, of the Dizzy clan of Black and Tans, to whom no one from the Hills had ever given the slightest respect. Tomorrow she'd tell the others all about it.

She wanted to talk with the Ancient but she was too tired, so she lay down at its paws with a soft, grateful sigh, and dozed off.

Ordinarily she would have been found by her family, or at least by the dawn hunters; if not by them, then certainly by other Kisdees coming down to eat at the Bottoms.

Instead, she was found much earlier, and by a poet.

"Spring steals into these happy Hills"
With newly minted leaf and fern,
Yellow bud forsythia, emerald frills,

The moon comes up – the moon comes up – the moon comes up – "

The mists had almost disappeared when down the slope came a Retriever, his hairs golden in the moonlight, his muzzle nudging away last year's leaves, nostrils sniffing.

Moody Sunshine Wordsworth recited the verse again and again, trying not only to finish it but also forget his aversion to the dark. Like Dizzy Birdsong Margaret, whom he was about to meet for the first time, he rarely went out at night. But it had been a bad day for poetry and he could not sleep, so he'd finally come up on his paws, stretching forward and then back. The brilliant moon had beckoned and he entered the woods, thinking to saunter a little way and return. Instead he continued, mesmerized by the enchanting light, whiskers twitching, tail curving in a slight upward sweep as it brushed against bare shrubs and limbs.

He returned to his old haunts, the dens of clans and neighbors he hadn't visited in years. He passed by Harrier Hollow, where the restless Harriers yipped as they slumbered, and by Deerhound Downs, where the gigantic dogs, second in size only to the Wolfhounds, thundered in their sleep, before making a quick beeline up Woodchuck Hill and there he was, on Golden Mesa, where his own family lived.

Golden Mesa! How long has it been, he wondered. But he knew the answer. Four cold, snowy winters without slumbering sweetly alongside other Moody Sunshine Goldens; four lively springs without circling around Vagabond with the others before they trotted out to hunt; four warm summers without panting quietly in the shade watching the new pups play tug-of-war with twigs and branches; four cool autumns without toppling into tall banks of newly fallen leaves; and now one more long, cold winter, the time of year when he felt loneliest of all.

His old home stood on top of a wide ridge, with stooping hemlocks, roots exposed in soft, crumbly cavities that were great to sleep in. After his mother had disappeared when he was just a pup, leaving him all alone, he'd enlarged a small gopher hollow into a cozy den layered with twigs and needles. Not an easy task for a dog that young, and certainly not easy with a twisted hind leg hovering uselessly in the air, and when you had to fight off occasional rushes by Swank and Flora, who loved to take you down. But he managed it, and later ran harder than all his cousins to strengthen his remaining legs, learned to ram them with the strong side of his body and bring them down, too. He used the same force on swalas as he got older and joined the daily hunt, always remembering to attack from his strong side, the one opposite his crippled leg.

By noon he'd be dozing with the rest of the family till visitors arrived later in the afternoon, for the Moody Sunshine Goldens were known for their hospitality. Neighbors from Mastiff Moors or Elk's Peak, or even Goldens from other families, would saunter up to the Mesa, droopy from their naps, and sit at the edge, looking politely away while waiting for permission to enter. Moody Sunshine Vagabond, the leader of the family, always barked fiercely, but behind him Mabel and Cicero were already digging out swala bones for everyone to share. While the young ones munched on fresh, savory grass, the older ones gathered around the visitors, exchanging gossip, listening to Vagabond as he proudly recited the morning kills. And if everyone knew that Vagabond usually exaggerat-ed, or took personal credit for kills that weren't his, no one said anything, the Goldens to honor their leader, the guests because they were guests. The sun would amble across the sky and everyone would amble with it, chasing down the pool of light, rolling on the grass to relieve some itch, hoping for a belly lick, waiting for Vagabond to give the signal that it was time to go down to the Bottoms.

The ridge on top of Wordsworth's brow deepened as it always did when he grew sad. Five winters of living alone without family or clan, five winters of exile for the Wobbler, Vagabond's name for him. The head of the Moody Sunshine Goldens couldn't laugh hard enough at how Wobbler walked with one back paw always suspended in the air, causing the opposite hip and flank to shimmy and roll. They were ashamed and wished his mother had done the right thing.

"What right thing?" he'd asked her, but instead of an-swering she simply snarled in the direction of the others, hov-ering over him protectively. She was his champion, never fail-ing him once till the morning she went out hunting and dis-appeared.

He surprised them all and survived. In fact, when they finally parted ways it was he who left them, or as Vagabond sanctimoniously put it, turned his back on his own family. He had left in anger, but there was no anger now. His nostrils twitched at the flecked base of a bare maple. It was Moody Sunshine Lena, he'd know her scent anywhere. She was the only one in the family who kept him company back then, wagging her tail companionably and giving him a playful shove with her flanks. But there was another scent above hers, an unfamiliar male smell, and Wordsworth growled softly. Did Lena belong to someone else now? *His* Lena? Plump and warm, smelling of rabbit and the twigs she loved to nibble on?

Don't be silly, he thought, lowering his muzzle, she was never *your* Lena. She was the only one who showed you any kindness, but when you stepped off the Mesa and tramped downhill in the direction of sunrise, she stayed here. What Kisdee in her right mind would choose to live alone with the Wobbler, companion to an exile and that most unnecessary thing in all of the Kiskadee Hills — a poet, the Bard of the Vale?

He sighed, took a last sniff, and disappeared down the far end, descending the slope right above the Black and Tans with his usual half-hopping gait, reciting the verse he'd been trying to complete earlier, at a loss for an idea, a word, a rhyme. The earth turned wet beneath his paws and he looked down, surprised to see cold mists rising. They parted like sheaves of long grass, and he saw her.

He didn't know it was Margaret; he couldn't even tell she was a Black and Tan. Parts of the body were torn off and the long, curly fur lay mangled on the ground like the soft gray hair of chipmunks after the crows had scavenged them. The head had swiveled sharply around, revealing a wide-open mouth that looked oddly vacant. He could see the ivory teeth, but no gums out front revealed by curling, snarling lips, no tongue, nothing to show she was ready to attack. It was as if the dog had opened her mouth to yawn and never closed it again.

Wordsworth blinked several times, wondering if he had gone to sleep after all, but each time he opened his eyes there lay the large, open cavity of the dog's mouth, his own paws growing sticky from the dark red pool trickling slowly down the ledge.

And now he felt terribly cold. Fog billowed up to his belly. His golden fur, always a reliable buffer against the cold, curled from the ice coursing through his veins. The two rocks before him had gleamed silver when he first arrived, but now one was getting darker.

The tip of his tail quivered, and he knew: Someone—something—was watching him. The mist rose higher and higher, up to his chest and now his back. He turned around. Nothing. But white eddies swirled around the hill above. Coils of rot and smoke snaked towards him, assailing his nostrils, causing his eyes to tear, delivering a biting frost that spread pain all over his shivering body. How was that possible? He was a Golden; Goldens were never cold.

He looked for the bright, cheerful moon and found it gone; when he looked back down they were staring at him.

Eyes? Not eyes like his own or other Kisdees, but green looped coils with black gashes across the center instead of round pupils. Nor could he see a nose or muzzle in that murky fog, just a crimson tongue that swept a slow, broad arc from under one eye to the other.

He couldn't move. The Black and Tans were close by, all he had to do was run down to where they slept, but his legs didn't budge. Only when the green eyes slowly closed his body came back to life. His hackles rose, head and tail shot up. He growled, crouched back, and was about to attack when the lids opened on the ringed eyes, and once again he couldn't move. He flexed his knees, he bared his teeth, the snarl rose from his belly, but he couldn't lunge.

And then the eyes grew bigger. Their master—whatever it was—crept slowly forward, his body concealed by the mist but smelling of fire and decay. The enormous red tongue continued its slow, back-and-forth loops, the wide arc the only indication of its gigantic hidden maw. Behind lay the Setter, head twisted, tail shredded, mouth an empty grin, and Wordsworth knew that was going to happen to him unless he did something. *Jump it, charge it, take it down!* There wasn't much hope for the last—the creature was enormous—but he had to try. Only his legs didn't move. He swallowed down a cry of terror for the eyes were close now, just behind the rocks that had turned black. And then the dark slashes in their middle disappeared and he was looking at himself, Wordsworth, inside the eyes. A long, high-pitched sound pierced the air.

"Wait!"

He twisted around and saw her, whined in awe and twisted back, heart pounding. He'd never seen one of them before, hadn't smelled or heard her coming, but he knew what she was. Most important, he knew he could trust her. He heard her light, panting breath behind him, saw a hint of pearly fur from the corner of his eye. But the danger was still out in front. The black gashes were back, his own reflected image had disappeared, and the green-ringed orbs now seemed to contemplate the one who'd just appeared, the lids dipping slightly, almost in curiosity.

"Soon it will blink," she said softly in his ear. "That's when you run."

"And you?"

"Do as I say."

But the eyes didn't shut. Instead they looked at her thoughtfully, the red tongue gone.

"I'll fight," he said in a low voice.

"You'll die," she replied. "I am not in danger. When he shuts his eyes, run back to the Vale."

The eyes blinked quickly, too quickly. A malevolent glint flickered momentarily, and then, slowly, as if guessing what she'd told him, they closed.

"Go." He didn't move. "Go!"

The green rings opened and grew bigger. The tongue re-appeared, sweeping back and forth, but not the black gashes. Instead he saw her in the center of those terrible eyes, the narrow muzzle, her yellow eyes, and the white moonlit fur. "It's after *you*," he whispered.

"Not yet," she murmured. He could feel her coat behind his, the hairs shivering, the two of them breathing as one. "He will close his eyes before he pounces, that's when you run."

"And you?"

"I'll meet you in the Vale, I promise. Run!"

But it seemed too late, for now gaseous fumes enveloped him. Ice still seemed to course through his veins even as he gasped for breath. The creature's head than bigger than he was, revealing now an arc of narrow, white teeth wider than he was nose to tail, and the eyes held *her* image there, thin and iridescent. They were not going to shut again, not till after it did to them what it did to —

They shut.

He ran.

His home was three hills over and he tore blindly past them: past Ridgeback Rise and Basenji Bluffs, Beagle Brae and Dobie Dells, even past Flathead Falls, where the Terriers babbled in their sleep. Small pebbles tumbled noisily down invisible ruts and culverts. He slid over slippery rocks and once, in his haste, even tumbled down a muddy embankment, getting sludge and clay in his fur. His crippled leg throbbed mercilessly, and so did his heart: What will happen to her?

I'll meet you in the Vale, I promise.

The wind turned; the night was reaching its coldest hour. He darted down Bloodroot Hill, breath turned to vapor. He was almost home, at the Vale, with only the dense brush to poke through before the clearing.

There was the large willow in the middle, a black overhang in pools of light. He could hear the water splashing on the rock on the far side where the stream ran, and far down below the rushing currents of the river. Otherwise all was quiet.

She wasn't there.

He made his way slowly towards the willow, heart thumping an echo of his worst fear. I shouldn't have left her, he thought again and again. And then he stopped.

Something approached the edge of the willow's shade. It was bigger than most Kisdees and paler than the moonlight. Two yellow eyes gleamed in the dark.

"You!" he breathed in relief.

✧✧✧

She walked towards him on her large webbed paws, never disturbing the ground's mantle of fallen leaves, her fur white, her smell strangely arid and sandy, incredibly warm. An Ancient.

Once they were wolves, bigger and more powerful than dogs like him, with bone-crushing jaws and large yellow eyes. Everyone feared them. With their narrow chests and powerful backs, they ran everywhere in hunt of food, leaping across wide chasms, eyes glinting, sharp fangs bared and ready to shear flesh from bone.

Dogs were their descendants, with muzzles not as long, jaws not as powerful. They had no need to wander in search of food for there were plenty of swalas in the Cliffs, antelopes small enough to be taken down by one hunter, their flesh delicious under the bitter, thick skin. The wolves had disappeared long ago before the Great Calamity, while the dogs settled in the Kiskadee Hills and were called Kisdees. But some wolves survived as Ancients, flesh-and-blood at night and spirit in the day, and on rare occasions — and only on the full moon — they came back.

She strode towards him stiff-legged and tall, her tail curled up and back, and he sank down on his belly. Her paws were gigantic alongside his muzzle, one on each side. And then, to his surprise, she bent over and licked him with a large, soft tongue. It flitted around the corners of his lips and then across his mouth, up one side of his muzzle and then down. She buried her black nose deep into the nape of his neck, scratching gently inside his golden hairs, and he moaned. Finally she turned around and walked off, so lightfooted her paws barely brushed the ground.

"Who are you?" he wondered, lifting his head.

"Ruwena."

It sounded like the whisper of air. He remembered his manners, rose onto his paws while remaining in a low crouch, keeping his chest just above the ground. "Welcome to Poet's Vale," he said. "My home is yours."

She looked away, following Kisdee etiquette, and he rose. He would have brought her a swala bone, or else taken her over to the small pool of spring water at the Vale's far end, but he already knew that she didn't eat or drink. A thin scar fell from the corner of one eye down the side of her muzzle. Ancients were supernatural beings who didn't grow old or sick, who always stayed the same. How else could she listen to sounds he could not hear, or suddenly appear on the ledge behind him where the dead Setter lay?

She gazed up at the dazzling moon, as though only now noticing how brilliant it was. "The moon is seeking its beloved," she murmured.

He grew flustered. "It's an honor and privilege for me —"

"Tell me the verse you were reciting earlier."

"What verse?"

She lowered her eyes. "The verse you declaimed back on Golden Mesa."

She's going to laugh, he thought. What does a great wolf, an Ancient, want with my poetry? He licked his lips nervously:

"Spring steals into these happy Hills
With newly minted leaf and fern,
Yellow bud forsythia, emerald frills,
The moon comes up – the moon comes up – "

His tail fell between his legs. Nothing like this had happened to him before. "I can't end the verse," he told her.

She looked away so as not to shame him. "At least, not yet. After all, you're not mistaken; the moon has indeed come up."

And now, for the first time since she'd emerged from under the willow, he remembered the mists and the body on the ledge beneath Golden Mesa. "What happened to the Setter?"

"You saw what happened to her." Her voice turned low and guttural.

"She was butchered. I've never seen anything like it. And that thing in the mist…" He hesitated, watching her carefully. "It seemed to know you."

A tremor went through her slender, powerful body.

"Why did it kill her?"

"It doesn't matter. There will be more."

"More of what?" She turned to look down towards where Bloodroot Hill met the river. Her fur twitched again and she growled, causing his heart to beat loudly. "What do you know? What do you see?"

"Your end. Dogs will disappear. You will become extinct, like us."

"Extinct?" He glanced around in bewilderment. The night was clear, the forest quiet; moonlight stroked his fur like love. "How? Who will do this?"

She replied softly, as though talking to herself. "He has waited patiently for a long time, gathering strength. Now he's ready."

"Ready for what? Who is he?"

"He's had many names; now he goes by Bludrun. An Ancient, like me."

"A wolf? That was no wolf!" She gave a brief growl and he looked quickly away. "Don't Ancients bring help and blessings to dogs?"

"This one's different, he's changed."

He remembered the green looped eyes with the black gashes, the red tongue where the muzzle should have been, and the mist coming in closer and closer. "You said he's ready. Ready for what?"

She listened to the river as though the answer to his question was in the white rush of snowmelt below. How beautiful she is, he thought. Were all Ancients like her? And yet her body looked pinched and gaunt, her fur almost gossamer against the naked willow branches, and there was that scar below one eye.

"Ready to put an end to you. To make dogs disappear, as we disappeared." Her voice deepened. "Once it was wolves who flew up and down these hills, the greatest hunters that ever lived. No one ran faster or leaped longer. Our territory stretched across the valleys towards where the sun rises, and down the Flats all the way to the Great Water where the sun sets. The elk stampeded in fright at one glimpse of us. We were caring mothers and loyal fathers; we protected our young. And still we died."

Wordsworth roused himself. "It was no wolf that did that, it was Magogs, and they've been dead a long time; they can't hurt anyone anymore."

Her nostrils wriggled with a scent he could not catch. "Their actions live on. Pain, rage, hate, revenge—those have not died."

He sat back on his haunches. Magogs had been extinct for years; that's why everything prospered. Water sparkled, birds sang, the sun laughed, prey abounded everywhere, all because there were no more tall, barbaric Magogs in the world. "Why tell me? Why not tell Enforcers? Why not tell Dreden?"

She approached him again, her enormous front paws—twice as big as his—bristling with hair, jaws narrow and stern. "It was not by chance that it was you who found Margaret."

He kept his eyes respectfully averted. "I am not an Enforcer or a guard. I live alone here in the Vale and recite verse." She said nothing and he licked his lips. "No one cares about me or even listens to me, including my own family. They laugh at me."

"I did not laugh. It's a new time now, poet, and you must tell them."

"Tell them what? That soon we'll be destroyed by a wolf that is not a wolf? They'll laugh at me harder than ever."

"They'll stop laughing soon enough."

"Why does he wish to kill us? He's an Ancient; we are his children."

She shuddered and raised her tail. "He has changed. Once he was different, but now he hates, only hates. That's why you must warn Kisdees. You are the messenger."

"They'll never listen to me. They despise me; they wish I'd never been born because of my leg."

"They are your brothers and sisters, your uncles and aunts."

"They disowned me a long time ago!"

"And you? Have you disowned them?"

Slowly he sank down on his belly, keeping his eyes on the shadow cast by the gigantic willow. Soon it would come into bloom, its long, fibrous leaves reaching down to tickle his ears. He'd come to love the Vale: cool, soothing, and lonely.

"I almost starved after my mother disappeared. The Rules say that family members must take care of orphan pups and bring them food. My uncles and aunts, as you call them, brought me nothing; they wanted me to die. I licked every scrap of food that fell on the ground, every morsel the others overlooked. I was skinny and weak, bruised by their kicks and bites. I could barely walk, and still I had to dig out my own den because no family would let me share theirs. I learned early to be careful, to jump back up on my paws every time someone took me down because if I stayed down they might give me the death bite. I learned to bare my teeth at everyone, including Vagabond, head of the family. No one thought I'd survive." He looked up respectfully but firmly. "You're right, I disowned them when I left to come here."

"And the dead Setter, carrion left on the ledge, to be skinned and feasted on by the Birds of Death—did you disown her, too?"

He shuddered. She had lain straight in his path, hidden by the mist, like some large canker clinging to a log. A hawk devouring a chipmunk, tearing out the hairs with its beak before opening up chest and belly, could not have been more thorough.

Something soft and warm now stroked his brow. Her tongue glided slowly, unhurriedly, over his body. It licked the furrow that lined his back and paused over the twisted leg, and then it stroked that too, and he thought he'd die from pleasure. It went up and down his other back leg, then across his flank and back towards his head. It dabbed at the corners of his mouth and then rolled up to his eyes. No one had done that since his mother disappeared. This was what he missed worst of all, someone to roll and play with, to pull on the fur of his cheek and neck and lick his face, all the normal things that Kisdees did to one another every day, and that no one did to him. Except her, Ruwena, an Ancient.

She pulled away and walked back. When she next spoke her stern yellow eyes searched his. "Go and find Daimyo's Fireside Stomping Beau."

Slowly he got up on his paws. "I know the Daimyos, an old, distinguished Akita family, but I never heard of Fireside Stomping Beau."

"You'll find him down in the Flats."

"There are no dogs down in the Flats!" She lowered her white, pointed muzzle and growled once again, and instantly he bowed his head, heart thumping. "Who is this Beau?"

"A Gawl."

Gawls live on the other side of the river, he thought to himself, they don't go down to the Flats. No one goes down there.

"Nevertheless, that's where he is," she said, as though reading his mind.

He chose his next words with care, still inclining his head respectfully. "You are an Ancient, much wiser than me, so you know what the Rules say about the Flats."

The Rules were clear. Kisdees could go anywhere. They could roam up and down the long ridgeline of the Hills; they could even go beyond the Cliffs and up to the distant Silver

Mountains. But they could not cross the River Curl, scale the broad, forested rise and then go all the way down to the end of the tree line and the beginning of the Flats.

In a flash she landed against his flanks, ears tall and lips pulled back, her breath hot above his neck. He saw the flash of teeth, knew her jaws could crush his neck with one bite. "The Rules don't matter, poet, your crippled leg doesn't matter. The past is past." She snorted. "Had you been a wolf pup, no wolf mother would have let you live."

She stepped back and he risked a glance up at her face. "Not even you?"

"Especially not me. That should make you strong. If you know that you could have died long ago, then what's there to fear? What's there to lose?" She raised her head and looked around her. "If you do nothing, nothing will protect you: not your verse, not the Vale, not the Noble One or Enforcers—not even me! You will die like the Black and Tan."

Like the Setter! He could feel the hair of his soft belly curl against the frost.

When she walked off he slowly rose up on his paws. She looked up at the moon again, ear tips twitching. "Beware of the black wolf, and find Beau quickly. Even now Bludrun grows bigger and stronger every day."

He looked around him at the Vale. She seemed to be talking about another world, a place far, far away. "And this Gawl will know about the danger?" he asked. "He will know what to do?"

Her yellow eyes didn't blink while the full moon gazed back unwaveringly, as though they were having a contest of wills. "Find him," she said.

"And what should I do then?"

The cold wind flattened the fur against her body. "I can only tell you your first step. That will guide you to the next, and that one will guide you to the one after."

Above them, the luminous branches of the weeping willow beckoned. "And the Vale? Can I come back here after I find him?"

"If you wish. Sooner or later, we lose everything. I have already given up much, and still more will be asked."

Later, in a place as distant and different from the Vale as day from night, he would remember her words. But not now. Now he thought only about himself, how he would never have her lightness and grace as she glided rather than walked towards the other end of the Vale, how he would always be clumsy and earthbound, the target of jeering and practical jokes.

She'd almost disappeared down the tree-dark slope when he stumbled up, shouting after her: "How will I find him?"

"In the Flats!" came the answer from below, though he couldn't see her anymore. "Look for him in the direction of sunrise!"

ONE

It was still dark when Wordsworth opened his eyes. His nose twitched and sniffed the crisp smell of night just before dawn, when the cold felt colder and the air dryer. He stretched forward and back. Spring had arrived a few weeks earlier and the snow covering the hillside was gone, leaving a cool, mysterious new earth under his paws. Even now the hunters and haulers were hurrying to the Kiskadee Cliffs to prepare for the dawn kills, but that was in the opposite direction of the Flats. The others were still slumbering, for sleep was usually sweetest in this tranquil, in-between time that marked the fading of darkness and the rise of dawn.

There was no path to the river and he didn't need one; he'd come down here to drink every day since moving to the Vale. But never before sunrise, so now, instead of skip-scampering down as he always did, he took slow, wary steps, his folded earflaps quivering each time a twig cracked, his nose sniffing suspiciously at every shivering leaf. Water from the melted snows cascaded in small falls around him.

Just before he reached the river's banks he heard the fast, hard pounding of hammering hooves. Swalas, he thought, drinking before returning to the Cliffs, where the hunters would be waiting. They were gone, but he would see some of them later at the Bottoms when he went down to eat, their eyes glassy, their carcasses tattered from being hauled such a long way.

The river had always soothed his lame back leg and even now, in the cold before dawn, he wanted to jump in. A large rock slanted high over the riverbank, its top leveled by wind and rain. He climbed it quietly to have a quick look-around, and instantly dropped down on his belly. He knew why the swalas had run.

An Enforcer stood silently below, staring towards sunrise. The moon, less golden than before, shone on him from the other direction, reflecting what Wordsworth already knew, that he was like all the other Enforcers, a Shepherd, the lower part of his head and back all black, plunging down to gold and white flanks, head and earflaps held high. He could smell the tart scent of terraberries that only Enforcers ate because they made them more aggressive. No one else was allowed to eat the tiny, sour, purple fruit; no one else wanted to.

Wordsworth hugged the top of the rock. His friend Birdy, the Giant Schnauzer, swore that Dreden, head of the Enforcers, had eyes everywhere; nothing escaped him. And now the Enforcer turned towards the other side of the river, revealing a flash of teeth as if he was grinning. Two shadows ran down the rise on the opposite bank. Gawls, the Golden thought, only they live on this side of the river. And the moon, as if by the Enforcer's command, disappeared.

There was no identifying them in the gloom, but one was big. Must be a Wolfhound Mixed, he thought, maybe even a

Tug-a-Lug. The other was much smaller. They reached the river and lapped the water fast and loud.

"What should we do?" asked the big dog in exasperation, a young female. "It's the second night in a row."

The shorter one just lapped more water.

"We were supposed to meet her at the —"

"Shhh," said her companion, a male, "the trees are listening."

"You're always nervous," she complained, speaking louder rather than softer.

"Not nervous, terrified."

"Stop teasing me. You know how I hate —"

"I'm dead serious. There isn't a day I don't wake up and think that this may be my last day on earth."

She snorted. "Death doesn't scare me. What's there to be afraid of? That I'll die and won't have to pull dead swalas down to the Bottoms anymore?"

"You're young."

"And you're — oh, I don't know what you are."

They sighed as though they'd had this argument before, lapping up more water. The small male was more mature, Wordsworth thought, but his voice was as fresh as a pup's, more youthful than his bigger companion's.

"I think we should go back there just in case —"

"No," the male said decisively. "It's been two nights now and she hasn't shown up."

"You think they found her?"

"I don't know. He said Charlotte's a tough Pit Bull, but it won't help her much if she's caught by Enforcers."

The moon came out from behind the clouds. Wordsworth raised his head slightly and almost started, for the female was staring straight up at him. But the splash of moonlight ended at the river, illuminating her alone, and he could see that she was indeed related to the Tug-a-Lugs, with her long head, muscular red body, and the wiry hair that crept over the eyes and came down below the mouth like a beard. Her muzzle seemed lopsided and a little bent. Still, she was not as big as the huge Tug-a-Lugs, who took pride in being the biggest dogs in the Hills. She was a combination of Wolfhound and —

Suddenly she was jerked into the shadows. "What are you doing?"

"Getting you back here, where it's safe."

"I've told you over and over, I can take care of myself. Besides, you know I love the moonlight."

"More than is good for you. Come on, it's time to get some rest."

"Can't we wait a little? Maybe she's lying somewhere, hurt."

"There are Enforcers out, I can feel it. You won't do Charlotte much good if they catch you."

"One day I won't run, from Enforcers or anyone else."

"Good. But right now, let's go."

With that there were two fewer shadows by the river. The night turned deadly quiet, the leaves stopped their rustling.

With a low growl the Enforcer emerged from the shadows and again Wordsworth saw the glint of teeth. He'd met Enforcers before but not one of them grinned like this one, who now looked across the river where the two Gawls had disappeared, tongue rolling over his lips in anticipation, teeth shining.

"Did you see them, Markus?"

Wordsworth flattened himself on the rock.

"I didn't hear you coming, Baas."

"Did you see them?" The voice was so calm and frosty that Wordsworth shivered. Nothing on earth could tempt him to look over the edge now.

The Enforcer repeated what he'd heard, word for word.

"So they don't yet know what's happened to our Prissy Miss Charlotte," Brancken Dukes Dreden, head of the Enforcers, said. None of the Enforcers consumed as many terraberries as he did, which resulted in a voice that was a little higher than theirs but as unwavering and glacial as an iceberg.

"We have them guessing." Markus waited for a response, but none came. "I could have caught them, Baas."

"You said there were two."

"Two, four, what does it matter? Mixeds are no match for an Enforcer."

"I'm after bigger game than those two, Markus. Much bigger game."

"They're helping Gawls escape."

"And someone is helping *them*," Dreden said. "That's the one I'm interested in."

The pounding in Wordsworth's chest intensified; he was sure they could hear it down below.

"The longer she's in the forest, the more dangerous she is, Baas," the first Enforcer said.

"Who do you have guarding her?"

"Brancken Dukes Conrad and Brancken Dukes Stark."

"Two Enforcers for one Mixed should be more than enough."

"It's the Friends I'm thinking of, Baas. They want Charlotte back."

Dreden growled. "They'll get Charlotte when we're good and ready. Or else we'll bring them someone else."

"They want someone like Charlotte—"

"They'll take what we give them," Dreden snapped. Then he sighed. "If there's anything I hate more than Gawls, it's our Friends. Every day, Markus, I give thanks that I was born to the Brancken Dukes and that I am an Enforcer, but everything has a price. Our price is having to deal with our Gawl cousins and our Friends." He growled again. "Let's keep her a little longer before we give her back."

"You think someone will still try to rescue her, Baas? The female, maybe?"

"Could you identify them?"

"I had to go downwind. But their own scent wasn't very strong and in the dark I couldn't see them, so we still don't know who they are."

"I may have a solution to that," Wordsworth heard, and the icy voice sent shudders all the way down to the tip of his tail.

"You always have solutions, Baas."

Wordsworth didn't move even after both Enforcers left. He shivered as the words reverberated in his head: *I'm after bigger game.* What game was that? The one who was helping Gawls escape, Dreden said, but escape from where? Gawls had lived peaceably enough on this side of the river for years. Besides, where would they escape?

The gray had paled and widened in the direction of sunrise; dawn was practically here and the safest thing to do was to go back to the Vale, take a little nap and then mull over what he'd heard. But inside he knew that if he didn't go down to the Flats now, he never would. So he finally slid down the rock, crossed the river, and scrambled up the rise on the other side, keeping to the shadows.

TWO

He was in Gawl country.

Long ago, a vicious Terrier Mixed called Senigawl had rebelled against purebred Kisdees. Those who joined him called themselves Gawls, but it didn't take long for the Enforcers, led by Brancken Dukes Andor, to put an end to all resistance, especially after they put an end to Senigawl. Only the name, Gawls, stuck, and that's how Kisdees usually referred to Mixeds.

Gawl country looked much like the rest of Kiskadee, gentle uphills and downhills, but it was actually the back end of the Hills that slowly slid down to the Flats. The ground here was hard and bouldered, the pine and beech trees taller and gloomier. Purebred Kisdees lived on the upper side of the River Curl while the Gawls lived on this side, banished here after the Senigawl revolt. Kisdees generally saw the River Curl as the lowest boundary of the Hills and didn't cross it, preferring to scamper up and down the higher slopes, but Gawls had to cross the river to reach their homes, and *their* lowest boundary was the tree line, which marked the end of the Kiskadee Hills and the beginning of the Flats.

This is where he was headed now, tail lowered, snout to the ground. Back in his hunting days he'd befriended a Gawl by the name of Bent, who had such short legs he wasn't much use pulling swalas from the Cliffs down to the Bottoms.

"Get to work!" Snowdog Samson, the big Samoyed in charge of the transport group, would yell, issuing a painful nip to Bent's rear haunches. The Gawl yelped and lost his balance, quickly clambering back up on his paws.

"Give him a chance, Samson," Wordsworth urged. "It's not his fault his legs are so short."

"What do you call that, anyway?" Snowdog Samson snorted. "It's a Terrier down below and a Doberman on top, but it's smaller than either, so it's neither. Hey, Deviant," he bellowed, "your mother should have sent you to the Land of the Gawls."

Gawls were often left by their mothers to die. They refused them milk and buried their bodies deep in the woods where no one would find them. Kisdees called it the Land of the Gawls.

As he cleared the rise and started down the long slope, Wordsworth wished it were summer, when curtains of silver and scarlet oak would veil him from view. Bank voles would scamper along in their grass runways and gray, silver-tipped squirrels would be busy building new nests in cavities created by woodpeckers, enough activity to distract anyone curious about the Golden Retriever scuttling down the hill to find a Gawl in the Flats.

What was the Mixed doing there and not at work with Bent and the others? And not just any Gawl, but one from the Daimyos. Who would have thought that someone from that family, so arrogant and proud of its pure bloodline, would give birth to a Gawl! And how did he get a name like that? The Daimyo Akitas had names like Tosa, Miyako, and Hachi. Nothing remotely like Beau. No Gawl puppies had ever been born in the Moody Sunshine family of Goldens, which Vagabond had been inordinately proud of. Till, of course, the Wobbler was born to Moody Sunshine Loreen. He was no Gawl, he was a pure Golden, but Vagabond was mortified nevertheless.

He didn't notice the large patch of gray up ahead but he could feel the change underfoot. The ground was growing level, which meant that he was leaving the Hills behind. His heart pounded. He came from generations of dogs who lived in the forest, knowing only the rise and fall of hillsides. The ground grew more and more even and finally he stopped. Before him were tall fir trees, their wintry trunks climbing up to the sky, and beyond them nothing. The hair on his back bristled as he took a few more steps beyond the tree line and stood alone, for the first time, outside the Kiskadee Hills.

A flat, crusty earth stretched far and wide before him. He blinked a few times and sniffed the ground and air in all directions. Back in the Hills forest smells assaulted his nostrils nonstop: evergreen needles, wet leaves, dead mice, grasshoppers, snakes, swalas, things that crawled and things that flew. There were no signs of life up ahead, no trees, shrubs, or even tall grass to hide in. He was a Kisdee, and Kisdees never traveled out in the open.

Water gurgled down the slope behind him, an invitation to retreat behind the tree line where it was safe. He heard it sloshing and bubbling, accompanied by an unfamiliar drone;

his earflaps twitched. If this were summer it might have been bumblebees, but not in a cold, early spring morning. He climbed a little way up and circled around to be upwind. The hum continued unabated, no sign of alarm. Furtively, he crept back down, hair moistened by a fine spray. The stream cascaded down the sharp slope onto a wide, stony shelf, hitting it loudly and casting small bubbles up in the air. Somewhere below the hum paused briefly, then resumed. There was a somewhat sour but pleasant wooden odor. He dropped down on a cold, spongy turf of moist leaves, crawled till he reached the green, rotting branches of a juniper bush spread out over the wet slope, and peered out.

The water fell and disappeared through a hollow in the ground, and sprawled alongside it, mouth gaping open at the gray sky, lay a Magog.

Wordsworth didn't move. He knew what it was though he'd never seen one in his life, because, of course, Magogs were extinct, or supposed to be. It was the thing Kisdees snarled about in recalling their long-ago history, the nightmarish creature mothers invoked when they warned their pups to behave or else, the beast that had destroyed itself and much of the world in the far past.

A Magog. A female, his nose quietly told him. She stretched out alongside the wet, muddy hollow, drops of water freckling her face. Short, yellow hair covered the top of her head while the rest of her body was covered by long, gray, rolling strips smelling of cypress.

She hummed and babbled to herself, which puzzled Wordsworth. Dogs didn't even wag their tails when there was no one about. And he didn't understand her gibberish, though Arden had taught them all Magogish language long ago till it had finally become their own.

He should run back up and tell everyone, or at least the Enforcers. A Magog here, by the Flats! It changed every-thing—in what way he didn't know, he couldn't know so soon—but he was sure it did. He almost pulled back when his ears picked up a high-pitched sound—*creeee creeee*—like the scratchy, scrapy wail of trees in the middle of a storm. He looked down the slope, and when he next looked at the Magog she was sitting up and gazing straight at him.

Instantly he turned aside; in the Hills you never looked anyone in the face. But her eyes didn't waver, just kept on staring, and a soft growl climbed up his belly. She raised her upper paw. He snarled a warning and she stopped, holding the hand in midair. But by then his earflaps were quivering for the creaking noise had stopped in favor of something far worse: voices. Down below in the Flats, coming up to the spring.

And now the Magog turned her eyes away. "Dog," she said.

He licked his lips. That word, at least, he knew. He regis-tered another smell now, rare and barely familiar, coming from light brown strands of fur that encircled her throat. At the same time his nostrils told him that those coming up the slope were also Magogs. Males.

"Dog," she said again. Her brows bolted up and her face narrowed imploringly even as she kept it turned away from him. "Dog," she repeated in distress, "dog, dog, dog, dog."

Wordsworth leaped up, felt a sharp sting in his front paw, and scrambled up the incline. The wet earth shrouded the pounding of his legs and he might have run all the way up to the river but for the pain in his foot. He crouched down to lick the blood oozing from where the sharp juniper needle had pierced his paw. The female had gone silent. He listened, but there was no sign she was coming after him.

Magogs, he repeated to himself again, Magogs are back. We thought they were gone forever, but they're back. Dreden has to know, everyone has to know. He imagined breaking the news, the Flathead Terriers scurrying back and forth along the Bottoms barking nonstop, the mothers urging their pups into the shelter of their trembling bellies, Enforcers, led by Dreden, pitiless and stern, and finally Priam the Noble One, with his Great Dane's dark, stately head and calm, relentless eyes. Priam would restore order. He'd remind Kisdees of their glorious history, of Arden's battles on their behalf, of the exodus to the Hills after Magogs had died, of how no one was hated and scorned by all living creatures more than Magogs.

His strength returned, as well as curiosity. The more information I can bring back with me the better, he thought, getting up on his paws. Slowly he made his furtive way down again, this time on the other side of the stream. As he approached the rocky shelf he went on his belly and burrowed under large banks of silent, wet leaves, slithering down until, slowly and quietly, he poked his nose out.

His nostrils recoiled. This was not the soft, slightly sour, tree bark smell of the female, but the scent of sweat and disease. Males.

"You're a pair of snails, both of you. Stop talking and hurry it up. I don't want to run into Dreden."

It was the speaker who looked like a snail, with a big, round, shell-like body between a small head and very short legs. Standing on his hind legs, he wiped his upper paws against his belly, looking at a round object atop the shelf, whiter and rounder than anything Wordsworth had ever seen. Reaching out with his two patchy paws, he slowly picked it up.

There were three of them, all Magogs. Long ago they were known as humans, friends, even best friends. But friends didn't own you. Friends didn't breed you or enslave you. Friends didn't claim you as family and then abandon or kill you. Friends didn't massacre entire breeds or cause the extinction of the Ancients. And friends didn't cause the Great Calamity, killing off their own species and so many others.

Yet here they were again, aberrant, clumsy, and mindless. Not only didn't they have all their legs on the ground, they also had no tail for communication or fur for warmth, unlike the female with yellow hair on her head. Their faces were the ashen color of the Mercurial Moaners, a clan of dirty shorthair retrievers known for their laziness, only these Magogs also had large red blotches. At first he thought they were like the patches natural to many Kisdee breeds, till he remembered that they hadn't appeared anywhere on the female.

"He's busy," said the Magog who lifted the water-filled container with his upper paws and hoisted it onto his shoulder before heading down towards the tree line. "Haven't you heard? A Gawl escaped from the Flats."

"What about you?" Snail asked another Magog leaning against the wet rock with a similar large container on the ground. "Taking a rest, are we?"

"Isn't *she*?" This one was short, with a nose that seemed bent and flattened from a fight, but which now motioned towards the juniper bush where Wordsworth himself had lain earlier, and where the young female now sat staring as though he was still there.

His heart pounded. All she had to do was repeat that word again and they'd know about him. He readied to spring up and disappear.

"Hey Summer," Bent Nose now said, "want to do a little work?"

The female just sat staring at the bush as before.

"You know she doesn't talk," Snail said with a grimace. He walked over and touched her, and she shrank instantly, looking away. "You're all wet, Summer! What's wrong with you, girl? Aren't you cold? It's freezing out here."

Instead of replying, she began to hum again, rocking back and forth as she squatted on her hind legs. She didn't have much protection other than the thin, gray strips of bark that covered her body. The other Magogs wore padded pelts over their pale, blotchy skin. A fetid smell came from those blotches, but not from the girl, whose skin was clear.

"Feeding these dogs is the worst job in the world," Bent Nose said, scratching under his arm.

"Who cares? Fill this last bucket up and let's move."

Wordsworth trembled at the word *dogs*, but the Magog just filled up the container and walked off like the first, only to stumble when Snail turned his foot sideways right in his path. The container fell and the water splashed out.

"Why'd you do that for?"

Snail laughed uproariously, his face getting rounder and rounder, and then quickly tightened up. "What's the matter, no sense of humor? Come on, we can't wait forever."

Wordsworth puzzled over the Magog's clumsiness and why Snail found it so funny. Didn't they know water was precious? Bent Nose refilled the container, muttering to himself, and walked down the slope, looking warily over his shoulder.

"Come on, Summer, you can't sit in the mud like this forever." When the girl didn't budge, didn't so much as turn her head to face him, Snail reached out to touch her shoulder. She screamed and jumped up, arms flapping up and down like a bird as she shrieked and hollered, scaring Wordsworth so much he would have run if the other Magogs hadn't rushed back. Snail grabbed the girl. She kicked him but he held on. "Shut up!" he bellowed. "Shut up!"

Instantly she quieted down, keeping her head turned away. Snail looked up towards the others and smiled, till she leaned down and bit his paw. He let go with a yell. "Get her!"

But she slipped deftly away and disappeared behind the trees.

"She's a kid, you apes," Snail cursed them, licking the blood on his hand. "What's the matter, can't you hold on to a kid?"

"She's a crazy deaf-mute, you know that. Nobody sees her for days. They say she hides out in Adamant Tor."

"Adamant Tor! Why would anybody want to go back there again?"

Snail continued licking his hand, muttering as they retreated down the slope, the noise muffling the dog's quieter footsteps. At the tree line he peered out after them. A flat platform rested on round hoops he'd never seen before, with two long, heavy stalks protruding out front. Several full water containers sat on top and he watched as two of the Magogs put the stalks on their shoulders and pulled forward. The hoops circled round, calling out *creeee creeee*, and the platform moved. Then it stopped.

"Hey," yelled Bent Nose to Snail, who'd remained in back, "you're supposed to push, remember? We pull, you push."

"I'll push when I'm good and ready," Snail hissed. "Can't you see I'm hurt?"

"You know what I heard?" the other Magog said. "Dogs once used to do this."

That got Bent Nose's attention. "Dogs pulled carts instead of us?"

"That's what Badger said. They'd tie them up to the cart and they'd pull it. It happened up north where they had lots of snow. Of course, you'd need a bunch of them to pull something this heavy."

"We have a whole bunch of them right here. So why aren't they bringing *us* water instead of us pulling like jackasses to bring it to them?"

"Let's get going," Snail said from behind the platform.

The two Magogs put the stalk-like objects back on their shoulders while Snail stepped back to pick up large leaves to wrap around the wound in his hand. "They really did that?" asked Bent Nose in a low voice. "Dogs really pulled things for us?"

"They were our slaves, we owned them."

"So what happened? Why aren't we putting them to work now?"

"We are, stupid, they're watching our crops," Snail said loudly behind them. "And they'll die if you don't start moving this minute and bring them water."

"Fine with me," muttered Bent.

"If they die there'll be nobody to protect the crops and we'll starve," his companion said.

"Don't worry, you won't starve," Snail told them. "Badger will kill you first."

That promise had its intended effect, for the two Magogs pulled the heavy platform while Snail pushed from behind. It rolled forward unsteadily onto the flat fields — *creeee creeee* — on top of hoops that revolved faster than Wordsworth's eyes could follow. Eventually they disappeared into the morning mist. Then the mist itself seemed to disappear and all was clear and still once again.

He sat back; nothing moved. Behind him dawn had come and gone, and a gray, rain-smelling morning had spread over the Hills. For a moment it was as though the Magogs had never returned, but were still extinct as everyone believed. Only they were back. Clumsy and flat-footed, with smelly, sickly blotches, loud, shrill voices, and coarse manners, they were back.

And already working us, he reflected, though how was not clear. Bent Nose was obviously ignorant of what every

Kisdee pup knew, that a long time ago Magogs owned dogs. Dogs hunted, carted heavy weights, and guarded homes. "Why?" pups would always ask. "Food," was the answer. "We did it to survive. Only sometimes we became food ourselves." And then they would be taught Arden's words till they could recite them by heart. *You were enslaved by Magogs. Never trust them. Never look upon them. Avoid them at all times, especially if they offer friendship.*

But Ruwena had said nothing of Magogs. She has to know they're here, Wordsworth thought, she's a wolf, she must hate them worse than we do. So why did she tell me to find another dog instead, a Gawl? Was she mistaken? Should he go back to the Hills, tell Enforcers what he saw, and return to the Vale?

Go and find Daimyo's Fireside Stomping Beau.

She was not mistaken. She knew about Gawls down in the Flats and she saved him from Bludrun. He had to trust her.

He took his first steps beyond the tree line and, mystified, contemplated rows of grooves that extended monotonously up and down the hard ground. He'd never seen such things in the Hills. Pink streaks already straddled the heavens. Where was he supposed to go?

Look for him in the direction of sunrise!

He ran, twisted hind paw dangling, gulping in the cold, sharp morning air, heart thumping loudly in his golden chest. The compact earth was hard on him, accustomed as he was to moist, leafy paths, and his legs ached. He paused to lick his pads and a silver beam caught his eye. It was the large rock face of Adamant Tor looming unmistakably high over the tree line, brooding over the Flats. The Magog had said that the young female hid there.

He looked up the tall, narrow, sandstone monolith rimmed by eternal clouds, remembering the Magog's words: "Why would anybody want to go back there again?"

What were Magogs doing on Adamant Tor?

And that's when he heard it.

"Aiffff! Aiffff!"

Aiffff? What's Aiffff?

He hurried one way, then the other, before coming to a halt. Up ahead, something large and flat protruded from the ground, climbing up in a slant, a smaller version of the rock he'd lain on by the river. Behind it stood a wooden post.

"Aiffff! Aiffff!"

A low growl climbed up from his belly. He lowered himself down on the ground and wondered if he should bark. A greeting? A warning? The ground was littered with tufts of hair and the remains of squirrels, mice, moles, and woodchucks. Why would a Daimyo Akita—even a Gawl—bother to kill such small animals?

He inched closer and an idea flashed in his mind: The thing that poked out of the ground was a den. No self-respecting Kisdee would have a den like that, visible from a long way off and barely providing protection from the rain and sun. He came closer and closer till a flicker of movement caused him to stop, and he saw a small dark tip trembling in the breeze. His eyes tracked it slowly down a black leaf that stood in the air. It was an earflap, a tall, erect triangle, slightly rounded on top. He followed it down to the head, which peered over the top of the den, staring back at him, and exclaimed.

A Mixed Akita! A Gawl, just like she said.

He appraised him quickly. Eyes and chin were Akita, but the head was too big and, most important, the color was black, which made it all wrong. An Akita mixed with what? A thin strand lay inert on the ground behind him as he looked straight ahead, eyes unblinking, and Wordsworth bristled, arching his back. Even a Gawl should have better manners than that.

"Are you Daimyo's Fireside Stomping Beau?" he demanded.

The Gawl said nothing.

Does he talk, Wordsworth wondered. The Gawls up in the Hills did, though they didn't say much. He approached closer. "I say, are you Daimyo's Fireside Stomping Beau?"

Nothing.

Even closer. "You look like the Daimyos," he offered, still keeping a safe distance. "Sort of."

The Gawl stretched slightly forward, his large nose leading the rest of his head as he sniffed the air in Wordsworth's direction. How dirty he was, his black hairs caked by dust and filth, and droppings everywhere! He's probably scared out of his wits, Wordsworth thought, edging closer. Gawls were so fearful by nature. "Why don't you say something? Can't you speak?"

The Gawl remained where he was, frowning and watching Wordsworth's every move. The Golden took a few more steps, and the Gawl jumped.

THREE

Great jaws clamped on his neck so hard he could feel the sharp teeth right under his ears. He scrambled, paws raking the bare earth, but the furry body pinned him down. He tried to growl, but the Gawl sprawled so heavily on top of him, large snout deep inside his gold hairs, that he could hardly breathe. He tried to sink his own teeth into the other's neck, legs flailing in the air. "Get off me! Get off!"

The Gawl shifted his weight and Wordsworth saw the corners of his lips twitch. He looked higher and saw a mad, happy gleam in his eyes as the Deviant jumped up and sat back. Wordsworth rolled over and tottered up, but the other lunged and brought him down again, producing a sound he had never heard before: *Eee, eee, eee, eee*!

That's his laugh, Wordsworth thought in amazement, glimpsing the big face and white, flashing teeth. He's playing with me. Up in the Hills it was forbidden for Gawls to even brush against purebred Kisdees. A surge of anger gave him strength. Thrusting his head up, he grabbed hold of the other's neck. "Get—off—me—right—now," he growled.

Instantly the Gawl jumped up, lowered his body, and pulled back his earflaps in submission. His eyes darted nervously in all directions, large forehead creased and wrinkled. Wordsworth got up slowly, hackles bristling.

"Are you, or are you not, Daimyo's Fireside Stomping Beau?"

"I am Fireside Stomping Beau from the Daimyo clan," the Gawl replied, brightening up.

He snarled. "Is this any way to greet visitors, especially Kisdees?"

"I was just playing," the Mixed said, wagging his full, furry tail apologetically before letting it drop.

Not an Akita tail, Wordsworth thought, noticing how it fell behind the Gawl's legs instead of curling over his back. He began to lick the dust and grime off his own fur, turning to face away as was customary, but jumped back when he heard a horrible sound — sniff sniff sniff, pause, sniff sniff sniff — and felt something long and moist along his flanks. "What are you doing?"

"I'm smelling you," the Gawl said, wagging his tail again, eyes flitting back and forth anxiously. "Just getting to know —"

"Don't."

The Gawl's tail froze in midair and fell behind his legs again. "Why?"

"No one does that kind of thing anymore."

"They don't? What do they do?"

Wordsworth bared his teeth before continuing his energetic grooming, while the Gawl carefully watched his every move, scraping the ground nervously with his paw. There was a white blotch on his chest and small white streaks above his paws. Not that *he* bothered to clean up, the Golden noticed. "You can't be from the Daimyos," he said, "they're known for their fastidiousness."

"What's that?"

"In fact, you're probably not from the Hills at all, are you? You belong to Magogs. You came with them."

"My name is Daimyo's Fireside Stomping Beau, and the Daimyos live up in the Hills," the Gawl insisted.

"So how come you're down here with Magogs? How long have you been here?"

"As long as I can remember."

A Magog-owned dog, Wordsworth thought disgustedly. He probably depends on them to clean him up. "You can't be a Daimyo, looking like that."

"Like what?"

"You're a Gawl, a Mixed. One of your parents may have been an Akita, but not the other."

The Gawl pawed the ground nervously again and this time his ear tips fluttered. "I am Daimyo's Fireside Stomping Beau," he repeated, "a purebred Akita from the Daimyos of the Hills."

"No you're not," Wordsworth told him. "The shape of your head is wrong, your tail is wrong, your forehead is wrong, and most important, your color's wrong. No Daimyo is black. No Akita up in the Hills is black. You're a Gawl, not that that's any excuse. Even Gawls don't sniff anyone's hindquarters anymore, that was finished with a long time ago. We rely more on our vision than on our smell. And everybody in the Hills, purebreds and Gawls, knows how to greet visitors."

"How do you do that?" His forehead, wider than pure-bred Akitas', was as wrinkled and furrowed as the Flats.

"When someone appears you first look away, then you see whether—oh, forget it."

"No one ever comes here other than Magogs."

Creeee creeee creeee! He saw the platform rolling on gigantic hoops, water sloshing. Quickly he circled the den, sniffing anxiously, eyes scanning the Flats for movement. Then he turned back to Beau, who was staring at his suspended back paw. "Do Magogs live here with you?"

"No, their dens are further back."

"They bring you water, right?"

"And food."

"What about the kills back there?" he asked, remembering the dead rodents he'd seen while creeping up towards the Gawl.

"They don't come here anymore; they know I always catch my prey." He wagged his tail eagerly. "You should have seen me ambush them! I'm fast."

"I don't believe it, you depend on Magogs for food." He couldn't hide his revulsion. Why would anyone, even a Gawl, stay with Magogs for their pitiful food and water? Long ago there was no choice, but things changed. Dogs that left Magogs and followed Arden to the Kiskadee Hills prospered, with peace and abundance everywhere, while all those that trusted Magogs died along with them in the Great Calamity. Only not all. He snarled softly. "When will your owners visit you next?"

"They're not my owners and I don't know!" His earflaps fluttered wildly, overcome by emotion. "What's wrong with your paw?"

Ignoring him, Wordsworth looked behind the wooden den and found containers like the one he'd seen earlier. "Do you sleep under here?"

"Sometimes, if it rains or if it's too hot." The Gawl walked a little way and raised his leg.

The Kisdee stared.

"I'm marking my territory," the Gawl explained, his black forehead creasing once again in puzzlement. "Don't *you* do that?" The Golden felt repelled and curious at the same time. It was said that long ago dogs had urinated to mark their territory. "How do *you* mark?" Beau asked eagerly. "I mean, since you can't stand on one of your back legs."

Wordsworth grimaced. *That*, at least, was one thing he didn't have to worry about. "I'm a purebred Kisdee from the Kiskadee Hills. We don't need to—as you say—mark our territory, we know where our home is. The Dobies are in Doby Dell, the Corgis in Humpback Crest, the Sheepdogs in the Green Ravine. I was born on Golden Mesa, where my family has lived for generations. No Mastiff or Ridgeback would dream of trespassing, we have our Rules."

"What's wrong with your paw?"

"I was born this way."

"Are all Goldens born like that?"

"Of course not," Wordsworth snapped. It didn't help that the Gawl was sniffing it from a distance, his large nostrils further dilated to reveal quick, tiny movements of hair.

"I bet you can't chase down squirrels and chipmunks with a leg like that."

"Why bother? That's the work of smaller Kisdees. I'm a Golden Retriever, not a Flathead."

"What's a Flathead?"

"Flatheads are Terriers because the tops of their heads are flat. They call us, the big hunters and guards, Curveheads."

"Do Flatheads and Curveheads fight?"

"Fight? Why should we fight?"

"Akitas are great fighters," said Beau, sitting up tall now, ears at full attention. "Especially Daimyos."

Wordsworth almost laughed out loud. How did this funny-looking Gawl, with the outlandishly big head, collapsing tail, and wrong color, just as Gawlish as could be, get the idea that he was a Daimyo Akita? Could the Magogs have told him? If so, then they had to know about the Daimyos, which meant that they'd been up in the Hills.

"What's the matter?" asked Beau, with an anxious wave of his tail.

"Kisdees haven't fought for generations. We don't have an enemy in the world."

"No fighting?"

"Not since Fearsome Arden returned from the Glade of Remorse and created the Great Alliance, putting an end to all wars."

"Daimyos fight," insisted the Gawl. "They fight Tug-a-Lugs."

"How did you know?" The Gawl was right. The one exception to the peace in Kiskadee was the feud between the Daimyos and the Tug-a-Lugs, which was as old as the Great

Alliance. "Anyway, it doesn't matter, most of the time even Daimyos don't fight. They live in peace like the rest of us."

The Gawl was clearly disappointed. "Then what do you do all day?"

"What do we do?" What a strange creature this Magogish dog was. "We work. The hunters hunt, the haulers bring the kills down to the Bottoms so that everyone can eat, and the guards guard. We do that every single day without stop."

"What do you do?"

"I hunt."

"You catch something with a leg like that?"

"Of course." He caught the slower, older swalas, which were not as tasty as the young, juicy ones. "But mostly I'm a poet."

"What's a poet?"

"I recite poems."

"What's that?"

Wordsworth pondered a moment. "When I say the truth through words, I create a poem."

"Don't you do that anyway when you talk?"

"I mean the deepest truth that I'm capable of."

Now it was the Gawl who seemed puzzled. In fact, thought Wordsworth, he looked much like his own family, the Moody Sunshine Goldens, had looked when he told them that he wanted to move to the Vale. *You're leaving your home for a poem?*

"Never mind," he said, glancing up at the morning sky. In the Hills the grass would be shimmering and the robins singing. Down here in the Flats nothing shimmered and nothing sang. And then he remembered why he was here. He eyed Beau carefully. "Don't you have something to tell me?"

The Gawl looked at him in bewilderment.

"Kisdees are in danger. A day will come when you will have to decide," he repeated.

Beau's eyes opened wide. "Decide what?"

"Don't you know?"

"No," said the Gawl, black brow furrowing.

"For that you must know the truth. What truth?"

The Gawl sat back, eyes narrowing into slits, thinking hard. Then he grinned. "I give up," he announced with a bounce of his tail, "tell me."

"You give up?" Wordsworth stared. She can't be mistaken, he thought. Beau wiggled his belly in friendship and the Golden growled. Something here made no sense. Was the Gawl keeping something from him? He didn't seem devious.

"What's the matter?" asked Beau.

The trees beckoned; there was still time to run back and up the slope without being discovered. Instead he sat back on his haunches and asked the question that had bothered him from the beginning. "Why are you here? Why aren't you up in the Hills along with the rest of us?"

"Because I'm tied up," Beau said matter-of-factly.

"Tied up? What does that mean?"

"It's hanging from my neck, can't you see?"

And for the first time, Wordsworth did see. In fact, he'd seen it earlier when he first caught sight of Beau lying on top of his den, but didn't know what the long, thin strand protruding from the Gawl's back was. It fell down after circling Beau's neck, coiling on the ground like a snake and twisting around the base of the den till it reached the wooden post, where it was fastened in knots.

He'd heard about the Magogish time when dogs were tied up, when they couldn't wander at will, running, hunting, playing wherever they wished. He could never imagine it but here it was, right in front of him. He approached Beau careful-ly, buried his nose in his neck and tried to nudge the wire. It didn't move. He licked it a few times, and just then Beau swiveled his head sharply to the side. The wire stirred and Wordsworth jumped back. "Can it take me, too?"

"No, Magogs put it around you. I'm just trying to do what I did back when I escaped."

"You escaped? You escaped this thing?"

The Gawl's eyes glittered. "Once."

"How?"

Beau's face shone. "I've been trying to escape every single day of my life. One morning there was a noise and I swung my head around quickly, and suddenly I was free. My head was free."

"What did you do?"

"I ran like the wind. I made it to the Hills and up to the river. Leaves were falling and I chased them in the air. Do they fall all the time? I felt the cool air in my fur and I ran and ran and—"

"What happened?"

"Enforcers caught me and brought me back here."

"Enforcers?" He stared in disbelief.

"Two of them." And now his lips tightened around his teeth and his eyes darkened. "They tracked me down and jumped me and then—"

"You're lying," Wordsworth said frostily. "You never left here, and Enforcers didn't bring you back to Magogs."

"I did, and they did." The tips of his tall earflaps started shaking in the air once again.

"No one even knows Magogs are here, no one knows you're here." Ruwena knew, a voice whispered inside. "No," he snarled, leaping up on his paws. "You stay with Magogs because you love them. They bring you stale food and smelly water, they give you this miserable den—and for that you love them!"

"I don't! I ran away. All my life I tried to escape, and when I finally did, Enforcers brought me back here." There was no mistaking the deep sadness inside Beau's eyes and Wordsworth noticed that one of the earflaps was torn down the middle. "I begged them to let me go, let me stay in the Hills, but they just laughed. They said they'd brought me down here as a pup and now they were bringing me back."

"You said you've been here all your life."

"I don't remember anything else, but one of them said he brought me down here right after I was born. Now I was a little more trouble but not much more, and he laughed. They called him Markus."

The grinning Enforcer by the river.

"He said I was so dumb I left tracks everywhere. I begged them to kill me instead of tying me up again, but Badger said I'll be dead soon enough."

"Who's Badger?"

"The head of the Magogs."

Badger will kill you first, Snail had warned Bent Nose. *They're watching our crops.* What were crops?

He tried to make sense of the crazy story he'd just heard. An Enforcer had taken a Gawl pup down to Magogs whom no one knew existed, let them tie something around his neck and left him down here, abandoned and alone! He must be making it up, he thought dully, maybe he heard Markus's name somewhere. But Beau also knew about the Daimyos. He knew about the river and the falling leaves. He was primitive and dirty, but he seemed guileless as a pup. "Was it Markus who said you were a Daimyo?"

Beau pawed the ground. "I remember someone telling me that long ago: *You are Daimyo's Fireside Stomping Beau.* Maybe it was my mother. She must have been a Daimyo if she said that, right?"

You're a Moody Sunshine Golden; don't let anybody tell you different. That's what his mother, Moody Sunshine Loreen, had told him. What was Beau's mother's name? Did she disappear, too? His stomach ached and rumbled. Up in the Hills he always ate grass or young green shoots when that happened, but there were none down here in the Flats.

Why, he asked himself, looking all around him. Why would Enforcers do this? Beau was a Gawl, but still a dog. Up in the Hills he'd be put to work with other Gawls, hauling swala carcasses down to the Bottoms. It wasn't much, but it was better than this. Anything was better than this. He thought of Bent Nose. If Magogs ever stopped bringing Beau water, he would die. He depended on them for his life as dogs had done long ago, the very thing Arden had warned against. Only he wasn't doing this from choice. Was this what Ruwena wanted him to discover?

"How many others are tied up this way?"

Beau didn't know. There must be more, Wordsworth thought, remembering the water containers he'd seen. And what about the Gawl who escaped and was captured by Enforcers, the one they called Charlotte? *The longer she's in the forest, the more dangerous she is. Somebody might see her.* And Markus had added, *They want Charlotte back.*

They'll get Charlotte when we're good and ready. Or else we'll bring them someone else. Dreden had said those words, which was most confounding of all. Dreden, who hated anything that wasn't pure, who hated the very name Magogs.

Beau whimpered and Wordsworth, deep in thought, at first didn't hear him. Finally he looked up. "What did you say?"

"Set me free."

He took a step back. "Are you crazy?"

"Set me free," implored Beau, mewling softly under small, pleading eyes.

A wave of pity swept over him. Beau was a Gawl, different from him, but no one deserved to be tied down here by Magogs. "Beau, I've already broken the Rules just coming down here."

"Set me free, please!"

"I don't know how." He began to walk away, but something landed on top of him. He fell on his side and rolled over onto his back, paws scratching the air, Beau's muzzle deep in his fur.

The Gawl gripped his neck hairs so hard he thought he'd choke to death. Summoning all his strength, he flung himself up and landed on his paws, but before he could straighten up Beau's teeth fastened around his neck once again and began to drag him on the ground. "Set me free," he muttered over and over again, "set me free."

"I don't know how," Wordsworth gasped. "I don't know how!"

He jumped back, pivoting so hard on his good back leg he almost fell flat, but stayed up and started to run. Too late! Behind him he could hear Beau leap up and prepare to pounce. He turned around, stiffening, just in time to see Beau violently twisted in midair, jerked savagely back, and thrown down on his side with a crash.

Wordsworth limped towards him. The Gawl lay paralyzed, looking out at the endless flat fields. Dangling over him was the thin wire, no longer in loose coils but drawn tautly from his neck to the wooden post. Wordsworth could make out the white of one eye, the dark pupil drowned in misery. He didn't look up.

"Beau."

"Help me," the Gawl said in a low voice. "Help me."

Wordsworth came closer.

"Don't leave me here alone, help me." But his voice was flat, as if he'd lost all hope. Then his ear grew taut, tip twisting slightly.

"What's the matter?"

The Gawl jumped up and Wordsworth leaped back. But Beau swiveled and looked out at the Flats, and the Golden followed his gaze. The air was so still it felt solid; he couldn't see a thing. But Beau stood rigid, almost mesmerized, tail frozen in place. He sniffed the air several times, paused, and then sniffed again. Was there something moving after all?

Creeee creeee creeee. It was large and cumbersome, raising dust, coming from the opposite direction of the Hills, rolling and creaking towards them.

No one moved.

The small dust storm changed direction and rolled towards sunset.

"They're not coming here," Beau said.

But by then Wordsworth was already running. He didn't mean to, he didn't want to, but his legs clobbered that packed, bare earth without asking, carrying him to the tree line, back to the Hills. The hard, wintry soil thumped back, but if there was pain he didn't feel it. A voice pounded again and again, in perfect rhythm with his paws: *They were our slaves, we owned them. Creeee creeee! We owned them, we owned them.*

"They're not coming here! Come back!"

He knew that Beau had lunged forward, only to be taken down hard by the wire around his neck, but it didn't matter. He practically flew on three good legs, ignoring the throbbing, rocky ground and the fierce hurt in his bad leg. Something sharp bit one of his pads, but only when he crossed the tree line and was back among the shadows did he finally bend down and lick it, and even then he could still hear the echo of Beau's last cry:

"They're—not—coming—here!"

FOUR

*I*t *was the old dream.*

It always started with the sound of hooves pounding the earth: swalas, their pungent smell causing the hunters to mewl in excitement as they rushed after the small antelopes in the daily race towards the Cliffs, for the Cliffs meant safety for the swalas and hunger for Kisdees. And he was running, too, alongside Mabel and Cicero, running on all four legs as fast and strong as the others, first the two front legs, and then the back two hitting the ground effortlessly and naturally, as though he'd done it all his life. He could feel the earth give way under him as he ran faster than everybody else, closing in on a young swala.

The wind sailed at his back and the air hummed. The Cliffs rushed towards him, he could see the caves dotting their tall rocks. Soon the young swala would reach its base and hop high onto a ledge above the dogs' heads, reaching safety. But he leaped first, feeling the back haunches of the antelope practically in his mouth. He snapped his jaws – on air. The antelope seemed to vault right over his head, landing on a high rock overhead while he crashed on his belly. Pain tore through his legs. Instead of the bitter flavor of swala skin he tasted dust and grit. He tried to rise, and fell flat on the ground. Mabel tittered behind him; then Cicero laughed, joined by the other Goldens. And as the guffaws spread, so did the pain, climbing now up to his flanks, his back, and then his neck so that he was completely paralyzed. He whimpered softly to himself but the others didn't hear, they were laughing too hard.

The sun was warm — and wet. Someone was licking his face. "Rise and shine, rise and shine," said the familiar gruff voice. Wordsworth opened his eyes and the large oblong head above him nodded happily. "We're sleeping late today, yes we are, yes we are." Then it disappeared. But as Wordsworth yawned and stretched, it continued: "I didn't see you at the Bottoms yesterday, no I did not."

He paused and gazed at Birdy from the corner of his eye. The pepper-and-salt Giant Schnauzer was grinning as usual, eyes scurrying back and forth in search of birds. His name was Werner, but everyone called him Birdy because he loved to chase birds. He'd go after pigeons walking stoutly on the ground, craning their short necks in search of seeds, or else he'd run round and round in circles, barking at flocks of small sparrows in the air. He was practically Wordsworth's only visitor and made no secret of the fact that his visits were due more to birds than to friendship, for Birdy, mouth open in an eternal jaunty grin, claimed that there were more birds at Poet's Vale than anywhere else in the Hills.

The sun had advanced in the sky, morning was well on its way. He'd slept through yesterday, last night, and half the morning. Drops fell on his face. It must have rained during the night for the gigantic willow was drying itself, shaking its branches free of water. He dug behind a maple on the other side of the clearing, Birdy looking away delicately as he did so, till he brought out two thick, warped swala bones. He nudged one over to his friend, who happily pulled it between his paws, went down on his stomach and gave two exploratory licks.

"Sleeping late this morning, yes we are," the Giant Schnauzer repeated good-naturedly. "Working on your po-e-try?" Birdy himself couldn't care less about poetry, but as a guest he had to make the proper inquiries.

Wordsworth munched on his bone and said nothing. He wasn't feeling particularly sociable, he needed time to think about what happened yesterday. Scenes flashed in his mind: Beau lying flat, brought down by a Magogish contraption coiled around his neck; the grinning Enforcer by the river; a young female Magog smelling of cypress with her upper paw pointing at him. Did all this really happen? Could he have imagined the large female Gawl at the river that night with the upturned russet head and long arched neck? *One day I won't run, from Enforcers or anyone else.*

He looked at Birdy. The Giant Schnauzer knew all the news and loved nothing more than to wander from family to family, clan to clan, sharing what he heard and picking up new tidbits of information. Now he prattled like he always did, high-spirited, good-natured, and a little foolish, licking his bone contentedly.

Wordsworth walked over to the stream at the end of the clearing. It reminded him of the small waterfall by the Flats and he looked down the slope. Beau was somewhere far below, with his large, black earflaps, one of which was torn down the middle, tips dancing in the air. He bent down to drink.

"Did you hear the news? Did you hear the news?"

Birdy's bearded, whiskered face brushed his own as the Giant Schnauzer drank too. Water dribbled from his hairs as, unable to restrain himself any longer, he whispered: "There was another killing. Yes sir, another killing." His short tail, angled high, waved back and forth in excitement.

Wordsworth looked up. "What are you talking about?"

"They found her yesterday. A Black and Tan Setter, Dizzy Birdsong Margaret. Birdsong," Birdy repeated happily, scanning the sky.

"*Another* killing? You mean there was one before?"

"You didn't know?" Birdy straightened up in a vain effort to appear grave, but he could not repress the glint in his oval eyes. Suddenly he was gone.

"Birdy!"

But his friend had espied a black-and-white chickadee that had just flown off a bare hickory branch onto the ground. He rushed it, and when it flew back up the tree he ran round and round and barked excitedly. Birdy's communications were usually punctuated by sudden enthusiastic bird chases and there was nothing anyone could do about it.

The Golden waited till Birdy returned after giving a delighted growl of frustration in the direction of the chickadee. "There have been two terrible killings in less than a week," he announced, as though there had been no interruption. "Two! Murdered. Massacred!" His eyes danced under the massive eyebrows, bushy whiskers twitching.

"There have been no killings in Kiskadee as long as I can remember."

"I know," Birdy said regretfully. "No fights, no battles, no violent deaths."

Kisdee families and clans fought and feuded, that was only natural. But ever since the Great Alliance nothing was permitted to get out of hand. Fighting, brawling and wrangling were fine; killing was strictly forbidden by Arden's First Rule. Even the feud between the Daimyos and the Tug-a-Lugs, many generations old, had resulted in occasional injuries when the two families met, but never any casualties.

"What happened?"

"I'll tell you what I heard," said Birdy, and off he ran again, this time after a couple of robins flying low across the Vale. They alighted on a tall branch, Birdy beneath them, tail wagging gleefully as if any moment they'd tumble down straight into his open jaws. Everyone liked Birdy well enough, but it was generally acknowledged that no self-respecting Kisdee would ever chase birds.

"I was this close," he complained when he came back, bending down to assuage his thirst. Then he sat back, drops running down his scraggly beard as he scrunched his un-kempt eyebrows. "The first was a Terrier, Ledoon's Famished Max. Yes, Famished Max."

"I don't think I know him."

"Nobody knew him. The Ledoons tend to stay by them-selves, feed a lot on rabbits back home at Grumble Grange. So nobody missed Max till a Gawl found his body a week ago on their side of the Curl. At least, what was left of it," he added, eyes glinting. "What was left of it," he repeated, louder this time.

"What do you mean?"

"I can't tell you."

"Okay." Wordsworth walked away.

Birdy hurried to catch up. "You promise not to tell anyone?"

"Promise." By now Birdy had told everything he knew to half the Kisdees in the Hills.

"He'd been devoured. Eaten! Eyes gone, tongue gone, throat cut, legs ripped, chest split, insides removed," recited Birdy, whiskers fluttering. "Some of it was left right by his body and *some of it was gone*!"

On other occasions Wordsworth would have laughed at the way Birdy's shaggy eyebrows twitched meaningfully. Luckily, custom dictated that he avert his glance, which he was all too glad to do now. A hawk circled high up, ignored by Birdy, who for some reason had never developed an interest in hawks. It swooped up and down, as if enjoying the freshness of a spring morning after rain. The trees soared up to the sunlight in joyful anticipation, like expectant mothers. It was a morning meant to be celebrated in verse.

"It could be a bear," he offered. "Bears are hungry when they wake up at the end of winter and —"

"Not a bear. Besides, there haven't been too many bears around the Hills lately." Birdy's teeth flashed. Everyone knew there were no big animals in the Hills anymore, no predators for Kisdees to worry about. Till now.

"Did they recognize the tracks?"

"It's one of us."

"What? That's impossible!" He thought of the two green, coiled eyes and the smell of fire and rot, shrouded by a misty, vaporous skin. And it had left dog tracks?

"Why do you say that?"

"I mean it's a violation of Arden's First Rule," he back-tracked. "Besides, it's—"

"Cannibalism," Birdy said happily. "They say that Bird-song Margaret looked worse than Famished Max even though a Setter's bigger and twice as fast. Yes sir, twice as—"

"Was it the same set of tracks?"

"It was. Cannibalism!" Birdy repeated happily again.

Wordsworth listened to the sound of water spilling down below "Who could it be?"

"Not a Kisdee. Kisdees don't eat each other."

"They did during the Ravages." When Kisdees had first arrived in the Hills, without Magogs to depend on, they couldn't find much prey. Worse, they'd forgotten how to hunt. The first to die off were the small dogs, who'd been toys for Magogs but couldn't fend for themselves in the wild. Soon entire breeds had disappeared.

"How I wish I was around then," whined Birdy. "Think of those years: the Great Calamity, the extinction of Magogs, dogs fighting each other to the bitter end. What a time to be alive!" He sighed, thinking of the excitement back then, before Arden had returned from the Glade of Remorse, founded the Great Alliance of Kisdees, taught dogs how to govern them-selves, and even found swalas in the Cliffs for them to hunt. Things had been humdrum ever since. But now there was danger once again, and his chest puffed out in pride. "That's why I'm on duty."

"What duty?"

"I've become a guard," and Birdy straightened up his forelegs and brought his elbows close in perfect Schnauzer alignment, before dropping on the ground and rolling on his back with a big guffaw.

"You, a guard!" Putting Birdy on duty against the killer in the mist was like telling Milly Marmaduke, head of the Daschunds, to lean against a tottering great white pine to prevent it from falling. "You're a hauler. You're supposed to bring swalas down to—"

"Not anymore, I'm not," sang Birdy, clambering back up on his paws. "They've got Gawls to do that. I'm guarding this side of Bloodroot Hill, yes I—"

"This place?" Wordsworth looked around in disbelief, searching for someone to guard against. Bloodroot Hill, overlooking the Vale, was small; no one lived there beside himself. "What exactly are you supposed to do?"

"Keep an eye on comings and goings, goings and comings."

"Like what?"

"Nothing," Birdy replied, eyebrows sinking in disappointment. "What's there to see around here? You don't think Rathbane is going to show up at the Vale, do you?"

"Rathbane?"

But Birdy was gone once again, barking shrilly at three crows. Wordsworth watched him give furious chase, zigzagging around the trees, darting deeper into the woods. Guards usually protected the kills from other animals, though these were few and far between since Kisdees had no predators. Except one. Bludrun, Ruwena called him that night, an Ancient, a wolf who wanted to destroy all dogs.

"Don't you want to know about him?" Birdy was asking, slightly panting.

"Rathbane?"

"Shhh," whispered Birdy in alarm, glancing in all directions. "You don't have to say his name out loud."

"They think it was him?"

"You should have seen the tracks!"

"You were there?"

"An Enforcer told me. No one's got giant paw prints like that except for him."

"I thought Rathbane was gone to the Land of the Gawls."

Everyone whispered when they talked about the Gawl Rathbane, born to the Tug-a-Lug clan of Wolfhounds. The biggest of the large Tug-a-Lugs, he was taken across the river like other Gawl pups, but refused to haul swalas and ran away. Dreden cornered him and the two fought. Rathbane lost the sight in one eye, but managed to break loose and was never caught. In fact, no one had ever seen him again. Dreden claimed he was dead, but tales began to spread. A young Beagle swore that she'd seen him in a cave at night, his blind eye blazing white. One of the Pointers had him crouching on the top branch of a tree, while an older Malamute spied him by the Cliffs one twilight, bearded head reddened by the sunset. Dreden had scoffed at all these stories.

"They're not saying that anymore," said Birdy, who always maintained that Rathbane was alive and well, a threat to the life and well-being of every Kisdee. "And everyone knows that he likes to drink blood."

"We all like it. What's better than a bloody, meaty bone?"

"He likes to drink *our* blood. Kisdee blood."

"Who says?"

"Zebu, my new boss. In fact, he says he saw him on the Gawl side of the river."

"Did he fight him?"

"He tried, but Rathbane disappeared."

"That's too bad."

The sarcasm wasn't lost on Birdy. "You better be careful when you talk like that, you better. Zebu's in charge of all the guards now and you know who's his brother."

He didn't need to be reminded. It was hard for him to hide his distaste. Enforcers were ruthless, but Zebu, Dreden's younger brother, had a special reputation for cruelty and humiliation. He smiled mischievously. "Aren't you scared, Birdy, being out there all by yourself?"

Birdy's grin disappeared. "Just between us," he whispered, whiskers trembling, "he could jump me when I'm all alone on Bloodroot Hill and — and —"

"Make you his next meal."

Birdy nodded tragically. He was a Giant Schnauzer, but he would be no match for Rathbane.

"He has only one eye," Wordsworth reminded him.

"He'd be a lot less dangerous if he had no eye, but that won't happen unless he drowns." When he saw his friend's confusion he added, "The Prophet said that Rathbane will lose all his vision if he is burned by water." Babylon, the Puli, had been prophesying all his life, but few Kisdees paid any attention to him other than Birdy.

"How do you get burned by water?"

"The Prophet didn't say," and Birdy ran back to the woods, following the irresistible knocking of an officious woodpecker.

So they were blaming the killings on Rathbane. He himself had never seen the giant, but it was common knowledge that Dreden hated him. The Gawl had managed to escape Enforcers despite losing sight in one eye. Was he really still alive? Where could he hide? Was he seeking revenge? Had he gone mad? That could happen to anyone who was alone for so long. That could happen to Beau.

He felt a familiar scratching in his throat, followed by a cough, and the words tumbled out before he knew it:

"He wavers between two worlds,"
Clinging first to life, then death,
Rules mightily both kingdoms
Of the darkness and the breath.

Unrepentant in dark shadows,
With an eye that will not blink,
He waits in dreadful silence,
Until – "

"Until we throttle him, I think."

Raucous laughter rang in the Vale as he jumped up and turned around. Mouth pulled back, sharp white teeth protruding under a curled lip. And the harsh, bitter scent of terraberries.

FIVE

"**A** small contribution to your little ballad, Lame Declaimer."

It wasn't Dreden. The Head of the Enforcers was too humorless to add a silly line like that, nor did he have that slight amused drawl. The Shepherd walking past him, sniffing derisively, was Zebu, his muzzle narrower and his head lower than his older brother's. Another large silhouette glided from behind a balsam fir into the clearing. Dark eyes glittered at Wordsworth, the black hair of his head gleaming in the sunlight. He opened his jaws and grinned. Markus.

Kisdee etiquette called for visitors to wait at the edge of others' territory till receiving permission to enter. Markus, like Zebu before him, didn't care about Kisdee etiquette and stepped briskly across the crisp brown leaves. The two Enforcers were almost identical; only Zebu, with his ample flanks and famous appetite, was heavier than the other. He now eyed with interest the two swala bones lying on the ground after taking in the Vale with an indifferent sweep of his head, his black and tawny tail in a still, downward curve. "He ran over the ridge. Probably thinks we didn't see him."

Markus growled.

"Don't get excited, the bird-chaser just needs a little talk." Zebu seemed lost in contemplation of the bones. "Most kind of the Bard of the Vale to leave us these, hey Markus?" And with that he stretched out on the ground and began to gnaw the very bone that Wordsworth had crunched earlier.

A growl rose from the Golden's belly at this gross violation of Kisdee conduct.

At first it didn't seem Zebu heard him, tongue happily wrapped around the bone. Then he raised his head and squinted impassively at the maples in the distance. "Something bothering you, Versifier? Let's see if I can put it into rhyme:

These bones are for friends, not for an Enforcer.
Markus and Zebu, don't come any closer.
Don't get too curt, don't get too wordy,
'Cause words, dear Markus, are for the Birdy!"

He laughed stridently, like a crow, before bending down once more. "Come and get your bone, Markus, these have a nice taste. Surprising, but so. Something in the soil, maybe."

Markus approached, but instead of getting down on his belly he looked at Wordsworth, his upper lip still raised to reveal sharp, white teeth. "He left his post," he said hoarsely, never losing his grin.

Zebu took a few more licks and sighed. "Like I said, he'll need a little talk. The new guards don't have our discipline, Markus, they weren't born to it. Unfortunate, but so. You know what my brother says: *Enforcers are bred, never taught.* It's a different time now. Kisdees are finally waking up to the danger they're in. Even senile, old Furrow Face has seen the light." Without so much as a sideways glance, he asked: "Something bothering you again, Versifier?"

Silver Bear Priam, a Great Dane with a massive square jaw, was the Noble One, head of the Kisdee Circle. The last bear seen in the Hills had once slashed his face with his claws, giving rise to the nickname Furrow Face, which Kisdees only used beyond Priam's hearing.

Zebu's teeth ground away at the bleached swala bone. "Let me guess," he said, his tongue making a long sweep under his upper jaw. "You disapprove of how I talk about our Noble One. But the truth is, everyone talks this way about Furrow Face, even in Circle meetings. You know why? Because he sleeps through them. You could make fun of him all you want and he doesn't hear a thing." He raised his voice and addressed the grinning Enforcer. "That's what happens, Markus, when Noble Ones stay on long past their time. Unfortunate, but so. Luckily, Furrow Face's time is finally running out."

Wordsworth's ears pricked up in surprise. Half loved, half feared, Priam had been the Kisdees' leader longer than any of his predecessors except for Arden himself. "Is the Noble One sick?"

Zebu contemplated the swala bone. "Sick? Maybe. Dying? Maybe. I think it's safe to say that he won't be the Noble One much longer."

"No one's ever challenged him before."

"Maybe there'll be a hunt soon," Zebu said pleasantly, never once looking towards him. "And speaking of hunt, Versifier, what were you doing in the forest two nights ago? You were seen on the upper slope above the Bottoms."

His tail tensed and his ears fell back. "I visited Golden Mesa."

"Missed the family, eh?" said Zebu, eyes still on the bone. "It's hard when a Kisdee doesn't stay with his clan, doesn't pay respects to the head of the family. Hard for us to keep an eye on him, too. Golden Mesa's not far from Setters Haven. Not far from where Dizzy Birdsong Margaret was found." Now, finally, he turned to Wordsworth. "You didn't happen to see her by any chance, Versifier?"

"I saw her."

"Dead or alive?" asked Zebu cheerfully.

"Dead."

"And what did you do?"

Wordsworth looked down at the swala bone between Zebu's paws. Should he tell him about Bludrun?

"You ran, didn't you? Or should I say that you wobbled fast? Rolled and shimmied downhill just as fast as your belly could take you?" Markus snickered. Zebu's voice dipped into an almost fatherly softness. "And tell me, Lame Declaimer, what did you do later that night?"

His heart sank. "I went down to the river."

"In the middle of the night? You recited so many verses you were thirsty?"

"As a matter of fact, I *was* thirsty. I wanted to—"

There was a high giggle and then his head exploded. At first all he saw was black for Markus was hanging over him, muzzle pressing tightly against his neck, teeth buried in his flesh. The Enforcer was in his fighting trance. Eyes shut, he seemed relaxed, even happy. Only his teeth ground deeper and harder, causing every nerve cell in Wordsworth's body to shrink and shrivel, till finally he cried out. But Markus didn't let him go till the cries turned into screeches and his legs crumbled under him.

He lay flat on his belly inside a dove-gray fog, tongue tasting dust. When the throbbing slowed down enough to clear his head, he saw Zebu sitting on his haunches close by, contemplating him serenely.

"You were at the river to meet the Gawls. Who are they?"

"I don't know, I just—" He felt Markus's hot breath over his neck. "I don't know! I never saw them before!"

"You just happened to be at the river when they showed up."

"They weren't meeting me, I don't know who they are." He saw Zebu's muzzle move slightly towards Markus and he braced himself for more pain. But Markus stayed where he was.

"They were meeting up with someone, or trying to," said Zebu. "There's a way we can find out the truth." He looked down Bloodroot Hill towards the river. "You and Markus heard the voices of two of our Gawl friends. You may have actually seen them. We need to know who they are. Obviously, they won't tell Markus anything, so that leaves you. You don't have to talk much with them, you get *them* to talk, and once you put the names to the voices you tell Markus and he'll do the rest."

So that was Dreden's solution. The Head of the Enforcers had seen him that night. "Why should they tell me anything? I'm not a Gawl."

"You're close enough," Zebu said with a grimace. He got up and stretched, black fur glittering in the sun. "It's a lot to ask; Gawls are such an affront to the eyes. Still, we have our duty. Markus and I do distasteful things on occasion, don't we, Markus?"

Markus seemed positively happy to do distasteful things. "You start today," he told Wordsworth hoarsely, with a grin. "Now." His forehead was pockmarked and scarred.

"Don't forget, this isn't the time for versifying. It's *their* voices we care about, not yours. Now move!" commanded Zebu.

His eyes gleamed and Wordsworth knew why. They wanted to watch him get up in his usual slow, awkward way and mock his upturned, ungainly hip. *If you know that you should have died long ago, there's nothing more to fear.* He kept his eyes down. "The Noble One gave me special dispensation to live here, hunt, and recite my poetry."

"We're not telling you to leave here, we're telling you to spy," Zebu replied good-naturedly, eyes glinting maliciously as they scrutinized Wordsworth's back leg. "Besides, everyone knows you're no good as a hunter."

"I bring down swalas."

"Slow ones, like you. Unfortunate, but so. Anyway, Furrow Face is not in charge. No work, no food; that's the new rule of the Hills. No more slackers with hearty appetites. No more bards or poets, no more lame declaimers talking to themselves." Zebu turned back to contemplate his bone. "There's too much talk, not enough action. Not enough deviants going to the Land of the Gawls. If your mother had kept that in mind, Versifier, she might still be around today."

He never felt the pressure on his back leg when he leaped up in the air; in fact he felt nothing till he crashed on top of

Zebu, and then he was aware of everything at the same time: the roar that burst out of his chest, the flare of pain, the snap of his teeth at Zebu's neck and the fangs reaching for the tawny throat. He would have connected, too, if Zebu hadn't hungered for the swala bone, turning his head an instant earlier and thus preserving his throat. With a snarl Markus pulled him off, but not before Wordsworth, scratching and tearing, tasted blood as his fangs pierced Zebu's neck just below the ear. And then he was on his back with Markus's teeth clamped around his neck, satisfied that the last thing he'd remember before he died would be the stale, sweet taste of Zebu's blood.

"Wait!"

Markus let go but kept his fangs hanging right over Wordsworth's throat.

"Let him go."

"He hurt you, Baas. Let me hurt him just a little before —"

"This cripple can't hurt me!" Zebu snarled.

Markus backed off quickly and Wordsworth rolled on his side. He tried to stand but crashed down again when his legs couldn't hold him up. The others watched, not laughing this time. He got up again more slowly to find Markus sitting close by, licking his chops. Zebu stood just steps away, close enough for Wordsworth to make out the crimson hairs on his neck below the wounded ear.

Instead of licking away the blood, Zebu smiled with particular malevolence. "You miss your mother, Versifier?"

"What did you mean," he panted, "that she'd still be around —"

"There's no room here for anyone like you. You can't hunt, you can't pull, you can't guard, you can't do anything but eat. Unfortunate, but—"

"She was a Kisdee. I'm a Kisdee!"

Zebu laughed. "As I said earlier, sometimes we must do distasteful things."

"What did you do? Why are you afraid to tell me?"

Zebu growled softly. "Don't use that word with me. You'll find out soon enough."

Wordsworth stared him full in the face, eyes full of hate. It was a clear insult, but he didn't care. He'd never hated anyone like this. He'd despised Vagabond, but even as a pup he knew that Vagabond wasn't big enough to hate. This was different.

"What do we do with him?" growled Markus.

The head of the guards got up and walked towards the edge of the Vale. "Let him live," he said over his shoulder. "The Baas wants him to do a job. Find out the identity of our scrambled cousins, Lame Declaimer. If you don't, you're our only suspect."

With that he disappeared, paws trampling down the old leaves as he climbed back up the slope.

"Report to me later when you come to eat at the Bottoms," Markus said. "Don't make me look for you." He was no longer grinning, but before leaving he picked up a hind leg as high as he could, marked the hickory that bordered the Vale, and then kicked back old, wrinkled leaves over it, making sure his scent would be around for a long time.

SIX

The icy river swirled. Wordsworth felt its rapid flow against his soft belly for only a moment before making his way to the shallows, where he could lie down in the water with his back dry, warming in the sun. He felt lightheaded and remembered he hadn't eaten. *No more slackers with hearty appetites.*

What did they do to Loreen? To the mother who didn't do the right thing, who nudged him with her nose to stand up, fight, get strong, survive? *Magogs owned us. They starved and drowned us; they killed off entire breeds. We are all precious. Kill to hunt; kill to eat. Never kill each other.* That was Arden's First Rule. But Moody Sunshine Loreen had gone hunting one day and didn't come back.

When he left Golden Mesa for Poet's Vale, Vagabond had waxed indignant; that meant fewer swala kills for the family, and consequently less standing. No normal Kisdee would choose to live alone, he said, this was a matter for the Kisdee Circle. So one rainy morning, for the first and only time in his life, he entered the Circle's cloistered thicket and asked permission from Silver Bear Priam, the Noble One, to live alone down in the Vale. Other Circle members were there, too, but he had eyes only for the Great Dane sitting back on the grassy mound with the scar cleaving his face, giving the eerie impression of a head made up of two badly fitting halves.

"Let me understand," said Priam gravely. "You say you will continue to hunt every day with the others, but you want to live alone to do this strange new thing, this poetry. What is poetry? Where does it come from?"

And he had waited, unafraid, until he felt the familiar catch in his throat and the dryness in his mouth:

"Words come not from what I know,
Only from what I don't know.
Inspiration can never be arrived at,
Nor emerge from this and that,

But from emptying myself of now and then,
Of past and future, where and when;
Take a backward step, watch mystery arise,
And stay confounded in everlasting surprise."

And confounded they were, for no one spoke.

"Words!" Goralac, the Bull Terrier and head of the Flatheads, finally exclaimed in his high-pitched voice. "It's just words."

"I believe he calls it a poem," Precocious Pariah, the Basenji, said.

Goralac sniffed. "I can talk as well as anybody —"

" — That's for sure!"

" — only I call it talk. Talk's talk."

"Your talk's talk; his talk's poetry," Priam said.

"Don't sound different to me," grumbled Goralac.

"Appearances can be deceiving." Scowling fiercely, the Noble One said there was no reason for any Kisdee not to live wherever he wanted, with his family or without, and added in parting: "You will be the Bard of the Hills." Instead Wordsworth became known as the Bard of the Vale, to the scornful merriment of just about everyone else in the Hills.

Geese honked overhead, returning home after winter, causing his earflaps to wave slightly. He loved the river, loved to feel the water cover up his belly and flanks, erasing all tension. When the sun was out he frolicked in it, paddling confidently against the current, creating bigger and bigger eddies with his splashing paws. But the sun now hid behind a cloud.

Zebu was going to kill him. No one could draw blood from the head of the guards, the brother of Brancken Dukes Dreden, and see the light of many days. He still lived only because he had a job to do, a job the Baas had ordered, but not for long.

He swam to the other side and climbed out onto the bank. *Find out the identity of our scrambled cousins.* Scrambled, Mixeds, Gawls. Some called them Dusties, because their fur was always caked with dust. Back in the time of Noble One Starry Slim Pomper, someone had reasoned that Gawls also ate, so why not put them to work? That's when working Kisdees like the Samoyeds and Malamutes, who once did the hauling work themselves, began to supervise Gawls, who did the actual pull and push of the small, dead antelopes across the long distance from the Cliffs down to the Bottoms. After all, being of mixed parentage, with no clear strengths and skills, what else could they do?

Only he had no idea where to find them when they weren't working. He walked in the direction of sunset, following a spongy trail matted with needles. The river ran below, getting stronger and wider, the water churning white at every dip. Soon the ground began to slope up towards a distant ridge of tall pines. Even from here he could see their forlorn tops towering over the neighboring maples. He left the trail and climbed. The forest felt particularly bare here, with little foliage above but with gigantic exposed roots below, which he clambered over. By now he was curious; he'd never explored this ridge before. The sun hadn't emerged from behind the clouds and there was a desolate chill in the air.

CR-R-R-R-ACK! A heavy tree limb smashed on the ground. He quickened his steps, sniffing warily over his shoulder. Bludrun had come in mist and silence, not in a clap of thunder or a shaking of the earth, but Rathbane? Rumors of the giant Gawl swirled in his mind, courtesy of Birdy. His jaws were said to be so immense he could swallow a swala whole, chewing it even as it struggled in his mouth. Upon his escape he'd sworn vengeance on all Kisdees.

Tangles of vine and thick brush blocked his climb. How did Gawls, known to be slow and lazy, make their way through all this? He pushed through a wall of brambles and nettles, sharp vines lacerating his wet fur. Ahead of him several trees had fallen one on top of the other, creating a pile-up of trunks. He climbed over them and stopped in his tracks.

The pines soared from a rise above him to a suddenly flawless blue sky, so tall and dense that the ground beneath was in shadow. And there, sound asleep, lay a small group of Gawls in different shapes and colors, huddled against each other for warmth. He could see liver spots on white, gray and rust together, longhair and shorthair, all jumbled together in deep rest. A few came from the mixing of two breeds, but most were well past that, Mixeds descended of Mixeds. *Our scrambled cousins.* Scrambled they were, heads against flanks, chests against backs, legs folded under other legs, oblivious, sleeping the sleep of the dead.

Crows cawed up high and every once in a while branches, dried out after the long winter, cracked and fell into the clearing like the one that had missed him before. But these Gawls never moved; theirs was the slumber of exhaustion.

"Our home is yours."

The oldest, oddest face he'd ever seen peered up from under the felled trunks. The muzzle was long and square, with pasty, wiry fur going in all directions. The ochre eyes were brown-rimmed and almost hidden by the profusion of rough hairs, the voice high, inquisitive, and familiar. It was the voice of the small Mixed he'd heard in the dark hours by the river.

"Trying to figure out what I am?" His cheerful, youthful voice contrasted greatly with his aged appearance. The corners of his mouth lifted in humor and one eye closed in a squint. "I'll tell you. I'm first-generation Gawl, so it's easy. Spinone and Springer Spaniel. My mother's the Spaniel, Dewy-Eyed Alicia. Know her?"

His body was no improvement on his head. The bottom part was all Spaniel, low-slung and short-legged. But from the neck up he was all Spinone, with the grumpy-looking face, bushy eyebrows, and tufts of hair that grew in all directions, covering his lips and eyes. His fur, once white with orange spots, was now threadbare, and he leaned clumsily to the side like a tree in a windstorm, ready to drop.

It's as if someone chose the worst fitting parts to make a new kind of dog, Wordsworth thought. He could imagine Zebu's disgust, hear the familiar drawl: *Can anyone tell me what this is? Can anyone tell me what it can do? No speed, no strength, no balance, just a body that's about to fall over and the ugliest face I've ever seen.*

The Gawl didn't seem the least bit discomfited by Wordsworth's inspection. He peered over his shoulder at the others sleeping beneath the trees. "Now some of my friends here have been mixed for generations, and that's a whole other problem."

"You mean it's hard to make them out?"

"Not necessarily. What I worry about is that *they* don't know who they are," the other said brightly. "You can get so mixed that you get mixed up, see?" And he looked at Wordsworth with lively curiosity as though it was he who was the aberration rather than the other way around. "What are you doing here?" he asked, squinting.

"I'm keeping a lookout on this side of the river. Things have happened—"

"You're not an Enforcer." It was a statement, not a question, accompanied by a frank, pleasant scrutiny. "I'm not sure we need protection—or spying—but it's not our decision, is it? Look, everyone killed so far has been a purebred Kisdee. Rathbane hates Kisdees, but I've never heard that he hates Gawls like him. Besides, if you Kisdees are so concerned about our safety, why don't you ask *us* to watch over this side of the river? We know it better than anyone else." His eyes squinted again. "Doesn't seem fair, does it? My mother didn't like the other Springer Spaniels so she decided to come together with my father, a Spinone. They had their little romance and went back to their families, free as birds. A short time later I was born along with four sisters and we were brought down here to live on the other side of the river and haul swalas every day for the rest of our lives."

There was no hint of self-pity, he was just stating the facts as everyone knew them. Wordsworth licked his lips in discomfort. He'd interceded on behalf of the Gawl Bent, but as with many Kisdees, it never occurred to him to question why Gawls lived apart from everybody else and did backbreaking work every day. "Who's up there?" he asked, glancing up at the pine grove.

"Our old ones, those close to death. Otherwise they'd be working, wouldn't they?"

Indeed, the Gawls huddled under the trees were truly old, their muzzles and flanks speckled with white, hair matted, tired resignation on all their faces. "So what are you doing here?"

"I'm also considered too old to work." Wordsworth eyed him narrowly. The small Gawl wasn't just old, he seemed ancient, but his mischievous, scrunched-up eyes and voice were those of a pup. "You don't believe me. My heart is young, my body's old. I'm the most mixed up Mixed you'll ever see."

"Are you making fun of me?" the Golden bristled.

"Not at all. Everybody's mixed. There's good and bad Kisdees and there's good and bad Gawls."

"If you're that old, how come you're not sleeping like them?" and Wordsworth motioned back to the top of the ridge.

"I don't like to sleep." The Mixed stretched his white-and-orange body first one way, then another, wincing visibly from stiffness. "That's all we do. Work—eat—sleep—work—eat—sleep. Do you know what I tell the others who pull dead swalas every day? If you keep looking down you'll forget to look up."

"What would they see if they looked up?"

"Depends. Maybe a hawk circling to make a kill; maybe clouds chasing each other. Or maybe just some big, angry Samoyed telling them to work harder."

Or the spiteful face of a Giant Schnauzer, Wordsworth thought. Birdy loved to bully Gawls. He'd become a hauler because he made a poor hunter, what with always being distracted by birds, and the Gawls working under him had been perfect targets for his peevishness and frustration. "What's your name?"

"Just Daniel."

"Because you don't have other names?"

"Gawls often have only one name, but I have two. And you're Moody Sunshine Wordsworth, the Bard of the Vale. Tell me, Wordsworth, do you agree that we're all mixed? For instance, what about Magogs? Do you think Magogs are mixed, too?"

He looked closely at the scrubby dog. "Magogs are extinct."

"Of course they are, but before that, when they were still around, don't you think they were probably mixed like everyone else? Why shouldn't there have been good Magogs and bad Magogs, short ones and tall ones? You're a poet. Do you think there is something that's not mixed, that's all good or all evil? Of course, your stories say that Fearsome Arden, the Liberator, was all good and that Magogs were all evil," he answered his own question sagaciously, brow wrinkling. "But in my experience, almost everything is like a swala. The skin tastes horrible, but the inside can surprise you." Swalas' skins were thick and bitter, and were always quickly removed to get at the sweet, tender flesh.

"What about Dreden?"

"He's mixed, too. He does his job, which means that he hates Gawls, Magogs, the blind, the lame, and everybody who's not a healthy purebred. But he's loyal to Kisdees. Now let me ask you one. What about Rathbane?"

"What about him?"

"The one they think is massacring and devouring your brothers and sisters."

He recalled the green-coiled eyes inside the mist. "Do you think it's him?"

Just Daniel sat back and shut his eyes. "Everyone says so, which makes it highly dubious. There are Ancients in the Hills. Wolves."

The Golden started. "You've seen them?"

"Others have. What are they doing here?"

"Looking out for us. Haven't they always done that?"

"Not in the old days, during the Great Slavery. Then they were wild predators who fed on many things, including dogs." He looked up at the pines waving across a yellow sky. "Just what do they suspect us of?"

"Who?"

"Dreden. Enforcers. If you tell me what information they want I'll tell you what I know."

They want to know your names, he thought, you and the tall female with the lopsided muzzle. Instead he looked up to where the old Gawls slept. The ground on the Kisdee side of the river was soft, with small caves and hollows that could be easily dug up and made into comfortable dens. Here little sunlight came through and the ground on which the Gawls slept was cold and stony, yet no one had moved the entire time he'd been there. A chill entered his heart. "Do they eat?"

"Some do. The young ones bring them food from the Bottoms. Some just want to die."

"Why?"

"Wouldn't you?"

He shuddered. He remembered the female in the moonlight, Markus grinning in the shadows. The words were out of his mouth before he knew it. "Be careful, the trees are listening."

Did Just Daniel blink as he heard his own words from that night repeated now? Did he even remember? His eyes, half covered by the unkempt hair, revealed nothing: "I'll keep that in mind, Moody Sunshine Wordsworth." And with that the Gawl slid under the fallen tree trunks and was gone.

His den must be underneath, the Golden thought as he hurried back down the ridge. His fur snagged on needles and his back leg ached, so as soon as he arrived at the Curl he went into the swirling river and sank on his belly.

What have I done, he wondered. The old taste of dirt and grit was in his mouth, familiar from the times he fell as a pup, a constant reminder of his *deformity*, as Zebu had put it. Warning Just Daniel made him an accomplice, but an accomplice to what? To saving that gutsy Pit Bull from the Flats? Had they ever tried to help Beau, whose earflaps fluttered at every mention of *Magogs*?

And now he recalled Just Daniel's droopy ears. They'd barely moved while the two had talked, but on several occasions their tips fluttered up just like Beau's, not towards the pine grove but somewhere behind his visitor. He was waiting for someone coming up the slope, Wordsworth thought. Was it the female?

It was a silly idea, but instantly his back leg felt better. He got out of the river and began to make his way down, paws gliding softly and quietly, avoiding the rustling of dry leaves. Soon he discerned a narrow, twisting path among the trees; it would be invisible once the leaves were out. He followed it downhill with a sprightliness he hadn't felt all day. There was no way he could miss her given how big she was, and his golden fur quivered with excitement.

But she didn't appear. Afternoon silence engulfed the forest, nothing moved. The ground began to flatten and the spaces between the trees broadened, and for the second time in his life he arrived at the tree line.

The Flats seemed more immense than yesterday. The sky was bleached white and the earth was dark, and to his amazement white and dark came together in a straight line in the far distance. Maybe this is what they mean by *horizon*, he thought; it looked as if the world ended there. But it couldn't because in that direction lay the Great Water and beyond the Great Water lay the Hills of Their Abode. All Kisdees knew that, though no one had ever seen them.

Disappointed, he retraced his steps. It was the warmest spring day yet and he was tired. A giant fir rose behind a cluster of rocks, with a tall pile of needles behind its thick trunk and low, drooping branches. He sank down, and the needles quickly covered his golden back, leaving only his nose out. If anything came up the path, he was well hidden. He could feel the breeze rushing uphill, causing a slight tickle in his fur, and knew he couldn't be scented by anyone coming down. Soon he was asleep.

But not for long. Heavy white paws landed on the dry, crisp leaves. They wobbled and slid, then straightened up again and made for the large rocks.

They never made it. Something whizzed in the air faster than any bird. The brown and white body flew up and immediately crashed on the ground.

"Going somewhere, Pit Bull?"

The Magog, head up in the air, chittered as he emerged from behind a large shrub. He strode forward with bared teeth, hands thrusting away silver spider webs before plummeting down his sides again. He chewed several times and spat out a grimy, brown swill that smelled of upchucked food and dry leaf. One of his cheeks bulged.

The Pit Bull snarled, but the Magog grinned through one corner of his mouth. "Well, blow me down! Looks like I've come just in time," and he took another step into the clearing. He held something in his hand, which Wordsworth recognized with a jolt as the wire that held Beau down in the Flats. One edge of it was in the Magog's hands and the other, he now saw, was around the Pit Bull's neck. "You're becoming a problem, Prissy Miss Charlotte."

The Pit Bull, white with cocoa patches, lay on her belly, pink tongue flicking occasionally over her lower lip trickling blood. The wire was coiled just below her spotted, half-folded ears. "I would have made it if not for those leaves, I can outrun anybody."

The Magog yanked the wire and she yelped. "You can't outrun this."

He approached closer, but remained at a safe distance. His head was wide and puffy, with the same bright red welts on his face that the other Magogs had. The mouth was narrow except for one bulging cheek, coming to a point where two small white teeth protruded from between fleshy lips. He wore the same thick coat as the others, dark and dirty, his feet covered by large thick pads while his hands were bare except for their red spots. He had no fur anywhere on his body.

"I'll break away again," the Gawl rasped.

"And I'll be there to tie you down. You know what happens then," and the creature chittered again, showing his two teeth.

"You don't scare me, Badger. I'm a Pit Bull, I'm strong."

"You're a Pit Bull and you're ugly."

"You're the one who's ugly, and you're sick, too. You can't keep me down, nothing can keep me down." And she thwacked her tail loudly on the ground.

The Magog's teeth gleamed. "That's some tail you got, Gawl. When you thump it like that everyone can hear you." Charlotte smacked her tail against her flanks again and the Magog lost his temper. "That's how I found you, you dumb Gawl! You're so stupid you don't know when to stop making all that noise."

Charlotte only lay back down on the ground, eyes shining in malice. *Whack! whack!* went her tail.

The Magog's eyes turned dark. Spitting out dark scum once again, he smiled. "I got an idea. Maybe this time we don't wait for the Enforcers, what do you say, Prissy Miss Charlotte? Where do you dogs get such stupid names anyway? Brancken Dukes Dreden, Silver Bear Priam. Even an ugly Gawl like you has a big name."

"You Magogs are ugly, not me. Nobody likes you, nobody in the whole world."

The Magog's welts seemed to redden. "You dogs think you own the world. But there was a time when *we* owned *you*, and those times will come again."

"Fat chance!"

"Oh yes, they're coming. And they're starting with you, Pit Bull, because you're a Gawl from the Flats. I own you already."

She snorted. "You couldn't own a cockroach."

Wordsworth held his breath. Why was she baiting and egging him on?

Ugly lines appeared around the Magog's mouth. Then he brightened. "It will all change soon enough. Besides, right now I have you. One Gawl more or less in the Flats doesn't matter, and you're my favorite kind of Gawl, Charlotte, because you're a Pit Bull, and there's only one thing to do with Pit Bulls. So let's save our friend, Dreden, a lot of trouble, what do you say?"

He turned his hand winding the wire; Charlotte snarled. He turned it again and the snarl became a cough. The Magog sniggered and turned the wire in his hand once more, this time slower. The Pit Bull gasped, trying to catch her breath. *What's he doing?* The Magog's grin widened perceptibly each time his hand moved a tiny bit, and now Charlotte's pink tongue fell out of the side of her mouth and her eyes bulged out of her sockets, and he understood. She was choking to death. A thin, yellow stream ran down between her legs.

He crouched back in a rage, ready to bring the creature down. This is what the stories said; this was how Magogs had always treated dogs. Instead, someone—black and tawny and smelling pungently of terraberries—smashed heavily into the Magog. Wordsworth quickly fell back on his belly, burrowing under the leaves, while the Magog crashed down on his back, forelegs flailing, screeching, "Don't, Dreden, don't!"

But Dreden's jaws clamped shut and the Magog howled as blood flowed down his arm. Then the howls turned into shrieks of fear as Dreden's bloody muzzle hovered over the welted face and the wet jaws opened.

"What are you doing here, Badger?" the Enforcer murmured hoarsely.

"The Gawl," he bellowed, "the Gawl was—"

"What are you doing up here, Magog?" Dreden snarled, showing his fangs.

"Please Dreden, I know, only—"

Dreden bent even lower, foam dripping from his lips onto the terrified face. "Tell me the rule, Magog," he hissed.

"Let me first—"

"Tell me the rule, Magog!"

"Never—" the Magog panted, "—never come into the Hills."

"Never!" Dreden whispered. "You hear me, Badger? Never. Where do Magogs stay, Badger?"

"In the Flats."

"Where do Magogs belong?"

"In — in the Flats."

"Nobody loves Magogs, Badger. Not the birds, not the trees, not the other animals, and certainly not Kisdees. You know why, don't you?"

"Most of us died! We almost disappeared! Have you no compassion?"

"None, Magog. The earth has turned on you. Arden warned us, and I warn you. Stay out of the Hills. Magogs deserve no mercy, and next time you'll get none."

The wire had loosened and Charlotte was taking quick, shallow breaths. But other Enforcers arrived, including one Wordsworth recognized instantly.

Badger raised one of his hands and wiped his face as he sat up, then rolled his forelegs backwards for balance as he stood up slowly. The welts on his cheeks were redder now and hate blazed from eyes that were the color of water. "I was only trying to help," he mumbled as he flipped back the wire with a flick of his long, supple claws. The other Enforcers pushed Charlotte up with their muzzles, none too gently. She fell back on the ground, but Markus snapped at her neck and she yelped, and they hurried her ahead of them up the slope.

Meantime, Badger rolled up his wire. It snagged on a knob at the base of the tree and he bent down to retrieve it. The Golden followed the tall head as it rose back up into the air and almost exclaimed aloud. Upwind from the others, motionless but completely visible, a large Tug-a-Lug Gawl stood still on top of a steep, rocky bank.

He froze. Dreden was no ordinary Enforcer. All it took was an unexpected breeze, the tiniest flicker of a leaf, and he would look up and see her. But she stood tall and silent, like the trees.

"We'll bring Charlotte to you this evening, the usual place," Dreden said.

"I still don't understand why you don't let me take her right now."

"We're different from you Magogs, we have our Rules. And if I ever see you again in these Hills, Badger, I will be the last thing you ever see."

Badger licked his lips. "You'd like killing me, Dreden, wouldn't you? But it's not my fault I'm sick. We have an understanding with you, we're partners. Where's your respect?"

"You're no partner of mine, Badger," Dreden growled. "No Magog is a partner of mine, nor of any Kisdee." With that he turned away.

The Magog clutched the wire, eyes narrowed into slits, and Wordsworth knew that at that moment what Badger wanted worse than anything was to have Dreden's neck in the wire. But the Head of the Enforcers ignored him, and Badger finally disappeared into the forest, followed by Markus.

He looked up towards where the large Gawl had stood and was surprised to find her gone. He thought only Enforcers knew how to appear and disappear so silently. How long was she watching us, he wondered. How long was she watching me?

"Don't, Dreden, please, don't hurt—"

But Dreden lunged. Markus, who'd just returned, barely had a chance to beg for mercy before the top half of his head disappeared between Dreden's open, foaming jaws. Wordsworth heard a terrifying screech. Then Dreden opened his jaws and raised his muzzle. "How did she get here?" he snarled.

"She got away from Brancken Dukes Conrad and Brancken Dukes Stark," Markus whimpered, hairs trembling under Dreden's wet jaws, eyes white with terror.

"How?"

"I don't know yet, I'll find out."

"And Brancken Dukes Alastor?"

"He went down to the Bottoms—" His voice rose urgently, "—they've been up a long time, Baas, they're tired—" but Dreden was already opening his jaws, "—I will administer punishment, Baas, they will all be punished!"

It did him no good. Dreden didn't move, only his jaws squeezed and squeezed. The Enforcer slumped. Blood dripped down the sides of his head and Wordsworth remembered the scars he'd seen earlier on his brow.

Finally, Markus struggled up on his paws. His tongue slid to the side of his mouth, tasting his own blood. "Do we bring her back to the Flats tonight, Baas?"

"There isn't much choice. I'd thought to use her as bait a little longer, but not now. Meet the Magogs in the usual place and let them take over. Tell the Pit Bull what will happen to her if she escapes a second time. Of course, Badger may kill her first. Magogs don't like Pit Bulls."

"Nobody likes Flatheads."

"They don't seem to mind other Flatheads, only Pit Bulls; it's something from the past. Badger can hardly wait to get that wire around her neck."

"I have a feeling we're not going to see Prissy Miss Charlotte ever again," said Markus, recovering his familiar grin.

He pawed the ground nervously. "Someone helped her escape, Baas."

"You found tracks?"

"Big ones; one of the big hounds." He licked his lips. "If I kill her right now, Baas, we won't have to meet Magogs tonight."

Dreden growled. "The Rules are clear, and so is our agreement with the *Friends*." His lips curled contemptuously. "We give them Gawls to use down in the Flats. If they escape once, we bring them back. If they escape a second time, you know what happens." He walked back towards the large rocks. "No one hates our scrambled cousins more than I do, Brancken Dukes Markus; no one would be happier if they all died. And I think I hate them most of all because it's on their account that we have to deal with dirt like Badger. But that was the Noble One's decision."

"It's time for a new Noble One, Baas, maybe an Enforcer this time."

"We have our job, let others do theirs. Don't forget to punish those who let the Gawl escape."

"They were tired, Baas, they've been up for a few days—"

"They'll sleep when they're dead."

Dreden disappeared. A grim Markus, licking his lips nervously, followed.

Wordsworth looked back up to where the Tug-a-Lug Gawl had stood. She's creating havoc for Enforcers, he thought admiringly. *Tell the Pit Bull what will happen to her if she escapes a second time.* What happens then?

He felt cracked inside, his world overturned. *We give them Gawls to use down in the Flats.* He repeated the words to himself again and again. Beau had told him the truth, Enforcers brought Gawls down to be slaves to Magogs. Why? It broke every rule that Arden had left behind, it ignored his warning to never trust Magogs. And Dreden had said that it was the Noble One himself, Silver Bear Priam, who'd done this. Not Dreden himself, who was known to loathe anyone who wasn't a purebred Kisdee, but Priam, the most respected Kisdee in the Hills, the one who'd made him the Bard of the Vale.

Only he didn't want to be a poet anymore, he wanted to do something, just like the Tug-a-Lug Gawl up above who'd freed Charlotte! Saying words, even beautiful ones, was not enough. Besides, what words were there to describe Charlotte's gasps when she was being throttled to death, he wondered dully. What words were there for what he saw in Beau's eyes?

A dark shadow skimmed the earth, vanishing quickly, then a second. The sun had begun its long descent. When the third appeared he looked up. Big birds were racing across the graying sky above him. He growled softly. Birds of Death were flying across the Flats in the direction of sunset.

SEVEN

Faster and faster the birds flew, becoming blots in the blue sky, and had Wordsworth hesitated briefly he would have lost them. Instead he followed them down beyond the tree line, running in the direction of the sun. His paws turned sore from the grassless earth but he didn't stop, for those birds meant only one thing: Something was dead out in the Flats.

It can't be Beau, he's in the other direction, he thought. His heart pounded as he tried to keep his head up to see where the birds had gone, but his neck still hurt from Markus's assault that morning and his head kept on dropping as he scuttled and bounced after the birds, feeling the weight of his stubbornly suspended back leg.

He would never have caught up with them. In fact, the first group was already gone when a second and then a third sailed over him, causing shadows to appear and disappear on the ground before him, converging towards a point in the distance. His breath came in quick, agitated pants. Just when he thought he'd have to stop, that he couldn't keep going, he saw the last birds swoop down to earth.

He crouched low, belly on the ground. Like most Kisdees, he had an instinctive hate for the Birds of Death, with their unfeathered reddish heads and hooked beaks. Every night, after Kisdees had left the Bottoms, they plummeted down to the riverbanks and ate the carcasses' remains. They were patient, waiting till nightfall when everyone had had their fill, but Kisdees hated them anyway for their voracious appetite, the way bones with meat and gristle were found stripped clean and shining white in the next morning's light.

They grunted and hissed. He raised his head and saw a thick wooden post like the one behind Beau's den, but there was no sign of any den like Beau's, only a low moan ending with a tiny whimper. He took a few slow, cautious steps, maintaining his low crouch.

A huge Gawl lay on the ground, a female. A mane of reddish brown framed her large head and a long tail curved over a thick, muscular back. She had a black snout and ear-flaps that fell flat. The powerful body was breathing quick, shallow breaths, her eyes shut. A desiccated tongue brushed over black, dry lips. She moaned again, louder this time.

The Birds of Death gathered a short distance away. The black feathers on their wings shone, their bare heads stared at him with undisguised hostility. Two suddenly advanced on long legs, their greedy necks protruding under short, hooked bills. He lunged at them and they flew back, but not far.

The Gawl was breathing fast, her large tongue lolling out of her mouth. Her next moan was short-lived and faded quickly, and Wordsworth realized that if she didn't get water soon she would die. Behind a low-spreading juniper shrub he found two Magogish containers like the ones that held Beau's food and water, empty. Did the Magogs forget about this Gawl?

He bent down and licked the cracked and broken lips; they felt dryer than the soil under his paws. He licked them again and again, and her eyes opened. Brown and deep-set, they showed no surprise at seeing another dog so close their whiskers touched. Then they shut. Behind him the Birds of Death hissed in displeasure. One advanced again and he lunged at the entire group. They flew up, squealing, and came down a little farther away, watching, waiting. They knew she had no more strength.

He ran back to the forest as fast as his legs could take him. He reached the tree line — this Gawl wasn't as far out in the Flats as Beau — and immediately heard the gurgling sound of the tiny waterfall. On the watch for Magogs, he circled warily, but there was only the rock shelf, its cold water streaming down luxuriously before disappearing underground.

Hot and thirsty, he lapped up some water, and then stared. Whenever he declaimed a verse the words emerged from somewhere in his belly. Now, too, something was trying to come up, not a word but an image, the picture of Gawls pulling kills across long distances with their teeth.

Pulling swalas was one thing; pulling water was something else.

A mound of wisteria vines leaned over the stream, their stems thick with leaves wet and glittering with spray. He bit off a large stem and shook it hard, water spraying across his face and chest. It's not enough, he thought, but what else can I do? He held the stem under the falling water till its leaves got thoroughly wet, his own neck hairs getting soaked, and ran back into the Flats. The wet stem was heavy in his mouth; he listened for the Birds of Death, but there was only silence up ahead.

The Gawl still lay on the ground. Quickly and gently he put the bough with wet leaves over her caked, dry lips. When there was no response he shook his chest and drops of water from his fur sprinkled her face.

The edges of her ears pricked up; half a pink tongue emerged between the dusty lips and licked the stem. Her mouth opened and she sucked the leaves, then chewed and ate both leaves and stem, eyes shut the entire time.

He flew back to the forest. Lapping water at the stream, he stopped out of sudden remorse. Who could imagine someone dying from thirst? There was always so much water in the Hills. He pulled off an even larger stem with thicker leaves and held it long and hard in his mouth under the white flow before hurrying back to the Flats. His neck hurt and it took a lot of effort not to drop anything. This time her eyes were open. She licked the wet leaves again and again, sucking in every last bit of moisture while staring him fully in the face.

He ran once more, and when he came back he knew he couldn't go again. She watched silently as he brought over the wet leaves and then crumpled a short distance away, exhausted.

When he opened his eyes she was sitting up. Her red and black matted fur shone in the afternoon sun and her lips were no longer crusted. Even sitting back on her haunches, she towered over him as he got up and stood a respectful distance away. "How long have you been without water?"

"Five days," she said in a croaking whisper.

He tried not to stare at the thing that glittered around her flanks. "They haven't brought you water in five days!"

"Ten," she whispered, licking her lips slowly. "There has been no water for ten days, since they brought me back here. I made it last for five days."

And then he understood. "You escaped?"

She raised her exhausted eyes up to the sky. "I ran away and they caught me, for the second time." A low sigh issued from her mouth, but she kept her eyes up.

So now he knew what happened to a Gawl that escaped the Flats for the second time. Dangling from her neck was no thin strand like the one that tied up Beau. Thick double coils were wrapped around her entire body, circling her legs, back, and front flanks several times before connecting with the thick wooden post coming out of the ground. They glittered in the sunlight, causing her to droop under their weight though she was a big dog. They'd shackled her so tightly that all she could do was stand in one place, sit, or lie down. Her skin puffed and swelled where the coils pressed tightly against it. *In the end they die anyway, only slower.* "Who did this to you?"

"Dreden." She finally looked at Wordsworth. "Not him personally, of course, it's Magogs who do the dirty work. But Dreden brought me here. *I will never see you again, Hanna, you are going to the Land of the Gawls.* Those were his last words to me." She gazed back up at the sky and the sun that shone brilliantly on her red, black, and golden fur. Clouds were gathering in the distance; it was going to rain.

"And the Magogs don't bring you water?"

She gave him a glance of pity and infinite patience, as though he was a pup. "I ran away twice. If you do that you're left to die."

It was a violation of Arden's First Rule against killing. Who knew of this back in the Hills? Dreden and his Enforcers, he thought. And the Noble One, Silver Bear Priam.

Hanna's thick, quivering nostrils sniffed the air. She wants it to rain, he thought miserably; she's conserving her strength. Her hairs trembled and she crouched back down, visibly tired, but raised her muzzle once again to sniff the dampening air.

"What will you do?"

"Nothing much *to* do." She turned and saw the look in his eyes. "Don't pity me, Kisdee. I've already lived longer than the others."

"What do you mean?"

She shut her eyes wearily, as though tired of all this talk. "What do you think happens to the Gawl pups they put down here? Most die young. It's not in us to stay chained down alone for a long time, so we either die or we escape."

"But it comes to the same thing. Once they catch you, then—"

"—they kill us. But it's not the same thing. As long as we think about escape, we live. When we stop thinking about that, we die." Again she saw the look in his eyes. "Don't pity me, Kisdee, you are more of a slave than I am." And with that she closed her eyes and put her head down between gigantic paws. Wrapped in the heavy coils, she couldn't even dig up a bed of cool soil on which to rest under the sun. She couldn't even curl up to sleep.

"I'll bring you more wet leaves," he said. Did she hear him? He stood over her a long time. If she were free I'd bring her to the stream, he thought. We'd run together in the woods; I'd show her the Vale. But Hanna went to sleep. He made one more trip and brought the biggest stem of wet leaves he could find. Her eyes were still closed when he came back, but her tongue came out to lick the leaves he gently lowered onto her face.

The Birds of Death, for now, were nowhere to be seen.

EIGHT

*H*e's down in the Flats again. Hanna lies senseless by the wooden post under the sun, her enormous golden body wrapped tightly in heavy chains. Her lips are caked dry and her breath is shallow.

Flying to the small waterfall, he pulls off a stem thick with leaves and dangles it under the water, feeling it get heavier in his mouth. As he runs back to the tree line he glances down; the leaves are trailing blood. He cries out and the stem falls out of his mouth, instantly shriveling into a clot of rotten foliage. He returns and finds another. The stream is cool as it soaks up the drooping leaves. Head held high, he turns back towards the clearing, smells the strong, sickening odor, and drops the stem once again.

Frantic, he rushes back to Hanna, but a swarm of the Birds of Death already covers the ground like a black cloud. Blood flows from its center onto the Flats. It begins to gush and churn like a river, covering his paws and rising up to his flanks. He tries to shake himself free but it climbs up to his neck.

All around him the Flats are awash in blood. He half wades, half swims to the tree line. Here the ground is dry, so he totters towards the trees, takes a breath of relief, and looks up. Blood is rolling down the slope in streams and rivers, widening and gathering speed, becoming red-black cataracts drowning everything in sight.

He moaned and woke up. His hairs were silky from sleep, not wet and sticky, and the willow protected him from a thundering rain that was pouring down. Dawn was still a long time away. The rain was falling on Hanna down in the Flats, lessening her thirst but drenching her at the same time, while he lay dry and comfortable. She couldn't last long like this even if he brought her water every day.

I ran away twice. If you do that you're left to die.

There were many, many Rules, but only one First Rule. Every Kisdee pup knew it. Fearsome Arden himself had declared it in the first gathering of Kisdees after his return from the Glade of Remorse. *The Magogs owned us. They starved and drowned us; they killed off entire breeds. We are all precious. Kill to hunt; kill to eat. Never kill each other.* But Hanna was being killed as surely as if a pack of Enforcers had gone for her throat. And what about the Pit Bull Charlotte? She, too, threatened to escape a second time, assuming she was still alive.

This is crazy, he thought to himself. We're all dogs. Who cares whether we're mixed or purebred, Shepherds or Retrievers or Wolfhounds or Ridgebacks?

He could hardly wait till the arrival of dawn The sky was thick gray with clouds soon to be nudged away by the sun, and he hurried down the slope, crossed the river, climbed the hill on the other side and then ran down the long incline to the Flats. At the bottom he paused by the rocky shelf. It was clear, without a hint of blood, rushing faster than before due to the rain. It was only a dream, he reassured himself as he hurried towards the wisteria, bit off another leafed stem, and held it under the cold surging water. She's not going to the Land of the Gawls, he promised himself, not as long as I move and breathe. The furrows in the Flats had become puddles. Sure enough, there was no black cloud up ahead, not a sign of the Birds of Death, and he took a big breath of relief before realizing she wasn't there.

Had he misjudged the place? No, there was the wooden post, there were the two empty containers lying on their sides. In fact, there were the chains and even the stems of leaves, now bare, for Hanna had consumed everything but the stems. Everything was as it had been yesterday, except for Hanna.

He ran in frenzied circles, eyes searching the ground again and again. The heavy rain had obliterated all tracks except for the large depression in the ground where she'd lain. There was nothing but the Flats, large, empty Flats, as vast and empty as the sky. He ran back towards the Hills and retraced his steps. It was no illusion, it was no nightmare. Hanna was gone.

Sinking on the ground by the heavy coils, he tried to sniff something, anything, but there was only the smell of wet earth. He moaned aloud, eyes open, unseeing. She's dead, he thought to himself, she's dead after all. I did what I could do and it wasn't enough. *You didn't do what you could do. You should have gone to the Bottoms and told everyone what you saw, even if Enforcers killed you for it. You should have told them about Priam's deal with Magogs and how they were letting Magogs enslave dogs again. You are the messenger, Ruwena said.*

But would this have saved Hanna? She needed food and water. Most of all, she needed freedom from those Magogish chains that shackled her to the ground. He remembered how hard she fought to rise up on her paws, her thick fur glowing golden red, shoulders and flanks tense against the pull of the chains, her eyes on the sun even while talking to him, as though any chance of freedom would come from up there, not from him. What would Gawls see if they looked up, he'd asked Just Daniel. What did Hanna see up in the sky? What did she look for? *Don't pity me, Kisdee, you're more of a slave than I am.*

Magogs could have come in their cloud of dust and he wouldn't have moved. Anguish lay so heavily on him that he could hardly think, hardly feel. All he could do was stretch out where she had lain the previous day, where she had died.

His fur was warm; the sun had climbed the sky. Wordsworth rose and looked around. Now what? Go back to the shelter of the trees, back to his old life at the Vale? He plodded away from the direction of the Hills, not knowing what he was looking for. Did the Magogs live in the Flats? Their stories said that long ago Magogs lived in big dens out in the open, without a tree in sight, easily visible to predators. And they lived alone, not in clans and families. Birdy would wonder why anybody wished to live where there were no birds, he thought. No birds, no forest, no hills, nothing.

But there was something.

"Aiffff! Aiffff!"

He stopped and turned towards sunrise, standing there for what felt like a lifetime, and right then he knew — without really knowing — that the time was now. He could run away again. He could go home and pretend that Hanna never exist-ed, that Beau never existed, that he'd never gone down to the Flats and seen what was done. Or—or what?

He ran. His back paw bounced under his hip as he raced over long furrows, slight bits of scrub and the telltale holes in the ground where gophers took shelter.

"Aiffff! Aiffff!"

It was the silliest bark he ever heard; no self-respecting Kisdee would be caught dead with a bark like that. The wind was at his back and the sun was beaming and, lame though he was, he was running towards some crazy impossible destina-tion.

Daimyo's Fireside Stomping Beau stood on the roof of his wooden den just like that first time, black hair glittering in the bright noon sunlight. Before Wordsworth could say anything Beau pounced, grabbing the ruff of the Golden's neck by his teeth, front legs straddling the other's chest.

"Beau!"

Wordsworth tried to roll away from him and get up on his paws, but Beau kept him pinned down, laughing his crazy laugh, *Eeee, eeee, eeee, eeee!*

"Beau!" Wordsworth arched his belly, back paws wig-gling in the air, and with one heave managed to roll over and jump up. "Listen to me, Beau, there's no time. You said you escaped once, remember? How? How did you escape?"

Beau paused, eyes wide. Before Wordsworth knew it the Gawl jumped him once again, landing on top of his chest, paws holding him down while he licked him repeatedly.

"Let go," Wordsworth mumbled, "there's no time, let go." They both jumped up. "How did you escape last time?"

"I don't know. I heard a sound, a rabbit maybe, and looked quickly over my shoulder. There was no rabbit, but there was no wire, too."

"Show me."

Beau turned quickly and looked over his shoulder. The wire never budged. He turned even quicker and looked over his other shoulder, then groaned with frustration. "They made it tighter."

"Who?"

"Magogs. I heard one saying to the other that the wire wasn't tight enough, that's how I escaped."

"Let me try to bite through it." Burying his head in Beau's neck, he took the sharp wire in his mouth and pulled hard, cringing at the harsh taste. Beau resisted, pulling back, but the wire didn't yield. "It's too strong. I don't think that even a Flathead could break this, and their jaws are stronger than ours."

He sat back on his haunches and stared at the Gawl's neck. Beau whimpered, eyes feverish with excitement. "Don't give up," he begged, "there must be something we can do."

Wordsworth circled and examined the wire once more as it rested tightly on the nape of Beau's neck, right above his back. It was a Magogish thing, clever and devilish just like Magogs, just like Badger, who actually carried it around with him, wound up and hidden. Beau whinnied again piteously, searching his face. "Tell me how they put this on you last time, after you were caught by Enforcers."

"They brought me down here. When I saw Magogs approach I started fighting and broke free, but the Enforcers jumped me and I fell on my side. One Enforcer had his teeth right at my throat while the other bit me hard above the leg. The Magogs walked over, laughing. They told the Enforcers they sure knew how to do their job. Then they brought the loop and pushed it over my head and down around my neck."

"They pushed it?"

"It was tight. When they began to slide it over me I resisted and the wire got stuck. They yelled, pushed it down harder, and cut one of my earflaps down the middle. Then they shoved it down till it fell around my neck." Beau licked his lips nervously. "Do you think we can't get it off?"

"No, I think we *can* get it off. What was pushed down can come up, but it's going to hurt."

"I don't care. I don't care if my head comes off, as long as that wire comes off too."

He took a deep breath. "Okay, lie down."

Beau sank on his belly. The afternoon sun shone on his sleek back as he bent his head while Wordsworth, hovering above him, nudged the wire up the back of his neck with his nose. It seemed to climb up easily enough till it reached the point where the head broadened, and there it stalled.

"A pure Akita isn't as broad on top as you are," he muttered to Beau, circling to the other side. Of course, a pure Akita wouldn't be in the Flats to begin with.

Beau grinned, looking slightly ridiculous with the wire wrapped around the top of his wrinkled head. But his breath was a little labored for the bottom of the wire was already scraping his neck.

"The whole thing will come off if I can get the top to slide over your head and ears." He tried to nudge the wire up on the other side, but it refused to budge. Grabbing it with his small front teeth, he slowly, painstakingly, pulled it to the ridge of Beau's head, where it stuck once more. Beau began to gag and Wordsworth instantly let go. The wire fell a short distance down the back.

"Don't stop," Beau rasped. "Don't stop."

"I don't want to strangle you —"

"Get it off, just get it off!"

Quickly he bit the wire and pulled it up again. This time it came all the way up to the top of Beau's head where it held fast behind his earflaps, which were lying back against his skull, curled at the tip. Beau began to gasp for breath, chest heaving, and his eyes turned glassy.

"Raise your earflaps, Beau."

The Gawl didn't move.

"Raise your earflaps, as if you've heard something," he urged again.

Nothing moved. The gasping stopped.

Fear clutched his belly. Beau looked out at the Flats, unseeing. Did he lose consciousness? He'd stopped breathing; only thin, white spittle dripped from the corner of his mouth. In fact, he looked uncannily like the Pit Bull, Charlotte, when the Magog had tried to strangle her.

"Beau! Beau!" He would have pulled the wire back down, but by now it was fastened so tightly over the Gawl's head he couldn't do that, either. Beau was dying, like Hanna.

Then the earflaps moved — not in one motion, but very very slowly, using up every last bit of strength the Gawl had. Slowly, agonizingly, they came up, and as they did their base narrowed.

He ran to the other side of Beau's head and tried to pull the wire hard across the narrowing base of the earflap. It didn't budge. Beau's chest was still, there was no heartbeat. Wordsworth pulled the wire so hard that the earflap tore and drops of blood spilled over the Gawl's motionless brow. He bent to lick it, and only then realized that the wire had slid over the ripped earflap. He rushed to the other side and pulled the wire down hard. It slid over the flap and now rested loosely on Beau's muzzle.

Beau was still.

Trying to ignore the terrible silence and the blood that dribbled from the lacerated throat and earflap, Wordsworth pulled the wire a last time. It slid down the sides of the Gawl's muzzle and fell on the ground.

Beau's eyes were shut. He didn't move.

Dead, Wordsworth thought despairingly. First Hanna, now Beau. He looked out across the fields. The dream had shown him, the Flats were soaked with blood. But not just the Flats, also the Hills shimmering emerald, the forest and slope, the Vale, his home. Everything was raw and terrible. We did this, he thought. Kisdees did this to other Kisdees. We're worse than Magogs.

He heard a brief wheeze. Were Beau's nostrils fluttering? A longer wheeze followed, and the big body started heaving and panting, gulping in air. Beau's eyes still didn't open and the splash of white on his chest was now red.

"Beau?"

The Gawl didn't answer, as though he still hadn't returned to the living. So Wordsworth licked the newly torn earflap, feeling it sag against his face. Then he sat down and licked the sides of Beau's head from the crown down to his throat, with deep red wounds on both sides. When he finally stopped Beau's eyes were still closed, but his breathing was regular. And now he, Wordsworth, felt more tired than he'd felt in his entire life. He lay down, closed his eyes, and fell instantly asleep.

NINE

When he opened his eyes the first thing he saw was the wire, black with blood, coiled on the ground just by his snout. He jumped back, tail outstretched in horror, then looked around. What happened to the Gawl?

The Flats were empty and silent as before, with no shadows to mark the sun's descent though it was early afternoon, not a breeze to disturb his hairs. But when he turned towards the Hills he caught a familiar scent and growled softly. A large black dot was dwindling, almost disappearing in the distant dust. With a snarl he sprang after him.

His legs pounded the hard ground and the hard ground pounded back. Up ahead, Beau paused for a moment, then speeded up. Wordsworth gave chase but the distance between them grew. He was running as he always did, one side of his body upraised and twisted, while Beau, younger and more light-footed, practically flew. But everything changed when they entered the woods, with their scratchy earth and carpet of pinecones. Beau's run soon became a gingerly walk, checked further by trees, shrubs, undergrowth, and stumps of all sizes, while Wordsworth felt right at home. He overtook the Gawl and jumped him.

The two snarled and wrestled, each springing up on his back legs to bring the other down. Wordsworth landed on top, bit down on Beau's blood-crusted neck, and the Gawl let out a shriek. "You ran away!"

"Let go! Let go!" Beau arched up and managed to get upright, but Wordsworth brought him down again. They rolled and wrestled, snarling and snapping, sunbeams slipping through the treetops, spotlighting gold and black simultaneously. They fought and fought, breathing harder all the time, till they broke apart, too tired to go on, and lay on the ground panting.

Wordsworth turned to Beau. The Gawl's eyes glinted feverishly, sharp fangs hanging over the sides of his loose lower lip. "I set you free and you ran."

"Of course I ran!" He spoke in a harsh rasp, throat still raw and bloody. He grabbed a small twig with his mouth and chewed it up, spitting out the wooden chunks. "I can finally run, jump, chase, roll on the ground, do whatever I want." And just to make his point, he got up, winced, walked a short distance away, paused at a hollow trunk and raised his back leg.

"Thanks for leaving a scent for Enforcers," Wordsworth called out after him. What did you expect, he asked himself, warm friendship? Undying gratitude and loyalty from a Gawl who still marks territory with his urine? Beau's eyes prowled restlessly in all directions. He's like a wild animal, the Golden thought, all speed and strength, and nothing else. He felt the cool forest earth under his belly, saw the small shadows along the tree line. Later they would lengthen, and it would be time to go to the Bottoms to —

He jumped up. I'm not going to the Bottoms to eat, he thought in alarm, in fact I'm probably never going to the Bottoms again. Markus's face grinned at him as surely as if the Enforcer was standing right there. *Report to me when you come to eat at the Bottoms.* Panic mushroomed inside. He hadn't gone to eat yesterday, never saw Markus. Were they looking for him? And now there was Beau. Did they already know about Beau?

He looked up just in time to see the Gawl, who'd been exploring a hollow at the base of a dead tree, suddenly dart up the slope. He leaped after him, only to smash into Beau's back flanks when the latter stopped abruptly by a fallen hickory. Beau whiffed quickly under the trunk — sniff sniff sniff, pause, sniff sniff sniff — before growling at Wordsworth. "What did you do that for? I almost had it."

"Had what?"

"The chipmunk. It went under the log. I would have caught —" Without finishing his sentence, without a glance over his shoulder, the Gawl made the fastest turnabout Wordsworth had ever seen, leaped, and snapped his jaws. He shook the body hard and laid it down, small, striped, and still writhing. "Eee, eee, eee, eee!"

"You went after a chipmunk? Why?"

"Why!" Beau's eyes shone, black fur full of brambles. "Because it ran, that's why. Don't you chase things when they run?"

"No."

"Besides, Akitas are great hunters. Eee, eee, eee, eee!"

"Akitas chase swalas, not little things in holes and burrows. Even Flatheads have more self-respect than that. You killed something that's too small to eat."

"I love chasing," said Beau stubbornly, the shiny eagerness still in his eyes. "It's like playing. Don't you play?"

"No," was the glum reply.

Beau turned incredulous. "You don't play? You don't chase? But you're free! What good is being free if you don't play and you don't chase?" His ears reared up and before Wordsworth could reply he ran back down to the dead maple by the pool, barking at the woodpecker making its own racket high above, and began to chew loudly on the surrounding new grass.

Wordsworth followed slowly. Considering he'd been chained all his life, Beau was remarkably fast. Nevertheless, Enforcers were going to catch him, it was just a matter of time. He already knew what they would do to Beau, but what would they do to him? He sniffed the air. The forest was peaceful and still now, but that could change in an instant.

"Wordsworth, why do you take Gawls down to the Flats?" Beau lay on his belly by the pool, chewing on a stalk of grass.

The Kisdee grimaced. "I didn't put you down in the Flats, I let you out."

"But why did Enforcers take me there to begin with?"

"Because you're a Gawl." And because our Noble One, for some incomprehensible reason, made a deal with Magogs, he thought.

"But most Gawls stay up in the Hills, don't they?"

He remembered the exhausted old Mixeds lying in the pine grove. "They're slaves to other Kisdees, Beau, like you were a slave to Magogs."

"But why? What's wrong with being a Mixed, or a Gawl?"

"Listen, Beau, we have to hide. Enforcers are probably looking for you already."

"Are you sure I'm a Gawl? Are you sure I'm not a pure Daimyo?"

He looked at Beau's dark pleading eyes, saw the raw, hairless, pink ring at the neck, heard the voice made harsh by the damage to his throat. After all that, Wordsworth thought, and he still wants to go back to the family that threw him out to begin with. "I'm sure. One of your parents is an Akita, maybe even a Daimyo Akita, but the other is not."

"How can you tell?"

"There are Rules about pure Akitas, just like there are Rules about pure Goldens. In fact, there are Rules about every-thing."

"What do they say about Akitas?"

"This isn't the right time, Beau, we must—"

"What do they say?"

He thought for a moment. "They say that Akitas should be intelligent and strong, capable of hunting large prey."

"That's me," Beau replied, cheering up immediately.

"Akitas should have a double coat to protect them in the cold and a broad, deep chest," he recited.

Beau pushed his chest out proudly.

"Their eyes should be deep-set. They should have strong shoulders, straight front legs, and wide back legs."

Beau bounded up and examined his reflection in the pool, tail wagging.

"Their paws face front and have thick pads."

Beau checked his paws and pads.

"Their full tail curls over the back or against their side."

Beau tried to curl his tail with little success; instead it fell over and behind his legs.

"And their head is supposed to be flat on top, cheeks full."

"How's mine?"

"Your head narrows under the eyes. Finally, the Rules are very clear when it comes to color. Akitas have only one color: white."

Beau looked back down at the water. "My face isn't white," he declared.

Wordsworth lost patience. "Most of you isn't white, Beau, except for small marks on your chest and legs. Not enough for an Akita, and certainly not for a Daimyo." Beau moved his head this way and that, searching high and low in the water for more white markings as he strained to broaden his jaws. "You're a Gawl and there's nothing you can do about it. Beau, do you know what they do to Gawls that escape a second time?" And he told him about Hanna.

Beau's hair bristled and the tips of his earflaps fluttered wildly. "We can run. It's a big forest, they won't find us."

"They'll catch us, it's just a matter of time. Enforcers are everywhere."

"There must be some place they're not, some place they don't check."

He was about to say no, and stopped. "Actually, there is," he conceded. "No one goes there, not even Enforcers."

"Is it far?"

"I can show it to you."

Beau whined in surprise as, instead of going further up the slope, the Golden led him back to the tree line. They turned and walked in the direction of sunrise, staying in the forest's shadow till the trees themselves came to an end. Both stopped and surveyed the rocky monolith that rose up in the distance. Its enormous white and yellow sandstone face, broad down below and narrower on top, with none of the soft curves or trees of the Hills, towered over the Flats. Lichen grew midway up, and then the stone swept up into one bare, gigantic crag turned alabaster by the sun. Only on top there were clouds.

"That's it?" asked Beau. "I've seen it from my den every day and always wondered what it was."

"It's called Adamant Tor, the abode of Fearsome Arden."

"Who's he?"

Beau's as ignorant as a pup, Wordsworth thought. "He appeared in the middle of the Great Calamity. Magogs had destroyed the world and were dying along with their dogs. Animals turned sick and great trees came down. Spring arrived but not the grass or flowers, the birds disappeared, and the sun hid all day behind clouds. It seemed as if all life was coming to an end when a great wolf appeared. He told the dogs that he could save them if they followed him. Most did not; they chose to stay with Magogs and died. But some did, and they are our forebears. Fearsome Arden brought them to the Kiskadee Hills and we became known as Kisdees, the last of the dogs on earth."

"And he lived on top up there?" Beau asked, looking up to the dusky summit of Adamant Tor.

"Not at first. He went up there when the Ravages began and Kisdees started killing each other. Our stories say that he spent a year of solitude at the Glade of Remorse, beneath the Turning Tree on top of Adamant Tor."

"Turning Tree?" Beau's eyes gleamed.

"It was Arden who turned. For a long time he grieved for the world that died in the Great Calamity, and especially for the Kisdees whom he'd freed from Magogs but who still thought and acted like them. He wondered if it wasn't too late, if life wasn't finally coming to an end after all. Instead, he made a turn, returned to the warring Kisdees to create the Great Alliance, and we've been at peace ever since. He discovered the swalas in the Cliffs, and we all prospered. He promised us that Ancients, great wolves like him, would be our guardians and protectors forever. But Adamant Tor is always covered with clouds because of Arden's grief. We consider it sacred; that's why no one goes there, including Enforcers."

Beau started running eagerly back and forth, but Wordsworth stared at the rock face, growling softly. "Why is this side of the mountain so dark? There's still plenty of sun." There were no clouds in the sky above them, not a hint of a storm, yet the sandstone that before had shone in the sunlight was rapidly getting darker. His tail tucked under on its own; he couldn't help recalling the two rocks, black as ebony, leaning over the dead Setter.

Just as quickly, the sandstone brightened up once again in the afternoon light and he felt silly. They returned to the forest and he hurried up the slope, but Beau ran helter-skelter, up and down, sniffing ecstatically under trees and ferns and overturning piles of old, dry leaves with his snout. He dug up the earth frantically for moles or else shoved his head into every hollow in search of chipmunks. For a while Wordsworth lost him completely as Beau raced after a ruffed grouse squawking loudly over their heads.

"You're doing exactly what she wants," he remonstrated when Beau returned. "She's luring you away from her nest on the ground."

"She has a nest on the *ground*?" Beau pointed his nose downward, snout whiffing and sniffling feverishly — sniff sniff sniff, pause, sniff sniff sniff — as he examined and re-examined the same patch of ground. He inhaled deeply under a bare shrub, committing the smell to memory, paused only briefly over a mound of brown leaves, as if he knew this smell from before, and came to a complete halt under a tall fir sapling, growling softly.

"What is it?"

"Large animal, thick hair, male." He sniffed some more. "Eats rats and gophers, has claws, and likes to go into water. Walks funny, too, like this," and he walked with a slight forward inflection.

"It's a badger, they have bowed legs. But you don't want to catch them, believe me."

"I want to catch everything!"

At the river Beau drank avidly and sighed. "This is the best water in the whole world." He walked in and sank onto his rump, a beatific expression on his face.

Wordsworth thought of Hanna and the wet-leafed stems he'd brought her. He remembered the parched lips and black tongue, the Birds of Death. He'd dreamed of bringing her to the River Curl and watch as she drank her fill and flopped around in the current. When he opened his eyes Beau was drying himself on the riverbank, whinnying in delight, his paws in the air while shining beads of water dangled from his whiskers. He pushed his rump this way and that, chuckling and chortling hoarsely, jumped up to go in once again, and stopped.

A head appeared above the brush on the other side of the river, followed instantly by a dark brown body. A splash and it was in the water, its long tail flat as it propelled through the current. A louder splash followed as Beau gave chase.

"Not now!" exclaimed Wordsworth. The muskrat could swim a long time underwater, helped not only by its tail but also by its webbed feet.

Beau was gone. The river frothed around them, and suddenly there was an enormous splash. The Gawl's black head came up holding the muskrat's long, scaly tail in his mouth, jaws clenched tight, trying hard not to break into a grin.

"Come on," Wordsworth said.

Beau opened his jaws and the tail slid silently into the water. He climbed up on the riverbank and shook his fur: "Eee, eee, eee, eee!"

✧✧✧

The lower slope of Adamant Tor started gently enough, cushioning their paws with leaves and pine needles, but the incline sharpened and the ground dried up. Soon Wordsworth was loosening grit and small stones and sending them flying. They arrived at the bottom of a tall, rocky escarpment that rose high up, seemingly forever.

He craned his neck; he'd never climbed rocks before. Swalas did that on the tips of their hooves, but not Kisdees. "No wonder no one climbs up Adamant—" He stopped. Maybe no one climbed up, but someone—something—was climbing down. A blanket of dust made things hard to see.

"It's a Magog," Beau growled even before the dust lifted, ear tips rigid, nose quivering, tail outstretched.

The Magog stretched his body down the wall, paws scraping and scrabbling till, with a short jump, he landed on a rocky outcropping on all fours, accompanied by a small storm of powdery dirt. When it lifted they could see him sprawled down the granite surface once more, legs scrambling in the air even longer this time before dropping down on a narrow shelf.

Beau growled again, upper lip curled. "I know that—"

With a loud, rumbling groan the shelf broke away, careening down the slope with a bang as it hit a large rock, and took the rock down with it. The Magog rolled after, stones loosening and cascading. Once again dust rose from the ground, spinning like a ball, following the flat shape that seemed smaller now, lurching and tumbling down till it finally crashed at the bottom.

"It's dead," Beau said, voice unnaturally loud in the silence as he drew near it, sniffing the ground.

"Are you sure?"

A male lay face down. His back legs were splayed out much like Curveheads' when they rested on their belly. This was the first time Wordsworth had seen one from up close and his eyes climbed up the bare, hoary legs, marveling at how it had no tail. Unlike the others, this one had no blotches on his arms and legs. Also unlike the others, he had a little fur on top of his head. Wordsworth licked it, the Magog twitched, and he jumped back. "It's alive!"

Beau growled, hackles rising.

"Do you recognize it?" he asked softly. "Is it one of those who chained you?"

"Who cares? A Magog is a Magog!"

The body shuddered. The male slowly shifted balance, pressing one foreleg into the ground and turning onto his back, revealing a lot more fur on his face. He had long, dark, wavy bristles that curled above his mouth. Certain hound breeds had bristles above their mouths, too, but not as lengthy as that. His lower lip hid beneath a thick patch of fur that came well down to his chest. He groaned and his eyes, the color of sky, opened. They stared at both dogs vacantly, leaving Wordsworth to wonder if he was blind. Then the pupils flickered to life and froze.

Beau snarled, baring his fangs.

"No," the Magog muttered.

"Wait, Beau! Don't—"

Too late. Beau crouched back, ready to spring—

"NOOOOOOOOO!" someone screamed behind them.

With a roar, Beau spun around and attacked. Wordsworth sniffed cypress, glimpsed yellow fur, and leaped. He barely reached Beau's flanks, but it was enough. The Gawl fell on his side, sprang up, and with a choked, raging snarl, jumped Wordsworth. The two dogs rolled across the rocks, raising a dust storm. "They chained me and left me there," Beau gasped. "I begged them to let me go, and you know what they did? They laughed!"

"If it was Badger lying here I wouldn't stop you," the Golden panted, "but it's—"

"They're all the same!" Wordsworth could see the stripe around his throat where the wire had been; he wondered if hair would ever grow there again. "You've never been put down there," Beau rasped. "You don't know what it's like when they put that wire around your neck and you can't move, can't run, can't eat and drink, can't run home to your family. It holds you down there day after day, year after year, all alone, and you know that's how you'll spend the rest of your life. If all this happened to you, you'd be sinking your teeth into their throats right now!"

"I never chained you. I never harmed you," a grizzled, low-pitched voice said behind them.

"CHARLIE!" The female rushed past them, hurled herself at the man who was now sitting up, and hugged him tightly.

Beau bared his teeth. "No! No!" she cried, but her eyes froze at the sight of red drops dribbling down from his torn throat. "Blood," she said, then added: "Wire not there," and her eyes filled with tears. "Wire not there," she repeated again, and hugged the male tightly.

"Isn't that a good thing, Summer?" the older Magog murmured, looking at Beau. His blue eyes sparkled and the fur above his lips curled even wider. "How did you get the wire off?" Without waiting for an answer, he bent over the girl's yellow hair. "You can talk now, Summer. You're among friends."

"No friends of yours," said Beau hoarsely. He snarled, turned, retraced the girl's steps with his snout, and disappeared around the bluff.

"Dog!" the girl said, turning to Wordsworth. He growled. "Dog!" she said again, louder this time.

"Tell her to stop."

"You tell her, she understands."

"The others said she can't talk."

"Oh, Summer talks, all right. In fact, sometimes you can't shut her up."

"Dog! Dog! Dog!"

Wordsworth barked out a warning.

"She likes you," the Magog said, unperturbed. She went down on all fours and slowly crept towards him. Wordsworth growled and she paused, perplexed. "Come here, Summer," and the other pulled her away gently. "She wants to touch you. That's pretty unusual; Summer hates touching anyone but Ophelia and me."

"Ophelia? Her mother?"

"Ophelia is not her mother."

Wordsworth heard a small snarl and looked up. There, on a tall overhang well out of reach, crouched a lynx.

It was a big one, light brown and yellow in the early spring. Lynx were rarely seen in the Hills; they knew how to remain hidden. There were the familiar tufts of hair by its ears and the ruff of fur around the face, its long legs bent as it watched him warily from its high perch. He snarled and the lynx responded, its growl lower and more savage than his own. He'd seen only one lynx till today, stretched out on top of a tree limb and looking calmly down at a party of hunters that had dashed right under it. He was bringing up the rear, as usual, had looked up and spotted it. A tale about Arden and the lynx flickered in his mind briefly, then disappeared.

"Ophelia, stop!" the Magog girl commanded.

"Did you say that the lynx lets the girl touch her?" Wordsworth demanded. "You're lying. No animal in the Hills hides itself like the lynx."

"Is that so?" the old Magog remarked.

Behind them the wall of rocks bent inwards, creating a small recess filled by large boulders fallen from the mountain-top. The girl, who seemed to understand completely, nimbly climbed up one large rock. Stretching herself vertically against the rock wall and moving from one tiny foothold to another, she gained the top. She sat and turned to the lynx, which had already shot up on its long legs and stared down at her with its yellow-green eyes, transfixed. The girl gazed back at it, and Wordsworth remembered how she hadn't once looked at Snail or any of the others by the Flats. The lynx climbed up the rocks with her broad paws, black-tipped tail flying, as though making her get-away. Then she circled back, descended, and gingerly approached the girl, sniffing carefully. When she came close enough Summer bent down and bumped heads with it. The two stroked each other's face and neck. "Ophelia, Ophelia," the girl purred.

He could hardly believe his eyes. Lynx didn't socialize with each other, never mind other species, and especially Magogs. But this girl seemed different from the others, he thought. If she'd stretched out her hands to grab it the lynx would have bolted. He remembered Badger rearing up on his hind legs, never realizing how aggressive this appeared to everyone else in the Hills. But the girl understood; that's why she crouched low when facing dogs.

Ophelia leaped away with a snarl and scrambled up a rock.

"What are they doing?" demanded Beau suddenly at his side, then added hoarsely, "I tracked the girl's smell to a big rock against the mountainside. She came from *inside* Adamant Tor."

"Ophelia!" the girl shouted, but the lynx was already high up. For a moment the feline eyes looked down at them; then she effortlessly bounded up and disappeared over another wide pile of rocks. "Bad! Bad!" the girl yelled at Beau.

"Summer, come here," the older Magog said firmly from where he was sitting on the ground. He reached for her with his arms till she came down and huddled against him, looking balefully at Beau. "Not inside Adamant Tor," he said calmly, "*under* Adamant Tor. We humans lived underneath."

Wordsworth was incredulous. None of their stories had said anything about this. Foxes, badgers, and rabbits lived under the ground, not Magogs.

"I was born underneath," continued the Magog called Charlie. "So were my parents and my parents' parents. For generations we lived there; we didn't know anything else. Until one day we came out to the sun, the sky, the grass and trees." The wrinkles in his face deepened with recollection and a few drops of water fell from his eyes. "I'm the oldest of us so I still remember that time. Most of the others, including Summer, were born above ground." He saw the look on Wordsworth's face even as the girl brushed away the wet drops with one of her paws. "It's how we survived the Calamity. As far as we know, everyone who lived outside died. But our ancestors, a small group, lived inside this mountain. We are their descendants, the only humans still living. For many generations we didn't dare go out; we were sure we would die. Still, there was always someone who knew the way out. In my generation, that was me."

"What caused you to finally leave the mountain?"

The Magog laughed sadly. "We got sick."

"Sick how?"

"We developed welts on our skin which smelled and itched. Men and women lost their hair, and we died young, much younger than humans did before the Calamity."

He examined the Magog with his plentiful gray fur. "But not you and her. Why?"

"I don't know," said Charlie, looking briefly at Summer before gazing up at Adamant Tor, which loomed over them.

He's lying, Wordsworth thought, but about what? Questions swarmed inside. Were these the only Magogs that survived or were there more inside, armies of them, with red welts on their bare skins, ready to come out into the Hills? Was he telling the truth about the sickness? These two didn't seem sick at all. Still, of the Magogs he'd seen so far, this one named Charlie was by far the oldest. "You're not supposed to be in the Hills. Aren't you afraid of Enforcers?"

The wrinkles deepened. "Enforcers track us by our shoes, but Summer and I don't wear any." He pressed the girl to him, but she broke free and went down on her four paws once again to look straight ahead at Wordsworth.

The dog gave a weak growl and sniffed curiously. A smell of lynx came from a braid of hairs the girl wore around her neck. She crept towards him.

"Let her touch you," Charlie said softly. "All her life she's wanted to touch dogs."

But Beau snarled and she jumped back, yowling in frustration. She looked away and began to hum.

"What's she doing?" muttered Beau.

"When things are too much for Summer, she hums. She's different from other Magogs, she thinks more like you do, in pictures. She depends more on touching than on seeing. She can feel afraid or angry, happy or sad; she's simpler than the rest of us. And like I said, she loves dogs more than she loves humans."

"No Magog loves dogs."

"We're not all like Badger."

"Badger," Summer said, putting her hand to her head as though feeling a sudden pain.

Charlie put his arm around her. "He hates Summer because she's different. He hates anybody who's different."

Like Dreden, Wordsworth thought. *Why shouldn't there have been good Magogs and bad Magogs, short ones and tall ones?* He looked up. The sun looked back from far down the side; the day was passing.

"Come, Summer." Charlie got up slowly, in obvious pain, but he looked away as he rose, following Kisdee etiquette. The girl watched Wordsworth, as though waiting for him to tell her what to do. "What is it, Summer?" Charlie asked kindly.

"He knows," she said, motioning to Wordsworth. "Dogs know. I wish I was a dog."

"You're not a dog, you're a human, only different."

"If I'm different, why can't I be a dog?"

Charlie just shook his head and picked up her hand. Slowly they walked down, Charlie favoring one side. The girl turned her head over her shoulder, keeping her eyes on Wordsworth till they disappeared behind a column of rocks.

"We should have killed them," Beau said. "They'll tell Badger."

Wordsworth looked up at the rocks above. "I wonder what he was doing here. Even if he wasn't lying and Magogs did live underneath for a long time, why was he coming down from the *top* of Adamant Tor?"

"You said no one ever comes here."

"That's what I was told. And looking up this sheer wall, I don't know how to get up there myself."

Beau's mood instantly changed. "*I* do," he said, eyes sparkling.

Wordsworth continued to examine the cliff. How can there be a glade up there, he wondered, the top has to be flat and dry. Then he thought of the girl. "Her coat is made of pond cypress, not fur," he mused. "You think it keeps her warm?"

But Beau wasn't there. Wordsworth searched up the tall escarpment of rocks, huge crags of smooth sandstone splayed one on top of another, reaching high into the afternoon sky.

"Here I am!" The Gawl appeared on a rocky ledge above him, grinning.

"How did you get up there?"

"Eee, eee, eee, eee!" was the happy reply. "I found it when I tracked the Magogs. If you go back where we came from there's a gap between two big boulders, and inside is a pile of rocks."

Wordsworth found it and climbed up to the ledge, dragging his bad leg up, only to find Beau gone again. When he called out, the Gawl hailed him from an outcrop further up, earflaps high, another grin on his face. "Come on!" he called out, clearly enjoying himself, and directed him to a cluster of three rocks that leaned against each other. The Gawl had made it in a few leaps, but he himself could only crawl and wriggle his way up.

Beau took the lead the rest of the way. Even when climbing any higher appeared impossible, when they stood at the foot of what looked like an insurmountable sweep of sandstone, Beau would circle, find his way through narrow ruptures and small crooks and hollows till he found something— a ledge, a cranny, another rocky shelf that was almost, but not quite, out of reach—and jump. While Wordsworth's body shook from the effort, his paws loosening streams of pebbles that echoed down a deeper and deeper chasm, Beau was strong and stable on his young, healthy legs, happily contemplating each new climb as if it were only a game.

How does he do it, the other wondered, helpless at the foot of another large slab of stone. He's been tied up his entire life! When he jumped his front legs made it, clawing and scratching, but his good back leg slid, taking him down till he fell. Quickly he rose, leaped once again and landed, crumbling onto his side, panting and shaking from fear and effort, bad leg throbbing.

"We're almost there," Beau said, tail wagging.

Bush and scrub dotted the ledges above them, giving him renewed strength as he limped up after the Gawl, who scampered up the highest boulders, tail waving from side to side.

When they reached the top Wordsworth looked down the deep abyss. How were they ever going to get back to the forest floor? The Magog had almost fallen to his death despite the long, soft fingers that gave him a better hold. Then he turned around and exclaimed.

They were standing at one end of the summit, its narrowest part. The rest was broader, dipping down into an immense glade, the Glade of Remorse. And the Glade of Remorse was green. Clumps of green-black tamaracks with clusters of needles stretched up to the afternoon sky, surrounded by groves of unfamiliar tall stalks with dense, furry heads. There were other plants with berries of all colors, some of which he recognized from the Hills where they wouldn't appear until summer, but here they were already out and several times taller, with peculiar large leaves that curled thickly around the stems. The ground was matted with moss, and strange flowers opened their purple and yellow petals to cool, sticky air that was eerily still. Most incredible of all was the damp. The smell of water was everywhere!

How could wetlands grow on top of sandstone and rock? It was as if the summit of Adamant Tor had caved in, creating a wet, verdant valley. Vapors rose from the ground, hiding and revealing the Glade by turn.

Beau stood at the other side of the rim, which at this end was a short walk away. Wordsworth joined him and looked down on the Flats below. He could see the Gawl's wooden den. There was another further off, and he wondered if that's where they'd put the Pit Bull Charlotte. Unless she was already dead.

The sun flashed gold and red. Beau's nostrils twitched intently. "Is there anything beyond the Flats?"

"Our stories talk about the Great Water and the Hills of Their Abode, where the Ancients live."

"Can we go there?"

"It's at the other end of the Great Water, which is too big for us to swim across. And to reach the Great Water we'd need to cross the Flats."

Beau sniffed cautiously in the direction of the Glade, a frown wrinkling his black forehead. The next moment he tore downhill and disappeared in the sea of green. Wordsworth plunged after him.

Crisp, cool spring had just arrived in the forest below, but here the air was warm and humid, as if they were in the thick of summer. Flowers, full-grown and open-petaled, scratched his legs and the white, furry tops of tall stalks poured their seeds over his fur each time he brushed past them. He saw poison sumac as high as trees and shivered from the coarse touch of tough, thick leaves that felt like no leaves in the Hills. His head struck low-hanging, slender branches again and again. Trees fallen against each other creaked and groaned, unable to lie in peace. When he reached the bottom of the slope the ground turned soggy. With every step the earth seemed to give way, and soon brown water seeped over his paws. Incredulous, he stopped and examined the layer of spongy moss on which he stood. All this on top of a sandstone mountain!

"How come it's raining?"

He jumped. "Can't you be quieter?" he whispered to Beau, who'd come up behind him.

"Why are you whispering?"

"I'm not whispering." They were in a grove of tamaracks, laces of mist enveloping the yellow trunks. Beau was right, it was raining, though down below the afternoon had been clear and dry.

"The trees talk here," the Gawl said.

"It's just their trunks scraping against each other."

"And there are no animals."

That's true, Wordsworth thought as both began to move more cautiously. There are plants and trees, but nothing else, no birds or crawlers. The trees creaked and the water bubbled at their feet, but other than that there was no noise at all. A familiar smell met his nostrils; he approached several trees and sniffed the pale gray bark. It was the same smell as the wooden layers that enveloped the Magog girl. This must be where she gets them, he thought.

His back leg fell and he scrabbled with his front paws. But the leg sank even deeper and now the crippled paw that he usually held high was in the water, too. He tried to scramble up, but the harder he tried the deeper sank his back legs. Then he felt Beau's jaws pulling him hard by the nape of his neck. He smelled the blood around the Gawl's throat and knew what this effort cost him. Finally he lay on the ground, panting. "A sinkhole?" he wondered aloud. He'd heard of one or two on the other side of the river far below them, created by heavy wet summers with long, rainy days.

But Beau wasn't listening. "It smells like fire," he growled, nostrils sniffing furiously.

"Fires can't burn here, there's too much water." He glanced around; there was no sign of blackened tree trunks. At the center of the glade, in the distance, the earth rose slightly, forming a low mound. A tree stood there alone and Wordsworth's heartbeat quickened. This had to be where Arden had stayed so long ago, at first consumed by doubt and grief, then transformed, determined to return below, form the Great Alliance, and change the world of dogs forever.

Silently they walked down, and soon Wordsworth, too, was able to make out the scent. There was water, decay, and smoke. He sniffed in disbelief, then fear. He knew this combination of rot and fire, he'd smelled it before. Something rubbed up against him and he jumped, but it was only the spike of a cattail rising on the margins of a stand of long grasses half-submerged in a watery ditch. The bank of the ditch was moist and dark, and there was no mistaking the deep, long, round indentations. Magogs' tracks. They were here, he thought, vaguely aware that Beau had run ahead towards the top of the mound. Beyond the ditch the earth was a fuzzy green as it first sloped down, then rose, wet and unusually bright. Up ahead Beau had come to a complete stop.

Wordsworth approached. The trunk of the tree was fat and gnarled with four long, thick branches, each bare and almost as big as a tamarack trunk, two on each side. A large black hollow had burned into the trunk below, and a deep furrow in the bark slashed its way between the hollow and the enormous tentacle branches.

Wordsworth went cold. Beau growled. "It looks like a Magog."

Was this the Turning Tree? Beau was right, it looked like a monstrous Magog. And yet, what else could it be, standing on the mound at the center of the Glade of Remorse? His thick hair was damp and his skin felt icy. The acrid smell of burn was stronger than ever, and it got worse as they moved up the mound closer to the tree, now joined by something else, the scent of blood and rotting flesh, and Beau growled again and ran up, Wordsworth right behind him. He'd never felt so cold in his entire life. He plowed into Beau's flanks for the Gawl had stopped. Wordsworth stepped around him and followed his gaze. Something large was lying on the ground in the center of the blackest, bloodiest grass he'd ever seen. Big and red and golden.

Hanna.

TEN

Hanna had been killed in the same way as Margaret, the Black and Tan. Her mouth was a wide-open, empty cavity. Some of her gleaming red hair had been torn off and there were deep bite marks around her neck.

One horrified glance revealed everything, and he knew he'd remember it for the rest of his life. Bludrun! Hanna was a big dog and more courageous than anyone he'd ever met, but after days of no food or water, crushed down by the chains, she'd be no match for Bludrun. Beau sniffed her feverishly; he, too, could smell the blood. Did she fight? She wanted to live so much! But he remembered how he himself couldn't move once the green eyes had opened, when he saw his own image in those eyes getting closer and closer.

Don't pity me, you're more of a slave than I am. Her last words to him. Probably her last words to anyone.

Earlier he'd told Beau that Adamant Tor was always covered with clouds because of grief. Now he looked up and couldn't see the sun. Beau was panting, tongue slipping out the side of his mouth. He's hot, Wordsworth thought, and I'm freezing.

Beau sniffed her nonstop. "She must be dead for days."

"That can't be, I saw her late yesterday down in the Flats." But Beau was right, the smell was stronger than that. "And how did she get here?"

"Maybe she escaped again."

"You should have seen those chains, and she was so weak!" He forced himself to look back at the bloody flanks. "Her flesh is fresh; that means that the blood stopped flowing not too long ago." This afternoon, he wondered, when the top of Adamant Tor turned dark though the sun was beaming straight at it?

Beau stiffened and his earflaps shot up. He followed the Gawl's gaze towards three pines whose long, dark branches grew practically horizontal to the ground. Then he himself jumped, lips parted to reveal the glitter of fangs. One of those branches was waving from side to side. Beau growled and rose up high on his paws. "Stay calm," he muttered.

Beau snarled. His tail shot straight out into the air.

"What are you —?"

Something hit him and he went down. He yanked his neck away to avoid the impending bite and heard a crash. Jumping up, he smelled a musky scent of balsam and saw the russet Wolfhound crushing Beau under her immense body, her fangs deep in his neck. He lunged and she shoved him away with a forceful sweep of her muscular hips. Beau screamed in agony for her fangs had found the torn flesh above his throat. When he attacked her again she twisted nimbly so that all he got was a mouthful of skin and hair before being flung off. How strong she was! She began to shake Beau by the neck and the Gawl shrieked.

"Pandora," said a familiar kindly voice.

Beau's head lolled to the side.

"Pandora, stop!"

She opened her mouth and the Gawl silently crumbled to the ground, neck crimson.

Wordsworth huddled over him. Pandora's deft moves were worthy of an Enforcer, for Beau didn't move. His throat wounds, crusted slightly, now hemorrhaged blood. Just Daniel appeared at his elbow but Wordsworth barely noticed. He'll die, he thought to himself. It's the second time today, and this time he'll die.

Did he say these words out loud? Maybe, for Just Daniel bent down and started licking Beau's neck. His tongue stroke the red cuts and lacerations in warm, wet, slow circles. Beau opened his eyes and the small Mixed doubled his efforts, brushing his tongue in long, soft curves all along the bloody throat. Beau shut his eyes, drained, and Wordsworth wondered if this was the end. Instead, the Gawl whimpered. He moved his head weakly, and Wordsworth saw that the bleeding had stopped. Just Daniel didn't budge, stroking the entire length of Beau's throat and neck, dribbling saliva on the raw half-circle once enveloped by Magogish wire. Beau groaned and arched his neck back, giving them both a clear view of the slashed throat. The groans turned into moans of relief, and when the small dog finally raised his head, the lacerations were gone. There were no sores, no trace of blood, no rawness anywhere. All that remained was a thin, pink band encircling the throat where the black hairs had torn off.

Wordsworth stared. "What did you do?"

"What anyone does when another is in pain," the old Gawl replied, examining Beau's torn earflaps.

"But his wounds are gone. How did you do that?"

Behind him someone growled a warning.

"It's all right, Pandora, he's a friend."

"I call no Kisdee friend," his companion spat malevolently.

Wordsworth turned around. Here was the Wolfhound he'd wanted to see again so much, and her name was Pandora. Her matted flanks smelled of balsam and her muzzle bent sideways. She looked back with hostile contempt.

"A Kisdee with a Gawl for company," Just Daniel murmured as Beau slowly got up. He sat back on his haunches and glanced from Beau to Wordsworth, and back again. "A Kisdee and a Gawl."

"Why did you attack him?" Wordsworth demanded. "He's a Gawl, like you."

"He's also a Daimyo," Pandora snarled. "I loathe Daimyos."

"And I hate Tug-a-Lugs," said Beau, nostrils flaring again and tail shooting up. "Nothing I'd like more than to get my teeth in—"

She almost leaped at Beau a second time but Wordsworth jumped between them. "Are you crazy!" He looked from one to the other. "Beau, you're a Gawl, remember? You're only partially a Daimyo *and* you're on the run. And she's not a pure Tug-a-Lug, either."

"What's the difference?" Pandora glared spitefully at Beau, her dark Wolfhound eyes shrouded by her wiry hair. In the Hills, any direct stare was an invitation to a fight. "I'm

Tug-a-Lug enough that I can't abide Daimyos. A Daimyo's a Daimyo's a—"

"You're being ridiculous, Pandora," said Just Daniel, getting up. "The Tug-a-Lugs don't claim you as family just like the Daimyos don't claim him. Why should you fight their feud? Someone's lying dead under that tree while you two—"

"And why is she dead?" demanded Beau. "Because of a murdering, butchering Tug-a—"

Pandora jumped Beau, who went crashing on the ground like before. This time, however, he managed to slip his head out from under her. She twisted, trying to reach his neck, and then they both looked up, startled.

"Someone's coming up the rocks," said Beau, earflaps pointing up, sniffing the air rapidly.

Pandora flew down the mound and crossed the Glade, curved tail waving. In no time she came back. "Enforcers," she told Just Daniel before turning on Beau, who was now up. "They're climbing up the rocks just like you said. Following you!"

"Maybe they're following *you*."

"We didn't come up the rocks."

"So how did you get here?" asked Wordsworth. She tossed him a scornful glance. "We're all in this together."

"Says who?"

"I saw the two of you by the river two nights ago."

She bared her teeth. "I knew you were a spy."

"I came down to the river and saw Markus standing on the bank. When the two of you came to drink he hid and heard everything you said."

"Can he identify us?" asked Just Daniel.

"I don't think so. At least, not yet."

"You mean, not till you identify us for him," snarled Pandora.

"Stop!" Just Daniel jumped between them, not the least bit discomfited by Pandora's fangs high over his neck. He scrunched up his eyes as if reaching a decision. "Okay," he wagged his hoary tail, "follow us."

"Where are you going?" she demanded.

"You know exactly where we're going," he replied calmly.

"You're going to show them the passage?"

"I'm not leaving them behind, we've had enough killing for one day. Let's go."

For a brief moment Wordsworth and Pandora exchanged glances. He didn't want to go with the Gawls either, but what choice did they have? She snarled, baring her sharp teeth, and ran down the mound. Wordsworth chased her across the Glade of Remorse to the opposite side of the rim. Half-submerged cattails brushed his paws, and at times his legs fell through the shallow ground and splashed in water. Beau followed and Just Daniel was last, trotting as fast as he could on his short legs. When they started to climb up to the rim once more Wordsworth stopped and looked back towards the black mound on which Hanna lay.

"There's nothing you can do for her now," Just Daniel said, running past him.

Beau's ears stood up tall. "They've reached the top, hurry."

Up the brief slope, the fog swallowed Beau and Just Daniel. Wordsworth followed and heard, "Go in."

Go in where, he wondered, facing the wall of rocks covered by layers of dry leaves, twigs, and withered branches. The mist curled and he saw Just Daniel standing patiently by a pile of dead foliage. Next to him was an opening: small, black, empty. His tail fell between his legs. "What's this?"

"We're going below."

"Below the rocks?"

"We know our way."

Down on his belly, he worked his way in. Ahead of him was only darkness.

"Come on!" he heard Pandora hiss.

He crawled further inside, the ground descending until, amazingly, he was able to stand. He took a few steps. Beau was right in front of him, listening. "They've arrived at the mound," he announced breathlessly.

Wordsworth turned around and saw the older Gawl, back flanks inside, prodding the dry leaves back together to conceal the opening, through which twilight still glimmered faintly.

"Help him," Pandora snapped.

But Just Daniel had obviously done this many times before. Just as quickly the light died, leaving them in total darkness. "After you."

"Where does this take us?"

"To the bottom."

Wordsworth heard Beau sniffing behind him while ahead Pandora disappeared. He ran into a wall, grazing his forehead.

"Let your friend go ahead of you," suggested Just Daniel. "He relies on his nose more than you do, he'll know the way."

Beau pulled ahead of him, striding confidently off to the side, and even as blood trickled down the side of his head Wordsworth couldn't help but wonder once again at Beau, who could hear and smell better than them and was as agile and fast as an Enforcer—all after being chained down all his life. How was that possible? And yet, he was sure Beau wasn't lying. For one thing, there was no mistaking his bitterness towards Magogs, matched only by his joy at being free in the Hills. Second, every smell and sound were new to him, and if they weren't going down this passage he would be hunting silly rodents under tree limbs and digging after rabbits long after they escaped through their runs. He was silly and brave, foolhardy and fast; he was not a liar.

Now Beau was sniffing the ground furiously as he made his way down. And down it was, for the passage was certainly sloping more and more sharply downhill.

"Easy does it," Just Daniel said softly.

Pandora and Beau had left them behind, battering their way forward, unconcerned by sharp-edged rocks and hard walls. Once Just Daniel emitted a brief cry of pain and Wordsworth sensed him bending forward and licking one of his paws. He was underground. *Underneath*, the Magog Charlie had said. Was this really how Magogs lived for so many years? How did they survive without light? Everyone knew that Magogs depended almost entirely on their vision.

And then he saw light, or at least a dim flicker. It came through a small opening below and ahead of them, half as big as his head. By the time he reached it Beau and Pandora had forged on. He looked through it and saw gray shadows of twilight blanketing the Flats.

"No one can make it up this side because it's a sheer sweep to the top, unlike the side you climbed," said Just Daniel calmly behind him. "But there are tiny openings in the rocks and they give us the light by which we find our way up and down."

So that's how these two came up to the summit, he thought. And maybe Charlie and the girl, Summer? The glimmer behind them disappeared, but a new one twinkled further down. The steep incline had become solid, hard-packed, as if someone had cleared the sharp-edged rocks away. He could make out Pandora advancing swiftly and confidently, filling the passageway with her great size. Beau matched her stride for stride, his nose leading the rest of his body, ears sharply angled, nostrils sniffing nonstop. He's stronger than I am, Wordsworth thought, and faster than I'll ever be. His own breathing was labored and his back hurt from holding his crippled leg up, causing the other legs to sway weakly.

He sensed rather than saw Just Daniel buckle and fall, then get up again. "I'm not as fast and limber as I used to be," he said with a self-mocking groan.

"Why not slow down?"

"Because Enforcers may be coming down the passage as we speak."

"You think they'll find it?"

"If not today, some other day. It's just a matter of time."

Wordsworth glanced over his shoulder, half expecting to see the glint of almond eyes, narrow muzzles and sharp, white teeth. When he faced front again Beau said, "We've reached the bottom."

Ahead of him Pandora pushed her large head forward, moving something away. Over Beau's shoulder Wordsworth could see the bare branches of the forest trees outlined softly in the twilight. He waited impatiently for Beau to jump out, but instead the Gawl looked to the side where the passage continued in still greater darkness, his nostrils still working nonstop. He took a few steps in that direction.

"Come on!" Pandora hissed.

"What is it?" Wordsworth asked.

"That smell is there."

He didn't ask what smell. He tried to sniff it himself, but all he got was the scent of cold wet earth and something very small and very dead. Beau growled softly. "How far does this go?" Wordsworth asked Just Daniel, who was waiting politely behind him.

"Who knows?"

"It's still going down, which means it continues beneath the forest floor. So where does it go?"

The small Mixed's ochre-rimmed eyes gazed at him expressionlessly. "It goes to the Land of the Gawls."

He bristled. "Let's get out, Beau."

Beau turned back and jumped out of the passage. Wordsworth leaped out after him, followed by Just Daniel. He and Beau watched as Pandora, using her long forehead and muzzle, bent and moved the brush back to block the opening.

ELEVEN

They were back in the pine grove.

The sun had gone down long ago and the Gawls were sleeping the sleep of the dead. There were many more of them now, huddling against each other in the dark just like their old ones, felled by hard labor and exhaustion, moaning in restless slumber as if aware that they didn't have long to sleep before rising to be at the Cliffs by dawn.

He and Beau had arrived earlier, just after it got dark, trudging behind Just Daniel with Pandora bringing up the rear, narrow eyes glowering beneath her bristly eyebrows. Word had gone out about a Gawl from the Flats and everyone had crowded around them—big and small, young and old, entire families—to stare at Beau. Just Daniel had stretched under one of the trees, his short legs collapsing under him. But first he'd muttered something to an old mixed Terrier who then disappeared from view and reappeared later, supervising younger dogs carrying meat-packed swala bones in their mouths. Wordsworth lay on his belly and chewed, noting that the Gawls brought the choicest bones to Just Daniel, who lay his head between his paws and went right to sleep.

"Where are you going now?" the old Gawl had asked them when they'd emerged onto the forest floor. When no one answered he said, "I guess you might as well come with us."

"You want them to come home with us?" Pandora demanded, incredulous.

"They're on the run; it sounds as though we might be, too."

"We're *not* on the run, why should we be?" The old anger was back in her eyes. "Unless *he* told them," and she jerked her head towards Wordsworth.

He sighed. "Pandora, they need help."

"*We* need help. What we don't need is a Kisdee hanging around us."

"A Kisdee with a Gawl. Wordsworth rescued a Gawl."

"How do you know it's not one of Dreden's tricks?"

"Dreden has easier ways to spy on us than by setting a Gawl free."

Pandora snorted, but she gave way. Bigger, younger, stronger, and angrier, she submitted to someone much smaller, older, and weaker, not something Tug-a-Lugs were known to do. But as soon as they arrived in the pine grove she disappeared.

Beau jumped at the bones with abandon, tearing apart the meat and gnawing the remains. The others watched open-eyed, urging him on, which he was only too happy to do, grinning widely as he chewed, eating so much that twice they brought him more. Finally, he finished up his enormous meal by lapping up half a pool of water, then frolicking on the ground with his paws in the air, much to everyone's admiration.

The pups followed Beau everywhere as he sniffed the ground fiercely — sniff sniff sniff, pause, sniff sniff sniff — before joining in their games, chasing and wrestling, accompanied by a loud, undignified commotion of screeches, yaps and yowls, Beau barking the loudest by far, usually from the bottom of a pile of flapping paws and rapping tails: "Aiffff! Aiffff! Eeeee, eeeeee, eeeee! Aiffff!"

When the pups tired and left, Beau jumped a Doberman Mixed, bringing him down in a crash of flanks and legs. But the dog leaped to his paws and snapped viciously, baring his sharp teeth before walking away.

"I guess he doesn't want to play," muttered a perplexed Beau, dark forehead furrowed.

"You didn't greet him properly."

The others had gone off to rest, leaving the two alone.

"Why do I have to greet him?"

"Because that's what everyone does in the Hills, even Gawls. Here, let me show you." Wordsworth wagged his tail invitingly.

"I don't want to greet, I want to play," groused Beau.

"First things first. Now, Beau, what do you do when you see someone?"

"Jump him."

"No, no, there is an etiquette for these meetings."

"Etiquette? What's an etiquette?"

"Etiquette is the proper way of doing things." He backed off in one direction while Beau, imitating him, backed off in the other. "Now, let's say we've just set eyes on each other. What do you do?"

Beau didn't know.

"You stop and assess the situation. Is the other bigger or smaller than you are? Is he or she more or less important? If he's smaller there's no contest and you can approach. But what happens if he's your size? Can you guess?"

Beau couldn't guess.

"The most important thing is not to stare at anyone straight in the face, otherwise you're looking for a fight. Always avert your eyes — it shows you're coming in peace — and wag your tail slightly, not too much. At that point the two of you can approach each other. Like this," and Wordsworth averted his eyes, wagged his tail slightly, and approached Beau respectfully but confidently.

"Now can I jump you?"

"No. Not before you give the invitation to play."

"I have to *invite* them to play?"

"This is how it's done, just watch." And Wordsworth lowered his front half down to the ground, rump staying high in the air, and wagged his golden tail.

"Then what?"

"If the other dog wants to play, he'll jump you."

Beau sat back on his haunches, thinking it over. "What happens if I meet someone who's bigger than me?"

"Bend your knees slightly, raise your underbelly a bit, and lower your head. That shows that you know he's bigger than you are and that you respect him. If you do that he'll usually leave you alone."

"You mean, like this?" And Beau bent his knees, raised his underbelly, lowered his head, and wagged his tail.

"Perfect."

He watched as Beau sauntered over to the others, trying out the different greeting postures and invitations to play. By now most were trying to sleep, but a few wagged their tails in friendship, only to be slammed hard by Beau. They snarled just like the Doberman and a puzzled Beau went on in search of other playmates. When he found no takers, he picked up a long, thick branch, clenched it in his jaws and ran around the grove smashing into various dogs with both ends. When that brought him no new friends, he crouched down and chewed up the wood, spitting it out in smaller pieces. Finally he dug a small hollow in the ground, lay down with paws in the air, rubbed himself first one way, then another, curled on his side, and fell asleep.

But not Wordsworth. Sleep wouldn't come. Each time he shut his eyes he was back in the underground passage, with the darkness and smell of being underneath. His heart beat furiously and fear whined in his belly. How could anyone live like that, knowing there was no sky above, just crushing sandstone rock? Finally he gave up, rose, and headed across the pine grove, walking gingerly around the slumbering bodies. He needn't have worried, most slept as though they'd never wake up. One or two opened their eyes and gave him a quick, sullen glance before closing them again. Kisdees were not welcome here.

He slipped silently down the slope in the direction of sunset once clearing the grove, one thought flashing repeatedly inside, which was that Just Daniel could buy himself and Pandora much-needed favor with Dreden if he was to send word that a Gawl from the Flats was taking shelter with them that night. Was this a trick? Were they being offered refuge now, only to be surrounded soon by Enforcers?

A cluster of rocks gleamed in the starlight beneath two balsam firs. Down below there were other larger rocks where a Pit Bull had thrashed around in a pile of needles, only to be caught. What happened to Charlotte? Did Badger send her to the Land of the Gawls? Why did Magogs hate Pit Bulls so much? And what was he doing here among an assortment of Gawls on the lower side of the river, sniffing nervously for the furtive scent of terraberries, instead of reciting poetry alone under the big, peaceful weeping willow?

Find Beau, she'd said.

And what do I do then?

Your heart will tell you. Whether you do it or not is another question.

His heart had told him to free Beau, but was that what Ruwena intended? Then why hadn't she told him to do that directly? And how can I be her messenger and warn Kisdees, he wondered, if Markus and Zebu will kill me on sight? And what'll happen to Beau?

I can only tell you your first step. That will guide you to the next, and that one will guide you to the one after.

He hoped so; right now he had no idea what to do. And he was homesick. Poet's Vale was lonely and simple. He had his poetry. There would be the dry catch in his throat, the cough, and the verses:

"Spring steals into these happy Hills
With newly minted leaf and fern,
Yellow bud forsythia, emerald frills,

The moon comes up – the moon comes up – the moon comes up – "

"What about the moon?"

He spun around. Pandora stood behind him, staring intently behind her scraggly hair. His heartbeat quickened and he licked his lips.

"Is that the end of the verse?" she demanded.

"I can't finish it," he replied awkwardly.

"Why not?"

"I don't know. I've never had that trouble before."

She stamped the ground with her paw. "It's a dumb verse."

This is why she smells of balsam, it occurred to him. This is her place, where we're standing now, her Poet's Vale. For the first time he noticed the narrow, pale shading around her eyes, which looked ghostly in the night.

"Why do you make up poems?" she demanded. "Why can't you just talk like everybody else?"

"It's not talk. When I talk I know what I'm going to say. When I declaim verse I surprise myself."

"By not finishing what you started?"

He tried to contain his irritation. "That's not what I mean. Even when the words come I don't know what they'll be till I say them."

"And that's good?"

"Don't you like surprises, Pandora?"

"No Gawl likes surprises. Good surprises don't happen to us, only bad ones."

"Like finding Beau and me on top of Adamant Tor? Or seeing me down below?" She snorted contemptuously. "It was you who helped the Pit Bull escape that day, wasn't it?"

"It wasn't *you*. You were too busy watching the Magog strangling her to death." Her eyes glittered. "'Course it was me. We ran to the Cliffs but they chased us, so we split up. She ran into Badger, who tried to kill her, and a lame Kisdee who watched."

He lost his patience. "Not to mention a Wolfhound Gawl who did nothing because she was too busy watching me!"

"I was looking for my chance."

"Dreden beat you to it."

The air vibrated between them. The night breeze was mild, but the balsam leaves swayed and wobbled. She shook her head and the wiry, russet hair covered her eyes once more. "You don't understand, Kisdee. I don't hate you for not helping the Pit Bull, I hate you for being what you are. A Kisdee is a Kisdee no matter what he does, even if he's managed to fool Just Daniel."

"Why does a big dog like you worry about what that runty old Gawl thinks?"

"Because that runty old Gawl is the head of all the Gawls in the Hills."

"Just Daniel?"

She snorted once again. "All you see is a small, broken-down Spaniel Mixed, but there's no one nobler in these Hills than him, including Priam, *your* Noble One." Her voice dripped with sarcasm but her eyes became both tender and incredibly sad. She looked down, as if to hide the anguish, and when she looked up again the rough tone was back. "What happens when the words don't come?" she demanded.

"I used to think that was the worst feeling in the world."

"What changed your mind?"

"When I saw Beau and Hanna in the Flats. That's when I knew there were worse things than that."

She thought it over for a moment, scraping the ground with her paw. "We have no poets. Can you imagine what Kisdees would say if I started reciting some silly words? *She's not this, she's not that, she's so mixed she doesn't know whether she's coming or going. All she knows is how to talk and how to eat.*"

Her voice sounded uncannily like Zebu's. "They say some of that about me, too, on account of my limp."

"I'm surprised they let you live."

Her coldness struck him like a blow. His top lip curled, the chilly night air licked his teeth. She's as icy as Dreden, he thought, suddenly feeling bone tired. There was no friendship here, no warmth, not the slightest stirs of sympathy. He started walking back uphill.

"Where are you going?" she demanded.

He gave no reply. The stars blinked down as he retraced his steps and thought back for the umpteenth time to the night when he'd first seen her, fearless in that supernatural light. *What's there to be afraid of? That your days might end and you won't have to pull dead swalas down to the Bottoms anymore?* Those words had pierced him then; they pierced him now. The moon was waning, the hillside luminous. *I've told you over and over again, I can take care of myself. Besides, you know I love the moonlight.*

More than is good —

A deep howl cut the night. It came from high up the Hills in the direction of sunrise. At the next one he jumped, for this one came from the pine grove. The response from the forest was immediate: one howl, then another, cries of grief. His hair stood on end. The night creatures stopped foraging and hunting; everyone listened.

At the next howl, louder and closer to home, he ran as fast as he could. But the Gawls had gotten to Beau first, throwing him down on his back, his paws splayed up in the air. They threw Wordsworth down, too, and the Doberman who'd snapped earlier at Beau now bent low, fangs touching the golden hairs.

"Spies!" he snarled, "I knew it," and he opened his powerful jaws.

"Stop!" The voice was soft, the impact instantaneous. The Doberman's muzzle shut while the others looked up towards the small shape that suddenly materialized among them. "What are you doing?" Just Daniel whispered, bending over the recumbent Beau. "Whom are you calling?"

"Dreden, who else?" answered the Doberman, as the others growled menacingly, hatred in their eyes.

"No," said Wordsworth. Just Daniel motioned and the Doberman slowly, reluctantly, let him get up. "Beau is not calling anyone, are you, Beau?"

The Gawl's eyes were white, pupils rolled sideways. "I heard it," he whispered.

"Heard what?"

"The howl. When I smelled the scent of sky, when I heard the sounds of the air."

"We all heard it," Wordsworth said, bewildered. "But why did you howl back? Everyone in the Hills must have heard you."

Beau said nothing. He turned his head one way, then another, in confusion. The Mixeds still crowded around them, ready to tear him to pieces.

"What's he talking about?" asked Just Daniel.

"I don't know. A long time ago, whenever a wolf died the family and clan would howl through the night."

Just Daniel looked at him strangely. "Hanna?" he asked suspiciously. "Hanna was no wolf. Who would howl for her?"

"Who cares? That's old history, no one does that in the Hills anymore," the Doberman snapped. "Certainly no dog, Kisdee or Gawl."

Just as he said that a single long howl resounded through the forest. It stopped abruptly, as if in question. All eyes turned to Beau, who now sat up, ears flung up and nose pointed to the sky, nostrils quivering loudly while moonlight glistened on his thick snout. He seemed to actually sniff it. Another howl pierced the night, and another, but Beau remained motionless and silent; only his nose still sniffed loudly the night air.

The howling stopped. Just Daniel looked warily at Beau. "You'll keep quiet now, won't you?"

"We should kill him," insisted the Doberman. "He's communicating with Enforcers."

"Let him be," Just Daniel said.

The Dobie Mixed shut his mouth with a snap and withdrew along with the others, growling angrily.

Beau lay back down on the ground, head between his front paws, while Wordsworth shook with anger. He'd just put all their lives in danger. Then Beau looked up and the Golden saw not just the familiar perplexed lines on his brow, but also a deep sadness in his eyes, as though there was something he was trying to understand, something he'd once known and had forgotten. His heart softened. "What is it, Beau? What did you smell when you looked up?"

"Moonlight," said his friend, and shut his eyes.

"What do you know about your friend?"

He was back by the collapsed tree trunks with Just Daniel, who was busy chewing on a gnawed twig in the middle of the pile. He sniffed the Gawl's old-age smell of sores and decay. "I was told by an Ancient to go find him in the Flats."

"A black wolf?" Just Daniel stopped his chewing.

"No, she was white, Ruwena." He looked at the other curiously. "What do you know about wolves?"

"A black one has been sighted several times, and not always on the full moon."

"But they only appear on the full moon."

"It appears they've changed their minds."

Wordsworth looked at him curiously. Ancients appeared but rarely in the past. It was considered an extraordinary sighting, not just for the lucky Kisdee who saw the wolf but for everyone, as if they were fulfilling Arden's promise to always be there for dogs. "What were you doing up on Adamant Tor today?"

"I could ask you the same question," and the small dog returned to the bare, gnarly shoot, occasionally depositing mashed pieces of bark on the ground.

"Were you meeting Magogs? You know the Rules against—"

"As well as Dreden knows them, not that it stops him."

"How can you trust them?"

"Who says I do?"

A new idea occurred to him. "Did the Magog Charlie kill Hanna? I saw his tracks up there."

"No. The tracks by her body were like ours, only much bigger." Just Daniel shivered. "The biggest dog or wolf doesn't have tracks like that. We heard a peculiar sound and followed it to her body."

"What kind of sound?"

"Like a long, shrill birdcall. When we found her she'd just been killed; we never saw who it was. I was examining her open mouth before you arrived."

"Her open mouth? Why?"

"To see if her tongue had been removed."

He looked at the Gawl in surprise, who looked back at him coolly, and suddenly he understood. He saw Hanna again on Adamant Tor, mouth gaping open. On the first night it was Dizzy Birdsong Margaret, her body laid out the same way. And what did Birdy tell him about the Terrier, Famished Max? The tongue had been missing, too. He'd forgotten what that meant. The Lake of Becoming lay at the foot of the Hills of Their Abode, where the Ancients lived. Kisdees who died and drank from its waters would become whole regardless of their wounds, and could join the Ancients. The only thing the Lake of Becoming did not heal was a wound to the tongue.

He contemplated Just Daniel with new respect. "Do the others know this?"

"I'm sure Dreden does."

There was nothing worse than losing forever the chance to be healed by the Lake of Becoming. Without a tongue, where did one go after death?

He stared at Just Daniel thoughtfully. "You have your tongue."

"Very perceptive, Moody Sunshine Wordsworth."

"I mean what you did to Beau. You licked him and his wounds disappeared. I've never seen anyone do that."

"The tongue kills, and the tongue gives life. Always remember that." Something small and pink wiggled out between the dog's two shriveled lips.

"You don't give straight answers, do you?"

"Not if I can help it."

Wordsworth went down on his belly, too. "They know you're freeing Gawls in the Flats."

"We don't free them."

"You help them escape."

"But we don't free them. We don't know what to do about the wires and chains, and it's too dangerous to venture out to the Flats."

"And Pandora? Does she also never go out to the Flats?"

The small dog groaned. "I never know what Pandora's really doing."

"She'd certainly like to see the last of me." He picked up a knobby piece of the twig the other had discarded and broke it in half with a snap of his teeth.

Now it was Just Daniel's turn to watch him thoughtfully. "When it comes to Kisdees, she has little to be grateful for. An Enforcer brought her here just days after she was born and dropped her from his mouth. She was scrawny and starved, maybe left by her mother to die, with bruises across her entire body. He said that they'd tossed her around for sport for a few days instead of bringing her straight to us, dislocating her jaw. She seemed almost dead, but as he left she stumbled after him on her tiny paws, yipping angrily. I was determined she'd live. I found Marfa Ringo Pentoniak, a Beagle Mixed who'd just given birth, and asked her to suckle Pandora." He laughed, showing his tiny teeth. "Of course, Pandora muscled the other pups away and eventually Marfa kicked her out, but by then Pandora was big enough to fend for herself."

"No one else here is as angry as she is."

"The rest of us learned to control our feelings better. And we're tired. Just staying alive takes work, which is what Kisdees are counting on to keep us quiet. But Pandora is stronger than anyone. She can be loyal and loving, and she can be as mean-tempered as an Enforcer. Her heart's in her eyes; she's incapable of lying. Most of the other Gawls have accepted their lot in life; she never will."

Long, deep wails came from the direction of Adamant Tor, loud enough to wake up every Kisdee in the Hills. Once again, the entire forest seemed to stop and listen. They, too, ceased their talk and lay on the ground, earflaps twitching. When the howling stopped Just Daniel got up stiffly.

"Funny thing the way your friend looked up at the moon," he said. "What could he sniff up there?" Without waiting for an answer he climbed stiffly up the slope.

TWELVE

He crossed the currents of foam to reach the Kisdee side of the river, keeping his body sideways and bounding carefully from one rock to another. This was hard on his back leg but he wasn't afraid. The river always felt like home, the place of coolness and dreams, where he could lose himself standing belly-deep while listening to the hum of dragonflies. He trotted alongside it for a while before following a tributary stream uphill. The Bottoms was actually bisected by the River Curl, with Kisdees on one side and Gawls on the other, but Kisdees always came down from the Hills above. That's how he would come, too.

Just Daniel had awoken him urgently that morning to tell him the news. He looked even older than before; his short legs tottered when he sat back on his haunches and his head drooped, as though he hadn't slept all night. "Pandora just came back from the Bottoms," he said without preamble. "Kisdees are gathering there right now, much earlier than usual. Dreden's making his move, I'm sure of it. You're not safe here, the sooner you leave, the better."

"Are Enforcers there, too?" he asked.

"No, and that's what's strange. There's no sign of them at the Bottoms. It makes me wonder if they're preparing to attack here."

"What about you?"

"I'm too old to run. You go, and take her with you."

"Me?" Pandora and Beau had just joined them, and her eyes widened under her frowzy hair. "I'm not going."

"Pandora, don't—"

"I'm staying right here." She arched her neck stubbornly, for an eerie moment reminding Wordsworth of Hanna.

"Where can we go?" asked Beau, looking longingly up at the pine grove. For one evening and a night he'd had a home. Perfect strangers had brought him real food and their pups had played with him. Till the howling in the middle of the night, he'd actually been welcomed.

"I don't know if any place is safe now, including here," said Just Daniel. "Unfortunately, Dreden can turn even those Gawls we trust. I'm sorry," he added dejectedly. "I've tried to find light in every darkness imaginable, but there's a shadow here growing bigger and bigger all the time. And it's not just Dreden. Something else is going on, something I don't understand. We need help."

Two white butterflies hopped repeatedly in the air, as though alighting on nonexistent flowers. Leaves fluttered and the air moved, pregnant with new beginnings, in deep contrast to the gloom they felt inside.

"Priam," Wordsworth said. "I'd like to talk to him."

"The Noble One?" Pandora demanded incredulously. "The one who made the deal with Magogs?"

"It sounds crazy, I know, but I met him once and he was different."

Pandora snorted.

"Different how?" asked Just Daniel.

"He listened better than anyone else I ever met. I want to tell him about Beau, Hanna, what I saw in the Flats—"

"Don't be a fool," Just Daniel snapped. "Priam knows about all that."

He's right, the Golden thought, feeling more confused than ever. "Enforcers don't like him. He's refused to post more guards in the Hills, he seems to resist many of their suggestions. Zebu said he was on his way out, and that might help us in some way. Besides," he added, "you said we needed help and I can't think of anyone else. If we continue to hide, Enforcers will find us, and they'll punish you two for helping us."

"And if you go to Priam you'll be killed," said Pandora, stamping the ground with her paw. "And maybe that'll be for the best."

"Pandora!" the small dog admonished.

She shook her bristly hair. "We were fine till they showed up, we were getting close."

"Close to what?" asked Wordsworth

The big, proud Wolfhound and the short, low-slung Mixed looked at each other, sharing a silent language only they knew.

"It sounds like Priam's our only chance," said Beau, who'd been silent all this time.

"He's responsible for sending you down to the Flats," Just Daniel told him.

"There must have been a reason," Wordsworth argued. "He's revered as one of the great Noble Ones —"

"Like all the rest of your great Kisdee Noble Ones," mocked Pandora, "like Engelhard's Sartorial Jacko and Starry Slim Pomper. You know what they did to Gawls? Beau, Enforcers will come here and send you back."

"I won't go back to the Flats," Beau's eyes glittered. "I'll hide in the forest, and if they find me I'll fight till the end, but I won't ever, ever go back to the Flats."

Silence ensued again. Pandora looked everywhere except at Wordsworth. Beau seemed calm — he'd made up his mind — and the Golden noticed a few white hairs on one side of his mouth.

Just Daniel sighed. "This is the craziest thing I've ever heard, but like you said, there's not much choice. All right, go and talk to Priam. You're either incredibly brave or incredibly stupid. Beau can stay up here. If you don't come back by midday we'll expect the worst and Beau will go into hiding." He rested his ochre-rimmed eyes on Wordsworth. "There are two things I ask. Don't tell Priam anything about Pandora and me. And if you must run, if you and Beau must escape, take Pandora with you."

If she comes, Wordsworth thought to himself now, trotting up the slope. Sparrows and robins frolicked above him. How he loved the small things of spring: bees and grasshoppers, the patter of raindrops and the speckles of shadow appearing in early afternoon. Pandora had nothing of spring about her, she was all winter: glacial, dour, and as hard as ice.

But he couldn't think about her now; ahead of him was a meeting with Priam — if he was lucky. He hadn't told the others that Zebu and Markus were probably on the lookout for him. Ordinarily he'd be spotted right away at the Bottoms, but Just Daniel had said that there were no Enforcers there.

Would Priam even remember him? He was taking a terrible risk; if he failed they would all die. But if he did nothing they would all die, too. Whatever happened, he had to avoid Enforcers at all costs, at least until he'd had his chance with the Noble One.

The river was out of sight, but he could still hear its sounds below. Long ago a violent storm had caused the Curl to flood, destroying the Terriers' dens closest to its banks and leaving the earth wet for months. He remembered how everyone had worked together to create new dens for the Flatheads, and his heart softened. There was a lot of good in the Hills, not just bad. Where else did so many families and clans come together to build dens for others? Where else did hunters kill game, only to leave it untouched till it had been hauled back to the Bottoms so that everyone—not just hunters—could eat?

He accompanied a brook that flowed downhill to the river in tiny, gurgling waterfalls. Birds chattered incessantly above his head, flying freely, building their nest far up out of harm's way. Spring signaled the return of many things: the forest and its panoply of green, wild turkeys, geese, fox and badger, and leaves and flowers—how he loved to chew on wild parsley and daisies! Then the Curl made a wide bend and his heart quickened. On both sides the Kiskadee Hills rose in a tight wedge, like one wide, outstretched hill that extended on either side of the river. But there were large mounds and hillocks, each of which was home to a different family and clan, familiar to him like the golden hairs of his body. The Ridgebacks lived at Ridgeback Rise. They preferred their own kind so it was natural that they'd live farthest away from the Bottoms. Next to them, for the same reason, were the Basenjis at Basenji Bluffs. On the other side of the Hill were the Dobies at Dobie Downs, and next to them the Malamutes. And now he was passing by Akita Vale. Home to the Daimyo Akitas.

He gazed down at the hollows dug deep into the slope, thinking how excited Beau would be to see them. Only he wouldn't see much. There were no bones strewn on the ground, no chewed up branches. Akitas were the neatest of all Kisdees, everything had its place and function, and the most aristocratic Akitas were the Daimyos. Pure white, small in number, refined to a fault, they fiercely protected their privacy and if you encroached on their territory they'd—

He stopped, heart beating rapidly. Rounding the bend slowly—the ascent from below was steep—and coming towards him was a Malamute.

He wagged his tail anxiously. Did word go out? Was he wanted, was he a fugitive? The other also stopped, picking up signs of nervousness. Wordsworth forced himself to walk slowly, pausing politely while looking away. He took a few more steps, suddenly recognized the wide, grizzled muzzle, and drew a big breath of relief. "Lalo!"

Awuna Mapa Lalo and his lifelong companion, Lala, were light gray Malamutes with white shading over their faces. Leader of the Awuna Mapa Malamutes, Lalo had been in charge of all the hauling and carting of swalas from the Cliffs for years. His muzzle and chest were grizzled now and a growth on the side of one eye caused it to sag, but he still had the powerful chest and shoulders that had once pushed and dragged heavy carcasses over hill and valley. His tail rolled at mid-staff as he approached and recognized Wordsworth, who licked the corners of his lips respectfully. They both wagged their tails once again and Lalo nodded courteously. "Lots of swalas," he said by way of conversation.

Wordsworth grunted a reply, which seemed satisfactory to Lalo, and remembered that Lalo no longer heard so well.

"Now's right time," the Malamute added mysteriously. "Migrations, y'know. Starting to wonder, myself."

"Starting to wonder?"

"Eh?"

"Starting to wonder what?"

"Swalas. Lack thereof."

The Golden thought he understood. There had been fewer kills of late, fewer swalas down at the Bottoms. The Flatheads worked hard to bring in more small prey, but foxes, raccoons, and rabbits were no compensation for the lack of swalas, which everyone loved to eat. Only it sounded as though today, at least, there were enough.

"I bring back what you bring down," Lalo added, letting out a brief cackle. In Lalo's universe there were no poets or versifiers, only hunters and haulers. "Funny things," he added.

"What?"

"Funny things."

"What are funny things?"

"Swalas, naturally."

"What's funny about them?"

"Don't learn. Hunters at Cliffs every dawn."

Swalas were all Lalo, Hauler-in-Chief, had ever been interested in. "You mean we've been hunting them at dawn for so long and still they keep on coming back?" Wordsworth hazarded. And now he recalled Birdy telling him that a younger Samoyed had replaced the Malamute. "Are you still working, Lalo?"

"Go out every day," Lalo said with a martial air. "Never sleep past dawn. No Kisdee should. Never tire, never retire. Lala in complete agreement." And he glanced over his shoulders in the direction of the Bottoms with an expression of deep grievance.

"You were the best Hauler-in-Chief they ever had."

Lalo snorted. "No chief now. Still go out there every day. Hauled and pulled, pulled and hauled. Never missed a day."

"What about the Gawls?"

"Worst thing in the world. No more haul and pull, pull and haul."

"But that's all Gawls do."

"Kisdees, I mean," Lalo said with a contemptuous sniff. "Forget haul and pull, forget to work, just give orders. Lala in complete agreement." And he glanced suspiciously at the Golden, as though expecting to be contradicted.

"So they brought in lots of swalas today," Wordsworth said, trying to change the subject.

"Evening."

"Evening?"

"This. General meeting," the old Malamute said, unconcerned.

"There's a general meeting this evening?" General meetings happened but rarely, and when they did every Kisdee was required to attend.

"Hunters back early," said Lalo ominously, muttering, "no work, no food. Lifelong philosophy. Lala in complete agreement. Not Circle. Extra duty."

Wordsworth was mystified. "Did you say extra duty?"

"Guard duty." Lalo shook his broad, white brow. "Guards everywhere. Enforcers everywhere. Hard on the young 'uns."

"They work too hard?"

"Hard work's good," Lalo's ruff quivered. "No haul and pull, just guard."

"The young Awuna Mapas are working as guard dogs?"

"Guards everywhere," Lalo griped. "'Gainst Magogs? 'Gainst Rathbane? No, 'gainst Kisdees!" And he gave another contemptuous snort.

"They're watching Kisdees," Wordsworth said aloud. "And tonight's general meeting —"

"Waste of time," Lalo growled. "Fight and argue, argue and fight. Wasn't always like this. No more pull and haul, just meet and guard, argue and fight. Lala in complete agreement." He scowled so hard that the eye with the growth on its side completely shut down.

"Why not give it a miss," suggested the other politely.

"Can't. New Noble One."

"Did you say new Noble One?"

Lalo grunted.

His heart beat fast. "What happened to Priam?"

"Retiring. Slow death, you ask me. Never tire, never re-tire. Lala in complete—"

"Who's taking his place?"

"General meeting," repeated Lalo, and Wordsworth final-ly understood that Priam's replacement would be revealed only later that evening. Stunned, he forgot about Lalo, who threw a final scowl in the direction of the Bottoms and a cour-teous, curt nod at Wordsworth. "Good hunting today," he congratulated him once again. The furrow between his eyes deepened as he added, "Funny thing, swalas. Never learn." He turned around with military briskness and walked away.

Wordsworth crept behind a thick, ancient oak and sat back. He felt overcome, numbed by this new development. The words that echoed in his mind weren't Lalo's, but some-one else's: *Luckily, Priam's time is running out. Maybe we'll have a hunt soon, eh, Markus?* So Zebu already knew that morning. What hunt was he talking about? Not that it mattered, with Priam out of the picture he and Beau were as good as dead. He should go back right now, get Beau, and go—where? How long could they last as fugitives in the Hills with Dreden's army of Enforcers and guards searching for them? He felt his heart trembling like a mouse in the talons of a hawk, soaring high up towards a painful death. It's the end for us, he thought, and for Just Daniel and Pandora, too. Someone is bound to betray them to Dreden, Just Daniel is practically ex-pecting it. What will they do to them?

"You're always doing the same thing, it's too big for you, lump head."

He curled up behind the large, mottled trunk just as two Bull Terriers appeared around the bend. The wind blew towards him, shielding his scent, but they still would have spotted him if not for the fact that one, short-legged and chubby, was busy huffing and puffing under an enormous swala bone laden with ribs, before dropping his burden on the ground.

"Now what?" his friend demanded.

"Time out, Pedro," the other said, sinking on the ground, panting.

"Another time out? How many time outs do you need, Karoo?"

"Enough to make it home," said his friend, pink tongue dropping out of his mouth and over his bottom jaw.

"You know what we have ahead of us, fly-brain? We have to go home, get our rest, and then it's back to the Bottoms for the hunt."

"I know, I know, but I can't help it if I always get hungry," moped his friend with the long, egg-shaped face, still breathing hard.

The other sat back solidly as Bull Terriers usually did, eyes vexatious and ebullient by turn. "Goralac picked us to help in the hunt. You know what that means? We'll be heroes. They'll talk about us all around the Hills. Pedro and Karoo, Pedro and Karoo, that's what they'll say. By tonight, for the first time in history, one of *us* will be the Noble One, not another Curvehead like before."

"Our day has come," agreed Karoo, taking a few furtive licks of the enormous bone on the ground. His body was white, like his friend, and the top of his muzzle was very pink.

"And don't tell me that because Curveheads are bigger than we are they're better hunters."

"I never said—"

"Curveheads say it," said Pedro, his tiny eyes indignant. "But not this time. They can't take it away from us. Goralac becomes the Noble One and you and I are heroes. And don't tell me Goralac's not a great hunter, that he's been part of the Circle so long he's forgotten how to hunt, because—"

"I never said he's not a great hunter, Pedro."

"And if he's not, who cares? You and I, Karoo, have gone head to head with the fox, teeth to teeth with the badger."

"I don't think we've ever gone up against a badger, Pedro."

"We'll help him. We'll make him the next Noble One and you know what? He'll be grateful. He better be." He gazed up the trail, lost in contemplation, then looked down. "What? Eating again, jiggle brain? Pick that up and let's dust. At this rate we'll never get to the hunt."

Karoo picked up the immense bone between strong, tight lips, almost pitched forward, and they walked away slowly. "This is one hunt that ain't gonna be underground," said Pedro as they climbed up the path, rounded the hill and disappeared.

Goralac the Noble One! Wordsworth, still crouched behind the tree, couldn't believe his ears. Officious and self-righteous, Goralac, the Bull Terrier who represented all the Terrier clans in the Circle, was full of the nervous energy and combativeness shared by so many of his relations who accused other Kisdees of disrespecting them while always bullying and insulting each other. Everyone knew that Priam had made Goralac an ally, as he'd done with other Circle members, flattering and cajoling, pandering to Goralac's ill humor and arrogance, all for the purpose of keeping the Circle intact. But that wasn't enough; now Goralac wanted to be the Noble One.

And those two were going to help him. How? And what did Pedro mean when he said that this hunt would not be underground? Flatheads always went underground after small animals.

The Rules were clear: Kisdees had to have a Noble One. That means that Priam remains the Noble One until the evening when his replacement takes over, Wordsworth thought. He got up gingerly, steadying his three legs on the ground. Feeling less hopeful but more resolute, he continued on the path down. It curved gently around the hill and disappeared into a grove of firs. He emerged onto a broad, grassy rectangle that sloped very gently down to the banks of the River Curl. Not as wide and bare as the Flats, it was still big and level enough to accommodate Kisdees from all over the Hills. This was where they gathered and ate; this was where the Kisdee Circle met.

The Bottoms.

THIRTEEN

Samoyeds, Shepherds, Terriers of all kinds, Pointers, Malamutes, Spaniels, Elkhounds, Griffons, Bullmastiffs, Rottwei-
lers, and more. He'd never seen so many Kisdees together in
one place.

Everyone knew that the enormous slope, declining slowly
to the river, had once been full of trees like the rest of the forest. But when Fearsome Arden returned from the Glade of
Remorse he stood where Wordsworth now stood, on a small
grassy outpost overlooking the distant water, growled quietly, and the trees below came crashing down, forming an open
embankment. Building an alliance of Kisdees, whose loyalty
till then had been only to their own families and clans, was no
simple matter, so Arden created the Bottoms, where all
Kisdees could eat together for generations to come. And indeed the place was littered with ancient tree trunks lying helter-skelter on the ground, providing the great plain's only
shade.

Wordsworth looked down at the enormous throng
sprawled below him, Flatheads and Curveheads, each breed
with its distinctive looks, markings, and personalities, all loyal

citizens of the Kiskadee Hills. As he was, not too long ago. And now, he wondered, making his way down towards the river where the kills were laid out, on the lookout for Zebu and Markus, was he still a loyal Kisdee citizen? He felt like a trespasser. Did the others think so, too? Could they see it in the tentative way he wagged his tail and the cautious walk, as though he'd already forgotten the feel of the Bottoms under his paws?

They stretched out everywhere, greeting and licking each other, taking a rest under the late morning sun, the shorthairs rolling on their backs to feel the warm rays on their bellies, the longhairs seeking shelter under the felled trunks. Mothers groomed their pups, protecting them with the length of their bodies. A family of Elkhounds barked vociferously at two Bassets, who gazed calmly back, while several young foxhounds lunged and rolled, their square cut muzzles perpetually open to reveal strong white teeth.

"Well, look who's here," he heard behind him. "It's Wobbler."

His first response was one of relief; at least it wasn't Markus. He wagged his tail and said, "Hi, Vagabond," licking his lips while trying to smile a greeting.

A large Golden Retriever with thin long lips that extended well up his muzzle in two black, disapproving lines stared him down, tail stationary. Other members of the family curled behind him in a length of gold. One or two of the young ones wagged their tails slowly as if in question, but the others averted their gaze.

"Come to eat or come to versify?" Sunshine Silo Vagabond asked. "Or both together?" Two pups giggled behind him. "Haven't seen you lately so I thought you'd begun to eat your words. You seem a little thin."

Wordsworth licked his lips again as his eyes scanned the slope. Not a hint of Markus, Zebu or any Enforcer anywhere, just as Pandora had reported, which was odd. All around him Kisdees were bright-eyed, chins and necks high with excitement. Is it the general meeting this evening, he wondered. Kisdees usually slept through such required gatherings. He stole a hungry glance at the kills by the water, but knew it wouldn't do to turn his back on the head of the family.

"I thought *we'd* be the thin ones, running out before dawn, jumping swalas, working for our food, but it looks like I'm wrong. Of course, we're eating more than usual," added Vagabond, licking his chops. "Lena had pups." That meant that once the Goldens came home they would regurgitate the food for the new pups that couldn't make it to the Bottoms.

He thought of Lena. If things had turned out differently, it might have been his pups waiting to be fed back on Golden Mesa. Would he be together with Lena now if he hadn't left? Would she have let a cripple father her pups?

"Laconic's the father, from the Ardent Barkers," Vagabond added. "Doesn't bark, doesn't growl or say a word. He's sneaky, if you ask me."

Of course, Vagabond distrusted any family member younger than him. Before Laconic there had been Fearless Flora, who would have challenged Vagabond for family leader if she hadn't broken a leg during a hunt. Then there had been Swank, who ultimately joined Simplicity and her family of the Stormy Goldens. It was just a matter of time before Laconic challenged Vagabond. One early morning,

Wordsworth thought, Vagabond would stand in the middle of Golden Mesa as he did every dawn, expecting the others to circle him, lick his muzzle, and whine and twitter in excitement, which was their daily routine before going out to hunt. Only this time Laconic would stand outside the circle and growl. Vagabond would do his best to ignore him, but soon the others would hush. One of the Goldens would step outside the circle and lick Laconic's muzzle, then another, and another. And when they were all gone, leaving Vagabond alone, Laconic would be the head of the Moody Sunshine Goldens. Unless, of course, Vagabond attacked him and the two fought it out, but this was highly unlikely. Vagabond was a bully, not a fighter.

"We could use more hunting help on account of Lena's pups, but I'm sure you're busy," Vagabond added, raising his voice so that the others could hear him. "Who's busier than the Bard of the Vale? He doesn't need a family, doesn't need a clan, he's happy all alone. Give us a verse, Bard, show us how hard you've been working."

He wished Vagabond would lower his voice; the last thing he needed now was to stand out. But the young ones were already chiming in with their high, yipping tones, "A verse! A verse!" and heads were beginning to turn. There was a wave of grunts and angry mutterings, all around him Kisdees frowned and growled, their noses quivering in dis-approval, and he wanted to sink into the ground and disap-pear till he realized he wasn't the one attracting all that atten-tion.

Up the riverbank glided what looked like a large black cloud. It was a Puli. His shoulders, chest, back and legs were so tightly wrapped in long dark cords of hair that he appeared to float rather than walk. In fact, the only thing that showed from under the thick braids was an occasional flapping pink tongue. The others quickly parted on either side of him at his approach, grimacing in distaste. He would have continued undisturbed, seemingly swimming in the air, if not for a young Ridgeback trying to impress his female friend, who raised his head with a grin, looked at his companion knowingly, and called out, "Tell us the news, Babylon! Give us the latest."

The Puli ignored him, advancing up the slope, head invisible behind the long black cords.

"Leave him alone," a Rottweiler muttered between mouthfuls of soft, young grass. "We all know the news."

"I want to hear the Prophet's news," said the Ridgeback with another grin at his companion. "The news from the future."

A female Afghan Hound, draped in a long dark silky coat, tittered. But the Rottweiler raised his head and glowered. "We've heard it all before. If I hear about Magogs one more—"

He was interrupted by a high-pitched, reedy wail that made him jump.

"Yeeeeeee! Yeeeeeee! Fear and retribution! Fear and retribution!" The wail came from the Puli as he passed close to the Goldens, who quickly looked away. "I have warned you of their evil, I have warned you of their devilry. Yeeeeeee! Yeeeeeee!" The strident keen went on as the Puli came to a stop, hidden head raised as though trying to see something on the other side of all that hair.

"Now you did it," said the Rottweiler to the Ridgeback.

"He's a Puli. Everyone knows that Pulis have future sight."

"Future sight," the other snorted. "How do they have any sight at all behind that hair?"

The young Afghan Hound giggled again, then stopped, self-conscious about her own ground-length coat.

"Arden knows the Three Times and the Ten Directions. Arden has warned us. *They'll tempt you with honeyed promises, they'll lure you with false friendship.* But they are our enemies. Magogs will destroy these Hills, they will destroy this Valley, they will destroy all Kisdees!"

Babylon had been prophesying for as long as anyone could remember, and always about the same thing. Most Kisdees reacted with bored disapproval, while a few played cruel pranks on him. Blinded by the cords of hair curtaining him off from the world, he'd been tripped and pushed frequently into the river, which in springtime ran so fast and deep that once his heavy strings of hair pulled him all the way down and he almost went to the Land of the Gawls.

"How are they going to do that if they're extinct?" the Ridgeback yelled.

"They *can* come back, you know," said an older Boxer, sitting elegantly on his haunches, flat face looking perpetually worried. "I heard somewhere that swalas were once considered to be extinct, till Fearful Arden found them again."

"Hey, Prophet, do you think maybe we're extinct only we don't know it?" the Ridgeback called out.

The jeering continued, and Wordsworth thought of Badger and Dreden, of Charlie and the girl Summer. He watched Babylon as the black apparition made his way across the crowd, drawing growls and epithets as he continued his wailing tirade: "Kisdees, long before your greed consumes you, Magogs will consume you. Long before your pride destroys you, Magogs will destroy you!"

"Look! A Magog!"

Wordsworth spun around and Birdy howled with laughter. He grinned sheepishly, so happy to see the Giant Schnauzer that he licked Birdy's face over and over again, ignoring the disapproving scowls on the faces of his family.

"Take it easy, take it easy," said Birdy. "Got to keep on the lookout, can't be distracted." Wordsworth looked around him cautiously. "Birds!" Birdy whispered gleefully, eyes scanning the sky. "Got to keep on the lookout for birds. Just don't tell the others, they think I'm always searching for Rathbane."

Some things don't change, Wordsworth thought, relaxing for the first time in days. "You mean you haven't found him yet?"

Birdy's bushy eyebrows twitched. "More important, he hasn't found *me*. And if my luck continues, nobody else will either." He looked around quickly. "You can't imagine what it's like, being a guard. At first I was patrolling Bloodroot Hill on top of the Vale, where nobody bothered me and there are lots of birds, but the other day Markus came looking and didn't find me, so you know where they put me? On Marmot Crest, right on top of Gravel Hill!"

"So?"

"So?" Birdy echoed in disbelief. "There are no birds there, that's what's so. Who am I supposed to chase? I wait all day long—all day long—and they never show up. There are no trees or shrubs, no owls or woodpeckers or robins, just a big flat hilltop that nobody ever visits—except me." He sighed. "Yessir, no one except me."

"Why don't you ask Markus to assign you someplace else?"

Birdy's narrow muzzle seemed to grow narrower. "Ask *Markus*? Markus the *Enforcer*?"

"Would he get angry?"

Birdy looked anxiously around him before replying, voice lowered. "Angry is good. I'm used to angry. It's when he grins that I start worrying, and when he's happy I'm positively terrified. No, I'd rather stay where I am than ask Markus for anything. And speaking of Markus, where have you been? I haven't seen you at the Bottoms; I even went to the Vale, yes I did. Yes I did," he repeated, as though Wordsworth had contradicted him. "And you know what I found?"

Wordsworth licked his lips. "What?"

"Two doves, two robins, one blue jay, lots of crows and sparrows, and best of all—wild turkeys. I chased the turkeys all the way up the hill and down the other side. Besides, you don't have to tell me where you've been, I know it already, yes I do."

"You do?"

"Markus told me. You're a guard, just like me. We're all on guard, yes we—"

"When did he tell you that?"

"A couple of days ago. Haven't seen him since. Seen everybody else," Birdy added, eyeing the crowd around him.

"Why are there so many Kisdees here? The general meeting is taking place only —"

"Meeting? They're not here for any meeting. They're here because of the hunt." Birdy saw Wordsworth's face. "The hunt, don't you know about the hunt? Where have you been?" He puffed up his already pronounced chest, trying to suppress his joy at once again being the source of important information. "The hunt for the lynx," he pronounced.

Wordsworth squinted. "The hunt for the lynx," he repeated. "Didn't that happen a long time ago?" Suddenly he understood, and his eyes widened. "That's what they used to do when they couldn't agree on a new Noble One."

Birdy's tail twitched convulsively. "Not just used to, not just used to. They're doing it tonight." He grinned happily.

"There hasn't been a hunt of the lynx in — in —"

"Too long, way too long." Birdy's voice turned petulant. "And it's all Furrow Face's fault. No one ever challenged him."

"And that's his fault?"

"But they are now," said Birdy excitedly. "This evening four hunters will hunt for the lynx and the winner will become the new Noble One. And guess what? Furrow Face isn't one of the four. No, he isn't."

Wordsworth's tail collapsed. "Are you sure? If he doesn't hunt, he can't win."

"Who wants him to win?"

I do, he thought, crestfallen. Without Priam we're lost, it doesn't matter who takes his place. "Is Dreden one of the four?"

"No, but he's the one who called for the hunt. The Enforcers are all up in the Hills guarding against you-know-
who. By tonight every single Kisdee will be at the Bottoms to
find out who won and greet the new Noble One, and night
time is when *he* is out and about." Birdy happily contemplated the bloody possibilities. "And there's food, yessirree, lots
and lots of swalas. I came down early to make sure I ate, you
know how it's been lately, but I could have come later, I could
have come any time. Yessirree, we're feasting tonight." And
Birdy looked down at the kills by the river, tongue sweeping
his upper lip, giving serious consideration to feasting right
now.

Wordsworth was no longer hungry. A hunt for the lynx!
There hadn't been such a hunt since Priam had become the
Noble One. The youngest of the contenders, he managed to
track down and kill the lynx before total darkness had fallen.
"I've heard of these hunts taking half the night," Sunshine's
Ominous Otto, the oldest member of the family, had recounted when Wordsworth was a pup. "So what do I do? I prepare
for a long night, settle down with swala bones, shut my eyes
to take a snooze, and when I open them what do I find? That I
almost missed the whole thing. Furrow Face came down the
Hills victorious after killing the lynx before the sun even set,
before the other hunters found the lynx's tracks. Everybody
cheers, of course, they make a big fuss, but inside they're disappointed because there was no contest, see? And Priam was
young then, a pup practically."

After that there had been no more hunts and no other
Noble Ones. Once in a while Wordsworth would hear some-

one sniping that it was time for a hunt for the lynx, but it never happened — till today. "Is Goralac one of the four?"

Birdy gave such a loud hoot that heads turned his way. "Does a Malamute pull?" he whispered. "Does a Mastiff guard? Does a Deerhound hunt? Does a Flathead run for office?" His white teeth shone in laughter behind his unruly beard. "Of course Goralac is one of the four. He's been waiting for this his entire life. Not that he'll win."

"How do you know?"

"Because he's a Flathead. Flatheads can't hunt."

"Of course Terriers can hunt. They're tough, especially underground."

"But the lynx doesn't go underground, the lynx stays aboveground, and there Goralac and his friends aren't as fast as us Curveheads. They're no good as trackers, and if you can't track the lynx you'll never find it. Already the Flatheads are complaining that Goralac should win automatically because no Flathead's ever been —"

"What do you mean, Goralac and his friends? Isn't he hunting alone?"

"Not anymore. They used to hunt alone, but some time ago, at Goralac's suggestion, they changed the Rules and now each hunter can bring two friends to help him hunt. He was planning for this, see, and he knew he'd need help. Of course, only the main hunter becomes the Noble One. Yessir, only the main hunter." He looked up yearningly at two cardinals that flew over his head.

"What did you say?"

"I said some time ago —"

"No, after that."

"Just that if they win only the main hunter becomes the Noble One."

We will make him the next Noble One and you know what? He'll be grateful.

Pedro's words echoed in his head. A new idea was taking shape inside.

Birdy, in the meantime, looked away pining for the woods. For Birdy the Bottoms had a great disadvantage: no trees, which meant no birds. When he couldn't take it any longer he would tear off up the slope and into the forest.

"When does the hunt begin?" Wordsworth asked quickly.

"Late afternoon," Birdy said, mesmerized by the cardinals hopping from one branch to another at the very perimeter of the woods.

There was no more talking to him, which was just as well since he had to find Priam as soon as possible. But first he had to eat. He made his way through the festive crowd down to the riverbanks. He'd never seen such a feast of swalas. Long bloody sides of them were stretched out on the grass, their open eyes young and sad. There were also foxes, raccoons, and a multitude of rabbits. The Terriers had done their bit for the great event, but Kisdees preferred swalas to anything else. The ground was littered with the small antelopes' horns, bones, and clumps of hair, but mostly he could see the discarded, bitter swatches of swala skin. He forced himself to eat, chewing on a swala's bloodied ribs. If his plan was going to work he'd need his strength. The Gawls ate on one side of the river, the Kisdees on the other, and as he squinted across he thought he saw the large russet shape of Pandora disappear into the trees. But it happened so fast he might have imagined it.

Finishing what he could eat, Wordsworth walked a short distance back up and paused in a pool of shade. Here several large trees had fallen like everywhere else on the Bottoms plain, but these had collapsed against one another, crisscrossing and overlapping on three sides, creating a cloistered thicket against the slope. This too was Arden's work, for the trunks and branches squeezing each other down closed the place off from prowling eyes. Climbing atop the tree trunks was strictly prohibited, for here the Kisdee Circle sat in deliberation, just as they had for many generations. Here is where he met Priam long ago, for the Noble One made this his home rather than Valley Gorge, where the other Great Danes lived.

Dried leaves from a multitude of seasons screened the enclosure's one opening. He paused nervously, pushed through, and stepped in.

Everything was just as he remembered it: the dense grass matting, the tiny pool of water fed by an underground spring, the deep shade from the branches overhead so that the sun seemed more distant here, the shadows more perpetual. In the middle, the grass had been worn down in different spots, revealing bare, brown earth. If you looked carefully you saw a circle of them, each patch usually occupied by the representative of an entire breed. They and their ancestors had sat on their respective patches since the time of the first Kisdee Circle, and over the years the grass had disappeared beneath the weight of their bodies and deliberations. On the other side of the entrance was the largest patch of all, where the Noble One sat. But he could see no sign of Priam, with his oblong head

and dark eyes. In fact, at first he saw no one inside and he began to wonder —

"The Bard of Kiskadee," she cooed. "What an unexpected
pleasure. My home is yours."

There was someone there after all.

FOURTEEN

A Saluki emerged from the shadow of a giant tree trunk. She was fawn and cream-colored, her body nimble, her white head tapering off towards a slender neck. Her tail, feathered but not matted, waved in friendship, the delicate hairs shimmering in the darkness of the shade. Her flanks and tiny ears were golden like his, eyes large and oval.

"Who are you?" he wondered.

"I am Anifa," she said, approaching the circle of patches.

Wordsworth forgot to look away as was proper. His nostrils quivered for she smelled of grass and willow, which reminded him of the Vale, and something else, the sweet scent of hyacinth, which was strange because it was too early for hyacinth.

"My family, the Tazis, like to stay with their own kind so most Kisdees don't know us. But that doesn't mean that I haven't heard of the Bard of Kiskadee." She tilted her head slightly and recited:

"It takes the bluster and the blast
Of a North Wind unsurpassed,

To tell the tale of the Silver Bear
Biding in the Bottoms' shady lair."

It was the first verse in a poem he'd dedicated to Priam on the Noble One's last birthday. "Who wasn't moved to hear this tribute? None deserved it more, and none spoke better. The rest of us use words that are forgettable; your verse reminds us of infinity. It helps us find our place in the long road of time." Her voice was high and breathless as she walked around the perimeter of the circle, eyes courteously averted.

He felt an ache inside. For a moment he recalled Sunshine Silo Vagabond and his perpetual rush of disapproval. How he'd yearned to be back with his family earlier, lie at their side, nuzzle against their soft golden hair and be nuzzled by them in turn, warm and safe forever. But Vagabond had laughed, calling him Wobbler. Nothing had changed in all these years, except for the gorgeous Saluki standing closer to him now, head bent humbly. "They tell me no Kisdee in his right mind chooses to live alone as a hermit."

Her soft hairs seemed to ripple and shimmer. "I'm something of a hermit myself."

"So why are you here?"

"Because of my duties. But I'm never happier than when I'm alone."

What a melodious voice she had. "Your duties?"

"I'm a member of the Circle."

"You?" He began to apologize, but she laughed it off.

"You really are a hermit. I was chosen at the last general meeting, to which you probably never came." Her tail wagged softly, feathery white hairs flying. "You're surprised?"

"Kisdees are a cautious lot; we usually vote for those we know."

She looked down modestly at the grass, which seemed to always grow here, even in the dead of winter. "And to what do we owe the honor of a visit by the Bard of Kiskadee?" she chimed.

"Perhaps—to me?" a voice said behind Wordsworth, who jumped.

A well-known fierce, oblong face peered into the enclosure.

"Noble One!"

The Great Dane said nothing, watching him inscrutably with deep-set eyes.

"Of course, you're here to see the Noble One." Anifa's tail wagged, bursts of sunlight flashing through its gauzy tip, eyes shining with light and warmth. Priam growled softly as she walked to the opening, gazing down demurely, but as she passed Wordsworth she gave him an encouraging brush of her flank and shimmering white tail, once again giving off the strong smell of hyacinth, causing an agitation of his own hairs and a loud throbbing in his chest. She kept her head down as she passed Priam, greeting him softly by name. He did not respond.

Wordsworth stood still.

"Anifa got your tongue?" the low voice rumbled sarcastically.

Priam stepped inside. The biggest Great Dane in the Hills, with a long face, deep muzzle, and square jaw, he was all dark gray except for his hoary whiskers. His chest and shoulders were massive, heart so loud and strong it seemed as if all Kiskadee could hear it. His eyes were dark and clear, hair short and glossy, revealing a deep scar that ran from the top of his head almost down to his chest which Kisdees often licked to show respect and obedience. He eyed him sternly, even suspiciously. Did he already know about Beau? Wordsworth wagged his tail and approached, stretching his neck forward to lick the scar, but Priam growled and he drew back. The Great Dane raised his head high and took a few more steps inside, eyes still cold and stony. He had the same smell Wordsworth remembered, a combination of warm dusty hair, acorns and nuts, as if the bear Priam vanquished long ago had imparted him his scent.

"So the Bard of Kiskadee comes to eulogize the Noble One," he said gruffly in a low, rumbling voice, walking to the circle of patches and sitting stiffly in his accustomed position by the pool of water. Before Wordsworth could reply he added, "You might as well sit down; this is not the time to stand on ceremony."

He settled carefully between the patches where the grass was dark and thick. He, after all, was not a member of the Circle. "You are all ceremony, Noble One."

"What do you mean?"

"The way you walk, the way you talk, the way you sit."

The Great Dane snorted. "That's what Goralac says. Whenever I suggest that we do without formalities Goralac says that I can afford to, but he can't." His teeth shone in a ghost of a smile. "I guess if you act like a clown you need all the help you can get."

"Where is he now?"

"Probably with his family, making preparations for the hunt, where else?"

There's no one else here, either, Wordsworth thought to himself. They've left him all alone, old and used up.

The Great Dane walked over to the other side of the small pool and burrowed inside a large cavity in one of the tree trunks, emerging with a swala bone in his mouth. Returning to his place, he deposited it between himself and Wordsworth, bent over, and licked the bone a few times. Wordsworth did likewise, heart leaping at this mark of special favor. "So, if you're not here to eulogize me, Poet, are you here to offer your congratulations?"

"On what?"

"On my forced retirement. They want a new era for Kiskadee and someone new to lead it. Not better, just new."

"Who wants that?"

"The contenders," said Priam, stretching the word out slowly and scornfully. "They say I've been Noble One long enough."

"How long?"

"An eternity." The leader of all Kisdees sat back, white whiskers quivering. "Most Great Danes don't live as long as I've been Noble One. The young generation complains that they don't remember a time without old Furrow Face." From the corner of his eye Wordsworth could see the silver markings across Priam's fierce muzzle and chest, and on his long, stalk-like legs. "An eternity is a long time," he murmured, "but this is not the time for me to leave."

"You are our great warrior."

"*Old* warrior, you mean." Priam stared dimly at the center of the Circle, lost in thought.

"They still honor you."

"Not all. Some have conspired against me."

"Who?"

Priam turned to him. "I thought you did. You were talking to her, weren't you?"

It took him a few heartbeats to understand. "Anifa? I never set eyes on her till I came here looking for you. Has she conspired against you?"

"Maybe. There are others."

"But what could Anifa do to *you*? She's new, she's young, she's—" For a brief moment he pictured the Saluki's oval eyes full of youth and sparkle.

"Anything else?" Priam asked sarcastically and Wordsworth looked away in embarrassment. The Noble One sighed. "It's the killings," he said gloomily. "The plotting is not new, but when the killings started they said I wasn't up to the task anymore."

"You've been our leader and champion. You fought the bear when everyone else fled. If there's anyone who could track down this monster and kill it, it's you." An enormous black bear, hungry and ornery after her long winter's slumber, had come upon a swala freshly killed by a Ridgeback. The Ridgeback fled, but Priam wouldn't surrender the kill. He lunged at the bear, which swiped at his face with her claw, cutting it open. Almost blind with blood, the Great Dane lunged again and again. The bear continued swiping at him, mauling and even chasing him away, but Priam attacked her each time she began to feed. Her cub arrived and Priam threatened it, causing the mother to come to its rescue and abandon the swala.

The Noble One raised his mighty dark head. "We've had five killings and—"

"Five! I heard about two."

"Dreden doesn't want Kisdees to know about the others. He says the hunters will stop going out to hunt and the guards will be afraid to guard."

"You're the only one who can lead here."

To his surprise, Priam yawned and his eyes half closed. "Wolves have been sighted in the Hills."

"The Ancients?"

"It seems so. There's talk of a black wolf."

Beware of the black wolf. "Arden told us to trust them, didn't he?" he said slowly, wondering if he should tell Priam about Ruwena's visit and warning. Only right now it was the hunt that mattered, for that was the only way he could save Beau and the others.

"They're the Ancients, our ancestors. In the past I've wondered how they felt about dogs making peace with the very same Magogs who hunted them to death."

"We didn't make peace with Magogs, we were their slaves."

Priam seemed to have trouble keeping his eyes open. "Kisdees are a curious lot," he mumbled. "We rely more on our eyes than we used to, which makes the night a time of fear and fantasy. When I was younger, of course, we had some large predators, but no longer." His eyes closed; he had dozed off.

Furrow Face sleeps through Circle meetings. You could make fun of him all you want and he doesn't hear a thing.

"The hunt for the lynx," Wordsworth said aloud.

Priam gave a snort. "What? What about it?"

"You're not one of the hunters, Noble One. Why?"

"Too much for me," Priam muttered, "can't do it anymore," and he yawned again.

"You *must* join the hunt," Wordsworth begged. "We can't be led by Goralac now."

"There are others," and Priam's eyes closed once again. "There's Marima, you know her? Big Borzoi. She's getting on in years, though. And Voldakov the Vizsla, a good hunter that one, and —"

"They're not you, Priam. You can find the lynx and kill it before the others even see it, you did once."

The Great Dane raised his head, revealing droopy, sleepy eyes. "I was much younger."

"They need you. They need a leader."

"They'll have Goralac. It's time for a Flathead —"

"They need a *real* leader."

"I'm too old, Wordsworth. I don't have the strength and stamina I had once." He sighed. "And I don't want to lose. They'll say that I couldn't accept old age gracefully, that I tried to outwit time. I'll come back tired and worn out, the laughing stock of the Hills."

Wordsworth swallowed. "What if you had help?"

"It wouldn't make much difference."

Now came the moment of truth, the point of no return. "I mean, very special help," he said, "the help of a very special hunter." Priam eyed him curiously. Not daring to meet the dark gaze, he related everything that had happened since the evening of the Ancient's visit. He told him about his encounter with Bludrun, his rescue by Ruwena and her instructions, his discovery of Magogs, the freeing of Beau and their climb up Adamant Tor. Most of all, he told him about Beau the hunter. He said nothing about Pandora and Just Daniel.

When he finished he looked up at Priam's face. The fatigue and lethargy were gone; what appeared instead were the stern eyes of a Noble One who had dispensed justice for many years—always according to the Rules. "And where is this Gawl now?" Priam asked thinly.

"I can't say." Wordsworth licked his lips and bent his head, and as he did so he heard a cry outside.

"You can't say?" Priam growled menacingly. "The only way that Gawl has remained free is because of help you're getting from others. Who are they?"

"I promised I wouldn't say." The noise outside was greater, a second cry, another, then several at once.

Priam's growl was like the rumble of the skies in a summer squall. Quickly Wordsworth lay on his belly. The old warrior jumped up on his round paws and the Golden froze, expecting to feel hot breath and sharp teeth against his neck. But Priam turned the other way, finally hearing the shouts and snarls, and watched the entrance expectantly.

Wordsworth heard a loud, deep snarl outside, followed by a hush. He jumped up, tail flattened between his legs. Someone was running to the enclosure. He shivered, feeling it was his own doom speeding towards him. The air quivered with an intense but silent hate, coming closer and closer. He smelled the sharp orange scent of terraberries, smelled something damp and cold, and realized it was his own fear. Pandora's words rang in his head: *If you go to Priam you'll be killed, and maybe that's best.*

The leaves of the entrance rustled and a head appeared. Black and white and tawny gold. A Shepherd, an Enforcer. Dreden.

FIFTEEN

Dreden stood still while everything else appeared to tremble; the very air was afraid. His neck and head were held so rigidly high that he seemed taller than any other Enforcer, causing others to always look up to him. And there was the pungent smell of terraberries, which quickly pervaded the enclosure and chased the morning breeze away.

To Wordsworth's surprise, Dreden didn't give him a glance. Instead he turned on Priam eyes glittering with hate, voice low and hard. "Enforcers patrolling the other side of the river have just found Zebu, Noble One. Dead."

"Dead!" The two exchanged stares. "Like the others?"

Dreden licked his lips intently.

Wordsworth huddled in his corner, afraid to move. Zebu — dead! Butchered like the others! He couldn't believe it. Those others were smaller and tamer; Hanna was big, but almost dead from deprivation. Zebu, on the other hand, was the biggest of all Enforcers, the one who put away large numbers of rabbits at the Bottoms every day, the one who loved a good fight.

Priam walked over to Dreden and licked his face in condolence. "May he be healed in the Lake of Becoming," he said.

"He won't," Dreden snapped. "His tongue is missing, just like the others."

Famished Max, Margaret the Black and Tan, Hanna, two others, and now the head of the guards.

"What evil spirit, what dark creature could do such a thing?"

"No spirit, Noble One," whispered Dreden, rage constricting into a serpent's hiss, lips curled to expose the gums above his front teeth, frenzied wrinkles appearing on top of his muzzle, "only one enormous Gawl who has hated us from the day he was born. A monster that preys on Kisdees as we prey on swalas and rabbits."

"And the tracks?"

"The same. Everything's the same, just like the others." White foam coated his under-lip and fell, drop by drop, down to his chest. "He removes their tongue. That means he knows our customs, Noble One. He is not new to the Hills, he knows everything—our habits, our families, where we sleep, where we eat. He not only killed my brother, he made sure he could never become whole. What monster hates like that?"

"And the sound? The piercing sound?"

"The same. Like a long birdcall."

Priam looked out through the leaves. "Why is it so quiet?"

"I sent my Enforcers to see what is left of my brother. I've ordered that they view the remains of each of Rathbane's victims till he's killed."

"Not caught?"

More froth fell onto Dreden's glossy coat. "I will kill him, Noble One."

"You will not wait for Babylon's prophecy to come true," Priam asked lightly, "that Rathbane will lose his second eye through burning by water?"

"Luckily Kisdees have Enforcers to rely on, not the ranting of a mad Puli. I will kill him, Noble One. What else do you do with a Gawl?" And with that, unmistakably, Dreden looked at Wordsworth.

Fear welled up in his belly. So Dreden knew after all.

But the head of the Enforcers turned back toward Priam. "We must have more guards, Noble One. Each family must provide more guards."

"And how will we eat?"

"They will have to hunt *and* guard. The old ones, too, will have to help." Dreden never raised his voice. Instead it dropped till it became a raspy, hissing whisper. "There is no time to lose, he is everywhere. We must have more guards."

Priam said nothing. But his head and shoulders rose almost imperceptibly as he walked over to the small pool and lapped. "Lalo of the Awuna Mapas was here this morning," he said. "And before that Bingley, of the Slugbed Airedales. And before him Grendel, who heads the sheepdog clans. And before him Alexia St. Bernard, and before her Rancorous Annabella of the Ibizan Podencos. They're complaining that you're taking all their young ones. Lalo says you've practically created a second army."

"Lalo lives in the past when things were different."

"Lalo is one of the great leaders of the Hills."

"Lalo doesn't know when it's time to die."

"Would you say the same of me, Enforcer?"

The two eyed each other across the enclosure till Dreden dropped his gaze. "I need guards to patrol the forest," he persisted.

The Great Dane walked back to the entrance, deep in thought. Wordsworth thought of Zebu lying dead on the other side of the river, in full view of his old comrades. What was he doing on the Gawls' side? Again Priam gazed out the entrance. He can't say no, thought Wordsworth, not after what happened to Zebu.

"The Hills are becoming a land of guards and Enforcers. You can't go anywhere without being watched."

Dreden pounded the ground impatiently with his paw. "There's no choice, Noble One."

And then, to Wordsworth's amazement, Priam yawned.

Dreden growled. "The Circle agrees with me, no one feels safe."

"And your activities haven't made them feel any safer. They are being watched and informed on, everyone's suspect."

"There's a lot to watch out for, Noble One."

But Priam's almond eyes were half closed, and suddenly he looked old. The once high-arched neck was bent and the tall head had slipped down to his chest. Zebu is—no, was—right, Wordsworth thought in surprise. Priam's not up to this anymore.

"Let me think about it," the Great Dane mumbled. "A little rest will do me good; after that—"

"I need permission *now*, Noble—"

"I can't give it now," Priam said petulantly, walking back to the circle. But instead of sitting on his large patch of earth he stretched out on the luxurious grass in the middle, clearly preparing to take a nap. Wordsworth looked down in embarrassment.

Dreden growled softly, almost inaudibly. "It's not just the killer Rathbane. There are Gawls plotting to —"

"There are always Gawls plotting something," said Priam, licking an invisible speck off one of his front legs.

Dreden's eyes rested on Wordsworth. Zebu had been arrogant and contemptuous; Dreden's was a simpler, purer kind of hate. "There are Kisdees helping them."

"Of course there are. Lalo would like nothing more than to stop using Gawls to haul the kills, he wants Kisdees to do all the labor. So what are you going to do, arrest Lalo?"

Dreden grunted. "Gawls are missing from the Flats."

"Gawls are missing," mused Priam, gazing over his shoulder at the pool behind him as though wondering whether he should get up again to take another drink. "Gawls have been going missing for quite a while. Have you caught them?"

Again Wordsworth felt the Enforcer's frozen gaze on him. "Not yet."

"Is this their first escape?"

"It's their last escape, Noble One."

"What are they?"

"A Pit Bull Gawl, Noble One —"

"What's his name?"

"A female, Prissy Miss Charlotte."

His heart leaped. Charlotte escaped again!

"We'll catch her soon, she's been hurt so she can't go far. And an Akita Gawl from the Daimyo family."

"A Gawl from the Daimyos, of all things." This seemed to wake Priam up. "Who would have guessed it? Daimyos are so refined, so arrogant. Can you imagine Odate's reaction when it was born?" Odate was head of the Daimyo Akitas.

"No one's immune to defilement. We'll find him, Noble One. But what about—"

"And his brothers and sisters?"

"The Gawl was born alone."

So Beau was right, his mother was a Daimyo Akita. Who was the father?

"The Daimyo leader, Karafuto, was the Noble One when I was a pup," Priam mused from his recumbent position on the grass. "What would you say, Dreden, if this Gawl you're searching for was descended from Karafuto, one of the greatest hunters that ever lived?"

Dreden strode across the enclosure towards where Anifa had stood, and faced Priam. "I'd say that Gawls are Gawls even if they come from the best families and have the most distinguished ancestors. I'd say it's a shame that such abominations have recently come from the purest of bloodlines. No one loathes them more than I do—apprehending them has always been the most unpleasant part of my job—and my Enforcers have tracked them down day and night to remove them from our sight. Only right now other things are more important."

Confronting a Noble One head to head was a severe breach of etiquette, but this Noble One had dozed off. By tonight, Wordsworth thought, someone new would be in charge; already he could see himself telling Beau the news — if he got out of here alive.

"Noble One," said Dreden aloud.

Priam snorted and opened his eyes. "We were talking about Gawls."

"No, Noble One, we were talking about getting more guards for—"

"You were saying these abominations appear in our oldest and most distinguished families. Why do you suppose that is?"

Dreden's lips curled in rage. "We have Rules in Kiskadee. Every time you have Rules you also have those who break them. More Kisdees than ever are violating limits imposed on us by nature. Instead of breeding inside their own clan they follow lustful instincts. No rules, no discipline, no integrity, just anarchy."

"Anarchy?"

"Hunters hunt. Haulers haul. Guards guard. Every family has its function, every clan has its purpose. A Gawl born to one parent who's a hunter and one parent who's a hauler isn't either, so he can't do anything except feed off the hard work of others. If you ask me, we have too many parasites already."

Everything happened fast. Wordsworth growled — he knew whom Dreden referred to — and with one leap Dreden was upon him. He heard a loud, vicious snarl, felt the Enforcer's hot breath and the stab of pain as sharp teeth sank into his neck. The Enforcer's teeth searched for the knot on top of his spine but he twisted sharply, escaping their grip, and lunged at Dreden's chest. He wasn't going without a fight. The Enforcer spun out of harm's way, but not before one of Wordsworth's fangs gashed his tawny front. Dreden howled with raged surprise and leaped at Wordsworth's crippled leg. His front legs collapsed, taking him down, and the head of the Enforcers snapped his jaws around his bad hip, causing Wordsworth to cry out.

There was a roar. Dreden backed off, but it was too late. With one leap the Great Dane stood muzzle to muzzle with the Enforcer. A thunderous snarl came from deep within Priam's body, the scar quivering down the side of his face, teeth gleaming. Instantly Dreden lowered his head in submission. Priam roared again and Dreden's head bent down lower.

"Who are your parasites, Enforcer? Old ones like me? Like Lalo?"

"This versifying cripple," came the guttural reply, "this lame idler who lives alone—"

Priam bent over Dreden, crushing the latter's head under his own. "I gave Wordsworth of the Moody Sunshine Goldens permission to live where he wished," he rumbled into Dreden's ear, sinking his teeth into the black-and-tawny neck.

"His mother should have sent him to the Land of the—" He never finished the sentence as Priam's teeth pressed deeper. "You're the Noble One," he gasped

"Do you question my judgment?"

Blood threaded its way down the side of Dreden's neck. "It's not my job to question your judgment," he panted.

Priam sighed almost regretfully before rising. "You've interrupted my nap." He walked back to his spot in the circle and sat on his haunches, watching grimly as Dreden slowly raised his head, moving it from side to side. "You like to intimidate, don't you, Dreden?"

The other's voice was steady now. He never bent down to lick the red drops that fell on his foreleg. "If I'm to be effective, I'm to be feared."

"I think respect should be enough."

"They can respect you, Noble One; they must fear me. Will you authorize more guards?"

But Priam was already lowering himself slowly and stiffly, feeling his joints, ready to resume his nap. Dreden looked disgusted, shook himself, and walked towards the opening. No longer did white foam drop from his lower lip; his mouth was a thin, stern, black line.

"One other thing," Priam said drowsily as Dreden was about to leave. "I want all Enforcers and guards back here at the Bottoms while the hunt takes place."

"Here?" Dreden searched Priam's face, but the large head was on the ground, eyes closed. "After what happened to Zebu the hunters for the lynx won't want to—"

"They'll take their chances. I'm more concerned about the Kisdees at the Bottoms. It'll be the biggest crowd ever assembled. I want all Enforcers and guards right here surrounding the Bottoms."

"The hunters won't like it—"

"They'll like it or they won't hunt lynx."

Dreden opened his mouth, then shut it again. "Yes, Noble One."

At the entrance the leaves rustled. Dreden eyed Priam, now asleep, before turning his narrow, icy eyes on the Golden one last time, and left.

Wordsworth got up on his paws with great difficulty. There was no blood; Dreden knew how to inflict serious damage without leaving a trace, and he could feel the agony in his back leg. He limped towards the entrance; he had to go back and warn them, tell them he'd failed.

"Where do you think you're going?" he heard behind him. Priam was standing, fully awake and alert. "So," the Noble One said, a satisfied gleam in his eye, "shall we talk about how you and your Gawl friend are going to help me hunt lynx?"

SIXTEEN

Λ

"**Y**ou knew?" Wordsworth stared at him in disbelief. "You had this in mind all the time?"

"Of course."

"And you're awake."

Priam snorted. "Awake? My problem is I can't sleep." He saw the other's incredulous expression. "That's just to put them off. Right now it's good for them to think I'm tired and senile. How's your leg?"

"Why do you want them to think that?"

But the Great Dane was already striding up and down, thoughts racing. "Lynx are becoming increasingly rare. They like to eat hares, only there are fewer hares. This may be the very last hunt for the lynx because soon there'll be no lynx left. One has been spotted hunting on the other side of the river."

"The Gawl side?"

"Where Zebu was killed," Priam murmured. "I wonder what he was doing there."

"Aren't Enforcers supposed to be everywhere?"

"In theory. In practice we've always left the Gawls alone. Dreden claims that Rathbane won't kill them; my guess is that he just doesn't care. Anyway, there's no time to lose, I must let them know that I'll join the hunt." He smiled, causing the scar on his face to widen. "Goralac will be disappointed. The Flatheads are agitating for him to become Noble One, but for that he'll have to win." He walked over and lapped water from the pool. "We'll cross the river and begin before sunset, when there's still some light to help us find tracks. Once the sun sets we rely more on our smell, which is where your friend, the Gawl, will come in. The lynx was sighted not far from Poplar Ridge late yesterday. Of course by now it's a long distance away, but that's where they'll start."

Priam was excited, fire in his eyes. And all this, Wordsworth thought uneasily, so that he could remain the Noble One. Of course, that had been his own idea from the beginning. As soon as he'd heard that each hunter could get help in the hunt he thought of Beau, with his enhanced sense of smell and superior hunting instincts. "What happens to Beau?" he asked nervously.

"If he's smart, nothing will happen to him. He won't get caught."

"How do you know?"

"Didn't you listen? No Enforcers or guards will be there. I just gave the order to bring them down to the Bottoms."

"What about the other hunters? They'll insist on some protection."

"Especially Goralac," Priam said gleefully. "He's terrified of being anywhere after sundown. But he won't dare complain now, it'll make him look bad." He was still striding back and forth excitedly. "Finally," he muttered, "finally it's chang-ing."

"What's changing?"

"Luck. My luck. Our luck."

"Ours?"

"You're coming with me. I'm allowed to take two hunt-ers. The Gawl is one and you'll be the other, only they won't know about the Gawl." He saw Wordsworth's face. "You're a hunter, aren't you?"

"Of course."

"If you don't keep hunting you'll forget everything you knew and become like Goralac." Priam grinned broadly, then looked down at Wordsworth's leg. "Can you make it? How badly did he hurt you?"

"I'll make it," the Golden muttered, though the pain in his back hip throbbed mercilessly.

"Good. Now, tell me about your Gawl friend. How can he be such a good hunter after being down in the Flats all this time?"

"His sense of smell is the sharpest I've ever seen, and he can catch any animal he goes after."

"In certain ways Gawls are more like our ancestors than we are. They don't see as well as we do, but their hearing and sniffing are sharper." His eyes glowed happily.

You'd think it was Priam who came up with this entire scheme, Wordsworth thought apprehensively. "You knew about how Enforcers put Gawls down in the Flats all along, you knew about Magogs. You made the deal with them."

"Of course I did." He caught a glimpse of Wordsworth's face and came to a halt. "This is not the right time, Poet. We have things to do."

"Enforcers are violating our Rules, they're giving Magogs dogs—"

"Gawls, Wordsworth, they're giving them Gawls."

"Why?"

"To prevent Magogs from coming into the Hills. Look," he said quickly, "I don't like it any more than you do. No one likes it, especially Dreden; he hates Magogs worse than anyone. But they're in our world whether we like it or not." He strode back to his spot in the circle and sat back on his haunches.

Wordsworth stepped forward. "Why don't the others know?"

"Because it would cause more fear and havoc." He sighed impatiently. "This is not your concern, but I guess you have a right to know. Soon after I became the Noble One, Enforcers spotted Magogs not far from Adamant Tor. At first no one believed it; like everyone else, we thought Magogs were extinct. But finally there was no doubt. It seems they'd been living underneath, as they say it, for centuries. Their ancestors were living like that before the Great Calamity, and that probably saved their lives."

"Magogs were never underground animals."

"That's what our stories said. Their story says that their ancestors were searching underneath for a great treasure. That was a terrible time for us," Priam said, eyes half closed in recollection. "I don't have to tell you that dogs fear no one like they do Magogs, and suddenly they're alive and in the Hills. Do you know where they lived underground?"

"Under Adamant Tor."

Priam looked at him closely. "For someone who's been living as a hermit, you're remarkably well informed. What do you make of it?"

"They've been on top, too, I saw their tracks in the Glade of Remorse. What are they doing in a place that is sacred to us?"

"You can also ask it the other way around: Why is our sacred place right on top of where they lived for so long?" He gazed around him at the leaf-shrouded den, darker now because clouds had crossed the bright skies. "They were starving when Enforcers first found them. After all that time underground they were no longer hunters, they couldn't track or kill swalas, or anything else for that matter. The first one I met was so thin and weak he could barely walk on his hind legs. For a while I even thought they'd go back to walking on fours, like everyone else."

"What did they eat?"

"Whatever comes from the ground."

"Nothing grows in the Flats, I've been there."

"Not now when the earth is frozen, but once it opens up they put in tiny things they call seeds, which grow out in the summer and become food. Hard to believe, but I've seen it myself. Of course it's not swalas. Sometimes one of them gets rabbit and they're as proud as could be. Their big problem was that forest animals would come down to the Flats and eat the food that grew there."

"Why couldn't they guard it?"

"They don't have our smell and hearing and they don't see at night. There were also not enough of them to work and guard day and night, so they came to us for help. I was young then, some might say inexperienced. Brancken Dukes Quinton was head of the Enforcers and he wanted to let then starve, or else chase them back underground. I decided differently. We told them we'd give them our own Gawls to put down in the Flats to keep intruders away, on one condition."

"That they never come up to the Hills." He thought of Hanna struggling up on her paws to see the sun, which now reappeared from behind the clouds, lingering straight above them. He thought of the wire coiled around Beau's neck and the raw, hairless ring it left on his flesh after it was removed. "You agreed to let them chain dogs down in the Flats, to be slaves to Magogs as we once were?"

"I did." Priam's eyes were dark and pitiless. "I thought about it then, and many times since. Magogs are animals, like us. Primitive, not as advanced, maybe not as intelligent, but they need to eat to survive, like us. They don't have our teeth, our speed, or our organization, they're terrible hunters. I knew that if they didn't get their food in the Flats they would come into the Hills, and we would fight each other to the end. Giving them dogs to use as slaves went against every instinct I possessed, even if the dogs were Gawls. But we've been through the Ravages ourselves, we know what we're capable of doing when we're hungry. Back then we were ready to kill each other over a few bones; Magogs would have done worse. Once, don't forget, they almost destroyed the world. So that was the deal I made with them: We would help them survive on condition that they remain in the Flats."

"Only they don't remain in the Flats."

Priam closed his eyes wearily. "They did till now. They have a new leader, Badger, an unreliable, repulsive character, I'm told. Dreden would like nothing more than to kill him, only whoever takes his place may be worse. For now, they are still in the Flats and we are in the Hills. The arrangement holds."

He raised his head in a show of authority, but what Wordsworth noticed was the frosted muzzle and chest. Priam was old; he was also tired. Briefly the Golden recalled the few white hairs Beau had that morning on the side of his face. "When will you tell the others?"

"I was going to tell Kisdees about Magogs, and then the killings began. There's so much fear and confusion already we can't tell them now."

So that was it. He approached Priam and sat down, facing him. They'd always known. They knew about Beau, Hanna, the Pit Bull, and countless other Gawls brought down to Magogs. How many had there been all these years? What do you think happens to the Gawl pups they put down here, Hanna asked him. *Most die young.* None of this was arbitrary or the work of malevolent malcontents, but orchestrated moves by a very calculating Noble One whom he'd always admired. And suddenly Wordsworth knew why Priam looked so tired and aged. Does he think about the Gawls he sentenced to a painful death for the benefit of Kisdees who are now ready to discard and forget him? "Could Magogs have something to do with the killings?"

"They don't make tracks like that. Enough of this," the Great Dane said, rising onto his paws, "we have work to do."

Wordsworth didn't move. "What about killing them?" he asked. "Magogs, I mean. They're few in number. Why not force them to go back? And if they come out, kill them."

Priam exhaled slowly. "It's what Quinton wanted me to do. Make Magogs really and truly extinct, once and for all, he said. Get rid of them, this is our chance."

"Is it better to give them our own Kisdees to help them survive?"

"I gave them Gawls, Wordsworth, good for nothing Gawls. Frankly, I doubt your friend will be of much help in the hunt, though I'll give him the benefit of the doubt. I've never met a Gawl who was good at anything."

Then you haven't met enough Gawls, Wordsworth wanted to say, but he kept quiet. Whatever happened, he didn't want Priam to change his mind. The hunt was Beau's only chance, and probably the only chance for Pandora and Just Daniel.

"Fact is, I'm still torn," Priam admitted, resting back on his haunches again. "There isn't a day that I haven't thought about this. Dreden would like nothing more than to lead Enforcers down to the Flats and kill every single Magog he could find. But I keep remembering our stories about how we came together with them long ago. We were hungry; they needed guards to warn them about predators, and a friendship developed."

"They made us slaves!"

"*We* made us slaves," Priam growled. "We depended on them for food, for shelter, and finally for everything. We lost our hunting skills and our independence. Wolves chose differently; they remained wild."

"And you know what Magogs did to them."

Priam sighed. "I know. Still, I don't want to make Magogs extinct, there's such a small group of them left. Maybe they won't make it and die on their own, but I'm not ready to send Enforcers down there to kill them off. I keep remembering that long, long ago dogs and Magogs made a pact, one that helped both of them survive and even flourish, till equals and friends turned into master and slave." He walked to the stream and lapped loudly. "Anyway, right now Magogs will have to wait because there's the hunt." He turned around. "Will you and your friend help me hunt lynx?"

"Yes."

"Good. This is what you have to do." And Priam began to speak softly but urgently. He was in full charge, with the old crispness and authority, everything clearly and dispassionately laid out. "Any questions?" he demanded when he finished.

"One. What about Beau?"

"You asked me that already. Nothing will happen—"

"What happens to Beau after the hunt?"

Priam's big tongue flicked over his to lip to brush away drops of water. "What do you mean?"

"Does he go free?"

"Free?"

"He can't be on the run forever. You heard Dreden, he'll catch up with him, and when he does…"

The Noble One walked over to his patch in the Circle and sat down once again. "I can't free him, Poet, I can't free a Gawl. Listen to me," he said loudly, for Wordsworth was about to remonstrate. "Dreden's right about one thing. Kisdees are afraid. Mothers won't leave their cubs, hunters are afraid to hunt. Some Kisdees won't come to eat at the Bottoms anymore. They're terrified of Rathbane or Bludrun or whoever the real killer is." He paused and glared at something invisible at the other side of the enclosure where Anifa had stood earlier. "At the Circle's last meeting someone suggested that all Gawls be killed as soon as they're born rather than taking them across the river."

"That's a violation of the First Rule!"

"I had that proposal dismissed—barely. Kisdees are terrified, they hate all Gawls. And the one who hates them most is Dreden. After Zebu's murder he'll stop at nothing to destroy them. Believe me, if I don't win tonight, there will be no one to stand between Dreden and the Gawls of the Hills."

"You're his boss," Wordsworth said.

"As long as I *am* his boss. His loyalty to the Noble One is unquestionable, that's why I trust him. He serves me even when he disagrees with me, as he'll serve the next Noble One, whoever he is. Or she."

"She?"

Priam gave him a hard look. "The one you were talking to as I came in."

"Anifa, a Noble One? She's young and inexperienced."

"And if she kills the lynx she'll win." Priam scowled, his eyes gazing beyond Wordsworth at some point only he could see. "Things are changing. The old times may soon be over. I won't always be here; others too will have to lead. The danger we're facing now may be nothing like what awaits us in the future, which is why I must go out this evening and hunt. I'm being watched and followed wherever I go, no place is safe anymore. Tonight I'll be freer than I've been in a long time.

Believe me, this evening will be more important than the fate of one Gawl."

He saw Beau's face in his mind, faith and trust in his small, dark brown eyes. *If they find me I'll fight till the end, but I won't ever, ever go back to the Flats.* And he saw Hanna. He hadn't been able to do anything for her. "Promise that if you win the hunt, you'll free him."

"What?"

His heart quickened; there was no backing down now. "He's a good hunter, better than anyone I've ever seen. Promise you'll free him when it's over."

Priam snarled softly. "You think I need him, Poet? You think I need you?"

"You probably don't need me, but you'll need Beau."

The snarl faded into a growl but Wordsworth still averted his eyes. When he looked back the Noble One was seated on his spot, contemplating the grass in the center. "I'll tell you what I'll do if I win tonight," Priam said slowly. "I'll issue an injunction against killing your Gawl friend. That means that no guard or Enforcer can touch him. I only ask that he stay with the other Gawls on the other side of the river."

"And what about them?"

"Who?"

"The other Gawls. They want to be free, too."

"Don't push me, Poet." Priam looked towards the entrance. Wordsworth saw that the afternoon sun was finally creeping down, heading towards late afternoon and then evening. "Kisdees are heading down to the Bottoms. They'll be here, safe and protected, while we'll hunt lynx in the Hills. I might catch and kill the lynx with your friend's help. Believe me, I'm the best chance he has. I'm the best chance Gawls have." He turned and their eyes met. "No one can change the Rules alone, the entire Circle must agree. But one thing I promise you. If I win the hunt tonight I'll break off the agreement I made with Magogs; no more dogs of any kind, not even Gawls, will be sent down to the Flats. And I'll make sure no one harms your friend."

Wordsworth hurried over to Priam and licked his scar happily. The Noble One's jaw relaxed, a large pink tongue making its first appearance as it swept in long, pleasurable arcs between his lips. "Don't forget, I must win the hunt to do that, and your friend has to help. And you," he added, motioning with his head to the Golden's back hip, "will have to run."

"I will, and so will he. He's tough and brave. Together we'll find the lynx and you'll kill it."

Success! Beau was going to gain his freedom, and there would be no more Gawls down in the Flats. No more Hannas, no more Beaus, no more Charlottes chained down by Magogish contraptions. The others will still be exiled to the other side of the river, they'll still have to work, but that, too, was bound to change. His eyes shone, hope and fantasy mingling in his imagination to a future time when Gawls would live, hunt, and work like everyone else instead of hauling swalas down from the Cliffs every day. Priam would remain the Noble One and his own family of Goldens would be proud of him; he could almost imagine Vagabond telling anyone who'd listen that he was the first to recognize the promise in Wobbler back when he was a pup. He would visit them on occasion but would still live in the Vale, reciting poems and teaching Beau new rules of etiquette. He was so excited he wanted to run around in circles chasing his tail, something he hadn't done since he was a pup, if not for the throbbing hip.

"Lately I've been thinking that long ago, during the time of the Magogs, dogs didn't talk," said Priam. "What came out of our mouths? Grunting, whining, and barking, not much else. Of course, Magogs spoke, but they had a special way of calling for us. They would bring their lips together and make a high-pitched sound that could be heard far away."

"The same sound they heard before the killings?" Wordsworth asked, bewildered.

"The very same," said Priam thoughtfully. "Isn't that interesting?"

SEVENTEEN

"I don't believe a word he says," Pandora declared.

He was back in the pine grove, where the light was dim even in the afternoon.

It hadn't been dim at first. As soon as he returned Beau had licked his face, danced and capered around him, whinnying in excitement at his friend's news, issuing several high-pitched *eee eee eees*! despite Wordsworth's warning not to tire himself out. The other Gawls had already gone down to the Bottoms to eat and wait for the night, leaving them alone till Pandora appeared, and as he proudly told her everything that had transpired he watched her eyes darken with the old, dull, stubborn suspicion.

"I don't trust Furrow Face," she said, shaking her unkempt hair. "He'll give you up."

"He promised."

"He's using you both and in the end he'll throw you away. Don't go with him, you can hide."

"They'll find us, Pandora," he entreated. "You should have seen Dreden after Zebu was killed, he wants to take his revenge, not just of Rathbane but of all Gawls. Priam is our best chance."

She snorted defiantly, earflaps flattening in malice. "It won't matter, don't you know that? He'll lose the hunt anyway."

"How do you know?" asked Beau.

"Because he's old! He's been sleeping in meetings, forgetting things, and going around talking nonsense."

"It's all a pose," Wordsworth said. "I saw him do it. I tell you, he can hardly wait for the hunt to begin."

"Everyone knows he's a senile, doddering fool. And of course, like all Kisdees, with no courage or honor. Isn't asking a Gawl to hunt with him against the Rules?"

"Not that I've heard," Wordsworth replied thinly. There was no one like Pandora to kill the joy in everything. Finally they had something to cheer about, even to celebrate! He'd hoped to see her long fleecy tail wave in friendship, maybe even respect. Maybe even something else.

"Will Beau join you in the hunt out in the open?" she asked slyly. "Will everyone see him?"

"Of course not, he's wanted."

"Furrow Face doesn't want anyone to know, right?" It's for his own good, Priam had said, specifying a meeting place for Beau. "How do you think the others will feel when they find out about Beau?"

"They're not going to find out." He tried to speak with confidence, but he could hear the droop in his voice. It was getting late. They should be resting before the night's hunt instead of arguing.

Pandora snorted and turned to Beau. "It's your life at stake. You know what they'll do to you if they catch you, right? You want to trust a Kisdee like Priam?"

"I trust this Kisdee," Beau said, wagging his tail towards Wordsworth. "Besides, it'll be fun to hunt for lynx. I've never done that before."

"Of course not," Pandora said spitefully. "In fact, you don't know what lynx smells like, so how can you track it down?"

Wordsworth's eyes widened. Of course! Beau had never smelled lynx in his life. Except—"Beau, do you remember the lynx with the Magog girl at the bottom of Adamant Tor?"

His friend growled. "It was high up. Before I could smell it, it was gone."

His heart fell. "So you can't identify its scent."

Pandora laughed harshly. "He's been down in the Flats his entire life, how could he know what lynx smells like?"

Beau looked from one forlorn face to the other filled with malice. "Maybe I smelled it down in the Flats."

"They don't go down to the Flats; lynx is rare everywhere. If you don't know the scent, Daimyo, you have nothing to go by."

His back hip hurt worse than ever as he felt Pandora's glittering, triumphant eyes. Was she taking pleasure in their downfall? How could anyone hate so much?

"I'll find it," Beau said quickly, gazing imploringly at Wordsworth.

"How?" she demanded.

"This way," said a familiar voice.

Just Daniel materialized from behind the trees, panting hard from running up the slope, wisps of hair falling over his face. Something protruded from his mouth and he deposited it on the ground in front of Beau. The Gawl smelled it curiously as Wordsworth's eyes widened in recognition.

"The Magog girl's lynx!" he exclaimed. "How did you get it?"

Instead of replying, Just Daniel watched as Beau thoroughly sniffed the strand of hairs that Wordsworth had first seen around Summer's neck, burying his nose repeatedly in them before trying to nudge them apart, smelling them anew from each direction with intense fascination. Then he looked at the Golden. "What happened to your back leg?" He told him about Dreden's attack on him. "You can't chase the lynx this way. Lie down."

It was getting late, time was running out, but the throbbing had only gotten worse. The small dog bent over him, pink tongue slipping out between thin, bearded lips. At first he felt nothing. Soon, however, a deep relaxation overcame him. Just Daniel's tongue circled around and around the center of the pain, sometimes gliding closer, then drifting away, and Wordsworth moaned. It was as if cool river water was washing over the fire in his back hip. The old Gawl took his time, making unhurried circles, edging closer and closer to the place that burned. When he finally found it there was a momentary blaze, but then it dulled into a painful twinge, then an ache, and finally a sore. He could feel the swelling subside and the skin mend. Soon even the soreness disappeared. In fact, his body seemed to vanish and he felt himself sinking into the ground.

"Wake up!"

He jumped; Beau and Just Daniel laughed. There wasn't a twinge, not even the slightest hurt. His hip felt looser than he ever remembered. "What did you do?"

"I told you before, what any other dog would do to someone that's hurt."

"Is it your tongue?"

Just Daniel didn't answer. "Enforcers have left the Hills," he said instead. "The only ones you'll have to worry about are the other hunters — and whatever else is out there."

"How do you know all this? And how did you get the lynx hair?"

"From a Magog called Charlie. He's old like me, so we have an understanding."

"And the girl?"

"He said the girl Summer is on the other side of Adamant Tor. Her lynx is with her, so Charlie's not concerned." He looked up over Wordsworth's head. "Pandora!"

The big Tug-a-Lug was walking away.

"Pandora!"

She swung around, neck arched. "Since when do we help Kisdees? And since when do we help Priam? He never did anything for us, you said so yourself." Her chest heaved with resentment, exuding the smell of balsam. "Some things never change."

Just Daniel licked her upper legs affectionately, which was as far as he could reach. "Never say never," he murmured.

She backed up the slope, eyes aflame. "You've said those words to me ever since I was born, but I've been hauling swalas every morning of my life. I don't know my family and they don't want to know me. Across the river they'll have their hunt for the lynx and their new Noble One, and what'll we have? Nothing, except for this pine grove, where we come to sleep and die. We'll be slaves till the end, which comes for some of us sooner than for —" She stopped, a look of guilt and horror in her eyes.

Just Daniel sighed. "For some of us sooner than for others," he said slowly.

"I didn't mean that," she said with deep remorse. "It's the last thing I want, you know that."

"I do know it," he said softly, "but it's true. It's been true for a long time."

She turned away with a mixture of defiance and self-reproach, Wordsworth and Beau looking on in bewilderment.

"My condition is advancing. You'll have to be ready."

"No!"

The two stood there as they always did, she wrathful and fierce, he calm and thoughtful, exchanging nuances in a language known only to them.

"What condition?" Beau finally asked.

Without taking his eyes off Pandora, Just Daniel said, "My body ages faster than others'."

"How old are you?"

"As a matter of fact, I'm probably just a little older than you, Beau."

"What!" Wordsworth couldn't believe it. Beau was all youthful energy, while Just Daniel was the opposite: weakness, exhaustion, old age.

"I've had this condition since I was young," said the small dog. "I became old while growing up, unlike others who first grow up and then become old."

They could all see: the matted beard that was now all ashen, the lumps of dead hair that made up his once-orange coat, eyelids that were always at least half closed, but mostly the slump of the entire front, the drooping tail and the short legs that seemed to get closer to the ground, as though any moment they'd cave in entirely. Just Daniel wasn't only old; he was a pile of bones waiting to be scavenged by the Birds of Death. And he was only a little older than Beau!

That accounts for his voice, Wordsworth thought, suddenly embarrassed by their scrutiny and looking quickly away. In fact, it accounts for many things: the youthful spirit, the fresh humor, the light heart—all in a crippled, dying body.

"Another thing we have you Kisdees to thank for," Pandora spat.

"How are we responsible for that?"

"We haul swalas for you, don't we? Where do you think the poison comes from? Just Daniel isn't the only one aging so fast, it's happening to other Gawls, too."

"But Kisdees eat swalas. Everyone eats swalas."

"Only not everyone sinks their teeth into their skins and pushes and pulls them down to the Bottoms."

And then he understood. "The skin is poisonous! That's why it's so bitter."

"You Kisdees remove the bitter skin right away before you eat," the older Gawl explained. "It comes off easily so you don't take in much poison. But we Gawls have our mouths in it all day."

That accounts for all the old ones they have, Wordsworth realized, looking up at the ones sleeping under the pines. And the same feeling he had when he first saw Hanna overcame him now: shame that he was a Kisdee, a dog who did this to other dogs. That morning, on the way to the Bottoms, he'd felt the old pride in this alliance of clans and families working for the good of all. But no, Kisdees worked only for their own good. Others didn't matter, so they could be exiled, enslaved, and even killed.

It wasn't always this way, he thought. Arden had said the swalas were for everyone. Not just the swalas, the Hills and forest, all of Kiskadee was for the dogs that had followed Him and left Magogs behind. He'd said nothing of purebreds and mixes, of slaves dragging the swalas down to the Bottoms and getting sick. Back then it didn't matter what breed or no breed you were, everyone hunted, everyone hauled, everyone ate and built dens wherever they wished. You weren't told to stay and work with your kind, there was no kind, there were only the dogs of the Kiskadee Hills. That was Arden's vision; then it all changed.

Kisdees are getting some of that poison, too, it now occurred to him. We may not have our teeth in swalas all day long, but some of that poison is entering us, too.

"It's worked out well for me," Just Daniel said tiredly. "As soon as Kisdees found out I had this condition they didn't want me to come to work. They don't want me anywhere near them."

"So they know about this?"

"I told you, Dreden knows everything. Priam, too."

"And does nothing to stop it," added Pandora in fury. "That's who you're going to help in the hunt today!" Rage and grief blazed in her eyes.

He gazed at her, recalling the Kisdees gathered at the Bottoms to feast and celebrate. I'm not so different from them, he told himself. I saw Gawls work as haulers from morning till night since I began to hunt and never wondered what it's like to do that every single day of your life. "Maybe you're right. Maybe we shouldn't help Priam, or anyone like him."

"It's too late for that," said Just Daniel, "you have to help him."

"Why? You didn't trust him this morning, and I don't trust him now. Pandora's right, he'd do anything to win the hunt, and he despises Gawls."

"You can't know what will happen tonight. Right now this is Beau's only chance, and maybe the only chance for the Gawls in the Flats. That's a lot better than nothing." He looked into Wordsworth's eyes and his tone softened. "You're starting to see a lot more than before, but this is not the time for doubts or misgivings, this is the time to act."

Wordsworth found himself repeating Pandora's question. "How can you trust him?"

"I don't, I trust *you.*"

I can only tell you your first step were Ruwena's words. *That will guide you to the next, and that one will guide you to the one after.*

"Why can't you heal yourself with your own tongue?" asked Beau.

Just Daniel laughed. "My tongue gives life and it gives death, Beau. You don't have one without the other. I've tried, but I just get older and crankier all the time." He looked up at Pandora. "Gawls will need a new leader soon."

"No!" She looked desolate. "You said the changes would happen in our lifetime."

"*Your* lifetime," he gently corrected her. "I knew mine would be too short. But you, Pandora, can live a full life. I don't know what will happen by the next sunrise, or the sunrise after that, but I am sure that you will not die in this pine grove. For you things will be different."

"You said there were more forces against us than we ever knew."

"But also *for* us. Some choose themselves, as we did. Others are chosen, even if they don't know it yet. Even if they don't know for what."

They stood there uncertainly. Shadows moved on the ground and Wordsworth looked up to see geese flying overhead. Pandora bent down and licked Just Daniel's face again and again. She straightened up and looked at Wordsworth. He could see it all in her narrow brown eyes — rage, hurt, suffering, shame. And something else. Before he knew it she came down and licked the edge of his mouth once. "Good luck," she said, and disappeared behind the trees.

He trembled. She showed affection to a Kisdee! And then he corrected himself: *Not to a Kisdee, to me.*

"There is something you must know," Just Daniel said, watching him carefully. "I don't know what good it will do you, but I've seen the poison in the swalas' skin someplace else. In Adamant Tor."

"*In* Adamant Tor?"

"Inside. Deep inside."

The Golden remembered their run down the passage. He'd looked at the darkness that continued at the end and Beau had complained about the smell. *Where does it go? To the Land of the Gawls.*

"Maybe I should have said the Land of the Magogs," Just Daniel said, smiling crookedly. "Magogs lived down there long ago. They dug up the ground and created Magogish things. That's where I saw the poison. The Magogs we know now are too primitive to have done that. What's deep down Adamant Tor is very, very old—and evil."

Wordsworth shivered, though the afternoon was still warm. "But swalas don't go underground, so how did they get it?"

"I don't know." He looked up towards where Pandora had disappeared. "I heard a story once. It said that Magogs found a treasure deep in the earth, but there was only a little so they dug deeper, looking for more, and found something else instead, which caused the Great Calamity. It's still there, inside that mountain. And it may be in them, too, because they have the red spots and sick, sour smell, and they die young. That's why they have no old ones, except for the Magog Charlie." He turned back to the Golden. "I remind you what I said this morning. Whatever happens, Pandora must live. Do you understand? No change will happen if she doesn't live."

"Does she also have the sickness?"

"She shows no sign of it. At least, not yet. Promise me that regardless of how she behaves, regardless of what she does, you'll make sure she lives."

"I promise," Wordsworth said fervently.

Just Daniel sighed. "It's almost time. There's nothing left to do but wish you good luck."

Wordsworth was overcome with emotion. He bent and licked the Gawl's old, uplifted face, and realized he'd never done this to a Gawl before. He'd licked Birdy and the pups back on Golden Mesa countless times, but not one of them had shown him friendship like this ancient Mixed. Beau, less circumspect, nuzzled and slobbered all over Just Daniel, his tongue drooling enthusiastically over the wiry hair. For a moment Just Daniel looked his true age. His face turned sweet and innocent, eyes fresh and full of wonder like the eyes of any young adult dog with his life ahead of him. He lay on the ground, his upper lip arched in a smile that revealed small white teeth.

Finally Beau sat back, grinning, and Just Daniel tottered up on his short Spaniel legs. "Be careful of the moon," he told Beau, "it's what I always tell Pandora. And you, Moody Sunshine Wordsworth," he added, walking away, "stay out of the water." Slowly, painfully, he climbed the slope, body sagging so low his wiry tail almost brushed the ground, till he disappeared.

"What did he mean by that?" wondered Beau.

Wordsworth looked up at the Mixeds sleeping in the pine grove and made a vow. If everything went as planned tonight and Priam kept his promise, it would be only a beginning. He would not rest, he would not return to his peaceful life in Poet's Vale, till all Gawls were free to live and work like other Kisdees. No more disease, no more premature deaths, no more exhaustion and exile to the other side of the river. Just Daniel would live to see the change, not just Pandora.

The sun was beginning its farewell. "Is it time to go?" asked Beau.

Wordsworth stretched first one way, then the other. He imagined the lynx waking up hungry. It, too, would first stretch and then sit back and lick itself clean before beginning to hunt. "Ready?"

Beau's eyes glittered and his tail wagged madly. "Ready."

And Wordsworth gave him Priam's instructions.

EIGHTEEN

They climbed the slope on the Mixed side of the Curl. Up high, the sun was visible behind the trees; below, Wordsworth could see his long shadow behind Priam's. The other hunters had run fast ahead and were long gone, but the Noble One seemed in no hurry. In fact, he was lagging well behind the Golden, panting from the effort, tongue lolling sideways. At this pace we'll never find the lynx, never mind kill it, Wordsworth thought to himself darkly, slowing down so that Priam could catch up.

Chipmunks were making their penultimate runs across tree limbs and into hollows and hawks circled the sky in a last attempt to get a meal. One part of the animal kingdom was preparing to retire while the other was stretching its muscles in anticipation of night. They belonged to the former, but their quarry was of the latter; they had to play by its rules.

"Do you know why we're hunting lynx?" Priam said, huffing and puffing at his side. "Let me tell you the story."

"Not now," Wordsworth mumbled under his breath.

"Like everything else, it started with Fearsome Arden. When Arden brought us to the Kiskadee Hills there wasn't enough food, as you know, so Arden went to find prey. He searched far and wide, and he took Lynx with him because Lynx had the sharpest eyesight of anyone in the Hills. In fact, back in Arden's time it could see through rocks and trees, and even down to where the foxes hid in their burrows. Lynx said he would help Arden on one condition: that dogs never kill lynx. The Ancients, the wolves, had preyed on it. Arden agreed.

"They arrived at the Cliffs and Lynx immediately saw all the swalas inside the caves, enough to feed Kisdees for generations. Arden couldn't tell they were there; as we all know, swalas have no scent. But Lynx said nothing, hoping that dogs would starve and disappear, and Arden returned unsuccessful. The Ravages got worse and eventually he went into exile on Adamant Tor. When he returned to form the Great Alliance, he went back to the Cliffs, and this time his eyesight had improved and he could see the swalas peering from the caves with their tall, protruding ears. He realized that Lynx had lied to him. He found it and attacked it, but just before he could give it the death bite Lynx reminded him of his promise. So Arden kept his word and didn't kill him, and we Kisdees, too, honor that promise and never hunt lynx. But Arden made one exception. When it's time for a Noble One to be chosen and the Circle can't agree, a hunt must take place, and the hunt is for lynx."

Wordsworth's fur felt heavy; it was going to rain. He wondered idly about the lynx Ophelia. How did she, an animal that avoided even its own kind, get so close to a Magog girl? Both were far away, which was just as well since tonight every lynx in the Hills would be in danger.

The sun had turned red when they reached Poplar Ridge. Here they found the other hunters: Voldakov, Marima, and Goralac. They saw Marima first. The leader of the Borzois, with her elegant long head and white, silky coat, greeted the Noble One respectfully. Not much younger than Priam, she had a mature, no-nonsense air about her. Her hunters, both Borzois, sniffed the ground and air, tails motionless in concentration. Voldakov, a chestnut-red Viszla in the prime of life, searched lower down alongside his two hunters, sleek and muscular like him. And on top of the ridge stood the Bull Terrier Goralac, with Karoo and Pedro. Goralac peered intently down at the valley below, his oval-shaped head looking in all directions as though he might actually see a lynx lurking in the open.

"Better late than never, Priam," he announced.

"Just winded a little from the climb," said the Great Dane, panting aloud. "After a rest I'll be as good as new."

"Think you can make it to the end? I'm concerned about your health." Goralac came down. "Why are you doing this?" he whispered loudly. "Someone your age!"

"I still have something left," Priam huffed and puffed.

"It's time to retire and let the young ones take over."

"You're not so young yourself, Goralac."

"And what's the cripple doing here? How much help can *he* give you?"

"Probably not as much as your helpers," said Priam, eyeing Karoo and Pedro, who were busy exploring the burrows under the ridge though everyone knew that lynx didn't go underground.

"It's our time now, Priam," Goralac growled.

"You have to win the hunt first."

The Bull Terrier's pink and white ears pointed up. "I wouldn't have had to win anything if not for you, the Circle was ready to back me."

"When there are other candidates the Rules are clear. A hunt must take place."

Goralac snarled softly. "You were the one behind it, I know your little plots. If I don't win tonight you'll be the one to blame."

Before Priam could answer one of Voldakov's hunters gave a loud snort. The gold-red Viszla hurried over and sniffed the ground carefully, eyes blinking fast, tail moving warily from side to side.

"Did you find it?" shouted Goralac. "Any news of the lynx?"

Voldakov said nothing; in an instant he and his hunters were gone. Marima's Borzois clambered down and sniffed. One of them gave her a watery glance and all three took off.

"What are you waiting for?" shouted Goralac at Pedro and Karoo, mutely awaiting his orders. "You want them to get an even bigger head start?"

The two hurried down so fast that Karoo slipped and fell, sending pebbles flying.

"Idiot!" Goralac cursed as he hurried over there, short tail twitching. "After them, after them!" The two Bull Terriers chased after the other Kisdees, while Goralac chased after them, leaving Wordsworth and Priam alone.

"That's what comes from trying to be king of the mountain," Priam said drily.

"How does he expect to win?"

"It's not completely his fault. Flatheads aren't used to hunting above-ground." A mischievous smile climbed on his dour face and a glint appeared in his eyes. "Now it's our turn. Let's go."

Priam began to run. Not after the others, but in the opposite direction, deeper into the Hills. Without a trace of weakness or uncertainty, head high and jaws firm, the Great Dane trotted fast across the uneven terrain. There was a jaunt to his pace and a slight parting of the lips.

"After a rest I'll be as good as new," Wordsworth imitated, panting.

"I'm finally moving! Do you know what it's like to be stuck in that enclosure day after day?"

"Why can't you leave it?"

"Because I'm followed wherever I go."

They started to climb towards Jack Pine Ridge, and suddenly Wordsworth remembered Anifa. If she was also competing in the hunt, where was she? He hadn't seen or heard of her since she'd left the enclosure that morning.

He remembered the scene down at the Bottoms, where the twilight feeding had begun early. More and more Kisdees had come down from the Hills, even reclusive clans like the Chow Chows and the Shar-Peis, retreating warily to their respective corners, barking out short warnings to stay away. He hadn't been able to eat. Neither had Forever Fighting Goralac, he noticed, surrounded by offerings of tender swala cuts placed right at his paws by well-wishers. "I'm a better hunter when I'm hungry," Goralac declared, pink tongue rolling jovially from one corner of his mouth to the other beneath his oval muzzle.

Someone licked Wordsworth's ear. Birdy's long black whiskers tickled his face as he whispered loud enough for everyone to hear: "I can't wait to see who wins. No, I can't! Just as we were getting used to the idea that a Flathead was finally going to become chief—guess what? New idea!" He laughed uproariously, and instantly, Birdy-like, became dead serious. "If Furrow Face wins there'll be hell to pay."

"If he wins he remains the Noble One, that's the Rule," a neighboring Bullmastiff said, raising his glum, square head.

"There'll be a lot of unhappy Flatheads running around." Birdy's tail wagged at the prospect of a civil war between Flatheads and Curveheads. "Goralac is furious. Says he's been betrayed."

"Betrayed! Flatheads like him should be grateful they're in the Circle to begin with," a female behind Wordsworth sniffed.

He swung around and saw an Akita. A Daimyo Akita. Tail curling over her back, she examined a thighbone she'd pulled earlier from a swala carcass. He stared, mentally ticking off the differences between her and Beau. Her face and eyes were smaller and more pointed, her tail curved over her back, and she was white, all white, with tiny ears and nostrils—smaller than other Kisdees'—of which the Daimyo Akitas were inordinately proud. Akitas were known to be standoffish, but Daimyos believed they were the Hills' true aristocrats and snubbed everyone, including other Akitas.

"Terriers have been part of the Kisdee Circle from the beginning," he told her, but the Daimyo didn't bother raising her head.

Birdy snorted loudly but kept his voice low. "That's Kiku, Odate's daughter, and as big a snob as her mother. It's a wonder she can hear anything with those ears."

Indeed Kiku, who was busy tearing off flesh from the thighbone and ignoring everyone around her, showed no sign of hearing either of them. She looks just like her mother, the head of the Daimyo clan, Wordsworth thought, recalling Beau's dirty black fur and wide-eyed, happy-go-lucky expression.

"Oh no, here he comes again," Birdy said amidst shouts and catcalls. It was Babylon, still veiled by his curtain of long hair, floating blindly up the bank. Wordsworth half expected him to bump into someone in his path.

"Hey Babylon," the Ridgeback from the morning yelled to the mass of dreadlocks, "tell us who's going to win tonight."

"That's right, Prophet," a young Newfie shouted, drooling from the corners of his mouth while his gray tail waved in a low arc. "You're supposed to know the future, right? How about the hunt? Who's going to win?"

"Voldakov," offered the Ridgeback.

"Goralac," the Newfie replied, eyes sparkling. "What'll you give me if I win?"

"A big fox skin," said the Ridgeback.

"What'll I do with a fox skin?" and the Newfie shook the thick fur covering him down to his webbed paws. The Ridgeback was abashed as the Newfies in the crowd rolled with laughter.

"Hunt for the lynx," the Prophet muttered beneath his cords of hair as he continued to cross the Bottoms in his funny gait. "Fools and imbeciles, it's Magogs you should worry about!"

"Hey Prophet, you need a fox skin?" the Newfie shouted, and this time everyone laughed, even the Ridgeback.

"Arden is coming," muttered the Puli as he half walked, half hovered across the Bottoms. "Arden will return."

"A prophet that foretells the past!" the Ridgeback cried out.

"What about tonight, Babylon? What's going to happen tonight?" The cries and catcalls went on till Babylon had disappeared.

"Prophets are never listened to," Wordsworth now mused aloud. "A little like poets." There was no answer. Priam was already nearing the top of the ridge, and it was his turn now to catch up.

Jack pine shrubs canopied the ground, their cones closed but smooth, providing excellent cover for hares. "The others will go to where the lynx was last seen," Priam had murmured earlier that day in the enclosure. "They may find an old scent, they may even find tracks, but they won't find lynx. Lynx will double back to Jack Pine Ridge in search of hares."

And this is where they found Beau, who immediately butted heads with Wordsworth, brushed his flanks and jabbed at his muzzle. Then he took a few eager steps towards Priam. Wordsworth held his breath. Don't jump him, he implored silently, and please, please don't sniff his hindquarters.

The Gawl hesitated, bent his knees slightly, raised his under-belly, and lowered his head as he averted his gaze. Words-worth let out a sigh of relief, but Priam growled, tail straight and motionless, eyes narrowing with aversion as they focused high above Beau's head.

Beau stopped in his tracks and looked uneasily at his friend: *Did I do anything wrong*? The Great Dane continued to growl quietly. Beau's eyes darted nervously from jack pine shrubs to a nearby tree stump, then back again, licking his lips.

"Don't come any closer, Gawl," Priam said, lips curling.

Now it was Beau's turn to growl. It was a low, hoarse rumble, like all the expressions coming out of his shredded white throat.

"No!" Wordsworth exclaimed.

"Tell your *friend*," Priam said, lacing the last word with sarcasm, "that staring at anyone is considered bad manners in the Hills, especially at one's betters."

"I'm not staring at my betters," Beau rasped.

A low roar rose from deep inside Priam's belly and he stepped forward. Beau did the same, coming so close that his muzzle almost touched the bottom of Priam's long, high-set neck, while the Great Dane's dark head hovered above him rigidly, and Wordsworth remembered what he'd done to Dreden. "What are you doing? You're fellow hunters!"

"He is not a fellow hunter," Priam replied in a clipped tone, snapping his jaws right over Beau's head.

"He's here to help you hunt lynx."

"I've changed my mind. Tell the Gawl to go home."

"He's got no home."

"Tell him to go anywhere, just not here," said Priam curtly, still keeping his eyes high. For contrary to Kisdee etiquette, Beau was standing tall on his paws, lifting his head up to make himself as big as possible. "He's an impudent Gawl who doesn't know his place."

"I know my place," Beau muttered right at the Noble One's neck.

The Noble One snarled. "Tell him to leave, for his own good."

"No."

Priam's voice tensed, though his eyes never moved from a spot above Beau. "No?"

"If Beau goes, I go with him." He shut his eyes. Their agreement was over. Any moment now there would be the sudden rush, the snarls mixed with yelps of pain.

But that's not what happened.

"He can stay till he locates the scent, then he goes." Wordsworth opened his eyes. Priam had taken a step back. "Ask him if he's caught the smell of lynx."

"Not yet," Beau replied. "I can smell hares, but no lynx."

Priam gave a disgusted snort and walked away.

Wordsworth nuzzled Beau and the two eagerly sniffed the ground. Under the jack pine shrubs well-kept runs and trails made intricate zigzags around trees and exposed roots. Interfering shrubs and twigs had been clipped off and lay on the side. There were different tracks of the many creatures that used the runs: squirrels, rabbits, chipmunks, and especially hares, whose prints from their large, furred hind legs he could easily identify. But no lynx.

That didn't seem to bother Beau: sniff-sniff-sniff, pause, sniff-sniff-sniff, pause, sniff-sniff-sniff. He seemed to live in his own ecstatic world, investigating the smells of all the animals that used the runways, rushing back and forth as though retracing everything that had taken place: the scampers between food and home, the scurrying from predators, the running and scrambling of day and night. His tail shot up as he sniffed under a fallen log, eyes gleaming, lips parted in intoxication; hares had rested there that day. And they were fast. Unlike rabbits, which hid in underground warrens at the first sign of danger, hares depended on their speed to outrun their hunters. The tidy paths helped them run faster.

Priam had disappeared into a tall, dense grove of white pines. Wordsworth followed him into the woods, only to find himself suddenly alone in the gloom.

"Why are you following me?"

He turned around with a jump.

The Noble One stood in a deep pool of shade, eyeing him gravely. "You should be searching for lynx, that's your job, you and your friend."

"I thought we'd be hunting together. You invited us to help—"

"I think inviting your friend was your idea, not that I think it'll do us much good. He's distracted and running all over the place, anyone can see he's never been trained."

"He's overwhelmed; his nose is more sensitive than ours."

"All the worse for me. He doesn't know the first thing about tracking."

"Give him a chance, Noble One."

"He's a Gawl, Wordsworth, he's not like us no matter what you say. Gawls are deficient."

"There's nothing deficient in Beau other than his torn-up throat and hoarse voice. Kisdees and Magogs did that to him."

Priam looked up at the gray crowns of the ancient trees. "Let me be, Wordsworth. I must—"

"Here!" they heard. "It's been here!"

They ran out to the clearing where Beau was furiously sniffing under one of the jack pine shrubs. "Ask him what he smells," directed Priam.

Beau's nostrils practically vibrated from tension.

"What is it?" asked Wordsworth impatiently.

"Don't know."

"Describe it."

"Fur, dust, hares, and something else. I got it—tree bark." Beau looked up at them expectantly.

"Lynx climb trees," Priam said. He nuzzled something on the ground. "Gray-brown hair."

Wordsworth sniffed and gave a start. It had the same smell as the strand of hair that Just Daniel had brought them earlier. The exact same smell.

"It ran down the other side," Beau shouted, running further down the ridge.

Hurrying after him, Wordsworth heard a slight rustle. He turned around to see Priam making his way back up towards the white pines. Before he could decide what to do, Beau cried out once more, this time in high-pitched alarm, and Priam turned back. The Gawl's hackles were rigid in the glow of sunset, ears fallen back. Wordsworth quickly sniffed around the stump. "It's from back there."

"Where?" demanded Priam.

"Adamant Tor."

"What were you doing on Adamant Tor?"

The scent was very faint and growing fainter; without Beau he'd never have smelled it. But there it was, something not of the forest or of the Hills. Quickly he recounted to Priam the events of the previous day.

"And you say that's here now?" Priam sniffed a few times. "I don't smell anything." He looked up at Beau. "Are you saying that this is the killer's smell? That Bludrun's here?"

"Something was here."

"Is he after *us*?" asked Wordsworth.

"I don't think so. I think it's hunting lynx."

"Lynx?" Priam looked at Beau, oval eyes narrowed with suspicion. "Why would Bludrun go after lynx?"

NINETEEN

They ran down the ridge. Beau's thick nostrils sniffed with intermittent pause, lips shut tight, earflaps folded back against his skull. Priam bounded right behind him, growling softly, forehead jutting forward, jaw square, vigilant eyes on Beau. Wordsworth came last. He could see the tracks of the hare as it ran in terror, the front feet smaller than the back, and the much bigger, broader tracks of the lynx. Funny, he'd always heard that lynx counted on a first pounce to capture its prey. The soft ground starkly revealed the two sets of tracks. Where was Bludrun?

They ran so fast they almost stepped over it.

At their feet, on a bed of dry leaves, lay a hare. Dead.

Beau sniffed it carefully. Large and already reddish brown, color changed from the white of winter, it lay on its back, large feet splayed, looking almost calm, and only when he turned it over with his nose did they see the blood at the back of the neck. "Lynx," he said, sniffing the air, "a female."

They could all see where she crouched before springing to give the death bite, for her paws left deep imprints in the ground. Her smell was stronger here and Wordsworth was sure. This was the Magog's lynx, Ophelia. "Where did she go?"

"A better question is, why isn't she here?" Priam growled. "Lynx kill hares in order to eat. This one killed and ran."

They searched the ground in deep shadow. There were the familiar large marks deep in the brown soil, continuing in an erratic zigzag downhill. She was speeding through the brush, going as fast as she could. "And the smell?" asked Wordsworth. "The heavy, smoky smell—is that here too?"

"It's following her," Beau said.

"How can that be?" demanded Priam. "There are only lynx tracks."

"There's a second scent."

"I can't smell it," said Priam sharply. "I've never heard of an animal that doesn't leave tracks." Sharp fangs appeared over his curled bottom lip as he turned to Wordsworth. "I don't trust anyone who tells me that something is here that only he can smell."

"Maybe it's a wolf. Ancients have no physical body during the day, maybe that's why there are no tracks."

"If they have no physical body they can't leave a scent, so what is this Gawl sniffing? Besides, Ancients only appear in the full moon."

"I sniffed it, too, on Adamant—"

"Well, I didn't," said Priam with an air of finality. "Not then and not now."

"Noble One!" Wordsworth implored.

The Great Dane arched his back. "He's a Gawl, Wordsworth. How do I know he's even taking us in the right direction? Chasing something that leaves no tracks? Enough. He found the tracks of the lynx; we'll continue the rest of the hunt without him." He turned to leave.

"The rest of which hunt?" asked Beau calmly, small ears twitching. "The hunt after lynx or the hunt after your killer? You didn't seem very interested in lynx back on the ridge even after we found her tracks. You're looking for someone else."

Priam snorted and walked a short distance away.

Beau spoke louder. "You need me to find the one you *are* hunting, the one who leaves no tracks."

"Everyone leaves tracks, Gawl."

But Beau stood silently, waiting. His black fur fluttered in the evening breeze but he himself didn't move, not a muscle quivered. He was so different from his usual restless, ever-sniffing self that Wordsworth also stopped in his tracks, his head tilted questioningly.

"Follow it," Priam growled softly behind him.

"Follow what?" Wordsworth asked.

"What does it matter? If the Gawl is right, they're both going in the same direction."

"And if he's not? Or if one changes direction? We're not hunting Bludrun, we're hunting lynx."

"Not anymore," said Priam, eyes pitiless. "Your friend guessed right, I've waited for this a long time. I'm going to find him and I'm going to kill him."

He remembered the green coiled eyes that froze him in place, the body invisible in the mist, the wide arc made by the large, hungry red tongue, and the whistle. The Magogish whistle. "You can't do this on your own, Priam, no one can. We agreed to help you so that you could remain the Noble—"

"You think I care about that?" Priam spun around with a roar. "You think I care more about the hunt than about that butcher, the one who's killed and mangled and mutilated our own Kisdees?"

"If you don't win the hunt for the lynx, Beau and I are as good as dead."

"We're wasting time. Besides, with any luck, we'll kill Bludrun *and* the lynx." Priam addressed Beau. "All right, I admit I need you. You obviously can smell things I can't. I also would rather have you out in front than behind my back. That way, if you betray us, I'll make sure to kill you even before I kill that monster. Understand? Now, which way?"

Beau was off before Priam finished talking, head lowered to the ground, then up in the air. Priam followed, tail up.

Wordsworth ran after them, paws pounding the cool, hard earth. So that's what it is, he thought; that's what it's been all along. Priam knew what he was doing from the beginning, he didn't need much persuasion. Inside he felt relieved, even proud. He hadn't been wrong in his instincts about the Noble One after all. But he couldn't avoid recalling Pandora's scornful words: *He's using you both and in the end he'll throw you away.*

The two dogs ahead exploded through the underbrush and Wordsworth saw that a path had already been made for them through the dense trees, a path littered with torn off branches and uprooted shrubs. Something had run amok, bringing down plants, bushes, and even tree limbs. Ophelia couldn't do that, though all could see her light, spread-out paw marks.

And it was Ophelia for sure. For as they'd left the dead hare he'd turned back in time to see a shadow withdraw into the aspens. She was uphill from him so he couldn't smell her, but there was no mistaking the tall shadow with waving strips of bark and short, yellow hair. It doesn't matter, he thought to himself as he chased after Priam and Beau. Summer is a Magog, we'll leave her far behind.

Up ahead Beau slowed down and Wordsworth saw blood in his tracks. The forest floor was tearing the Gawl's pads, which were not as hard as theirs. He shivered. Sundown always brought the cold with it, but this clamminess was something else, like sweat freezing in his fur. And the air was getting heavier and more vaporous. A dim, hazy moon was rising in the twilit sky, often obliterated by fast-moving clouds. They began to cough.

"Why are you stopping?" Priam demanded.

"It's hot," said Beau thickly, his white-pink tongue lolling over the side.

"Hot?" Wordsworth couldn't believe his ears. Both he and Priam were shivering from cold, but Beau looked queer and was panting. Priam rushed forward. Fog had rolled down around them and it continued to rise and fall, as though undecided, like the mists on top of Adamant Tor. He'd been cold there too, while Beau had complained of the heat.

Priam disappeared into the fog, Wordsworth after him, smoke filling his nostrils. He saw a hazy shape up ahead slipping behind a phantom tree. Beau was somewhere behind them, slowed down by his sore pads. The moss and ferns were wet under the Golden's paws. He ran helter-skelter, not sure where to go, till he practically ran into the Great Dane, a looming shadow in the gloom. The curtain of fog went up once again to reveal that they were standing in the middle of a clearing dotted with broken stumps surrounded by tall, bare elms, the ground full of last season's ragged leaves and surprisingly long grass. There wasn't the slightest breeze, yet wisps of fog swirled and spun in a bizarre dance, enveloping and revealing in turn the thick trees with their large, swooping limbs, waving and shaking in air that didn't move.

The Great Dane circled the large clearing nervously, as though ready to run but not sure where or why. The fog was still rising, all was still. Wordsworth squinted at the trees along the edge of the clearing. Something creaked behind him and he jerked around. It came from a low, heavy stump behind him. The bark had been seared, leaving a sooty, ridged surface.

"Where's Beau?"

No sooner had Priam asked the question than the Gawl rushed into the clearing, flopping and stamping, and immediately sank down to lick his bleeding paws.

"What's making that noise?" Priam wondered.

They could both hear it, loud, shrill sounds that came not out of the upright elms, whose drooping branches fluttered wildly, swaying and shivering in silence, but from the low, broken-off trunks in the clearing, remnants of once great trees, which rasped and creaked. Priam crossed the clearing, but Wordsworth stopped in his tracks. From the corner of his eye he noticed that Beau had left off licking his pads and was looking up, not at the trees but at the wan features of a hazy moon. It had blurred and waned since that first night, made less visible by the twilit fog, but a moment later the mist lifted and light washed the top of the Gawl's broad, deep head and upturned muzzle. Wordsworth could almost see the fast, tiny movement of his snout as Beau sniffed the moonlight.

Beau jumped up with a shout.

Wordsworth didn't remember moving, but several long leaps brought them both back to the edge of the clearing, and instinctively the two withdrew further in till Beau paused. "Where's Priam?"

"He ran to the other side. Priam!"

The Noble One emerged from the tall trees on the opposite side and walked towards them.

"No!"

Beau yelled something else but Wordsworth never heard it. There was a tremendous crack, like lightning striking the ground, and Beau flew from his side. The rest happened all at once, but the obscure light caused it to appear in fragments. In one, Priam stood in the middle of the clearing, head and neck tilted forward as he snarled at the Gawl dashing towards him. In the next, Beau leaped up and hit him hard in the chest, sending them both sprawling as one of the tall elms crashed down with a thunderous blow.

Wordsworth was thrown off his legs. There were more cracks, each louder than the last as the tall, bare trees smashed on the shaking ground. The earth thundered worse than the sky, convulsing so hard he was sure it would split open and swallow him whole.

Instead it turned silent, and that was worse. He got up. The clearing had disappeared; what remained was a burial ground, with enormous gray trunks prone on the ground, their heavy, mottled limbs collapsed in a pile. Each tree had crushed the other beneath its weight, sometimes breaking it into pieces, transforming the entire glade into a vast, criss-crossed jumble of craggy bark and broken branches.

It took a moment to find his voice. "Priam! Beau!"

He stared at the fallen elms, knowing that no one stand-ing in that clearing could have survived. The bark of each had been sheared off, the white insides serrated like an ugly wound. It occurred to him that the trees had been butchered much like Margaret and Hanna. He walked a few steps one way, then another, trying to ward off a giant wave of despair. "Priam! Beau!"

"Aiffff! Aiffff!"

"Beau!"

It was the highest-pitched, most ridiculous bark he'd ever heard, and he'd never been so happy to hear anything in his entire life.

A pair of black legs with white paws slowly emerged from under an enormous pile of branches. They were fol-lowed by black flanks and a tail that never curled, and finally tall earflaps above a black head and a white-patched chest. Beau wobbled, stretching front and back. To Wordsworth's disbelief, a dark gray hillock rose behind him in the shape of Priam. The Great Dane tottered and almost fell, but recovered and remained standing, eyeing his body tentatively, as though uncertain it was still working.

"You're alive!" Wordsworth leaped over limbs and branches, his brown eyes shining with joy. "I saw a tree fall right on top of you."

"It did," Beau said, shaking his fur, "but not right on top."

Beau had sent himself and Priam sprawling on the ground just as the tree fell. Had one of them been standing it would have meant instant death. Had the tree hit the ground flat it would have crushed them; instead it had landed atop another fallen trunk, leaving a narrow space underneath, exactly where the two had fallen. Wordsworth examined the spot. There was nothing extra. If the tree had sagged a little further down his friends would never have gotten up again.

"How did you know?" Priam's voice was cold and peremptory. "How did you know this was going to happen?"

"I didn't." Beau looked up at the sky where the tops of the trees should have been. "I just knew that we shouldn't stand in the middle of the clearing."

"Who told you?"

"No one. I just knew."

In the silence they could hear the final lone creaks and moans of the dying trees. Beau's brow wrinkled in confusion, the same confusion that had been there the previous night when Just Daniel asked him why he'd howled.

Priam looked dazed. He walked away, motioning for Wordsworth to follow. When they reached the other side of the clearing he looked at him darkly. "One thing is certain, whoever did this is no Gawl."

"Did you really think the killer was Rathbane?"

"Dreden always said so; I had my doubts. Now I know it's impossible. But then who is it? Who is this Bludrun? Where are the tracks? He almost killed us."

"Almost, thanks to Beau."

"Thanks to Beau," Priam repeated in an odd voice. He looked at Wordsworth. "Let me ask you a question. Why do this?"

"What do you mean?"

"Why doesn't he just kill us and be done with it? If he can bring down an entire forest of elms, killing and devouring us should be easy."

"He just tried."

"Did he really? What if our butcher doesn't want us dead? What if he wants me to trust your Gawl friend?"

"Why would he do that?"

Priam sighed. "I don't know. I hope we find out before the night's over." He gazed at the felled trunks around him. "I didn't know he could do this," his voice lowered in awe. Then his eyes focused on Beau, who was sniffing the long grass at the far corner in search of a scent.

"Noble One, let's find the lynx," said Wordsworth. "Kill it, and then bring Dreden and his Enforcers here."

"And what will they do?"

"What will *we* do? At least there'll be more of them, and they're better prepared."

"You can't prepare for something like this." His fierce eyes softened. "I know, you want me to take it step by step, it's how we always do things, but not this time. Don't you see? Bludrun is at hand. We can kill him and end the terror tonight." Wordsworth was about to say something but Priam cut him off. "Look at your friend, the Gawl. You said he wanted to be free more than anything. Free to do what? To stop going to eat at the Bottoms because you're afraid of what you'll meet on your way home? To look over your shoulder for the rest of your life? To be free we must find Bludrun and kill him. We three, not Dreden and his Enforcers. It falls on us."

He thought of Margaret's tattered body on the ledge, the rocks black under the full moon, the mists opening and closing, the emerald eyes. Not hungry eyes that killed for food, but cold and dispassionate, eyes that loved killing. *Some choose themselves, as we did. Others are chosen, even if they don't know it yet. Even if they don't know for what.* He met Priam's dark gaze. "Let's get him," he said.

Beau gave a shout.

Wordsworth's tail shot up. "Where to?"

"The river," Beau called out, "and he still seems to be after lynx."

They reached the Curl.

Up here it was broad and deep and they swam to the other bank. Beau limped on his battered paws upriver alongside the water. Wordsworth was relieved; the Curl was his daily friend and companion. The spring melts had flooded the banks, creating deep pools, causing the others to walk inland while he trod in the water. The bottom half of him shuddered exquisitely, his hair getting limp and heavy while his head, neck and back were exposed to the cool air.

How did you know? How did you know this was going to happen?

Beau had sniffed the moonlight just as he'd done the night before. Is that where he got his information? Did moonlight have a scent?

The water revitalized him. Bludrun was chasing the lynx, so there was still a chance Priam would kill both. The river crept up his legs. It was deeper here, almost up to his thighs. Submerged weeds caressed his legs deliciously, he could feel their matted surface under his paws while they stroked his fur. I *could* swim, he considered with a tinge of pleasure. His front legs came up to paw at the water surface and he felt the weeds tickling his belly. They embraced his back legs and he sighed from pleasure, but they didn't let go. His front legs came down and were immediately enfolded. The wet, cold weeds clasped his legs tighter and tighter, squeezing hard, and began to pull him down.

TWENTY

"**H**urry up!" Priam called out.

Beau turned back, tail quickening into a friendly wag. He paused, sniffed the air curiously in his friend's direction, and ran over.

"Stay there!" cried Wordsworth. He lowered his voice. "I can't get out. The weeds are pulling me down." He held down a whimper, for the river now reached his belly.

Beau's eyes widened and he stepped off the bank.

"No!" Priam yelled. The Gawl jumped back. "If you go in you'll go down too, that's what he wants."

The water climbed up Wordsworth's flanks.

"We can't just let him drown without—"

"Can you move your legs at all?" Priam asked.

Wordsworth tried pulling up a front leg, but in response the silky weeds pulled his back legs down so forcefully that in an instant the water had reached the top of his flanks.

"We have to do something, he's drowning!"

Priam cast about in desperate search for clues, for an idea. "Help me, Beau," he yelled, bounding towards a tall hickory on the bank. The trunk had split in two and one long, heavy half vaulted across the bank and over the pool at a precarious angle, though it was still held in place by the tree's roots. Priam climbed atop the low-hanging limb; it creaked a little under his weight, but didn't move.

"Come on, Beau!" he shouted.

The Gawl looked uneasily at the other end of the tree limb hanging over the deadly river, leaped up and stood next to Priam, legs shaking. The hanging limb sagged a little. Slowly, putting one paw behind the other, Priam began to walk back. The limb drooped.

In the river Wordsworth raised his head as high as possible. The water had climbed up to his neck.

"It's not enough, come towards me," Priam shouted to Beau, and the Gawl made his way forward while Priam slowly backed away from him, edging closer and closer to the end which dangled over the hungry, treacherous water. The limb creaked heavily. The Noble One and the Gawl gazed at each other as one stepped forward and the other back, earflaps high in the air, listening for just a hint of the crack that would splinter the tree limb from the rest of the trunk. Where Beau stood the limb still hung over land, but Priam was already standing above the river, inching backwards, trying to bring it down.

The water had already climbed over the Golden's muzzle, covering his tiny nostrils. He held his breath, took a last look at Priam and Beau suspended high in the air, and shut his eyes.

Beau gave a desperate bark, there was a tremendous crack, and the river went crazy. A white wave reared and Wordsworth sank. Icy water poured into his nostrils. The dark got darker, his back legs shot out from under him and he sank. But his front legs were suddenly free. They punched and scrabbled, poking at the water till he broke through the surface and gulped air. One swallow and down he went again, but only a little way this time, coming back up once more.

He lapped up the air, and only then realized that nothing was pulling him down. Jabbing with his paws, he swam, swallowed water, swam some more, and felt solid land under his feet. He tottered out, legs shaking violently, and collapsed on the ground.

When he opened his eyes Priam was standing over him, water streaming down the short, glossy hair of his muscled legs. He could feel the solid riverbank under his wet body. "The weeds," he said, and instantly began to cough. His stomach heaved. Raising himself a little, he retched out water, choking and gagging.

"He must know how much you like water," Priam said dryly.

Stay out of the water, Moody Sunshine Wordsworth. The Golden retched some more. How did Just Daniel know? Or Bludrun, for that matter? "What did you do?"

"I guessed that the weeds were hexed into grabbing anything that came in. It could have been you or me, a log or a swala. It was you. I hoped that when that heavy tree limb fell into the water it would catch their attention; it's bigger than you are. Or was."

Wordsworth followed his gaze and gave a cry of surprise. Little remained of the long limb that before had leaned over the bank. It had been pulled into the river, which was busy sucking in the rest of the massive gray trunk.

He felt something warm and moist. Beau was licking his face, whinnying in joy, his tongue passing over his lips still dribbling with water. "I thought we lost you for sure," he said between licks. "And when that limb fell in, I thought we lost Priam."

"You barked just as the limb tore off the tree and I leaped towards shore," said the Great Dane.

In silence they gazed again at the Curl. All that remained of the enormous fallen hickory were eddies on the water surface. The Golden thought of the silky weeds wrapped around the heavy trunk, remembering how softly and sensuously they'd stroked his hair.

The Noble One growled. "How do you feel?"

Slowly Wordsworth stood up on all fours and shook his fur. Priam, he saw, took some stiff steps and winced, his hind legs almost crumbling to the ground. He must have hurt himself jumping to shore, the Golden thought.

"I smell them," said Beau, "both of them."

"There," Priam said, motioning with his big head. Wordsworth looked up the slope, which now rose slowly in broad terraces up to the Cliffs, the home of swalas. It was a mystery how the terraces had come to being, carved into the hillside by channels that even now coursed down to the river, replenishing it with snowmelt. Only now he couldn't see the terraces, he could only hear the water running down the channels, because higher up the slope everything was shrouded in mist.

Beau limped painfully while Priam grimaced with every step of his hind legs. Wordsworth looked over his shoulder a last time at the river. Its surface was purple and completely smooth, without a trace of what had fallen in. That same moment something disappeared behind the trees on the other side and he marveled at how fast she was. Magogs weren't supposed to be so quick on their feet.

The sunlight had almost completely disappeared and now heavy, threatening rain clouds hovered above the forest. Beau hobbled rather than ran up the terraces in a straight line towards the foot of the Cliffs; to Wordsworth it seemed that one last effort was all they had left. Up ahead he could see the blocks of ancient stone so immense that their tops were still gray from the last rays of sun, their rims thin red lines, while their base, dotted by swalas' caves and burrows, sank into evening shade.

The base of the Cliffs widened in one direction, narrowed in the other. Beau, nose to the ground, turned towards sunset where the shelf widened, nostrils sniffing nonstop. But Priam halted.

"She's here!" Beau called out a few steps ahead, looking down to where a tall bluff jutted out like a promontory over the terraced slope.

"Are you sure?" the Great Dane asked tensely, sniffing in the opposite direction.

"I'm sure," Beau said breathlessly, hurrying back. "The smell is so strong she must be just ahead of us."

"And Bludrun?" Priam asked.

Beau hesitated.

"I think Bludrun's *there*," said Priam. They followed his gaze up towards the Cliffs. "The rot and fire smell is in this direction, not where you're taking us." He growled softly. "He's there, waiting for us. For me."

The twilight shades were climbing up the crags, the red at the top had almost disappeared. "He's no longer chasing lynx," said Wordsworth in a low voice, his hackles up.

Beau's earflaps fell back as he charged forward. "Let's go!"

But Wordsworth and Priam froze.

A black shape ran down the embankment where Beau had originally headed, rounded the bluff and disappeared. Wordsworth saw the large head and paws and yellow eyes, and knew what it was. They all knew. It was a black wolf, an Ancient in its nightly physical form, flying after the lynx.

Priam ran after her.

"Noble One!"

He didn't stop and they ran in pursuit. Wordsworth could smell the Ancient in the dark: arid, sandy, incredibly warm, unlike the Hills this damp evening-turned-night and so like Ruwena, gliding on the ground so evenly and lightly it seemed she was almost flying. But she was black, far bigger than the white wolf. Her thick tail rose up and pointed to the sky, waving, and her front legs stretched forward in impossibly long strides.

Why was she appearing this night, when there was no full moon?

They came to a stop before the big protruding bluff.

"Where did it go?" asked Priam. "Where did the wolf go?"

Something shrieked. They froze. The echo rebounded from cliff to cliff and was interrupted by a scream, this time cut short.

With a snarl Priam leaped up and began climbing the bluff. They could hear the scraping of his paws against the rock as they clambered up after him, slipping and falling, his harsh breath by now so labored it seemed the Great Dane's lungs might give way. Wordsworth's own twisted leg throbbed.

Priam disappeared. Several more steps up revealed a wide groove in the rock that rounded the bend high up and jumbled down to the wide shelf on the other side. Echoes of the last, brief, high-pitched cry no longer reverberated; something else now took its place, an oddly familiar low drone. They got back down the big bluff and into a clearing.

A forest of white pines, bathed in gray, had climbed up the slope and ended here. Something else did, too, at the foot of one of the tall trees. Ophelia.

The lynx's legs were long and her feet large, hardly the most graceful animal, and black tufts of hair surrounded her ears. Her tail was short, with a solid black tip. Her large yellow eyes were open. Her claws were out; she'd been ready to fight. To no avail. She'd been killed just like the Kisdees, just like Hanna, her eyes open wide in horror, her mouth parted in one last scream.

The drone came from the Magog girl who'd reached the lynx before them. Seated next to it, she hummed in that way Wordsworth remembered when he'd first seen her by the stream close to the Flats, her body seesawing front and back, her arms folded across. She hummed without stop, not even looking at Ophelia dead at her feet, her eyes fixed, frozen, open wide.

Beau sniffed crazily around the lynx, growling. Wordsworth's hackles rose. The smell of burn and rot was there, and it was freezing.

"Who killed it?" demanded Priam. "The Magog? The wolf?"

Beau edged his snout under the ears and the blood-drenched ruff. The girl continued to hum, staring into the darkness, ignoring Beau completely.

"Summer," Wordsworth said, remembering her name.

It was as if they were not there. Her hands folded across her chest scratched her arms so hard he could smell the blood.

"Who killed it?" Priam asked again, his voice rising in rage.

"There are different smells here," Beau said, bewildered. "There's the Magog, the Ancient, the heat and rot, and something else I don't recognize at all."

"The Magog didn't kill it, she loved it," said Wordsworth. He could smell the cedar that she wore around her body. "Summer, who killed Ophelia? Who killed her?"

The girl continued to hum.

His heart softened inside. "You saw it, didn't you, Summer? You saw Bludrun."

She hummed louder, shutting her eyes as he spoke.

"Where is he?" he asked her.

He heard a snarl. Priam was staring up at the bluff they'd rounded earlier, and behind it, the Cliffs. "He's where he always was," he said slowly. "Back there, waiting for us."

A frenzied, loud howl broke out of the Great Dane; an answering howl came back from the Cliffs, lingering and lower pitched. Both howls echoed back and forth, but Priam was already gone in a rush of paws. Wordsworth and Beau chased after him, scrabbling back up the groove in the tall bluff and then rolling down on the other side. The hunt and lynx were forgotten. The one who'd been there all along was up ahead. *Once he was different, but now he hates, only hates.*

Priam was far ahead of them and Wordsworth wondered how the old hunter could run so fast. He smelled the blood dripping from Beau's paws and his own back leg scraped uselessly against the rocks, slowing him down. Behind them lay a dead lynx they hadn't killed, ahead was a very alive Bludrun. He stumbled several times but kept going. Soon he could no longer catch Priam's scent.

The shelf climbed, narrowing to a ledge, and the Cliffs climbed with it. Caves and grottoes dotted their base. The incline grew, causing their breaths to come out faster and shallower. Priam must slow down, he thought. He's been lurching forward since the mishap by the river, he can't run far.

Wordsworth stopped. The peaks lingered in gray as they waited for darkness to climb from the bottom, except for the one right before them. Like the others, it made a broad sweep rather than narrowing to a point, but unlike the others, its top lay concealed in black shadow. The fur on his back rose once again. He looked over his shoulder at the sky, hoping against hope that there would be something that cast such a shadow.

There was nothing. "He's here," he said softly. His legs shook. "Noble One!"

The fog rolled and thickened ahead of them.

"The smell," groaned Beau behind him. Wordsworth could smell it too, harsh and bitter, not of this earth, much stronger now than before. Beau's legs collapsed and he rolled on the ground, panting hard, whimpering, "It burns, it burns!"

The smell seemed to spread through Wordsworth's entire body, poisoning his lungs, causing his eyes to water and overpowering his nose. He saw nothing but mist, and he was cold, so cold, just like in the Glade of Remorse. His fur seemed to curl up into a ball.

"Priam!" he called out again, but his voice came out as a low-pitched wheeze.

The earth rumbled, agitating small pebbles on the ledge. The fog parted, revealing two eyes: shiny green, malevolent coils, each with a black vertical slash. They looked at him unblinkingly just as they had that first night, intelligent, indifferent. The mist didn't move so much as expanded towards him, bringing those terrible eyes closer. This time there was no Ruwena to save them. Behind him Beau whimpered.

It will blink soon. That's when you run.

Filmy tendrils wove around his fur, leaving icicles among his hairs. Frost covered his head and his tail fell because he had no strength to hold it up. Icy numbness spread through his body; he wanted to shut his eyes and slip into a dream. Stay awake, he told himself; wait for him to blink.

Bludrun blinked. Instantly he felt his brain working again, the muscles tense and ready to run. But the green orbs opened sooner than he expected, and he gasped. For they no longer contained black slits in their centers, but rather a long, gray head and a muzzle flecked with white under deep, tired eyes.

They shut and the fog collected itself, reared up, and floated up the ledge.

"It's going after Priam," Wordsworth said at the same time that he heard a low, tearing vibration. A thin fissure appeared across the ledge. "Quick, Beau!"

But it was too late, for the earth rumbled, its crusty surface cracked open. A breach appeared, then widened as the ground fell away at their very paws, causing them to leap back rather than forward, and then collapse when they couldn't stay upright. When they finally got up again, they were standing at the edge of a deep chasm that cut across the narrow ledge.

"Priam, come back!" Wordsworth called out in fright. But the other side was already shrouded in mist. He strained his eyes, trying to pierce the darkness while Beau ran up and down the side of the abyss. The Gawl lunged up the Cliffs in an effort to find some way up and across, paws clawing at the immense rocks and leaving bloody tracks on their smooth surface before he slid back down, whining in frustration. Again and again he tried to find a way up, to no avail.

The two sat back, sniffing the air anxiously. Wordsworth fixed his eyes straight ahead, hoping to see Priam emerge from the darkness, head sharply set off, jaw square, neck tall. But there was no sign of the Great Dane. The ledge continued on the other side of the chasm, hidden by mist.

It felt like a long time later when he heard Beau say, "You must go back. The others will come and find the lynx." He sounded like he was talking from far away.

"They weren't anywhere close to us."

"Someone killed her; someone will find her. I can't go back there so I'll wait for him here."

Wordsworth didn't want to leave; he never felt closer to Priam than he did that moment, waiting for his return. But Beau was right. He turned back and walked down, the Cliffs looming silently over him. He could lift his back leg again, but inside his heart was black and ready to burst. He climbed up the bluff once again and found the path that circled to the other side.

He knew Summer was gone even before arriving at the clearing, for there was no humming. The moon reappeared, throwing off a light sufficient for him to see that the Magog girl was not there, with her cedar smell and the look of frozen terror. What had she seen? Where was she now?

There were no signs of blood, only the limp body of the lynx, more ghostly than before, her final snarl a grin forever. Ophelia's head had been nearly severed. As a hunter, he'd learned how to give the death bite with a quick rip of the life cord connecting the swala's head and body. Severing a head was something else entirely.

Someone emerged from behind the cliff and walked towards him. And even as his heart leaped at the thought that maybe it was Priam, the smell of hyacinth told him who it really was, for she was smaller, with a tail that curled over her back, glistening white at the tip, and golden flanks that suddenly bent over and rolled in the carcass of the lynx.

"Not a bad kill," she observed to Wordsworth pleasantly as she got back on her paws, "only harder than I thought. She put up quite a fight."

He stood there stupidly, his long muzzle pointed at Anifa, mouth wide open. "You killed her?"

"Who else? It wasn't you, was it?" He couldn't speak. "And I don't think it was Priam. By the way, where is our *former* Noble One?" She gazed over his shoulder while he stood there mutely. "It doesn't matter, does it? Wherever he is, he's late. Close, but not close enough."

"But—" But we didn't sniff you, he wanted to say. We smelled Bludrun, we smelled the lynx, we even caught the scent of the black wolf, but we never smelled *you.*

"Didn't think I could do it?" Anifa demanded, her tawny body streaked with Ophelia's blood.

"There was no sign of you. No smell, no tracks—"

"Obviously, neither of you are great trackers," she said airily. "Frankly, I'm surprised to see you here. Well, not you, Wordsworth, but certainly your friend Priam. I didn't think he'd make it this far." Again she peered over his shoulder. "And he hasn't, has he?" She eyed Wordsworth and smiled, her beautiful low voice suddenly pealing into high laughter. "I wonder, did he bring the Bard of Kiskadee with him to declaim a celebratory verse right on the spot, over the dead lynx?"

He licked his black lips.

"Would you like to do that for me?" She sidled over to him and rubbed against his flanks, smearing him with some of the lynx's blood.

Wordsworth stared, head pounding. When did she pick up Ophelia's tracks? The whole way here, from Jack Pine Ridge to the foot of the Cliffs, none of them had seen or smelled her. Beau had smelled something unfamiliar here, but nothing along the route the lynx had taken. He started when he thought of Beau, who was back on the ledge. On no account must Anifa discover him.

"What's this?" he heard a familiar voice behind him, accompanied by much panting.

Goralac shoved him out of the way with his muscle-bound shoulders and bent over the lynx. Behind him came his two exhausted helpers, Karoo shuffling last of all, ready to collapse.

"Who did this?" Goralac snapped, small eyes filled with rage. He looked from Anifa to Wordsworth. "Where's Furrow Face? Did he kill the lynx? I'll kill the—"

"Furrow Face isn't here," Anifa said lazily. "He never got here. He's probably resting somewhere far, far away."

Goralac's broad, flat forehead wrinkled. "But then—but then—"

"That's right," the Saluki said, her eyes wide with merriment. "I killed the lynx."

Goralac's small eyes blew wide open and his bottom lip, always hidden, seemed to disappear completely as his jaw dropped. "But how—where did you pick up the smell? We never saw you back—"

"Of course you didn't," Anifa snapped, her tone changing instantly. "Because I was tracking this lynx. I found her tracks up at Jack Pine Ridge and followed them all the way here."

"So that's where you went," another voice said. It belonged to Voldakov, who had just arrived with his Viszla companions, their pace so smooth and light no one had heard them. Right behind him Marima followed more decorously with her Borzoi sisters. The rust-colored hunter seemed so spry and energetic it looked like he could hunt all night. He walked over and looked down at Ophelia long and hard. He exchanged glances with Wordsworth, peered at Goralac, and gazed towards Anifa. "Good guess," he said. "We lost one lynx's scent some distance after Poplar Ridge and never found it again."

"From the beginning my plan was to start at Jack Pine and hunt from there." She turned from one to the other, challenging them to contradict her.

She couldn't have, Wordsworth thought. We'd have smelled her.

Goralac growled. Voldakov bent his lean, narrow head in acknowledgment. He examined Ophelia's mangled neck. "I never knew Salukis could be such killers," he murmured.

"So you picked up its tracks at Jack Pine Ridge. How do we know you killed it?" Marima demanded, holding aloft her narrow, white head.

"That's what I'd like to know," from Goralac.

"She has the lynx's blood all over her," Voldakov noted.

"So does he," Goralac said, unceremoniously pushing Wordsworth forward with his large head so that the others could see him.

"She could have rolled in the lynx after it was dead." Marima's nose sniffed curiously, her intelligent, mature eyes settling first on one face, then another.

Goralac growled again.

"Let's ask the Bard of Kiskadee," Anifa said, her voice carrying a slight tinge of sarcasm. She looked at Wordsworth, her long, feathered tail waving, and demanded, "What did you find when you arrived here?"

"We found the lynx, dead," said Wordsworth slowly.

"We?" Goralac demanded.

"Priam and I."

"Did Priam kill the lynx?" asked Anifa.

He looked down. "It was already dead when we came."

"Because *I* killed it," she said imperiously. "These are my tracks around it. I went away to slake my thirst, and when I came back I found Priam's helper here." The others gazed down but it was too dark to see anything. Anifa smiled. "Any other questions?" she cooed.

"Just one," said Voldakov. "Where is Priam?"

TWENTY-ONE

"**Y**eah, where is he?" demanded Goralac, looking at Wordsworth. "You say he came and left. Let's hear his story. Maybe he'll claim he killed the lynx."

"If Priam didn't kill the lynx he won't say he did," said Marima mildly.

Voldakov kept his eyes on Wordsworth, saying nothing.

"I left him back up the ledge," the Golden said slowly. "I don't know where he is now, but I can show you where we separated." They'll make a lot of noise and Beau will hide, he thought, it'll be easy in the dark. But what will he tell them when they reach the chasm?

It was eerily quiet. The tall rocks were ghosts in the cool streams of distant moonlight. They walked behind him along the base of the Cliffs, each deep in his own thoughts. Only Goralac, in his eagerness and disappointment, flopped and stumbled, muttering to himself.

Voldakov walked alongside Wordsworth. "How did you find us?" the Golden asked in a low voice.

"We saw bloody tracks along the river. There were three sets of tracks and I wondered who else was with you; now I know it was Anifa."

Wordsworth said nothing. They reached the point where they'd first seen the black wolf. What happened to her, he wondered now for the first time. We were about to go the other way after Bludrun when she appeared and we chased her, and found the dead lynx instead. But where did *she* go?

The group continued up the ledge, the big Cliffs keeping vigil alongside, Wordsworth straining hard for the first sign of Beau. Not that Beau would wait to be discovered; he'd hear them easily long before they spotted him. They climbed up for what seemed an eternity. By now they should have arrived at the chasm that slashed the ledge. He glanced around furtively in case he'd missed something, but there was no other way up the narrow shelf. His legs shook; the ground felt solid enough beneath his paws, but he knew that in an instant it could open up.

The ledge narrowed almost to a point. Does it end here, he wondered in confusion. Where's Beau? But no, it merely circled another enormous bluff, kin to the one that overlooked the dead lynx. They didn't have to climb this one—the path went around—so he walked ahead, followed by the others in single file. And as he rounded the bend the path suddenly flattened and widened into a broad passage, bordered by the Cliffs on one side and the terraced slope on the other.

Obstructed by the Cliffs, the moon gave very little light, but the little it gave seemed to shine exclusively on Beau. His earflaps were up, tips high, not fluttering in their direction at all. Wordsworth heard *Gawl!* as the others took in the black—not white—Akita standing in complete silence.

Run! he wanted to shout. *Why are you just standing there?* Beau didn't move. Wordsworth heard another gasp behind him, for the moon, playing its tricks, had shifted its light. Something lay on the ground next to Beau.

The others rushed forward; the Flathead Karoo whined from fear. Goralac, for once, was completely silent. They gazed in horror. When he himself finally came forward he took one look and turned away.

It wasn't as bad as the others. Priam's neck was black with blood, but his muzzle was closed, with no hint that his tongue was missing. His once formidable eyes were now open, grim, and lifeless, the wide scar that once furrowed his face, licked respectfully by so many Kisdees, now a thin, faint line. His body had been oddly spared, but blood gushed out of the torn neck, creating a pool around his body. Like Hanna, Wordsworth thought.

Anifa was the first to recover. "Who did this?" she growled.

Beau stepped towards them and they recoiled.

Goralac snorted in embarrassment. "Lower those ears," he hissed.

"Let him talk," said Voldakov.

"I don't like it when Gawls have those flaps up. Sign of insolence, if you ask me."

"Speak!" commanded Anifa.

"I found him like that," Beau said in his hoarse voice. "The fog was just lifting."

"We don't care about the weather," fumed Goralac.

"What were you doing here?"

"Isn't it obvious?" a terrible familiar voice asked behind them.

No one had heard Dreden approach. Silently and smoothly, he glided inside the group, and Wordsworth heard more footsteps behind him. He didn't have to turn around; he could smell the overpowering scent of terraberries. Enforcers surrounded them.

"What do you mean?" asked Voldakov.

"One Gawl helps another."

"You think *he* killed Priam?" Goralac was incredulous. "I know Furrow Face was old and decrepit, but this one—"

"He helped another kill Priam." Dreden turned from one to the other. They were all silent. The moon had gone again, hidden by thicker clouds, but Wordsworth imagined the Enforcer's eyes glinting mercilessly. "Look at our Noble One. See his neck ripped to shreds. Do Kisdees kill like that? Who do you think killed Priam? And this Gawl helped him. That's why he escaped from the Flats."

"No!" said Wordsworth. "He was with us. He helped us hunt the lynx."

Their faces betrayed only one thing: disbelief. Goralac recovered his voice first. "Priam invited a *Gawl* to help him hunt lynx?"

"No, not just lynx," he said quickly, "the killer of the Hills. That's who he was hunting all evening long, that's why he joined the hunt to begin with."

"Strange, I thought he joined the hunt because he wanted to remain the Noble One," said Goralac. "It's clever and convenient for him to use a Gawl. They're freaks, of course, but we all know they have better hearing and smell than we do."

"It was my idea," Wordsworth said, and instantly felt Dreden's eyes on him.

"If Priam wanted to hunt Rathbane, why do it during a hunt for the lynx?" Voldakov asked quietly.

"He said that at other times he was always being followed."

"Followed? The Noble One? By whom?" Marima's large, sad eyes rested on him.

"I don't know."

Voldakov looked thoughtful. Beau still stood conspicuously in the middle of the circle. Why doesn't he run, Wordsworth wondered in despair. But Beau was completely motionless. Like a guard, he thought. Like an Enforcer.

"So that's why Furrow Face joined the hunt so late," said Goralac, getting more and more agitated. "At first he was adamantly against it, and then he changed his mind. He knew he couldn't do it on his own, or with the help of that one," motioning with his head towards Wordsworth.

"This Gawl is a runaway from the Flats," said Dreden silkily. "Who told Priam about him?"

Wordsworth hesitated "I did "

"And how did you know about him?"

"Because I freed him."

The first drops of rain finally began to fall.

✧✧✧

There were flashes of lightning and thunder as they trekked back to the Bottoms. His fur got so wet that water trickled continuously from his belly to the ground and it was a struggle to stay up; his legs couldn't stop shaking from exhaustion. He often stumbled, only to be bitten hard on his flank by one of the Enforcers that surrounded him. No one said a word. Voldakov walked in pensive silence. Marima was sad; she was an old friend of Priam for many years. Goralac griped and muttered, his tough bravado gone. They walked as if in a dream.

He, too, felt as though he was walking in his sleep. The pain in his back leg was excruciating, but hardly mattered. All he could think of was the Great Dane's body at the end of the ledge. The blood hadn't stopped flowing; each surge followed another, as though Priam had secret reservoirs of life inside his old, failing body. Dazed, he would shake his head suddenly as if he just remembered where he was, spraying rain all around him. No, it wasn't possible; Priam didn't die. Others came and went, Priam stayed on. White covered his muzzle and speckled his flanks, but he stayed on.

What ifs assailed him from all directions, one in particular. What if, upon reaching the Cliffs, they hadn't followed the black wolf? What if all of them had gone together after Bludrun instead of Priam finally confronting him alone? Old, bone weary, and alone. Against Bludrun! Killer and butcher! He remembered the cold, dispassionate coiled eyes; rage filled his chest and the hair on his back bristled with hatred. Instantly the Enforcers growled and crowded tighter against him. But the hate didn't disappear. He could feel it coursing through his body as part of his own blood, reaching everywhere, biding its time. One day I'll kill you, he vowed silently. One day I'll avenge Priam.

The ground got muddy. He slipped and fell, and the Enforcers stopped and waited, their eyes expressionless as he struggled back on his paws. He was a cripple to them, less than a clod of earth, a pebble they were slowly and patiently moving downhill. They brought him to the enclosure at the Bottoms and quickly ushered him inside, but not before a flash of lightning told him that all the Kisdees were still outside on the enormous riverbank, families and clans filling every bit of space. The rain hadn't driven them away; no one had left.

He kept his eyes averted from the small round clearing where Priam had sat in Circle meetings over many years. Enforcers came in, never taking their eyes off him even when a great cry outside shattered the night. What were they saying? And what happened to Beau? He'd lost sight of his friend on the way down. Did they return him down to the Flats, trussed up in chains like Hanna? Did they decide to end it quickly right there by the Cliffs? *I will kill him, Noble One. What else do you do with a Gawl?*

He heard another deafening cry. It rumbled like thunder, starting in one place and spreading in all directions till it came back together again in one wave, one name echoing again and again. This time he recognized it: *Anifa!* They're telling them she won the hunt, he thought. There were other, more raucous cries, too, and it occurred to him that the Flatheads were angry.

The smell of orange terraberries grew stronger. An Enforcer entered the enclosure, looked at Wordsworth, and grinned. "Aren't you glad to see your old boss?" Markus showed his white teeth in the dark. "The one you were supposed to report to?"

Wordsworth growled. "Where's Beau? What did you do to Beau?"

"We had an agreement," Markus said, ignoring his question. "You were going to keep an eye on our cousins across the river and report in every day." He grinned. "But finally you made it; better late than never. Time to go."

"Go where?"

"To the Land of the Gawls. Don't you want to see all your friends?" And Markus's grin widened appreciably, revealing his fangs.

They killed Beau! Rage exploded inside and he rushed Markus. But he never made it; his back leg gave way and he sank to the ground. Instantly Markus's teeth fastened behind his ear. Pain enveloped him like a mist. Markus ground down harder, and though he couldn't see the Enforcer's face he knew it wore a pleasant expression, that Markus wasn't vicious or angry, that in fact he was quite relaxed, eyes closed as in a trance. Nor did he let go when Wordsworth screamed. Instead, using the pressure of his fangs, he pulled the Golden up on his paws.

"You know who else you'll find in the Land of the Gawls?" Markus's eyes gleamed. "Your mother, Moody Sunshine Loreen. Don't you want to see her?"

"What happened to her?" he panted.

"You should know, you're a lot like her. Rash, impulsive, doesn't do what she's told. We tried talking to her, tried reasoning with her that no true Kisdee mother lets a crippled

pup live. She threw herself at me for even making the suggestion, so I gave her the death bite. But don't worry," murmured
the Enforcer happily, "you'll see her soon," and with his powerful muzzle he pushed Wordsworth out of the enclosure.

He was back out in the storm, his neck thudding with
pain. The other Enforcers pressed hard against him, forcing
him up the slope that overlooked the Bottoms. Lightning
flashed and he recognized Anifa's gold flanks from afar, the
white hair of her tail gleaming, Dreden standing alongside.
And he knew that now it was his turn, he was to be killed in
front of everyone, made an example of. He paused, only to
jump with a yelp when Markus's fangs bit his flanks hard.
Slowly he climbed to the top of the slope and turned around.

Below him stood the Kisdees of the Hills. Anyone he'd ever known and everyone he hadn't, all the families and clans—
Flatheads and Curveheads, Hounds and Haulers—were there.
He hadn't realized there were so many. Families that rarely
frequented the Bottoms—the white-and-red Ibizans, the spotted Dalmatians, the shy Greyhounds—were there. In the bright
flashes of lightning he could see his own Retrievers, and for a
moment he thought he saw Vagabond, with his lustrous gold-
en hair. Nor could he miss the enormous wolfhound Tug-a-
Lugs, standing and glowering on the side just above the enclosure, and he heard the voice of their leader, McDoon's Riverbend Corley, thundering above the others: "I cannae believe it
of Priam, I cannae!"

"It doesn't matter what you believe, this is what we saw.
He was using a Gawl—a Gawl!—to hunt for him." Dreden
didn't need to shout. His merciless eyes scanned the faces below and they all hushed in disbelief, though no one dared

contradict him. No one, that is, except the head of the big Tug-a-Lugs.

"What does Priam need a Gawl fer?" demanded Corley. "He's the greatest hunter we've ever had. I should know, I hunted with him fer a long time, and he didn't need me own help."

"He was old, Corley, and—"

"I'm old too, but ye want to tell me I can't hunt?" The other Tug-a-Lugs laughed, showing white teeth above their beards. "Do I have me eyes? Do I have me teeth? What's true fer me's true fer Priam. It's a mistake, I tell ye!"

"It was no mistake," shouted Goralac, standing apart from the others. "He hunted with a Gawl. He violated—"

"I want proof!" yelled Corley. "I don't want no guff from any Flathead 'bout a Noble 'Un, nor from some Saluki I never heard of, I want proof!"

"Here's your proof," said Dreden, and a wall of Enforcers moved aside, revealing Beau just as the lightning, as if on command, flashed.

Wordsworth's heart leaped. Beau was alive. Covered with blood, but alive. For a moment he almost forgot where he was and the terrible danger he was in. A great relief overcame him, as though a burden of shame and guilt had fallen off. He knew where his loyalty lay, knew it clearer now than before. With that same clarity he heard an intake of breath as the Kisdees saw Beau for the first time, an Akita who was the wrong color, with a square head and full cheeks, and a tail that did not curve over his back. It was how he'd seen him that first time in the Flats, an aberration that at best evoked disdain, and at worst, fierce loathing.

He tried to see Beau's face but Dreden stood between them. There was no gloating in Dreden's face, just the same frozen features congealed to eternity. He'd hidden Beau till he could show him for maximum effect, and there was no question that he succeeded. Silence fell on the Kisdees. Even McDoon's Riverbend Corley grew quiet, his scraggly tail twitching.

"He says his name is Daimyo's Fireside Stomping Beau," announced Dreden icily, and the remorseless lightning flashed on Beau once again. "Tell me, Daimyos, what do you know of this?"

"Nothing," came a female voice from the back. It was an Akita, so white she shone in the dark, and Wordsworth recognized Odate, the head of the Daimyo family. "As anyone can see," she added with great distaste, "he's no Daimyo. No Gawl is ever a Daimyo."

"No Gawl is ever a Kisdee," growled Dreden. "Yet the Noble One Priam broke our Rules for this one. And do you know how the Gawl repaid him? He killed Priam, he killed the Noble One. Tell me, Kisdees, what should we do with this Gawl?"

"Kill!" they shouted. "Kill him!"

"I cannae believe it!" shouted Corley. "That ugly Gawl could not bring down such a one as Priam."

"You're right, Tug-a-Lug," snarled Dreden, and this time his eyes were filled with hate. "No Gawl like him could bring down Priam. But another Gawl could, with the help of this one. This one lured Priam on the pretext of finding the lynx to where the other waited, much bigger, much more terrifying, a Gawl with one eye that butchers and devours—"

"Kill!"

"The same one that preyed on your brothers and sisters, your children, my brother! Say, Kisdees, what should we do with Rathbane?"

"Kill!" they yelled, their eyes feverish in the lightning.

"And what should we do with this one?"

"Kill!"

"No!"

Suddenly there was no roar, only eyes, a multitude of them, fastened on him. His heart pounded, his mouth was dry. He tried hard not to lick his lips. "It's true, Beau was with us for the hunt. But it wasn't a hunt for the lynx. It was a hunt for the one who's been killing Kisdees in these Hills."

"A Gawl!" Goralac scoffed. "A Gawl helping a Noble One track Rathbane, another Gawl? Why?"

"Because Beau is a great hunter."

"A better tracker than an Enforcer?" Dreden snorted.

"Priam didn't care where he got help, he wanted only to kill the monster responsible for the killings. That's why he died."

"Why would this Gawl help Priam track down and kill another Gawl?" Goralac demanded.

It wasn't another Gawl, he wanted to say, but they'd never believe him. "Because he'd been chained down in the Flats by Magogs and Enforcers, and Priam was going to set him free."

If he'd said something less outlandish they might have jeered and mocked, but this was so extraordinary that all turned silent, as though he talked of another world or another time. There was bafflement in their wide-open eyes.

"Why don't you ask Dreden about Magogs," he told them. "Ask him why Enforcers help Magogs tie dogs down to protect their food. Ask him why Enforcers are violating the Rules."

For a moment no one said anything. But lightning flashed and he saw something in their eyes: the old terror of Magogs and the dawning of some primal knowledge they'd tried to deny all this time. They'd always known it would come down to this. Magogs would be back.

"There are no more Magogs!" a Flathead, member of the Lonesome Lobos Border Terriers, shouted.

"Ask any Enforcer," he yelled back. "Ask them what they do with certain Gawl puppies. They don't leave them across the river, they bring them all the way down to the Flats and deliver them to Magogs, and they remain Magogs' slaves forever, isolated and tied down, unable to move, unable to hunt or haul. Ask them! Look on their faces and ask them. Ask Dreden!"

And that's what they did. Those who stood close to Enforcers searched their faces. Caught by surprise, the Enforcers licked their lips. A couple dropped their tails while others growled quietly. Then all eyes moved to Dreden. The head of the Enforcers raised his head proudly.

"Is it true?" asked a Red Terrier up front in a small voice. Her sad eyes looked up at Dreden over her long, narrow muzzle as though they already knew the answer.

Dreden looked pitilessly down at their faces.

Pandemonium broke out. A few in the back, well out of harm's way, yelled and barked at Dreden, but most just snapped and bellowed at each other. It was as if with that one glance all was clear, their worst fears realized. And suddenly, almost everyone had seen Magogs.

"I knew it, I knew it!" a young mountain dog from the Beguiling Berners said, his enormous tongue falling out of his mouth excitedly. "I saw Magogish tracks a couple of times but no one believed me!"

"I saw one on the other side of the river," a golden-eyed female Greyhound from the Bashful Barkers said softly. "It had lots of gray fur and six legs, though it used only four. Kind of like a big bug."

"Magogs don't have six legs," a Bullmastiff told her mournfully. "Unless they evolved."

"Babylon warned us!" the Ridgeback who previously mocked him now hollered. "He warned us they were coming back!"

"Remember, Jerusha, when we followed that rabbit down into the tunnels under Sycamore Bend and we heard those heavy steps and I looked out?" one Dachshund said to his companion. "I saw a Magog that time. It was such a shock I couldn't sleep for a week, remember? You said I was imagining things!"

"Who knew?" Jerusha barked shrilly. "Who knew?"

"The Prophet knew," the Ridgeback said solemnly. "I always said he knew."

"I saw two by Mastiff Moors," reflected a Bassett, member of the famous Hurrying Hounds, as he slowly chewed on a new grass stem. "When I barked they stretched out their wings and flew down the Hills, like big hawks."

"Didn't used to fly," said the grumpy Bullmastiff.

"I looked up and saw one looking back down at me from the top of a tree," a Foxhound said. "Didn't they live there once, long ago?"

"There are no Magogs!" the Lonesome Lobos Flathead yelled over and over. "They've been extinct for generations."

"Babylon told us, he told us!"

Wordsworth felt a sudden chill and looked up to find Dreden's frozen wasteland eyes on him.

"Wait a minute, wait a minute!" expostulated Goralac, running back and forth across the top of the slope in frustration, legs so short it looked as though his white, oval body was rolling back and forth. They started to laugh. "What's this got to do with the hunt? Priam's dead, the lynx is dead, and this Gawl—this Gawl—" he broke off, not knowing what to say.

"Sounds like this Gawl saw what happened," drawled a Rottweiler loud enough for everyone to hear.

"But the Rules are the Rules!" exclaimed Goralac. "The Gawl had no business in the hunt."

The other Flatheads murmured their agreement, their box-like faces turning first this way, then that, but Wordsworth saw his chance. "This Gawl risked his life for us!" he declared loudly

"He is not a Kisdee!" someone shouted from the crowd.

"He is a Kisdee," Wordsworth said. "He is born of a Kisdee father and a Kisdee mother. He lived, if only for the shortest time, in one of our dens and was fed our food."

"The Rules say–"

"Nowhere in the Rules does it say that a Gawl is not a Kisdee. Gawls are Kisdees like us—and slaves." There was a murmur in the crowd. "Slaves to us, and slaves to Magogs who can't hunt their own food." The murmur grew louder, like a fierce wind spreading from the forest to the riverbank. "Slaves to be tied down, unable to move! To lie on the hard earth under the sun with little shelter while we repose on soft grass under the trees. Never to eat fresh kill, never to drink fresh water from the river, and worst of all, never to speak to another Kisdee. To live alone in this miserable way for the rest of their very short lives. And for whose benefit? For the benefit of Magogs!" He addressed their upraised faces. "Is this what we do to dogs?"

For a moment no one said anything. Then someone shouted: "No!"

"Dogs are not slaves!" cried out the Rottweiler.

"But wha' about the Rules?" It was old Corley again. "We cannae forget the Rules."

"The Rules were made by us, and can be changed by us. That's what Priam was going to do. He was going to kill the lynx, he was going to kill the murderer, and he was going to free all Kisdees—including Gawls. He gave his life for us, but had he lived he would be facing you now and telling you that all Kisdees should live in peace, purebred and Mixeds. All Kisdees should eat swalas at the Bottoms and drink water from the river. Priam would stand here tonight and tell you that all Kisdees should be free."

The night burst into uproar. He couldn't hear what they were saying. Some yelled, their faces betraying everything from rage to enthusiastic agreement. Others expostulated with their family and neighbors. The noise was terrific. They forgot about the hunt, they forgot about the storm. They argued and shouted, their bodies shaking furiously, while the young ones barked nonstop. He felt someone watching him intently, turned, and met deep-set eyes almost hidden by long eyebrows and a shaggy beard. Wordsworth wagged his tail, but Birdy gave no sign of friendship.

It's happening, he thought with a sudden surge of joy. He could feel it in his bones. He would save Beau and finish what they'd set out to do. Priam had said it himself: *I won't always be here. Others, too, will have to lead.* He glanced over quickly in Beau's direction, but Beau stood exactly as he'd stood on top of the ledge over Priam's body, rigid and silent, his brow smooth and unwrinkled, as though what was happening below didn't concern him in the least.

"But Priam is *not* facing you here tonight," said a voice next to Wordsworth. It spoke so softly that Wordsworth didn't think anyone heard it besides him. But the Kisdees grew quiet, their faces glancing up uneasily.

It was the Kisdee that smelled of hyacinth, the Saluki, Anifa.

TWENTY-TWO

"I am here tonight, not Priam," she said, stepping forward and raising her feathery tail over her back. "*I* killed the lynx, not Priam. And Priam is not here because he's dead." She raised her voice. "I am a member of the Circle, and I never heard Priam say that he wished to change the Rules concerning Gawls. Dreden, you've attended every Circle meeting. Have you ever heard Priam express this wish?"

"Never, Noble One," Dreden said fiercely.

"And you, Goralac," she called out. "Have you ever heard Priam speak of this?"

Goralac snorted, though it was not clear whether this was in response to Anifa's question or to Anifa generally.

The Saluki spoke more slowly. "It seems as if no one but the Bard of the Vale has heard this from Priam." There were a few cackles from the crowd. "And what proof has he given?" She posed with a raised head, coughed importantly and licked her lips:

> "*Spring steals into these happy Hills*
> *With newly minted leaf and fern,*
> *Yellow bud forsythia, emerald frills,*

The moon comes up – the moon comes up – the moon comes
up – "

She paused, smiled, and looked at them expectantly. "Unfortunately, our crippled poet can't finish his verse," she said sadly.

The laughter rose slowly, like a wave.

"But he finished this one. How about this for proof?

Deepwoods Rushing Emma sounded the alarm
'Gainst Magogs in the furrowed Fields below.
Freedom! cried our warriors, and feared no harm
As they dealt the Tall Ones an awful blow."

It had been one of his first efforts, nothing he was proud of now, and they laughed. In fact, they laughed so uproariously that some fell on the ground, or else rolled on their backs to let someone tickle their bellies, which was the best laugh of all. The Terriers especially tittered and snickered loudly, drooling from the corners of their mouths.

Finally they quieted down and she continued.

"Our Bard says that Rules were made by Kisdees like us, and can therefore be changed. But there was a reason why these Rules were made." Her tail waved confidently, its long, silky, white hairs falling down like a shower of stars, her eyes glittering like jewels in the darkness. Her voice carried, though she wasn't speaking loudly. In fact, it was a pleasant, unhurried tone that effortlessly drew them all in. "Fearsome Arden brought us here long, long ago from the Old Place, where we were caged and imprisoned, where we could not hunt for our own food or drink water from the river. Where Magogs ruled, either killing us in mass or chirping over us as if we were pups. All of us were slaves, even those who rebelled and escaped, but still faced death by slow starvation or through the violence of Magogs. Until Arden came."

They listened in rapt attention. It was the old story, the tale they loved, as much a part of them as their very bones.

"And he led us here. Many died on the way. The old were too frail; the young were taken by mountain lions. We were so weak we could hardly protect them from coyotes. But a few of us arrived in these Hills, where the forest was full of game and the River Curl flowed year-round. Yet we couldn't see the game and in our hearts we brought the Old Place with us. Soon we started fighting. You know how it was. It started with the Tug-a-Lugs. They fought with the Daimyos over a kill. Others joined the fight, and before we knew it, the Ravages began. We fought over everything: territory, food, water. And when the winters came and there was less food, we did the only thing we knew: kill or be killed. We believed that for a few to live, many had to die. We were starving, we were desperate. We almost disappeared."

The Kisdees growled.

"Then Fearsome Arden came back and created the Great Alliance. He taught us to hunt together, to cart the kills down to the Bottoms together, to guard together. The hunters went out to hunt, the haulers went out to haul, the guards guarded. All worked for the sake of all. And in this way we had food — not just for some, but for everyone, for young and old, males and females. And we had safety and security, because Enforcers watched out for us, making sure no Kisdee was threatened again. The coyotes hid from our faces; the mountain lions left. There was food, there was safety, there was peace."

"There was food, there was safety, there was peace," they chanted after her.

"There were no more us and them, no more you and me, no more enemies, all of us were one great—"

"Not all, Noble 'Un!" a raspy voice spoke out. Old Corley rose and instantly towered over them. "Ye're right, we're one great circle—with an exception, that being the scurrilous, nefarious, pusillanimous Daimyos. Words haven't been invented you can hold to 'em. We Tug-a-Lugs have been claiming the Daimyos for generations, and we plan to be claiming them fer many more, don't 'e, lads?"

"Aye!" rose the chorus from the Wolfhound Tug-a-Lugs, rearing up to their feet with a yell that resounded across the Bottoms. They grinned at each other in self-congratulations before quieting down, at which point a lone voice spoke up.

"As is customary for them, the Thugs are taking this important meeting hostage." Odate rose on her paws. She was not as big as Corley; she didn't have to be. Her white fur gleamed. She looked around gracefully, her words slow and languid. "They use every opportunity to show their bad manners and lack of respect, not just for Daimyos but for all dogs. You should have expelled them long ago from the Kisdee Circle, but even if you haven't, we Daimyos have not forgotten our vow to rid the Hills of these flea-bitten Thugs. Naturally we will work and cooperate with Kisdees, but not with hoodlums and barbarians."

"Don't let 'em fool ye!" Corley shot up with alacrity. "All this pissin' and—not meanin' no cheek, Noble 'Un—and—"

"Silence!" yelled Anifa.

McDoon's Corley opened his mouth, shut it and sat back. Anifa stared at Odate, who stared boldly back before sniffing and sitting down too. The Saluki walked back and forth along the top of the slope, Enforcers scurrying out of her way. She turned from the Tug-a-Lugs at one end to the Daimyos at the other, her long tail waving menacingly.

"The Kisdee Circle does not expel anyone—including the Tug-a-Lugs and Daimyos who have endangered the peace of these Hills since the beginning. You see how quickly we go back to fighting and killing? These two families have never made peace all these years—and why? Because of a swala skin one of them found and then lost to the other long, long ago."

The crowd started laughing.

"It's no laughing matter," she commanded. "That's how all Kisdees once behaved. Now we have many swala skins, but once we killed each other for much, much less." She continued walking silently, followed by spellbound eyes, before facing them again. "No one knew this better than Arden. He brought all the families and clans together and told us that we were all Kisdees. All worked for the benefit of all; none were excluded. Am I speaking fact, Kisdees?"

"Fact!" they thundered back.

"And none are excluded, so long as they work. All of us—Boxers and Shepherds, Deerhounds and Malamutes—come together to eat at the Bottoms and meet in the Circle."

"All Kisdees together!" they chanted. "All Kisdees together!"

"Here in the Hills we live in peace and harmony among our families and clans, with full bellies summer and winter, with work we do freely instead of slaving for Magogs. No-where else has this happened. Am I speaking fact, Kisdees?"

"Fact, Noble One!" Their eyes glittered, their tongues hung out of their mouths.

"The Glorious One warned us that Magogs were our worst enemies. But we were betrayed. And the one who be-trayed us was he we loved most, he we admired most, for whom we would have given our lives. You know who—"

"How dare ye!" Corley McDoon thundered. "How dare ye impugn the name of the noblest of Noble Ones, the greatest of hunters, the one of the scar?"

"He used a Gawl for the hunt," said Goralac. "He broke the Rules of the hunt."

"He did worse than that," said Anifa, looking straight at the big Tug-a-Lug. "He made peace with Magogs!" There was a rumbling below but she went on. "He made peace with our archenemies. He could have killed them; instead, he saved their food by using Gawls. I despise Gawls, but if it were me, I'd rather let the whole lot die before handing any over to save the life of one Magog!"

The Kisdees growled their assent.

"There had to be a reason!" Tug-a-Lug Corley insisted. "Priam was no fool, he did things fer a reason."

"Shall we find out?" she suggested softly. "Dreden!"

The Enforcer didn't move, only his eyes glinted in the dark. It rained and rained, and still no one budged. "The No-ble One is right," he growled. "The Magogs were starving. Sometimes they would go up to the Hills in search of food. I demanded we put an end to them completely, but he refused. Instead of killing them, he helped them live."

"There had to be a reason," insisted Corley.

"You're right," Anifa replied, "and that reason was that we lost our grit." Her voice got softer and slower, pulling them in. "We lost our vigilance; we lost our hate. These are not the same Magogs as before, swaggering like kings. These Magogs crawled out from under the ground where they'd lived for years like worms, like slugs, like vermin. We should have killed them on the spot, destroyed every male and female, every young one they had, finally made them as extinct as they did to our Ancients, as they did to so many others, as they almost did to us. Do you doubt that I would have done that?"

"Nay, I don't doubt it," Corley muttered. "I don't like to speak bad of the dead. It's not the Gawls I care fer, I just cannae believe Priam let Magogs live."

"That's what happens when you get soft and generous, when you forget where you came from and what they did to you. He left it to us to clean up his mess—to me!" Her tail waved imperiously. "We will destroy them. Not a one will escape." She peered down, eyes glinting. "Who will defend them? Who wishes to defend Magogs?"

"Kill them!" a Flathead shouted, instantly joined by others. "Kill!"

There was no hiding the look of satisfaction in her eyes. "Slowly," she said softly. "It was simpler before. But we are hunters, we know the value of patience, and I promise you this, Kisdees," she growled. "Your Noble One, *this* Noble One, will lead you against the Magogs. We will destroy them and finally eliminate them from this earth."

"Kill!" they cried again and again, and now the tops of the trees higher up in the forest shook and shivered.

"There was something else the Glorious One told us," Anifa said to the enormous crowd, eyes sparkling. Instantly they quieted down. "He said the Alliance would only hold if we all did our work, the work we were *bred* to do." She flung her head up, her white and gold tail leaping up too. "Setters!"

A loud growl came from the back where the clan of setter families had settled for the evening.

"Briards!"

A louder growl came up from the opposite side of the Bottoms, and though the Briards' eyes were half covered by their long locks, they flashed like small flames.

"Terriers!" A yelp arose from the innumerable Terriers right in front of her.

"All of you have your skills; all of you have your jobs. Briards guard; Terriers hunt for small game; Setters hunt for big game. You have these skills because you were born to them," she declared. "I am a Saluki. Look at me. I was born to hunt. My body is lean so that I can run fast. My flanks are low so that I can more easily jump and leap. I was born for endurance, speed, and strength—not just me, all Salukis. Dreden is a Shepherd. Look at him. He is solid, his eyes alert. His strides are long to cover ground quickly. He is loyal and devoted to a fault. The Enforcers are all Shepherds. They would die for Dreden, and Dreden would die for me, just like he was ready to die for Priam. And why? Because he was born to it. He was born to guard. Kisdees," she addressed the throng, eyes flashing, "tell me, what is most important? What is our precious gift?"

"Our breeding," they repeated loudly.

"Our pure breeding," she said.

"Our pure breeding," they repeated

"Without our pure breeding we have no skills. We have no hunters, no haulers, and no guards. What is our life worth then? Long ago we had many mixed breeds, a father from one clan, a mother from another, their children all Mixeds. There were no pure hunters, no pure haulers, and no pure guards, only Mixeds without any skills at all. That's when we starved. We fell prey to other animals, we died in the winters. We fought each other—for a bone, for a cave, a swala skin. There was never any peace, never any discipline, never any order."

"No peace, no discipline, no order," they repeated after her.

"Look at this Mixed!"

They contemplated Beau in silence. He stood as he'd stood all evening, still and impassive. Wordsworth could see the pale, hairless ring around his throat from where he'd finally torn off the wire.

"He calls himself a Daimyo, but tell me," she commanded, "is he all white like the Daimyos?"

They laughed.

"See his head, see his tail. He still marks his territory with urine, yet the Bard of the Vale calls him a Kisdee."

They jeered, eyes fixed malevolently on Beau.

"We were all like that once," Wordsworth shouted, but no one listened.

"Yes, he's ugly," said Anifa happily, "but that's not the real problem. Tell me, if he were allowed to live among us, could he hunt?"

"No," came the answering roar, especially from the hunt-ers.

"Can he haul or guard?"

"No!"

"Is there anything he can do?"

"No!"

"Oh, but you're wrong," Anifa said. "There is one thing he *can* do. He can eat. See how big and fat he is already. He has been fed too well down in the Flats." They laughed. The lightning flashes returned, revealing curled lips and sharp, white teeth. "He is cowardly and useless, like all other Gawls. Even if they haul our food back to the Bottoms, they eat more than they haul. Tell me, Kisdees, do you wish to free Gawls? Do you want a few to work from morning to night to support the many who do nothing but eat, till there is no one left to work, no one left to guard? If that is your wish, Kisdees, tell your Noble One and she will do as you ask."

"No!"

"There are fewer swalas now. We are not yet hungry, but once, long ago, we were very hungry. Tell me, Kisdees, do you want more Gawls to eat our precious food?"

"No!" they roared.

"What should be done with him?"

"Send him to the Land of the Gawls!" a Flathead yelled out.

"Send him to the Land of the Gawls!" they repeated in a deafening cry, leaping up on their paws.

Anifa turned to Wordsworth, venom in her eyes. "And what should be done to those who give them their *freedom*?" she hissed.

"Send them to the Land of the Gawls!" they roared again.

"And what should be done to those who give them refuge?" snarled Dreden. He stepped back, the lightning flashed, and the breath froze inside Wordsworth. There, dwarfed by the black silhouettes of two Enforcers, stood Just Daniel.

He leaped forward, catching those around him by surprise. In three bounds he stood over the old Mixed, looking with horror at his broken white-and-orange body smeared with dirt and blood. His face was so swollen that his eyes were shut and globs of drool fell out of his half-broken, sagging jaws. He shook, ready to collapse at any moment. "What did they do to you?" Wordsworth whispered.

Markus jumped him from the back and pulled him down. He twisted sideways, but it was no use. Markus seemed positively jolly as he sank his teeth into Wordsworth's neck, drew back, and then stabbed his neck again and again.

"Kill!" shouted the Kisdees in unison.

"This one had accomplices," snarled Dreden, eyes mad with hatred. "Mixed accomplices who betray us from within while they eat our precious food and drink our water. What shall we do with them when we find them?"

The thunder roared across the sky, but not louder than the Kisdees at the Bottoms, who roared back: "Kill!"

Pandora, Wordsworth thought, trying to get up in the confusion. What happened to Pandora?

That moment a family of Huskies, snapping and snarling below them, streams of drool dripping down the corners of their mouths, broke ranks, leaped up the short slope, and jumped Beau. Someone screamed. Markus left Wordsworth as Enforcers leaped into the fray, but more Kisdees pushed their way to the front, snarling, lunging, their white fangs showing in the shafts of light, pushed in turn by those behind them, shouting, "Kill him! Kill the Gawl!"

A Rottweiler jumped Wordsworth. The Golden snapped at his attacker's leg and the other yelped. But now he felt the hot, wet breath of muzzles on all sides. He looked for mercy down at the assembly of Kisdees and once again met Birdy's shaggy, fear-filled eyes. Birdy looked away.

"We can't hold them," he heard Dreden say. As he struggled to stay up he could see the Head of the Enforcers facing Anifa, waiting for her orders.

"Give them the Gawl," she said softly, "let them tear him to pieces."

"No!" Wordsworth screamed.

"Kill us—and you die!" a voice rang out.

The Kisdees paused. Eyes full of hate and menace, they looked up the slope, then at each other, then back at the small group standing on the rise, and began to laugh. They laughed harder and harder, some even falling down again, mouths open in merriment. It was Just Daniel. They motioned to him again and again, howling with laughter. His short legs hardly held up his hunched body and only one puffy eye opened under his scraggly hairs. The lightning revealed ugly splotches of raw skin and bloody, sticky hair, making him more laughable to those below. With the low-slung Spaniel part of him barely holding up the larger Spinone flanks, neck and head, and his squinting one eye, he seemed a caricature of a Gawl, a pathetic joke. They settled back, ready for some entertainment.

"You pretend we're different, you call us Mixeds or Gawls," he said loudly. "But who created us if not for you? Who gave us birth?" They stopped laughing. A few growled softly. "You are our parents, our brothers, sisters, cousins." The head of the Gawls raised his still youthful and strong voice: "You are our family."

"No!" they shouted back.

"Yes!" he countered defiantly, eye shining. "You're family to Beau and you're family to me."

There was no mistaking the revulsion on their faces. Be quiet, Wordsworth pleaded with him silently.

"He's mad!" said Anifa, the disgust audible in her voice. "Ugly and mad."

"Yes, I'm mad," said Just Daniel, and to Wordsworth's astonishment, he smiled, revealing missing teeth in his mouth. "What can you expect? I am Mixed, which means that I am many things. I am old before my time. I have seen things blacker than night, and lighter than the white water of the Curl; I know that where there is death there is also life. So while I am many things, there is one thing I am not, Kisdees. I am not afraid!"

"We will make you afraid," someone yelled from the crowd. With a roar the others showed curled lips and white teeth. They wanted to make him whine and whimper, go down on his belly and cringe in the face of their violence.

But Just Daniel remained standing, squinting in the direction of his heckler. The lightning flashed, and he smiled. "Ah, a Spaniel, a relative. Come, Spinones! Spaniels! You are my families. Come and greet your long-lost son."

With a roar of rage Spinones and Spaniels scrambled forward, pushing others out of their way in their rush to tear the Mixed apart, their flanks heaving, tails sharp-pointed, lips curled and jaws snapping, murder in their eyes. Why is he doing this, Wordsworth wondered in horror, surrounded by a tight cordon of Enforcers. The Bottoms was now a river of rage more violent than the churning Curl below.

But Just Daniel went on unafraid, his one open eye flashing. "Your Noble One told you the story of Arden and these Hills—all falsehood and lies. Only once did she speak truth, and that was when she said that nowhere else has this happened. And you know why, Kisdees?" he taunted them. "Because you make slaves of your own children and grandchildren! And she is right, nowhere else in the entire world does this happen. Even Magogs—you hear me, Kisdees—even Magogs don't enslave their own children and—"

They broke through. Just Daniel disappeared under a yelping, snarling pile of bodies. The Enforcers rushed forward and Wordsworth was thrown down, head smashed against something hard. He snarled and tried to push himself up, but this time a giant weight bore down on him and crushed him to the ground. There was a high-pitched scream—Beau, he thought hopelessly—followed by an enormous light and the loudest crack he ever heard. Then sharp pain. Darkness.

TWENTY-THREE

Someone licked his face and he smiled. It was probably Birdy, telling him the sun was overhead, time to get up. He felt it again, followed by a sharp, painful jab. He leaped up, snarling.

Only he couldn't leap up for his legs crumbled beneath him and he fell back down. But it was enough to cause the malevolent hairless head above the pink, unfeathered neck to dart back. The Bird of Death unfurled its wings with a cry and flew up, landing among its less daring friends a short distance away. They watched him dispassionately, black wings folded at their side, eyes cool and aloof, as if to say this was nothing to take personally. They were just waiting for him to die.

He tried to get up again, tottered, and fell. What's wrong, he wondered. The sun felt good on his sore body but he was thirsty. He licked his dry lips, reached sideways to lick his back paw, but instead tasted something hard and bitter. He jumped up, staggered, but this time remained on his paws. Then he saw it, felt it, and knew, in a burst of shock and re-vulsion, that he was wrapped in Hanna's chain.

Horrified, he pulled away with all his might against the coils securing his chest, first one way, then another, to no avail. He bit down on the chain that snaked around his front leg but immediately recoiled. The taste burned his mouth, an abomination not of the forest or of the Hills. He bit down on it again and pulled, but the more he pulled it away from the front the more it bit his back, finally piercing his skin. When he saw the blood he went wild. He growled and snarled, pulling harder and harder, insensitive to pain, but the chain just rubbed deeper into his flesh and more blood flowed. Now he understood how hard it must have been for Hanna to stay up on her paws, for the chain was lulling him into giving up, collapsing on the ground, and waiting for death. It took all his will power to stay up on his legs.

When he turned, the chain immediately pulled on his neck, grazing his skin. Yes, he was in Hanna's place in the Flats. There was the low-spreading juniper shrub and an empty Magogish container far away. He took a step forward and felt something under his paws. There, half buried in the ground, were the stems of the once dripping branches he'd brought to wet Hanna's mouth. He remembered how her tongue had emerged between thick, dry lips to feel the drops of water.

Slowly, painfully, he turned around. There were the Hills in the distance, where Kisdees lived, where he once lived. On the other side, waiting patiently, were the Birds of Death. And where was Wordsworth, or someone like him, to bring him water-moistened stems and branches? He licked his dry, dusty lips. What he would do for just one wet leaf to relieve his thirsty, parched mouth!

It wouldn't save him, just as he had not saved her. He hadn't saved anyone, including Beau. It all came back to him, the storm, the raging Kisdees, Anifa and her glittering eyes. *Give them the Gawl, let them tear him to pieces.* He collapsed on his belly. They'd done it. They'd finally broken ranks, the line of Enforcers gave way. He remembered seeing Beau and Just Daniel going down, the triumph in Anifa's eyes, the sickening scream broken off at the end.

Kisdees haven't fought for generations. We don't have an enemy in the world. How disappointed Beau had been to hear those words the first time they met. Beau was a Daimyo, he wanted to fight Tug-a-Lugs. And he, Wordsworth, had laughed at him. Just as Markus had laughed that night, jaws clamped around his neck, as though this was jolly entertainment, while his friend, Birdy, looked away.

And then there was the one who never looked away, the most mixed of all the Mixeds. Small, drab, graceless, ancient, curious, and optimistic. Never say never, Just Daniel had told Pandora. Old before his time, his body had been poisoned by slavery but not his spirit. The change will come, he'd promised her, his funny ochre eyes glowing with confidence. But the only change that came was that he died, Wordsworth thought miserably, torn to pieces by enraged Kisdees.

Even in his present condition he could feel shame gnawing inside. Kisdees, his Kisdees, had done that. Not to a Magog but to a Mixed, a dog they saw, worked with, and ate with, every day of their lives. And they as good as did that to him, too, for here he was, chained down and sentenced to die a slow death because he freed a Gawl.

No, he thought tiredly, because I never fit in from the beginning, because I was different. *There's no room here for anyone like you.* His own family didn't want him, but a new family did — all Gawls and misfits, and even ne'er-do-wells like Birdy who'd looked away when he needed him.

Why did Just Daniel taunt them? Because he'd heard Anifa order Dreden to give Kisdees the Gawl. He incited them, getting them so angry that they forgot about Beau and hurled their rage at him, rushing in, taking him down, and...

Some choose themselves; others are chosen, even if they don't know it yet. Even if they don't know for what.

And Pandora? Did she see what they'd done to her beloved Daniel? Dead, a voice whispered inside. No, no, he argued furiously with himself, she can't be dead. *Whatever happens, she must live.* He promised.

He squinted up at the sky. It was sunny, blue and merciless, not a hint of a cloud anywhere. Rain had come down the night of the hunt, but what night was that? There was a humming in his head. Gingerly, he licked the packed, brown earth, causing his already black, dry tongue to chafe badly. *How long have I been here?*

He tried to rock himself up once more, but this time the chain didn't give and with a groan he lay back. How he hated the touch of the Flats, the lack of soft underbrush and dead leaves. How he missed the velvet feel of the forest. He glanced up, wishing not just for rain but also for a tree, a shadow of branches, the feel of fluttering leaves though he knew it was too early. Dying down here in the Flats, so far from home, was the most terrible thing of all.

At least you died back in the forest, he told Priam quietly, shutting his eyes. But the Noble One's butchered body appeared vividly in his mind and he opened them again. The blood had flowed, but the tongue hadn't been touched. Was it because Beau had appeared? Or was it Dreden? The Head of the Enforcers was told to stay down at the Bottoms during the hunt, but ever vigilant, ever watchful, ever loyal Dreden arrived at the Cliffs right after Priam was killed. How did he know when to come—and where? Did he wait along with his Enforcers nearby? But that made no sense; more than anything, Dreden hated Rathbane. He hated Gawls.

His thoughts went round and round in his head till they made him dizzy. He groaned, or thought he did, but no sound came out. Set me free, Beau had begged him, not crying even once as the wire's sharp edge bit deeper and deeper into his throat. Beau had tracked the lynx. He sniffed its scent and led them after it till they found its body. But he hadn't caught Anifa's scent till it was too late. Why didn't he run, Wordsworth wondered dully. Why did he stand next to Priam's body till they all came? He must have heard them, just as he must have known what was going to happen as he faced the jeering Kisdees at the Bottoms, nothing but hate and white, snarling teeth wherever he looked. He must have known that soon, very soon…

The merciless sun beat down on his head and he finally fell asleep.

He dreamed of water. Not the gray and white spring currents of the River Curl, churning in serpentine around the Hills, but of blue,

clear water. With his last ounce of strength he crawled towards the edge. He felt the blood boiling in his veins, the heat roasting him dry. Strange, for this had been such a cool spring. But he was hot and thirsty, and he crept towards the calm, quiet water, lowered his head to drink, and then shot up and spat the water out. It was salty.

His eyes opened. His tongue was heavy, almost hard, with no taste of salt. There was a loud humming in his head and his vision was blurry. The Birds of Death had neared, casting their shadow on him. They didn't move as he budged; they were no longer afraid.

He wanted to stand once more. He wanted to feel the air in his thick fur, the breeze curling his whiskers, wanted to feel the life and strength of his body. He thought of Hanna, who'd gotten up to raise her eyes to the sky again and again, and now he too, with a final exertion, rose onto his paws. He looked around for the last time. In three directions there were only flat fields. Nothing moved anywhere; no one was coming to bring him food and water for they had brought him down here to die. He turned towards the Hills. He couldn't see them anymore, but if he shut his eyes he could catch a glimpse of greenery, of shade, of forests and birds. Of home.

There was no anger in his heart. In fact, the air felt sweet, big and soft and open. He sank on his belly for the last time and the dust settled in his throat. *Soon,* he thought through the thickening haze, *soon.* He felt the approach of the Birds of Death. But inside he tried to focus on Ruwena, the Ancient who'd visited him and told him to go down to the Flats that mysterious, shiny night. He could see her gleaming, yellow eyes demanding everything.

Kisdees must know the truth, and you must tell it to them.

I'm dying! There's no more time.

She watched him gravely, saying nothing. And then she did what he'd yearned for so much that first night: She bent over and licked his ravaged, dusty face. Her tongue spoke of another world where no heat and thirst existed, where not even death existed. Wolf and dog met once again in the feel of her long, soft tongue on his powdery muzzle; he could almost see that first primeval meeting long ago, the rough, scraggy dogs running alongside the Ancients, howling together on bare, twilit mountain ridges that looked nothing like the Hills, and chasing a large horned animal pounding the ground with its hooves, much bigger than any swala.

Where is this place, he wondered, numbed and dazed, before shutting his eyes.

TWENTY-FOUR

A cool breeze stroked his face and he swallowed. The pain in his throat was gone. He swallowed again and licked his lips. They were no longer caked and swollen.

He opened his eyes. His hair felt fresh. It was night, cold and silent. He raised his head and saw no sign of the Birds of Death. He turned back, saw something from the corner of his eye, and his heart stopped.

He'd heard of Kisdees seeing things before they died, chasing fantasies and dreams with their last breaths till they dropped of exhaustion. He shut his eyes and opened them again. It was still there. The container he'd seen before, lying far away by the underbrush, was now just a step away.

He got up on his paws and fell. He got up again, legs shaking, and this time stayed up. He took a step, peered inside the container and instantly something cold and wet splashed his face. He opened his lips and lapped, and lapped, and lapped.

Water. Cold water. Not stale and brackish, but fresh from the River Curl; he'd know it anywhere. He drank till there was none left. He stepped back, licking his lips, feeling the stiffness and pain in his legs, and that's when it hit him. Nothing dragged him down. There was nothing on his body, no coils wound tightly around his chest and across his flanks and legs. The chain lay on the ground near where he'd collapsed and he watched it warily, but it lay still.

He sniffed carefully all around the water container and the chain just to make sure, but he'd known the smell immediately. He'd known it when he woke and sniffed the powerful aroma of cedar all over his flanks. His belly caved in from squeamishness at the thought of those hands combing up and down his body, loosening the chains. He licked his front and back flanks at great length till he could stretch his aching limbs. The Birds of Death had seen it all, knew the game was up, and flew away. He glanced up at the stars and took one last look at the coils and lonesome shrub in the middle of the large, empty Flats, and began limping towards the forest.

It was slow going. His body was dotted with wounds from the Enforcers' sharp fangs and he had lain flat and fettered, unable to move, for a long time. Finally he saw the tree line before him, and as soon as he crossed over his delicate hair quivered with joy. He was back in the forest, with its ridged trees and hollow logs, the caves and dens, the hidden paths, old, crispy leaves crunching underfoot. He whined with pleasure as the bare lower branches scratched the top of his head and thought, I'm home again.

There was the pool from which he'd fetched water for Hanna a lifetime ago. The storm had transformed the merry gurgle into a small waterfall and he squatted in the icy water till it covered his back, then shook himself off and rolled on the ground to dry. He was weak, for he hadn't eaten since be-

fore the hunt. Wishing the sun were overhead to warm his
wet fur, he took shelter behind a large mossy rock and quickly
fell asleep.

A snapping, crunching sound awoke him. He was sure he
was dreaming, for it was just like the noise of teeth tearing
meat and gristle, clattering against bone, that he knew from
the Bottoms at twilight. Then he jumped up, disappeared behind the trees, looped around the waterfall noiselessly, gliding down on the other side, and peered up over a log.

Chomp chomp munch munch r-r-rip! A familiar black shape
stood beneath a gray, bare hemlock. The tips of its ears were
white though they were now bent low along with the rest of
the head, happily buried in the fresh remains of a dead raccoon. Another lay right beside it.

"Beau!"

With a terrific snarl the Gawl leaped up, and the next
moment he jumped Wordsworth. The two fell on the ground,
whinnying in joy, *eee, eee, eee, eee* and *aiffff! aiffff!* echoing wildly in the forest. Beau wore his familiar, silly grin, his whiskers
full of bits of raccoon flesh, fur, and blood. They yanked each
other's hair, rubbed bellies, and licked each other's face.

"You killed two raccoons?"

"Not me," said Beau, "they were already dead when I got
here."

Two young raccoons, still fur-fat from winter, had been
freshly killed, eyes glassy through black and white masks,
their bushy, ringed tails flat on the ground. Beau returned to
the bloody remains of the first and the Golden plunged his
muzzle into the other.

When they finished Beau jumped him again and they rolled and rolled. "This is the happiest moment of my life," Wordsworth said, finally getting up. "I was sure you were dead."

"Enforcers told me you were dead," said Beau, panting happily, eyes ecstatic.

"What happened? I was sure they—"

"Tore me to pieces? It wasn't me they jumped, it was Just Daniel. By the time they got to me the Enforcers had me surrounded and no one could crash through."

"But I heard Anifa say to give you over to them."

"Dreden said that rules were rules, and that chaining me down in the Flats was going to be a slow, terrible death anyway. They took me down there, Magogs put heavy coils on my body and left me no food or water. I tried to escape but I couldn't. I must have gone unconscious, and when I woke up I was free. He freed me."

"He? You mean, a Magog?"

"Of course not," Beau said, tail wagging vehemently, "a dog."

He sat back, bewildered. "A dog freed you, not a Magog?"

"I know what I smelled. It was a dog, a big male."

If the Magog girl didn't free Beau, who did? A sudden, wild hope flamed inside. "Maybe it wasn't a *he*."

"He marked the chain. It's a he."

Now he was even more perplexed. "Kisdees don't mark."

"He was very big and he ate a rabbit before he freed me. I must have fainted, but I remember a voice telling me to drink. When I opened my eyes there was no one there, but I saw the water so I drank. I went back to sleep and when I woke up there were no more coils around me, so I ran here."

Wordsworth walked around and around, questions spinning in his head as he watched his friend make quick shrift of the remains of the raccoon, licking its furry skin before burying his nose in it. "And you didn't kill these raccoons?"

Beau's pink tongue swept over his lips. "I found them like this, dead by the stream."

They were nearly full grown, the Golden noted, big enough to fight. Kisdees had been run off by raccoons, sore and bleeding, but someone had killed these two quite recently, to judge from their freshness, and never touched them.

He looked up at the bright spring moon. They should have been dead; instead they were alive and back in the forest, belly full. But not Just Daniel. And Pandora, he wondered. What did they do to Pandora?

"We have to hide somewhere," Beau said, sitting back, earflaps up.

Wordsworth remembered the last time they were here, when he explained to Beau about purebreds and Gawls. "You have white hairs on both sides of your muzzle now," he said warily. "You're not sick, are you? You're not getting old like Just Daniel?"

Beau wagged his tail. "I haven't eaten any swalas, and certainly no swala skins. Can we go to the Vale? They can't know yet that we escaped."

"They will very soon and that'll be the first place they'll look."

"We can't hide with the Mixeds anymore. What about the caves in the Cliffs?"

"There are hunters there every dawn."

"There's only one place left," Beau muttered. His tail didn't wag this time.

"They found us up there before."

"We have to go somewhere. At least the water up there will cover our tracks, and there are lots of places to hide."

Wordsworth shut his eyes. What he wouldn't give to rest by the pool of water, or at Poet's Vale under the weeping willow, squeezed snugly on a pile of dead leaves. What he wouldn't give to never return to Adamant Tor.

"It will give us a little time," Beau said. "We can't stay here."

As they drank again Wordsworth saw the moon's reflection in the pool; it had begun its long decline. Beau ran quietly up the slope while Wordsworth cast a last look at the white hemlocks and licked the cool, slumbering air. Suddenly he wondered if he'd ever see the Hills again.

They reached the base of the monolith, and as they climbed the lower, pebbled slope he thought again about how this mountain, surrounded by such green hills, had become dust and stone, except for the peculiar waterlogged, marshy top. Once they reached the tall, rocky escarpment Beau sniffed his way through breaks and crannies, leaping up ledges just like before while Wordsworth tried hard not to fall, watching with trepidation as his paws loosened streams of stones and gravel.

At the top, they made their way towards the opposite side of the rim. Moonlight beamed down on the broad, dark plain of the Flats and on Beau sniffing silently at his side. Be careful of the moon, Just Daniel had warned Beau. Who else did he say that to? Beau's tall ears twitched uncertainly.

Wordsworth swept his lips with his tongue. "How did you miss her?" he asked.

"Who?"

"Anifa. She said she tracked down the lynx from Jack Pine Ridge, just like us."

"She couldn't have," Beau growled. "The first time I smelled her was when we stood over the dead lynx. Even then, I didn't know whose scent it was."

"The moonlight didn't tell you?"

Beau looked at him in surprise. "I sniff with my nose, like you."

"So what does the moonlight do?"

His friend licked his lips beneath the few white hairs on both sides of his muzzle. "It tells me things. When the light hits my head I raise my snout, smell it, and sometimes I *know*. Like what happened back in the clearing with Priam. I knew something was going to happen there, but I didn't know what."

"And the howling that night when we stayed with the Gawls? Who was it?"

"I don't know. Only " he bent his head first in one direction, then another, looking as bewildered as he did that night. "I think he was trying to tell me something."

"Who?"

Beau looked at Wordsworth. "Doesn't the moon talk to you?"

"No, nor to anyone I know." He watched Beau bend his head this way and that once again. What do you know about

Beau, Just Daniel had asked him. "Does the moon tell you anything now?"

"No," was the forlorn reply. "In fact, my head feels heavy just like it did the last time we were here. I'm hot and thirsty, and I feel sick."

"Is that how you felt that night on the ledge? I came back with the others—I was sure you'd hear us and run—and instead you just stood there by Priam's body."

Beau looked down into the darkness of the Flats. "After you left I waited right at the edge where the ground fell off. Then I heard a high-pitched sound, like—"

"A long birdcall?"

Beau looked at him strangely. "No, like the whistle of a Magog."

"How do you know about that?"

"Whenever Magogs came to feed me one of them would make a funny high sound with his mouth. That's their whistle."

Do you know how they called for us? With something they called a whistle. They would bring their lips together and make a high-pitched sound that could be heard far away.

"I ran up and down the ledge but I couldn't jump across. For a moment I hurried down the Cliffs after you, and when I got back I saw that the break had closed up and the ledge continued like before. So I went after him." His white whiskers twitched. "The first thing I saw was the fog. The smell was there again, as if something was rotting and burning at the same time. That's when I turned dizzy and hot, like I do here. I saw Priam on the ground. Gobs of blood came out of him, but he was alive."

"Alive!"

"His eyes were shut and he was taking slow, heavy breaths. I licked his neck and he realized I was there. He opened his eyes and made some sounds. I bent over him —"

"What did he say?"

"I could hardly make out the words. I heard *one we've been expecting*. His eyes closed and I thought he was gone, but then he began to growl, or tried to. Every time he made a sound the blood would gush out of his throat. Again he said something, I couldn't hear the first words, just *according to plan*. He was in terrible pain, he was dying. I told him to rest till you came, but that just seemed to upset him and cause more blood to rush out. He took a last breath, said *No time*, and died."

Wordsworth turned back to the dark Flats. Priam had tried to give them a message. Things had gone according to plan and there was one he'd been expecting. Who was it? And how could things go according to plan if Priam was dead? "Why did you wait?"

"The fog was there. It wasn't finished with him, it was still hungry."

He remembered the terrible scene: Priam lying motion-less, Beau standing guard like a rock. Why would Bludrun make a Magogish sound like a whistle? He saw the two green, coiled eyes with the black vertical slash, the tendrils of fog reaching out towards Priam, and the blood coursed through his veins. His muscles flexed, his body trembled, and he made himself a promise. *I don't know what this night will bring,* he vowed silently, *but if I need one more reason to live, one more thing to do before the end, it's to avenge Priam.*

The moon lit up the dusty, barren summit on which they stood. "We shouldn't stay here," Beau finally said. "We'll be better hidden down below."

He let Beau run ahead down the slope as he followed more slowly. His back leg was hurting, a sure sign that the rest of him was now better and stronger. The dry earth turned sodden and began to sink under their weight, and long, wet grass stroke their paws. The fuzzy tops of invisible stalks brushed against their flanks. Mist enveloped invisible trees, creating shadows that creaked and groaned, a chilly reminder of the clearing where everything had come down on top of Priam and Beau. Back down in the forest the night was clear and the moon was out; here on Adamant Tor it started to rain.

They heard a snarl behind a grove of tamaracks and froze. At the second snarl Wordsworth rushed forward, lips parted, heart thudding in sudden joy. He ran across the Glade of Remorse and up the large mound capped by the Turning Tree, with its Magogish fore and hind legs and a hollow circle above in the shape of a face.

On the other side of the mound was Pandora, pinned to the ground by Markus and two Enforcers. She twisted and snapped, trying to get back on her feet, lips white with spittle, eyes filled with hate. Taller than the Enforcers, she shoved off the ground with her paws, heaving herself up with such power that she almost lifted one of her attackers off his legs, but the other bit deep into her thigh and down she tumbled again with a roar. Her head and chest bounced up and she bit him hard on his nose. He yelped, shook his head loose, and then all three were on her, trussing her up so tightly that for a moment it seemed she'd stopped breathing. A grin that Wordsworth knew well appeared on Markus's face. He shut his eyes in anticipation as he bent down towards Pandora's neck.

He never made it. The two dogs leaped on the Enforcers with a snarl, hitting them so hard they all crumpled on the ground behind Pandora. Wordsworth was exhilarated — she was alive! — and felt the blood rush through his body. He would save her, just as he'd promised. Markus jumped him while the others attacked Beau, and all rolled off the mound in a frenzy of legs, teeth, and snarls.

The two Enforcers crouched, ready to attack, as Wordsworth and Beau scrambled up. But the Enforcer closest to the Golden suddenly shrank, his grim eyes clouding in puzzlement. Then they widened, panic-stricken, as his back legs sank in the mud. He tried to scramble up but instead sank further down. The Golden tried to lift his own front paw, but the other caved in. "Don't move!" he shouted.

Beau and the other Enforcer froze.

"We're in a sinkhole. If you move or struggle, your legs will go under."

Beau whinnied but remained motionless. The two Enforcers scrabbled and strained, causing their back flanks to disappear, so that now only their chest and head showed above the mud. They stopped and stared forward resolutely.

With a roar, Pandora flew at the Enforcer next to Beau, lunging at his chest with her own powerful front while keeping her legs on the ground. The Enforcer exclaimed, fell over on his side, and was instantly gone. The dark sludge bubbled briefly, then turned calm.

"No, Pandora!"

But he was too late. The Enforcer beside him flailed, panic-stricken, as Pandora jumped him with her front legs, thrusting him back. His brief cry was cut off. The mud took him smoothly and placidly, with hardly a ripple to show where he'd gone.

Wordsworth looked up at her in horror, but she snorted and began to walk back up the mound. "Where are you going?" he shouted.

Pausing under the Turning Tree, she looked back. "Just Daniel told me that bones dissolve quickly here because it's so wet."

"Pandora!"

"You have a choice: Move, and you'll sink quickly. Don't move, and you'll drown slowly, or else Enforcers will get you. It'll be slow going for Markus because I chewed up his leg, so I think the mud will take you first."

Indeed, Markus was gone. Wordsworth tried to raise one of his paws, and the other leg sank deeper in. The muddy, sucking surface seemed calm, but each time it yielded one or two bubbles he sank a little deeper in. If it wasn't swallowing him as fast as the river waters during the hunt, the outcome was just as certain.

Pandora retraced her steps down the mound, maintaining a safe distance from them. Behind her the Magog-like Turning Tree grinned like death. "On the other hand," she said with the old malicious glint in her eyes, "maybe I'll watch a little."

He smelled her musky balsam as he looked up at the muzzle an Enforcer had bent out of shape long ago. "Why are you doing this?"

"It's what traitors deserve," she said softly. "You were working for them all the time. I told Just Daniel but he wouldn't listen, he trusted you." Her lip curled in bitter contempt. "I was on your side of the river after the hunt. I mixed with the Kisdees; nobody noticed me in the dark. I crept by the enclosure and heard Markus say that the two of you had an agreement, that you were supposed to keep an eye on us and report in every day."

"You're lying," said Beau. One of his front paws was submerged deeper than the other, so that he seemed to be leaning sideways.

"She's not lying," said Wordsworth, trying not to panic as the black, viscous surface gurgled briefly. "That's what they sent me for originally, but I never told them anything. You heard that yourself, Pandora, he said I never told him anything."

She snarled. "You're the reason Just Daniel died. He gave his life for both of you. He trusted you, he sheltered you, and he was killed." The mud bubbled briefly as it rose and now licked his back haunches, but Pandora was already walking away. "Time for me to do something valuable, like killing Enforcers. This is only the beginning. I'll show them how —"

The air buzzed, a flashing beam hit her, and she went down. Instantly she tried to clamber up on her paws, looking wildly around her. There was a grunting and a chittering, and from behind the tamaracks emerged the Magog, Badger. In his hand he held one end of the wire; the other was now wrapped around Pandora's neck. She twisted, trying to grab it in her mouth, but he spun it the other way and she collapsed.

"Fighting won't do you any good," he said, showing his teeth. When she stopped thrashing around his voice lowered into a tease. "You know how this works, don't you, Gawl? You can't escape this, no dog can." He spat out something brown and evil-smelling even as he continued to chew on a roll of wet leaf in his mouth.

He tittered once again, and only then saw the two dogs in the sinkhole below the mound. His red-striped face widened with surprise. "Well, blow me down! It's the famous runaway and his noble savior! Dreden's looking everywhere for you two, and here you are, stuck like grass to the ground." One side of his mouth stretched into a grin, the other clutching and chewing the balled up leaves. He spat once again. "He'll be glad to see you; maybe a new development in our relationship. But first things first." He turned back to Pandora and his lip curled. "Tell me where it is." His pale, striped hand turned, and Pandora screeched. "Don't waste my time, Gawl. That ugly mutt friend of yours knew, only he's dead, so you tell me where it is."

Wordsworth lunged, but his back legs sank so deep that mud covered him up to his chest.

"You want me to make it tighter?" Badger demanded. "Another couple of turns and you won't be able to talk even if you want to."

"I don't—"

Badger's hand jerked and Pandora twitched and coughed violently. "It's here somewhere, it has to be. This is the only place that's so wet all the time, and Daniel knew! That ugly mutt knew, and you know, too!"

He twisted his hand again; her scream was cut short and Wordsworth roared. Out of patience, Badger jerked the wire hard. Pandora's throat gurgled and her eyes turned white. Panic overtook the Golden. His front legs scrabbled in a frenzy, causing his back to sink instantly. *She must live, promise me that.* But one more twist of the Magog's wrist and Pandora would die. Already she lay on the ground unconscious, the wire shutting out all air. He roared in agony, and that moment Badger screamed and dropped the wire.

A white dog with brown spots had grabbed a hold of his arm. He shook it hard, trying to throw her off, but Prissy Miss Charlotte held on so tightly with her strong jaws that it was he who fell on the ground. He kicked her but she didn't seem to feel it. Blood dripped and Badger yelled, but Charlotte just clenched her teeth tighter, looking wide-eyed at Badger. Her jaws settled in for the long haul till, with a brief sideways glance, she espied the two dogs in the mud. Her eyes rose in pleasant surprise. Leaving Badger on the ground to nurse his bloodied arm, she jumped around and headed towards Beau.

"Leave them," Pandora said, taking deep drafts of air once the wire around her neck had slackened.

"He's a Gawl," Charlotte replied, looking one moment bright-eyed at Beau and the next moment suspiciously at Wordsworth. "What's the matter with you? Why are you just standing there?"

"We're in a sink hole, we can't get out," Beau told her.

"They're cowards and deceivers, let them drown," commanded Pandora.

"I'm not letting any Gawl drown," Charlotte said. She whacked her tail in excitement and sniffed the mud.

"Do as I say!"

"I didn't leave the Flats to do what you or anybody else says," Charlotte added.

Leaning over Beau, she wrapped her jaws around the thickest part of his neck fur and pulled. Beau winced and his front legs scrabbled for traction, to no avail. But the Pit Bull planted her front legs solidly on the ground and began to jerk backwards. Her white chest was powerful, but Wordsworth saw a large lump around what looked like a protruding splinter, and realized that her brown eyes weren't big with excitement but rather pain. She pulled hard, and slowly Beau's body began to move. Her eyes widened some more—how can she do this, wondered Wordsworth—and then, with a yelp, Beau's front paws and flanks were on the ground. Charlotte kept on pulling, but now Beau could work his own front muscles, and with a final yank he hoisted himself up. He turned towards Wordsworth.

"He's a Kisdee," Charlotte said, "why bother?"

But Beau did just what she had done. He bent forward, grabbed a hold of Wordsworth's thick fur with his teeth, and began to pull. The Golden tried to relax even as he felt the throbbing at his neck. At first nothing happened. Beau pulled hard but the mud held fast to the Golden's legs and flanks and he didn't move an inch. *Come on*, he prayed silently, *come on*.

"You're not pulling hard enough," the Pit Bull said.

Beau let go of Wordsworth's fur and the mud gurgled around the sinking dog. "You think you can do better?" Beau panted.

"I *know* I can do better." And with that she bent towards Wordsworth, clenching her teeth around his neck fur so hard that he cried out. Charlotte didn't care. She tightened her grip and tensed her white, bowed legs, emitting a low drone of pain from the side of her mouth as she pulled. Still, nothing happened, except that now the bone splinter had burst through the skin and blood was dribbling down her white-and-brown flanks. Charlotte gave several powerful jerks and Wordsworth thought his head was coming off. But that moment the mud let go of his forelegs. The front of his body rose up as he tore and scrambled with his paws till they felt hard ground underneath.

"You can take it from here," the Pit Bull wheezed, letting go of his fur. He wriggled and climbed, propelling the rest of his body out of the sinkhole and collapsing on the ground. Beau licked him happily, and stiffened. He turned around. Up the mound Badger held something in his hand. He struggled onto his feet, growling at the Magogish contraption, two thin wooden bars tied together with each sharp end pointed in a different direction. Badger's arm twisted around his body. What's he doing, he wondered.

He didn't find out, at least not then, for just as Badger's arm untwisted and shot forward someone jumped the Magog and he fell back. "Let go, Charlie! Let go of me!"

It was the old Magog with fur above and below his mouth. He sprawled over Badger, while behind him stood the girl.

"Get out of my way, Charlie!" Badger pushed him aside.

The old man rolled and sat up, holding the odd contraption in his hands. "Not this way, Badger." The other made a grab for it but Charlie withdrew his arm quickly, holding it to his side.

"We're not underneath anymore, Charlie," Badger snarled, "we have to survive."

"Not with wires or stars, they won't help."

"They help a lot. Tell me, is her life more important than mine?" he gestured to Pandora. "Or the rest of us? But you don't care, why should you? You and that wild animal are not sick like everybody else." His welts were redder than ever as he picked up the end of the wire with his other hand and pulled it once again, jerking Pandora flat on her belly.

"Let her go, Badger."

"Not before I drag the secret out of her. She knows where it is."

"Just Daniel knew, not her. Anyway, it's not here."

"How do you know?"

"It's not here, Badger." Charlie's sky pale eyes didn't blink.

Badger pulled the wire. "You're lying, it must be here. This is where we were back then before the Calamity, this must be where they found it. I want it, I want to get well."

"Not by torturing someone, Badger."

"It's not a someone, it's a dog! We owned them once, remember? We did anything we wanted with them. She knows the secret and I'm getting it."

"No!" exclaimed Summer. She ran towards the wire, but with Pandora lying at one end and Badger holding the other she didn't know what to do, so she grabbed the taut wire with both hands. And as she did so, she saw Wordsworth on the other side of the mound. She let go of the wire, smiled, and walked over towards him. "Dog!" she said.

Behind her Badger still raged. "Do you know what it's like to live with these blotches covering my skin? Nobody'll come close to me!"

"They're all sick, Badger —"

"Not like me! Nobody's sick like me. They'll listen but they won't touch me, they're all afraid. I want to be healthy like you, like that crazy girl!"

But Wordsworth wasn't listening anymore, for the girl Summer was fast approaching, her hand outstretched. "Dog!" she repeated happily, oblivious to what lay between them, deep and hissing, ready to suck her in.

"Go away," he told her. Beau and Charlotte growled.

But she didn't stop. "Dog!" she exclaimed.

"There's a sink hole," he shouted, but she didn't stop.

Everything happened fast, so fast it was hard to follow. The Magog Charlie jumped up to his feet and ran towards them, shouting, "Summer, come here!"

Behind him Badger picked up the Magogish object on the ground. Again his arm went around in a twist, jerked back, and with a flick of the wrist he sent it whistling towards them. The air swished as the strange object spun through it. It wasn't clear whom Badger aimed at. The old man looked back, raised his arms to block it, grunted and doubled back, falling onto his rump right under the Turning Tree.

Summer ran to him as Charlie bent forward and picked up the thing that had hit him. Stationary, it looked harmless enough, two thin, sharp-pointed wooden bars tied together so that one was horizontal and one upright. But launched sideways by Badger, it had hurtled as fast as a speeding star before piercing Charlie's stomach.

The dogs could smell the blood. The old Magog sighed and leaned back against the tree. "What have you done, Badger?" he mumbled.

Badger stared. "I wasn't aiming it at you," he said, licking his lips.

Charlie breathed with difficulty. "We've never hurt each other, not like this. We lived under that mountain, and no one ever hurt anyone else." He spoke with increasing difficulty, head sagging forward. A red spot appeared on the front of his padded skin and began to spread.

Badger stared at it. "We're not underneath anymore," he muttered. He looked up and saw the dogs' eyes on him. "You hear that?" he shouted. "We're not underneath anymore. We're above ground now, we're back!" With another flick of his wrist he tossed up the wire from where it had hung loosely around Pandora and quickly wound it up.

Beau raised his head and sniffed. "Enforcers are coming up," he growled.

Badger started walking down the mound.

"Leaving so soon?" taunted Charlotte.

He turned around, lip curled in hate. "Don't worry, Pit Bull, I'll be back. Only you'll never live long enough to see it, not with those broken ribs. What I didn't finish, Dreden will finish for me."

Charlotte chased him down the mound but stopped, rasping loudly. So that's what he did to her, Wordsworth thought, that's why she's in so much pain. His heart ached and he looked up at the sky; the moon was sinking towards the horizon but there was no sign of dawn yet. He remembered Just Daniel's words that first morning when they met: *Why shouldn't there have been good Magogs and bad Magogs, short ones and tall ones?* Magogs fought and even killed each other. Just like us, he thought now.

There was silence under the Turning Tree where the two Magogs now sat. The blood smell was overpowering. Charlie slumped forward while the girl sat next to him, arms crossed around her chest, and began to hum.

"Summer—" Charlie began, but she hummed even louder. He expelled a hoarse, shallow breath. "Try, Summer, just try."

She hummed some more. "They don't know."

"Someone will know," he said with a failing voice, raising his arm with a sigh and wrapping it around her.

"Wordsworth knows. Dogs know. I wish I was a dog."

"You're a human, Summer, a very special human." Charlie tried to laugh but coughed instead, spewing out pink spittle, and Wordsworth knew that he would soon be dead.

"Go before Enforcers get up here," he told them.

Charlotte and Beau darted back and forth restlessly, but Wordsworth didn't move. "I can't leave her, she saved my life," he told the old Magog. "She set me free down at the Flats."

"Summer can take care of herself, she knows her way around Adamant Tor." She continued humming quietly as he put a hand on her blonde fur. "Let her stay with me a little more, it won't take long, then she'll go." He slumped further down. "It's all right," he mumbled. "I lived to see the sun and the stars. I lived to see the sky my parents talked about but never saw."

Still, he couldn't leave. There was something about the dying old man and the young girl that moved him deeply, not just the violence and injustice of it all but something else he couldn't name. He approached Summer, trembling. The girl stopped her hum and stretched out her hand. He sniffed it with great deliberation: acorns, dust, cypress bark, heat, and none of the sour, diseased smell he got from the other Magogs. Her pale, open fingers radiated warmth as she slowly reached up to his head; one finger stretched out tentatively and found the groove on his brow. Gradually, it traced its way down the bridge of his nose to his muzzle and back up. She craned forward, her finger circling the top of his head and down along the ridge of his body towards his tail. Her touch was unhurried and sweet. He heard a hum, and when he opened his eyes he saw that the girl's were shut, her face beatific, and she was humming the same low-pitched song he'd heard when he first found her lying by the small waterfall above the Flats. For the briefest moment he let himself relax. What did this remind him of? His mother, Loreen, licking him as a pup? No, something much older than that, an ancient, primitive touch that every hair in his body yearned for.

"They've reached the top," Beau said.

Pandora, who'd lain low all this time, jumped up, preparing to run. He pulled away from the girl, who exclaimed in surprise and disappointment, and took some steps after the big Tug-a-Lug. Pandora turned and snapped at him. "Go back to your Magog friends, Kisdee."

"The girl freed me, Pandora."

"Not me," said Beau at his side. "A dog freed me."

"Of course a dog freed you, you're a Gawl," Pandora said, shaking her russet head so that her hairs no longer covered her eyes. "The one who freed you is the one who frees all Gawls, the one who freed Charlotte from the Flats twice."

For a moment they stared stupidly at her. Then, in one burst of clarity, he knew.

"Rathbane," the Pit Bull said at their side, eyes gleaming.

We don't free them. For one thing, we don't know what to do about the wires, and for another, it's too dangerous to go out to the Flats.

"Rathbane freed the Gawls, sent them into the Hills, and we would bring them up Adamant Tor because no one ever came here," Pandora said, lifting her muzzle to smell the coming Enforcers. "And then we would show them the passage that he showed us a long time ago."

He freed Hanna, Wordsworth thought. They brought her up here, too, only she was killed.

"He's the one they say is killing Kisdees," Beau said.

"It's not him, but good riddance just the same."

"Did Just Daniel know who the killer is?" Wordsworth asked.

At first she said nothing. When she finally turned back to face him her eyes were grim and sad. "Just Daniel knew everything, but he wouldn't tell me except to say once that it's the beloved of the moon. I thought he was teasing me because he knew how much I liked the moonlight."

The moon is looking for its beloved. That's what Ruwena said as she looked up at the sky full of light that night. He raised his head towards the moon and instead found himself looking straight at the black, hollow face of the Magogish tree on top of the mound. Under it sat Charlie, head fallen forward, and the girl Summer, with arms crossed as she hummed. *This is where we were back then before the Calamity, this must be where they found it.* Found what? "Come with us, Pandora," he urged.

She inhaled the crisp night air. "I'll take my chances in the Hills, I know them better than anyone."

"What about the Gawls? They need a new leader."

"I'm never going back to that pine grove," she snapped, turning to leave. "I'm never dragging another swala down to the Bottoms."

"Wait," Beau said. "What did Badger want from you? What was he looking for?"

"The same thing they're all looking for," she said over her shoulder. "The cure to their disease."

"Enforcers are coming down!" Charlotte said.

Beau's nostrils puckered and sniffed. "She's right, let's go."

"Come with us, Pandora," he implored.

"With you? Never!"

She bounded away with several large leaps, stagnant water splashing under her paws.

His heart sank. So much had happened, so much had changed, except for one thing: He was a Kisdee; she was never going to forgive him for that. "What are you going to do?" he called out.

Her voice sounded distant; she had already disappeared in the mist. "Kill some Enforcers!"

"There's no time," said Beau. "Are you coming or not?"

Beau led the way as they flew down the mound and across the Glade. Wordsworth was slower on account of his leg, but Charlotte was slower still and he wondered how she would catch up with broken ribs.

They got to the other side of the rim and the large pile of rocks covered with moss and dead leaves. Beau buried his head in the crackling leaves, searching for the opening. He flattened himself on his belly and disappeared. Wordsworth let Charlotte follow. Her lips were parted in excitement but her breath was heavy. The blood had stopped dripping but the bulge around the bone splinter that came out of her chest seemed even bigger than before. How much pain could someone take, he wondered, even a Pit Bull like her?

At first they crawled, then the passage widened enough so that they could walk. Charlotte, shorter than both of them, was already standing, sniffing the darkness as hard as she could as they made their way down. He was tired and his bad leg dragged. He turned back to give it a lick, hit his head against the wall, and at the same time smelled familiar scents: moss, mildew, granite, and terraberries. Enforcers. This time they'd found the passage.

Sniff sniff sniff, pause, sniff sniff sniff. Beau forged forward, tail up. Wordsworth wondered when they'd see a little light from the small cracks in the rocks like last time, and realized it was still night outside. In a while the hunters would rise and go to the Cliffs, waiting for the swalas to return from the river.

Ahead of him Charlotte ran smack into Beau, who'd come to a stop. There was a flicker of gray a long way down. We've reached the other end, he thought, licking his lips thirstily. Beau hurried forward. The ground grew level and the light from the other end dispelled the gloom of the passageway. His spirits rose.

Beau reached the opening; in their eagerness, both Charlotte and Wordsworth ran into him. "Why aren't you jumping out?"

Beau gave no answer.

He raised his head to peer over his friend's shoulder and saw acorns and moss, the green gray earth, the ghostly tilt of branches and the flutter of leaves in the dim, predawn air, and a shadow. Framed by a low-flung shrub, not bothering to hide, stood Dreden.

TWENTY-FIVE

The warm, tawny fur contrasted with the coldness on the Enforcer's face, his white belly hairs trembling with relentless purpose. There was no compassion or even a hint of mercy in Dreden's eyes. "Why isn't he coming for us?" Wordsworth wondered, standing just behind Beau.

"He doesn't have to." Beau's earflaps flipped once again the other way, and Wordsworth understood. The other Enforcers were chasing them down from the other end.

This was it then.

"I'll fight them to the end," said Charlotte, sitting down glumly, earflaps quietly folded, awaiting the final battle. "No one's taking me back to the Flats!"

Beau stepped out of the opening, standing on the forest floor, and Dreden crouched with a snarl, ready to tear him to pieces. Beau began to growl back, then stopped, gazing out to the distance. Wordsworth looked, too. There were the trees, the young bushes of spring, the moon ready to set behind the hills, the grass sparkling in—

The moon. The waning moon. Its beams shimmered in a long slant through the woods, alighting on the gray, naked bark of a still wintry maple, the shivering tips of leaves, and the edge of Beau's snout, which was sniffing the moonlight feverishly, hairs dancing.

The snarling stopped; Beau froze. A shadow appeared on the maple trunk. It crossed right in front of Dreden, almost touching him, but the Head of the Enforcers didn't move. Then it came towards Beau, who whined softly.

A black wolf. The one they'd seen at twilight in the hunt with Priam. She was twice as long as Dreden, taller and heavier. She paused in front of Beau, who now whimpered and looked down. The passage in which they stood was narrow, but she nimbly passed by him and Charlotte and ran down the passageway that continued in darkness under the forest floor.

As one, they turned and chased after her.

This darkness was different from the one they'd just left. This one was underneath the forest itself, blacker than any night he'd ever seen. *Where does it lead? To the Land of the Gawls.*

"Hurry!" Beau urged, invisible up ahead.

Enforcers were behind them with Dreden probably in the lead. They ran silently, but he could hear the soft, relentless slap-slap of their paws and if he turned around he was sure to smell the scent of terraberries. Pain shot up his back leg, but he reminded himself that Charlotte hurt a lot worse and was keeping up, for all he could see was the white tip of her tail. The passageway was narrow and he seemed to run from one wall smack into another, getting scratched and bruised, till he got the hang of it and hugged the wall with the side of his body, following the curve of the rocks as they plunged under the ground. Sharp edges tore his skin. Once Charlotte paused and raised her head, the tips of her white and brown earflaps turned back. "Enforcers," she said as calmly as if announcing rain.

It was so black they could have been climbing up to the night sky. Instead they were going the other way, down to the very bowels of the earth. A small hope still fluttered in his heart that they might find another way out of the passage and emerge onto the moist brown soil and low green spikes of new grass, that they would breathe the fresh air of—

The floor disappeared. Front legs flailing in the air, he went sliding. The incline was short, and then it, too, disappeared and he fell into pitch-dark space before crashing down on his side.

They landed on mounds of black, powdery dust, which probably saved their lives. But there was the smell, horribly familiar: fire and rot, smoke and decay all mixed together, worse this time than ever before.

He got up gingerly and looked around for signs of Bludrun, venomous curls of mist or a high-pitched, Magogish whistle, but vapors of thick smoke enveloped them. Beau burst into coughs and Charlotte couldn't get up. The bulge through which the bone protruded had opened up completely and her chest quickly became a large daub of crimson, her lifeblood spilling out, just like the Magog Charlie's. For a moment despair filled his heart.

She didn't cry out once. Instead she raised her white, brown-spotted head, licked her lips with a desiccated tongue, and asked, "What happened? What's that smell?"

He looked at her dumbly, and then it hit him. He could see. Pearly light came from the far end of an enormous cavern that sloped gently down at its other end. He coughed from the smoke, feeling hot and thirsty, wondering where the light was coming from so deep underground.

At least he couldn't hear Enforcers anymore.

Charlotte dragged herself up and inched forward towards Beau, head down, gagging and coughing, leaving a puddle of blood behind her. She can't go on like this, he thought to himself, no one can lose so much blood and have so much pain. He followed, walking through a heavy fog thick with a stench that seemed to penetrate every pore of his body. The vapors lifted briefly, revealing a small opal pool at the very end of the cavern. But ahead the two Gawls had dropped on the ground. There was a pounding in his ears and his body burned. The black gravel on the floor of the cavern irritated his paws. It accumulated in large piles alternating with deep, wide craters he had to carefully avoid.

"Get up, Charlotte," he said hoarsely when he reached the Pit Bull.

"I need water," she panted.

"There's a pool on the other side."

"I didn't see anything, are you sure?"

He looked again. Water shimmered through the swirls of smoke and stinging heat at the other end.

"Look! Look!" Beau gasped, lying a short distance away.

It took forever just to reach him. Something lay next to Beau and he sniffed curiously the round object with deep sockets, half covered by the tiny black granules on the floor. "What is it?"

Beau mumbled something. He took a few more steps and saw it all, not just the skull but the rest of the bones. Magogs. Dead.

The cavern was full of the remains of Magogs, their bones in fragments but their skulls intact, with hollow openings where their eyes and mouths should have been. Stretched out on top of layers of small black pellets, their arms—or what remained of them—reached forward, hands spread out.

Magogs dug up the ground and created things, that's where I saw the poison.

"I can't move," Beau gasped, "I can't breathe."

"We must get out of here, this place is full of poison." His own head pounded and he felt as though his body was turning to liquid. He was so thirsty.

He looked again at the Magogs. Their arms stretched out, heads facing forward. Towards the opal water.

I have seen things blacker than night, and lighter than the spring water of the Curl. I know that where there is death there is also life.

He was here, he thought. Just Daniel was here, and he'd gotten out.

"Beau, we have to reach the pool."

The Gawl's breath was breaking up. "Can't," he murmured.

"Get down to the water, Beau."

The Gawl raised his dazed head, white tongue falling out the side of his mouth. "I need air," he panted, "I need water."

Wordsworth looked from him to Charlotte. They can't die down here, he cried silently. "Come on, Fireside Stomping Beau, you're a Daimyo. Daimyos never give up!"

Beau scrabbled up on his paws, swayed, stayed up, and took a step forward. Then another, and another, his head sinking further and further down to his chest.

Wordsworth hurried back to the Pit Bull. "Come on, Charlotte," he urged, nudging at her neck with his muzzle.

Nothing moved. Was she dead? A pale tongue emerged slowly from between her lips.

The smell of the blood under her body jammed his senses. "Get up, Charlotte."

She rose, limped forward, and fell again. She had no more strength. Ahead Beau was tottering down to the small pool, but not Charlotte, who was now finally whimpering in pain.

"You've come so far, it can't end here." He tried to nudge her up with his muzzle, but she was solid as a rock. "There's water ahead," he urged. "Just a little more."

"I'm dying."

"You're a Pit Bull, Charlotte, you're tough. If you have to die, die outside under the sky and the trees, not in this underground bone yard!"

He pushed her again, this time from behind, and she scrambled onto her legs, paws clawing the ground. She almost came down again, but that moment the tips of her earflaps hooked forward, capturing the sound of Beau lapping water. Her pink tongue rolled over the side of her bottom lip. She came down on her belly and he thought she'd given up, but instead she began to crawl, dragging herself forward with her powerful, wounded chest, emitting soft, high-pitched mewls of pain.

Slowly, slowly, she crept forward while he pushed her from behind with his muzzle. The opal water beckoned them forward. What if I'm wrong, he wondered. What if it, too, is poison?

The Magog skeletons lay all around them, pitched forward towards the water.

They were almost there when she stopped. Her body convulsed; she was nearing the end. It was now or never. Wordsworth gave her one last, powerful shove with his muzzle. He meant for her to reach the pool's edge; instead she toppled in. "Charlotte!"

He jumped in after her, sure she would drown.

But Charlotte didn't drown. He went down but came right up again, only to see her swimming on top of the water, her small pink tongue lapping thirstily. How buoyant she was, a heavy Pit Bull like that! He, too, swam easily, and suddenly he realized that his back leg, the paralyzed, useless leg, was paddling. It came up and pushed forward in the water just like the other, feeling light and agile. Impossible, a voice said inside, but he didn't care. The water licked the crippled leg so sweetly that all he could do was groan in pleasure. The heaviness that had been with him since birth, the relentless load slowing him down and making him so different from the others, these were all gone. Instead his back leg felt supple, almost weightless, part and parcel of his body instead of something extraneous, dragged around or held up, always threatening to fall.

This is how the others feel, he realized, this is how they move. And then he stopped paddling altogether for the water held him up. A deep peace enveloped him and he shut his eyes. He heard Charlotte climb out of the pool and wondered how she managed it, with the protruding bone and her life-blood streaming out of her, and then realized there was no trace of blood in the water.

"Charlotte, your chest! What happened?"

He looked out. Beau stood near the edge of the pool, legs strong, eyes shiny as they rested on Charlotte, who was walking towards him. The Pit Bull's chest was white again, no bulging bone, no drip-drip blood, not a hint of the deep wound draining her life away. Her eyes no longer wore their mist of pain; they looked back at Beau, clear, untroubled, happy.

That moment the water broke under him and he sank. He scrabbled to come up to the surface again. Instantly he felt his back leg turn heavy, and he knew the old paralysis was back. He couldn't move it up or down, couldn't push it forward as the other did in the water. It was heavy and useless, like before.

He climbed out of the pool, crushed, bewildered, and looked at the water. What happened, he wanted to cry out. For a moment it was all healed and I could walk and run, I could be like the others! Maybe Charlotte drank a lot more of the water than he did; quickly he bent down to lap more. A cool, strong energy swept through his body, but when he tried to stand evenly on all four his back leg curled once again, unable to take any weight, and hung suspended in the air, paw folded. He was still a cripple.

Beau came forward, tail wagging, and tried to sniff his back leg, but Wordsworth twisted away with a snarl and his friend backed off. Charlotte looked away. He knew what they were thinking. The pool was magical. It hadn't just cured Charlotte, it had made her stronger and healthier, too. Only now he realized how battered she'd been even before Enforcers had hurt her, hungry and exposed for so long in the Flats, but no longer. Beau, too, was full of his old spark and vigor, the wear and tear of the last days miraculously evaporated after drinking the water in the pool. Only he was still a cripple.

The tongue kills, and the tongue gives life. Always remember that.

Just Daniel's tongue had done both, healing others while killing him at the same time. Was this the place where he'd gotten his powers? Was this pool of water what Badger was looking for? And if it healed others, why not him?

He walked back and sniffed once again the remains of the dead Magogs. What killed them? Carefully he sniffed the black, gravelly pellets that lay all around them, that smelled of smoke and decay. Like Bludrun, he thought.

What were Magogs doing deep under the earth? And if this was the poison that killed them, was it getting into the Hills? Is this what was in the swalas they ate every day? But swalas didn't come down here and they certainly didn't have this scent. One question led to another and then another, swirling round and round in his head. But something seemed clear. The disease that killed Magogs was here, and also— maybe—the cure.

Just not his cure.

He rejoined the others.

"So how do we get out of here?" Charlotte asked, practical as always, tail whacking.

They were surrounded by tall cavern walls that disappeared into darkness.

"Magogs must have built passageways out of here," surmised Beau.

"But that was a long time ago. Tell me," Wordsworth turned to him, "why did you rush us here?"

"We all ran after the black wolf," Charlotte reminded him.

"I saw you sniff the moonlight when we first tried to get out, before she appeared. Why? What did it tell you?"

"I suddenly knew we had to get here by the time the moon set," replied Beau. "That's why I told you to hurry."

"But where's here?"

Beau's forehead furrowed in bewilderment. "I don't know."

"I hate to point out the obvious," drawled Charlotte, "but there's no moon here. We're underground, remember? How would we know when the moon sets?"

Wordsworth searched the cavern again but could see nothing, no passageway, no opening, nothing but walls that loomed so high they couldn't see the top. The black wolf had distracted Dreden long enough to help them make their escape, but Ruwena had warned him about her. Had she brought them here to die?

As long as we think about escape, we live, Hanna had said. Besides, he thought, something—someone—had pointed them here. There were a few more white hairs on Beau's muzzle, and now he was sure. Some of Beau's black hair turned white each time he sniffed the moonlight. But who—or what—spoke to him?

Then his mind cleared, and he knew. The moon. It had been there all the time, from that first night when it was full, enticing him forward to find Margaret, to the moment when it hovered over Dreden, sending Beau a message. And it was in his verse from the beginning, the verse he couldn't finish.

"Spring steals into these happy Hills
With newly minted leaf and fern,
Yellow bud forsythia, emerald frills,
The moon comes up – the moon comes up – "

He knew the ending in every bone in his body:

" – even in unstarred caverns underground,
Gleaming at the weary marge of hope,
Not to make the darkness dimmer
But to kindly show us how to grope

Our way among the briers,
On cold-heart stone and rocky clay,
Choose life-death's soft, eternal rush
That never yields or goes astray."

Charlotte gave a skeptical twitch of her tail. "That sounds awfully – "

She was flung on her back. The cavern shook with a deafening roar, hurling the others across the floor and almost into the pool. The walls quaked, large rocks swaying, and the three dogs buried their whimpering heads in their paws for there was no shelter anywhere from the avalanche of stones raining down on them. For a moment he wondered if Adamant Tor was finally crumbling from the poisons it had accumulated.

It stopped. At first he couldn't see anything because of the dust. Finally he made out Beau, upright, walking towards the cavern wall, and then blinked in disbelief. Beau had raised his head, and the new white hairs on his black muzzle quivered at the end of a pale, silver beam. Wordsworth followed the thin, shimmering beacon through the opening to its source. A moon hung suspended at the very edge of a wide, empty sky.

Charlotte was the first to regain her voice. "We're not underground anymore! We're out!"

"The voice said to be ready when the moon set," Beau marveled.

But he had no time to marvel long, for the next moment Charlotte rushed and toppled him. The Pit Bull barked and barked, and soon the two Gawls rolled on the cavern floor. Beau's joyful *eeee eeeee eeees* alternated with the smacks of Charlotte's tail, and each time he tried to rise up she lunged and brought him back down with her Pit Bull strength.

Wordsworth didn't move. "The moon isn't setting, it's rising," he said in a curious voice. The other two paused from their play and looked up. "It was night time on Adamant Tor. When we saw Dreden it was almost dawn and the moon was going down. Here it's rising."

The gray opening was only several bounds away. A moment ago they'd been anxious to get out, but now they stayed put, searching it warily from a distance. There was no doubt about it, the sky was getting darker. Night was starting once again.

"Were we under Adamant Tor all day and didn't know it?" Beau wondered.

"Maybe," Wordsworth replied slowly. "And maybe we're on the other side. The moon has set in the Hills, and it's rising here."

"Where's here?"

The opening revealed a wide, twilit vista empty of trees, hills, and forest. Large, chimerical rocks loomed in the dimness and they could barely make out tall, narrow peaks far away that were different from the Cliffs back home.

"What is this place?" Beau asked again.

Slowly Charlotte started whacking her tail. Then she whacked it faster and louder. "The Land of the Gawls," she announced with a happy grin.

Wordsworth shuddered. He looked again towards the mouth of the cave and saw billows of white smoke climbing up to the dusky sky from one of the faraway peaks. And then the peaks were gone. A face appeared at the cave's opening, a face similar to the one they'd seen before but smaller, the fur yellow-brown, the muzzle thin.

The three dogs stared silently at the Ancient; the Ancient stared right back. Then it raised its muzzle and curled its lips, revealing sharp fangs. It gave a low, dangerous growl, and was gone.

"It's not her," said Beau disappointedly, "it's not the black wolf who brought us to the lynx and saved us from Dreden."

She brought us to a dead lynx, Wordsworth thought, and now we're here. Apprehension twitched inside his belly whenever he thought of her.

"Ancients always help dogs, everyone knows that," said Charlotte with a brief thwack of her tail. Having made up her mind, she leaped towards the opening. Beau leaped after her.

He didn't move.

"We can't stay here," Beau told him, standing on the ledge with Charlotte. "The voice said to hurry. I don't know what will happen if we don't get out, maybe the cave will close again."

He's right, Wordsworth thought. Pictures flashed in his mind: the Hills, an abandoned Poet's Vale, scraggly Birdy, Priam lying dead in the pool of blood, the Bottoms full of Kisdees now led by Anifa and Dreden. One picture most of all: Pandora, the perpetually angry eyes half covered by hair, the smell of musky fir, the matted russet flanks. He remembered his promise to Just Daniel. *Whatever happens, Pandora must live.* But she didn't want him to protect her. She didn't want him at all.

He stepped forward, tail waving slowly behind him. Charlotte and Beau ran gleefully towards the fresh night air while he bounded onto the warm, rocky ledge and looked down on a savannah golden in moonlight.

ACKNOWLEDGMENTS

I am indebted to writers, scientists, and animals who have helped me to clarify my relationship to dogs and other companion species not as that of a human being to furry toddlers, but as equal — and different — fellow voyagers.

To Anna Cottle, Claudia Gere, and Mary Alice Kier, who gave me their gifts of trust, confidence, marketing acumen, and most important of all, the challenge to rewrite, re-vision, and always return to not-knowing.

To family, fellow writers, and friends who, over the years, ask those all-important questions: *How's the writing? How's the book?*

GLOSSARY

Ancients. Wolves that have become spirits living in the Peaks of Their Abode. A few sometimes appear to Kisdees.

Great Calamity. A catastrophe that took place long before the events of the book, wiping out most Magogs.

Curveheads. Kisdees that are not Terriers.

Enforcers. Purebred German Shepherds from the Brancken Dukes family who enforce the Rules in the Kiskadee Hills.

Flatheads. Kisdees that are Terriers.

Gawls. Mixed dogs born to Kisdee parents who are exiled to the other side of the River Curl.

Great Alliance. The alliance of all Kisdee families and clans created by Fearsome Arden.

Guards. Kisdees from all families recruited to help the Enforcers.

Kisdee Circle. The group governing Kisdees made up of representatives from all Kisdee breeds.

Kisdees. Dogs liberated from Magogs by Fearsome Arden and brought to the Kiskadee Hills.

Magogs. Humans.

Noble One. The Head of the Kisdee Circle, and therefore the Head of all Kisdees.

Ravages. A time of war and bloodshed among Kisdees as they struggled to survive after coming to the Kiskadee Hills.

Rules. The Rules governing all Kisdee conduct, established by Fearsome Arden. Arden's First Rule prohibits killing other dogs.

Swalas. Small antelopes that live in caves on the Cliffs.